THE DISCOVERIES OF

ARTHUR GREY

THE MINOTAUR RIDDLE

by V. K. FINNISH

THE
DISCOVERIES OF ARTHUR GREY
SERIES

BOOK 1   The Society's Traitor

BOOK 2   The Minotaur Riddle

THE DISCOVERIES OF

ARTHUR GREY

THE MINOTAUR RIDDLE

K. FINNISH

HAT PUBLISHING, LTD

TAIN FALLS, COLORADO

Published by Panama Hat Publishing, Ltd.
Edited by Kellie M. Hultgren

www.panamahatpublishing.com

Publisher's Cataloging-in-Publication Data

Finnish, V. K.
 The minotaur riddle / by V.K. Finnish. — 1st ed.
  p. cm. — (The discoveries of Arthur Grey ; 2)
 SUMMARY: Twelve-year-old Arthur Grey gets more than he bargained for when he discovers the truth about the legendary Labyrinth and what it holds.

 ISBN 978-0-9852202-3-5 (hardcover)
 ISBN 978-0-9852202-4-2 (paperback)
 ISBN 978-0-9852202-5-9 (ebook)

 1. Secret societies—Greece—Juvenile fiction. 2. Minotaur (Greek mythology)—Juvenile fiction. 3. Labyrinths—Juvenile fiction.
[1. Secret societies—Fiction. 2. Minotaur (Greek mythology)—Fiction.
3. Animals, Mythical—Fiction. 4. Labyrinths—Fiction. 5. Greece—Fictio
6. Adventure and adventurers—Fiction. 7. Fantasy.] I. Title. II. Series:
Finnish, V. K. Discoveries of Arthur Grey ; 2.

PZ7.F49843Min 2013
[Fic]—dc23

First Edition: June 2013

The text of this book is set in 12-pt Adobe Garamond Pro
on acid-free paper from a renewable, responsibly managed fo

Here's to my dad,
who believed that I could,
and told me his stories so I'd write a book.
And here's to my Eeyore dad whom I will miss,
who gave me the chance
to make my books live.

CONTENTS

PROLOGUE   The Lizard at Bay   1

ONE   Time to Go   17

TWO   The First Mysteries   31

THREE   Welcome to Origins   42

FOUR   Let the Games Begin   60

FIVE   Translationary Troubles   80

SIX   The Investor   88

SEVEN   Detour   106

EIGHT   The Joust Ghost   125

NINE   A Jolly Rescue   152

TEN   Danger on Crete   167

ELEVEN   The Wisdom of Prometheus   178

CONTENTS

TWELVE Knossos Palace 202

THIRTEEN A Library Lesson Ruined 230

FOURTEEN The Spiral Office 245

FIFTEEN Poseidon's View 261

SIXTEEN Stuck on a Journey 272

SEVENTEEN Release of Asterion 294

EIGHTEEN The Donation 309

THE DISCOVERIES OF

ARTHUR GREY

THE MINOTAUR RIDDLE

THE LIZARD AT BAY

Grey and cold surround us. The wind howls through the trees, rattling the few dry, colorless leaves that still cling to their branches, and I shiver. Nothing else in the forest before us moves, not even a squirrel. That is a bad omen. I adjust the bow slung over my shoulder and pull my cloak closed. Behind me, several voices sing.

> *We've been called to wander,*
> *On a troublous road.*
> *A fortnight through cold dunes we went,*
> *O'er an ice bridge without snow.*
> *On Lady Anna's errand,*
> *We've faced dangers steep,*

Past floating mountains and wicked waves,
Till journey be complete.

"The men are ready, Lord Llachau," growls Bram. I look up. *Llachau.* After several months of going by this name, I should be used to it, but I am not. As much as this journey is an adventure, part of me cannot wait for it to be over so the men will stop calling me Llachau and I can go back to being my real self—Amr.

But, for now, we are in the depths of the forest on our way to the king of all this land, and I am giving orders to a company of men twice as old as I am and not allowed to call me by my real name.

Vows we made to gods and men,
And those we will not spurn,
Though dead we may be borne back home,
Hero songs we will have earned.

"Very good," I say, and I try to sound as deep and commanding as Bram. After all, I am nearly fifteen years old. My black wolf Ingulf leans his hefty body against my leg, and I scratch at his ears, feeling reassured. "Then we will continue the day's march."

Bram makes a grimace that reveals several missing teeth through his wiry black beard. He is as big as a bear and has many battle scars. Most people are afraid of him, but I have known him all my life and trust him to watch my back.

But as of yet we're stoutly souls,
And to home will soon fare forth.
Then light the fires, roast the meat,
And sorrows we'll drink no more!

As Bram turns to grunt orders to the laughing men, I tighten the strings of my pack and toss it into the wagon. I give a pat to Falla, the sturdy horse that has been pulling our belongings since we left my home of Tarn on the Lake. "Just a little further," I whisper to the poor beast. "We're not far now. We'll reach the walls of Din Arth in less than a fortnight, I'm sure." She nudges me with her nose and stamps a broad hoof. I know she is eager for journey's end too. We have already traveled over frigid land and icy bridges, over the Great Sea, and through bare forests since leaving our home in the Old North.

Bram gives me a curt nod, so I pull up the hood of my thick cloak and adjust the belt holding my dagger and sword. Then I stride out into the road. The ground glistens with the morning's fresh snowfall. For a minute, I pretend I am the leader of an army, even though it is only an army of ten men. I picture myself as the High King of Din Arth, marching before an army of thousands.

But a sudden cold wind whips at my blue cloak, spitting icy snow at my face, and too quickly I go back to feeling small and nervous, just a boy on an errand too big for him. I grab at the flapping fabric and yank the ends back over myself. Embarrassed, I glance over my shoulder, making sure no one saw me—particularly not the green-clad young lady now adjusting her own pack in the party behind ours.

"She's not looking at you."

With a sniff, I glare down at the great wolf trotting lazily beside me. "What makes you think I care?"

He raises his clever amber eyes and snorts a cloud of icy breath from his nose. I can tell he is grinning. "You forget how well I can read you by now," he says.

Anyone who sees Ingulf thinks he is nothing but a tame wolf, if a bit on the large side. Only my own household knows that Ingulf and I can talk to each other. After all, he is my Fetch and we have had a special bond since birth. Unfortunately, he is also a know-it-all who has noticed how it annoys me that the maiden Bóchra pays no attention to me.

I risk one more glance at the lady before I lose sight of her amongst her own clan. She is the real reason we are on this journey. She came to the realm of Tarn asking for our help in finding out the truth about the rumors of the high king's treachery. Treachery. We are supposed to be on friendly terms with him—even loyal to him—because of the old wars he helped to stop. But if he is trying to steal relics from the realms around him . . . it could mean war for all of us. The Lady Muirgen of the Green Isle sent her handmaiden Bóchra to plead for our help.

I gaze up at the frost-covered tree branches and frown. Bram does not allow me to speak to Bóchra, nor anyone in her company of seven men—well, mostly men. One other is a woman. Strangely, that maid follows Bóchra like a servant. A handmaiden with her own maid? That seems odd to me. They are a quiet bunch, usually taking up the rear guard, speaking to each other in their own language, not taking meals with the rest of us. For a lady's maid, Bóchra certainly is bossy to her own people. And it's curious that she carries that locket. I want to ask her about it, but she is proud and speaks to no one of my party but Bram, as he is mostly in charge. It bothers me that I can't tell her I'm son to the Lady Anna. She never even notices me.

"I wonder if the high king will be there when we arrive," I say aloud, staring ahead at the road we are following, so Ingulf gets the hint that he is not to mention Bóchra or I will have to kick him. "I suppose his fortifications must be greater than our own back in Tarn. I hope he agrees to see us. I've been practicing what I'm to say. Do you think he will grant our request for the Tyrfing Sword?"

"I hope so. It is not his to keep, since it belongs to your grandfathers. Lady Anna said he knows this. Also, don't forget that we have gifts in exchange." Ingulf nods toward the wagon. "And those gifts are not treasures to be sniffed at—even by a high king!"

He is right, of course. But I still wonder how the king came to have the Sword in the first place. Songs are sung about it and prophesies spoken of it. Before I was born, it was pulled from the great silver tree in my own land. I wish my lady mother would have given me the answers to these secrets. After all, this part of the reason I am to be found marching along this forsaken road, leagues on leagues from my childhood home and being called *Lord Llachau* by my mother's most trusted advisor.

I shove my hands deeper into the folds of my cloak and kick my boots through the heavy snow. Mother did not want me to go. She did not want to think I was ready for this journey. But I had turned fourteen, almost a man. In the end, it was brusque Bram who came to my aid. Bram had stood firm and told Mother, "Amr should get further training away from home. His skill with the bow is beyond anything else I can teach him. He is old enough to do his part." Bram's compliment must have impressed Mother, for he is extremely hard to please.

Mother always takes Bram's advice, but this time she did it reluctantly. And still she would not tell me anything about the Sword except that I must speak of it to no one—not even Bram— and that no one else is to know who I am. Then she made Bram accompany me. But Bram said that I must take my rightful responsibility as chief of the expedition.

So our plan is this: I will meet with the high king and give him our gifts and request the Sword. If he does not give it willingly, then I am to offer him my loyalty and service in his court—to be one of his own men—as a gift from the Lady Anna. This idea makes my skin prickle, because it means Ingulf and I might never return home. But if ever I get the Sword, I am to Guard it right away with every protective curse and rune I know.

"Stop worrying," Ingulf tells me. "We will get it." He always knows what I am thinking.

"I know we will. But I hope it's sooner than later."

Before Ingulf can respond, another voice cuts in. "What is going on there, Lord Llachau?"

I jump and look up in embarrassment when I realize it is Bram's hulking shadow that now engulfs us. "Ah." I clear my throat. "Nothing."

"Nothing is carrying you very quickly, then."

A glance behind shows me that we are well ahead of the rest of the company. "Sorry, sir." I slow down.

"*Sorry* doesn't raise dead men," Bram growls. "Be wise, not sorry. Tell me that you've at least learned that after all my years of hounding you."

At this, I smirk teasingly. Bram forgets I am not his student anymore. "What if I say no? Shall we have a duel?" I lay my hand on the sword hilt at my side.

But Bram does not grin back.

Hesitantly, I let my hand fall. "All right," I mumble. "I understand—be wise. But," I add, "don't forget I have Ingulf. He's an excellent guard."

At that moment, there is a shout from behind and the *twang* of an arrow loosed. Before I can even blink, I am knocked flat over as Bram shields me with his body and several more arrows fly.

Then I hear laughter and see a dead bird drop from the sky, an arrow in it.

"Supper for today," one of the men shouts. Ah. So, it is just my men hunting pheasants. Relieved, I grin at them. It was a good shot.

But Bram takes three long strides and snatches up the bird carcass. "Enough," he growls and yanks out his dagger, waving it like a madman. "What do you think you are doing? Do not be so careless that you forget your duty!"

I exchange a startled glance with Ingulf. This behavior is grim even for Bram.

"I only meant to give us a head start on supper," one man begins nervously.

"But we ought to be keeping our eyes on the trees and brush—not the sky," Bram interrupts with a growl. "Remember what the folk at the last house said."

At this, I burst out laughing. "What? Is that all? You don't believe those old grandmothers' tales, do you?" Beside me, Ingulf snuffles. "They were kind old women, but they were rather silly."

Bram squints an eye. "Not all old women's tales are nonsense. It's not just they who warn of dangers here. The land outside the towers of Din Arth is known to be full of highwaymen and worse. We'd do well to keep our eyes open."

I stare at Bram in disbelief, but remain quiet like the others. Our journey feels heavy again. I glance back at the large man and wonder why he is taking old women's nonsense so seriously.

"What do you suppose he senses?" Ingulf asks me, turning his bulky head toward the trees on either side of us and sniffing the air.

I shrug, but make sure my hands have free access to sword and bow. It isn't like Bram to pay attention to idle hearsay. I suddenly remember that Mother has always said it's better to trust Bram's sense over our own eyes. I try to focus on the land around us. As I do, I begin to feel tense.

The ground at my feet slopes into a narrow dell. Straight across from me, the sun is a dim orange glow sinking behind the sea of trees. I take a deep breath and lead the march downward.

The bottom of the dell is murky, and the air feels still and wet. The snow is deeper around my shins. I can hear the creaking of the wagon behind me.

Suddenly, Bram jerks up his arm and pulls the horse to a halt, looking around like an animal sensing danger.

At my side, Ingulf crouches and lays his ears back. "Enemies!" he barks, just as Bram shouts, "Prepare!" and yanks his sword from its sheath with a sharp *shrang!*

I jerk out my own weapon as a crowd of thieves leap like angry giant insects out of evergreen bushes and from behind trees. Our company of ten is easily surrounded.

From all around me come shouts, and snow like sparks showers from the trees. I whack one man hard in the jaw with the pommel of my sword and narrowly avoid a slashing dagger on my right. Out of the corner of my eye, I see a tall, black-hooded man just outside the ring of attackers. He wears a large gold crest on a chain around his neck, and a long brown lizard clings to it, its tail hanging across the man's chest. I am so startled by this strange sight that I receive a clout in the mouth from someone's fist before my brain reminds me that I am in the middle of a battle.

Ingulf springs to my side, teeth bared and fur bristling. Recovering, I lean against a tree and aim a two-footed kick at the behind of a particularly fat thief, sending him rolling into two other bandits to knock them down. Then I am back on my feet.

Breathing heavily, I whirl and run toward the wagon. I need to protect the treasure, or our whole journey will have been in vain. But how can we defend it against so many enemies? We are only ten—eighteen, if Maiden Bóchra's company catches up—and there are at least fifty of these bandits! Still, these thieves won't be able to take the treasures unless they kill both me and Bram, because we Guarded it with protective curses.

All at once, I feel something heavy land on my head and I tumble forward, hitting my shoulder against the wagon wheel. I shove myself back up and look toward the wagon. I see the brown lizard scrambling over the bags.

Before I can do anything, a piercing cry rings through the woods and the battle seems to stop for a moment. Then I hear Bram's roar, and everything moves again. Bóchra and her company have arrived, and her men aim arrows at the bandits' heads. But the lizard rummaging through the wagon does not notice this. I leap onto the wagon and snatch at the creature. It snaps at my hand and scurries off. Is it possible that it can see the treasure that we Guarded?

"Amr!"

At the sound of Ingulf's call, I spin around just as a knife slashes at my leg—it rips through my breeches and grazes my skin. With a roar of pain, I kick at the head of the bandit standing on the wheel. He flips back, and I swing my bow around, nocking an arrow, and fire a well-aimed shot at him. He does not get up again. Since I am high up, I have a good view of the battle. I shoot a few arrows at the enemy, hitting every target. But then I see Bóchra—she is fighting with a small-sword. Her movements are skilled and smooth. Then, out of nowhere, the brown lizard leaps onto her. No one else seems to notice what is happening.

I jump down from the wagon and run toward them, aiming an arrow. But the maiden is thrashing wildly, and I can't get a good shot. The lizard clings to her cloak, snatching with long claws at the locket around her neck.

"Stop!" I bellow and grab at the lizard with both hands. But the creature whips its spiny tail at my fingers, slashing them. Blood and skin spatter the white snow at my feet. Still, I manage to rip the lizard off the lady's cloak before I cannot hold onto it any longer. I drop it and try to draw my sword, but before my bloodied fingers can close around the hilt, the lizard vaults at my face.

Suddenly, there is a flapping of deep blue wings and the lizard is snatched mid-spring by dark bird claws, carried a ways off, and thrown into a thorny bush. I try to watch it, but its coloring hides it as it scuttles away in the bushes. Above, the dark raven screeches threateningly at the lizard. Bram is rushing toward me, sweat dripping down the sides of his head, blood trickling from a wound on his arm, his eyes glaring at the place where the lizard landed.

And then it is over. Six of the highwaymen have been captured, but another nine lie dead. One of my own company has been killed, and several others are badly wounded. But most of the bandits have escaped, along with the leader and his lizard, it seems. I feel blood slipping down the corner of my mouth, and my knuckles are cut to the bone.

Ingulf comes whimpering to me, dragging his front paw, and slouches at my feet. "I failed you," he mourns. "I did not reach you in time."

"Stop it." I turn my eyes to him, and I feel like a failure, too. "At least you saved me having my leg sliced off. But I did nothing except get my hand torn up. The lady's raven—it took care of the foul lizard."

Slowly, I rise and turn to see if the maiden Bóchra is all right. Her hood has fallen back, and her long chestnut hair, plaited with a single green strand, is disheveled. The long scar angling down her cheek gleams. Around her neck, undamaged by the lizard's attack, hangs a chain bearing the silver locket etched with delicate designs and symbols. The last of the sun's rays glint off its surface, making it look like scalding hot metal. But she does not look at me.

"Are you all right?" I ask her. She only nods curtly, flipping her locket back beneath her cloak. I wait for her to offer thanks for my help.

Instead, she snips, "You be the boy who spoke up in the Lady Anna's hall. You let the lizard escape."

At the word *boy*, anger blazes up inside me. "My apologies. Next time I'll be sure to hold on to it until it completely slices my hand off." I lift my hand, which is still gushing blood.

At least she has enough manners to blush at her rudeness. She even looks at me. I do not care if she is going to snap at me. "One should be grateful for help—even if it's from a mere boy," I seethe. I straighten and move to clutch my dagger hilt, but wince at the pain in my knuckles. So much for my manly appearance. All the anger smokes away, and I squeeze my palm in an attempt to ease the burning pain.

"You're right," she murmurs at last. "I owe you my thanks."

I nod and try to turn away from her bright green eyes, but it takes me longer than I like.

"Let me see your hand."

I pause uncertainly and glance around. Bram is busy with the wounded men, and Belta, his boar, guards the prisoners. Finally, I hold out my hand. "Are you gifted with healing?"

"I have some skill." She motions me over to a fallen tree and alights on the edge, taking a bag from her belt. With a shrug, I follow and sit beside her, keeping my stiffening fingers up. Tingles go through me as she touches my hand. Then she sprinkles some powder from her bag onto my injury. It stings terribly, and my eyes water, but I grit my teeth and do not cry out. She murmurs over my hand as the powder soaks into the blood. It still hurts, but the pain is less as she wraps my hand in bandages. I wonder if she is a healer in her own country. It strikes me that she has been gone from her land much longer than I have been from mine.

"Do you miss your homeland?" I ask.

She looks at me with suspicion, then uncertainty. Finally, she shakes escaped strands of hair back from her face and tilts her chin. "Aye," she says slowly.

"What is it like there?"

A faraway look glosses over her eyes, and a small smile creeps over her lips. "There be waterfalls there, hidden like jewels," she murmurs. "And stairways to the clouds, built by giants. In the morning the sunrise gleams through the lifting mist, like a window opening on wide green lands, and the rivers are musical. There be magic in the earth. Ierne, we call my land." She looks at me in surprise, as if she had forgotten I was still there.

My mother's handmaidens never spoke this way. At that moment, her dark raven flutters down and settles on her lap. Now the truth hits me like a club—her fighting technique, her healing skills, her words, her pride. She is no mere servant. "Why do you go by the name Bóchra?" I demand.

"What do you mean?" she asks a little too quickly.

"You aren't a handmaid to the Lady Muirgen." I look into her face and see fear there—fear of being found out. "You *are* the Lady Muirgen." For a moment, the words make me feel stronger—she is afraid of me now. A shudder runs through me. What am I thinking? This is something we have in common. We should be friends, not enemies.

She is about to protest, so I hurry on. "It's all right. I won't tell anyone. I have a secret as well." I feel my heart pumping hard in my chest and my cloak feels too hot. "My name is not Llachau. I am Amr, son of Lady Anna." A great relief flows through me as I say that. My real name. It feels good not to pretend. And to know the truth.

It seems that minutes pass as she stares at me in silence. "You and I are not so different," I insist. "Both away from our homes, forced to hide our names, fighting for peace and justice." I hesitate, wondering if I'm going too far, but not able to stop myself. "Why do you really think the high king is a traitor? Didn't he help stop the old Ravager from taking over? Why would he do that and then become a Ravager himself?"

Something about her relaxes, and she smiles sadly. "A man may start down a road with good intentions. But greed can turn him down the wrong path." She looks searchingly at me with her bright eyes. "He already has three sacred objects and has been searching for the Aurora Cauldron. Two nights ago, I received word that he has news of a mighty horn in the east."

I shrug. "So he has been greedy? But why was it so important for you to come yourself to stop him?"

She pauses before answering slowly. "The high king has something of my family's, and he refuses to give it up without . . . an exchange."

An exchange? I lean forward eagerly. "Then that is another thing we have in common. I too must make an exchange." But before I can ask what kind of exchange she must make, pain shoots down my arm as a large hand clamps tightly on my shoulder. I look up to see Bram's rigid face.

Holding me, Bram grunts, "Is the maiden well? Is your company fit to move on? I would like to get to a more secure place before nightfall."

She leaps to her feet, causing her raven to take flight. "Yes—were . . . were you able to get any information from the prisoners?"

"None. They will not speak. We planned to leave them here, tied up, if you think that would suit your lady's will."

She nods once and, without looking at me, flits away.

Still gripping my shoulder, Bram firmly turns me the other direction. "Instruct your men to be swift in tending their wounds. Does your lordship agree that we are in need of speed?"

"Are we going on then?" I gasp, hurrying on my injured leg to stay with Bram's long strides.

"You mean you aren't making all the decisions?" Bram snarls suddenly, startling me into silence. "*No one is to know who you are,*" he hisses. "You fool boy. Are you trying to ruin everything? Did you forget we are on an errand to a king—not on a children's picnic?"

So he had heard our conversation. I frown, dismayed. Why is everyone treating me like an infant? Does he think I am trusting the lady on a fanciful whim? "I know she is another Guardian," I snap in my defense.

Bram jerks his head sideways, one dark bushy eyebrow raised.

"That raven is her Fetch, like Ingulf is mine and Belta is yours," I continue in a rush. "And she is Guarding a locket."

But instead of acting pleased at my observation, Bram roughly grabs my arm, his face alarmingly twisted. "What about those thieves, boy? Why did they leave us when we were so outnumbered? They were looking for something. Those men were *Seekers!*" The words spit out of his mouth like sharp knives, and shivers that have nothing to do with the cold run through me. "If they find out you're a Relic Guardian, our whole world will fall back into the very turmoil that Lady Anna and myself and many others have battled to destroy! You are to tell *no one* who you are, to speak of Relics to *no one!*"

I stare at him, torn between fear of this unexpected side of Bram and anger at being treated like a traitor. But a curiosity strikes me about Bram's rage, and I wonder if, for all his senses, he has never noticed the lady's locket.

For a minute, Bram doesn't speak, but stands, his bear-sized chest heaving with fierce breathing. All at once, he releases me and looks forward again. His voice is a growl, but calm now. "Make sure you heed the Lady Anna's instructions to let no one know your identity, my lord. As in all things, she has her reasons for them."

By this I understand, with a heated feeling of confusion and unfairness, that the conversation is over.

THE MINOTAUR RIDDLE

1

TIME TO GO

The night was cool and deep, not a speck of sun left in the sky. On the ground, however, so many lights twinkled from houses and offices and stores that you might have thought the stars had fallen to the earth. At the Regal Garden Inn, lights still peeked through many curtained windows, and from room number two-twenty-six, the sound of laughing voices drifted into the night.

"Okay, okay. You'll like this one, kiddo. What gets up in the morning, goes to bed at night, and can force you to take off your coat?"

"Take off my coat?"

"That's right."

"Uhhh . . . a troll?"

"A troll? Trolls don't get up in the morning, dopey."

"Oh, right. Um, then, I dunno. A genie?"

"No way."

"I give up."

"It's the sun. Get it? When it shines hot, it makes you take off your coat."

"Ohh, the sun! I knew that, I really did."

"No you didn't. And you know what that means."

"No, no. Come on, that's not fair, Dad."

"Yes, sir, you lost fair and square. It's the rule. Now, take the fizz!"

A sudden *pop!* pierced the room, followed by a sharp hiss and then a confused eruption of spraying and laughter and barking.

Arthur Grey fell over the couch, drenched in foaming soda pop from his tousled brown hair to his striped socks and clutching his sides as he laughed.

"You, sir, have been fizzed." Etson Grey laughed as he tossed aside the now-empty glass bottle labeled "Fizzy-Winks Fizzy Soda." But he suddenly stopped laughing and looked around the room.

Arthur looked too. The walls, the television, the couch, the tan-and-green carpet, the desk and everything on it were bubbling with sticky, fizzy brown liquid. The rest of the room was covered with crumpled papers, popcorn, candy wrappers, used amusement park tickets, drinking straws and little orange cocktail umbrellas, suitcases, and random piles of balled-up clothes. "Uh-oh," Arthur groaned. "The hotel cleaning people aren't going to like this." He looked at his dad, who looked back at him.

They both fell onto the couch laughing again.

"Oh, brother," snorted Griffin. He rolled his eyes, tucked his tail beneath him, and began licking soda out of his fur.

The last week had been one of the best of Arthur's entire life. He and Etson had spent the Christmas holidays roaming the United States, staying in nice hotels with pools, playing arcades, seeing hockey games, and sneaking the dog into all of those places. For Arthur's birthday, Etson had taken him to Disney World in Florida. Between events, Etson had told funny stories about things that had happened at work, like people accidentally turning themselves orange or getting their neighbor stuck in freezing goo or causing their hair to disappear. It had definitely been a week Arthur would never forget.

In fact, the whole last year had been the most awesome in all his previous eleven years combined. It had all started with being kidnapped by his own dad, Etson Grey, whom he hadn't seen for five years, and then finding out the reason was that Etson worked for a secret society.

Well, actually it started right before that. When Arthur found Griffin.

Griffin was Arthur's Siberian husky. But Griffin was no ordinary dog. He was Arthur's Fetch, the animal companion with whom he had a special link. They had been separated for years without knowing about each other and had only met again last year. And Arthur was different than other twelve-year-olds: he was a Guardian. He could hide things so no one else could see them, an ability he had inherited from his mom, though he didn't understand it much. He had only found out about that secret last year too. There was only one other person who knew the whole truth about Arthur. . . .

"Well," Etson said at last, rubbing his neck and surveying the room again. "I guess we should clean up a little, huh? At least so we don't stick to the walls when we walk by?" He leaned on the wall and pretended to be stuck to it.

Arthur laughed.

Etson flipped open the nearest suitcase. He paused to take out a yellow piece of paper crinkled at the bottom of the suitcase. The paper turned bright red at his touch. "Yow!" He dropped it and stuck his fingers in his mouth. "Stupid Tricky Note—remind me not to get the ones that burn anymore." He slapped the suitcase closed and glared at the note, which had "Mom" written on it. "Oh yeah, I almost forgot. Hey, do me a favor, kiddo. Write a letter to your grandma. She's been pestering me about you."

"Gree?" Arthur asked in surprise. "Have you talked to her?"

"Yeah, well, I've gotta see her every now and again, right? I went over there before Winter Solstice. She wanted to see you and make sure you were eating well and all that. I told her you'd write a letter." He snickered as if at an inside joke.

Arthur pushed away any guilty feelings about his sudden departure from home over a year ago. "Yeah, okay. How is she?"

"Oh, you know my mother. Same as always. But don't worry about her. She says a neighborhood girl keeps her company. Heidi or Patricia or something."

"Penelope," Arthur said, and his stomach gave a turn.

Penelope Riffert had been Arthur's best friend back in Wisconsin. He left without saying good-bye to her.

"Yeah, Penelope. That was it."

"Okay. And do we have to pack? Tomorrow's New Year's Eve, right?" Arthur glanced at the clock above the television. It showed 10:52 p.m.

"Right." Etson also glanced at the clock. Then his eyes widened. "Oh, Pharos Lighthouse, I forgot!" He scrambled back to the suitcase, flung it open, and began stuffing clothes into it. "We're going to have to hurry. I can't believe I forgot how many time zones behind we are here!"

"Huh? But we have till tomorrow, don't we?"

"Where did I put my *Telecator*? Good grief, no. Time zones, you see. It's already almost eleven at night here, which means it's nearly six tomorrow morning there. Wait. No, we're in the Pacific time zone, so it's . . . great Holy Grails . . . *eight* in the morning there! That only gives us one hour to pack, get there, sail to the island, and find where the Initiates are meeting." Etson slammed the suitcase shut and yanked on the zipper. Then he paused. "Oh, wait a second. Don't they all sail together? Now that I think about it, I'm pretty sure they do. Phew! We don't have to worry about that part. We only have to pack, get there, and meet them at the landing shore. In that case, we've got time. I think I'll go shave."

Arthur and Griffin watched Etson mosey off into the bathroom. Griffin shook his head. "There's no such thing as *normal* with him, is there?"

Arthur grinned. "There's nothing normal about *any* of my

life, so I guess it's all right." And Griffin couldn't argue with that. After all, there weren't many people who could talk with their dogs, whose dads worked for the Historia Society, and who had spent a year learning about goblins and gnomes and magical birds, how to feed a cockatrice and milk a glowing cow, and then finished it all by finding a place no one believed in: Paititi, the lost city of gold.

Arthur reached into a pile of clothes to toss them in his bag. "Ouch!" he yelped, jerking his hand back. A small streak of blood now decorated his finger where something sharp had cut it. He squeezed his eyes shut as a stinging pain shot through his left eye for a few seconds. With a wince, he glanced over his shoulder to make sure Etson wasn't there to see what had happened. Then he frowned back at his finger. It now showed no sign of a cut.

From the floor, Griffin gave a grunt. "Did you just hurt your paw?" he demanded. "Because I thought I felt something in my front right."

Arthur waved him off. "Yeah. Nevermind. It healed up as usual. I just wish it wouldn't make my eye hurt." He returned to gathering his stuff. He didn't have too much to pack, though his bag and his trusty adventure belt pouches were definitely fuller than they had ever been. When he first left the old manor in Wisconsin where he used to live with his grandmother, he had only the clothes on his body, his belt, and Griffin. Now he had added so many things.

He twirled a feather—from the alicanto bird he had helped save in Peru. The feather was fiery red and glittering gold on one side, but the other side was sky blue with flecks of silver. He could hardly believe his adventures at the Conservatorium had been less than two weeks ago.

Next were the gifts Etson had given him last year. He dropped a fat book, *Muppledeim's Nearly Complete Encyclopedia of Non-Mythical Creatures and Plants*, into a large box. For a moment, Arthur considered his Walrus's Navigational Pocket Knife. With its mapping feature, it had helped him find his way out of maddening underground tunnels not long ago. He knew it was a dependable tool. Confidently, he slid it into his belt pouch.

On top of the *Muppledeim's* book, he tossed this year's twelfth-birthday gifts from Etson: a remote-controlled camera collar for Griffin and a set of invisible-ink pens.

Carefully, Arthur opened an ornately decorated cloth-bound book to the first page, where the words *Secrets of the Andes* and a dazzling painting of a golden sun face peered up at him. The book was handwritten and decorated throughout with the most amazing, lifelike drawings, made by his mother Helena, who had died when Arthur was only two years old. His adventurer friend Nicholas Hobbs had given the book to him. Arthur grinned, remembering the first time he met Hobbs. It was back in Wisconsin, and the Australian had stood out like a Christmas tree in July in his long, weather-stained traveling coat, well-used Panama hat, and twinkling grin. Arthur gently placed the book in with his other things.

Lastly, he tossed in his award. It was a medal in the shape of an exotic green and purple flower with the words, *Initiate of Conservation* embossed on it. It meant he had completed his year at the Conservatorium.

After packing these into his box, Arthur closed the lid. Then he began folding the box smaller and smaller until it fit nicely into his bag.

"How does it do that?" Griffin asked for the hundredth time in the last week, sniffing at the now-small box.

Arthur shrugged. "It's the box Penelope gave me," he said. Penelope had found it in a bin of donations from Arthur's old house. But he didn't think she knew it had this magical way of folding up small, even with things inside it. Penelope had always missed noticing things like that—she didn't like adventure.

Griffin cocked his head. "I remember her. She was nice and smelled like toothpaste. Don't you miss her?"

Arthur's brain immediately clouded over with a vivid picture of Penelope's round brown eyes behind her glasses, her two brown braids hanging over her shoulders—but most of all, her skeptical frown, which Arthur had turned away from last Christmas Eve and hadn't seen since. "Whatever," he grunted. "She didn't care about the stuff I do, like finding treasures or traveling around the world. Why would I miss her?"

The truth was, sometimes Arthur did think of Penelope. She'd been his best friend for four years, after all. She had followed him through plenty of goofy Robin Hood acts and searches for stories in her dad's bookstore and snooping away from Gree's nosy housekeeper. But that was before Penelope went all grown-up on him. Before she decided to stay behind.

"Aren't you going to put the locket in the box?" asked Griffin, interrupting Arthur's brooding.

"No, you know I won't." From around his neck Arthur lifted up a moon-silver locket decorated with very fine markings. He had found it at Ivor Manor and supposed it had belonged to his mother, Helena Grey. He hadn't shown it to anyone—not even his dad—not since the Peruvian wise woman had warned him to keep it safe. Arthur had tried offhandedly several times to ask Etson if his mom had owned any special jewelry. Etson, however, couldn't think of anything, and that ended the conversation. The locket was strangely linked to the dreams Arthur had begun having on his eleventh birthday.

"I had another dream on my birthday, you know," he told Griffin as he studied the locket.

Griffin's ears twitched. "Did you? You never mentioned it. Was it the same as the first dream?"

Arthur shook his head. "No. It was different. But it had the same people. The boy with the wolf and the green-cloaked lady. There were bandits and a battle and a lizard." He shuddered. It had been a very vivid dream, like the first one.

"What was the battle for?"

"For treasures, I think. No, wait." He paused. "Actually, I feel like it had something to do with the locket. This exact locket."

"And still no luck finding a way to open that thing, huh?"

Arthur glanced at the locket again. "No. It doesn't open. At least, not that I could ever figure out."

"Well, what was the dream about?"

"That boy with the wolf." For some reason, Arthur couldn't remember the names, but the images were very clear. "He's a Guardian, like me, and so is the green-cloaked lady." He cocked his head. "I wonder if it could be real."

Griffin snorted. "Real? From what you've told me, it doesn't sound like the way things are in modern times. High kings and daggers and castles. Are you sure it's not from a story?"

Arthur raised an eyebrow. "A story?"

"Yeah. Maybe your mom or somebody told you a story when you were a little baby and now you're dreaming about it."

A little shiver tingled through Arthur. He cleared his throat. "I guess it's possible . . . "

At that moment, the bathroom door opened. Arthur quickly dropped the locket beneath his shirt as Etson stepped out, patting his clean-shaven face with a hand towel. Etson stopped. "You packed already?" he asked, surveying the room.

"Um, mostly."

"Excellent. Well, I put in a request for a HistoriTaxi. We're in a bit of a rush, so I'm not going to risk a Transportal today."

Arthur felt his ears grow warm. He knew Etson was remembering the last time they tried to take a long-distance Transportal. Instead of dropping them near the Inka Palace Hotel in Peru, the transporting doorway had left them lost in the middle of a jungle. And since Etson couldn't find anything wrong with the device, it must have somehow been Arthur's fault. Although, afterward, Arthur had a strong suspicion that his mysterious locket had something to do with it.

At ten minutes till midnight, Arthur stood shivering outside the hotel with his bag and Griffin, waiting for Etson to pay and check out of the hotel.

"Okay," Etson said as he strode through the automatic doors, glancing at his Telecator watch. "Let's go to the back of the parking lot. It should be here any minute." He pulled his wheeled suitcase behind him as he hurried away from the well-lit hotel entrance.

Arthur and Griffin exchanged puzzled looks. "Uh, what should be here?"

"Why, the Borak Express, of course," Etson answered, glaring from the night sky back to his Telecator.

Arthur opened his mouth to ask what on earth a Borak was, but stopped when a glimmering light suddenly appeared in the dark sky. He watched it curiously. As it came closer he could hear what sounded like a very low airplane.

Etson blew out a breath. "Thank goodness. Here it comes."

What flew toward them could have been part of a magical circus. It was the strangest donkey Arthur had ever seen, and it was almost as big as an elephant. Arthur and Griffin jumped out of the way of the creature's wide, leathery wings as it clopped to a stop, its wings folding and its enormous, colorful tail fanning upward. Arthur stared open-mouthed. The creature had a bristly mane that was braided down its neck and glittered with Christmas ornaments. On the animal's back was a square, shimmering purple tent with gold tassels and embroidery. Hanging at its side was a sign that read:

THE MINOTAUR RIDDLE

Arthur and Griffin jumped when the tent wall split open and a small, plump man with a droopy black mustache and a tall red hat hopped out. They could hear awful elevator-jazz music coming from inside, the kind that reminded Arthur of the dentist's office. But he got a peek of purple and green cushions and a yellow lava lamp inside.

"Who rang for the Borak Express?" the man demanded, waving a clipboard as if it were a threatening sword. He looked sharply at the three before him. "You?" He aimed the clipboard at them.

"Yes," said Etson, eyeing the clipboard warily.

"Ah, good, sir." The man grinned and twitched his mustache. "Then climb aboard. We are heading for . . . " He looked down at his clipboard. "Ah, the Main Hall, then."

Etson hefted up his suitcase. "How long will it take?"

The man straightened his hat. "Ah then. Not more than ten minutes."

"Ten minutes?" Etson frowned. "Hey, I need to be there at nine o'clock their time. My Initiate's got his orientation. Can't you cut a few corners to speed things up?"

The man raised his eyebrows till they were hidden by his hat. "Look then, sir. It is over ten thousand kilometers to Greece. You want take airplanes and see how long that takes? Much more than ten minutes! And do you know how difficult it is made that Chuki here is always wanting to stop for snacking on peanuts every time we pass airplanes? I tell you, we'll go as fast as we can, but I can't make promises, especially if you're having a dog along. The dogs are a distraction, you know. And they cost extra." He pointed the clipboard at Etson's chest.

"Okay, okay," sighed Etson. "Come on, kiddo. Let's go."

Arthur settled on a green cushion squashed between Etson and Griffin. The tent smelled of hay and too much perfume, and the awful tinny music (which Arthur was sure came out of a potted plant behind him) made him want to bang his head on a wall. He was just thinking that the driver was lucky to be outside the tent and wondering how exactly he would get the strange Borak creature to take off when the driver yanked back the curtains and hopped inside. He swooshed off his tall hat, smoothed his hair over the shiny bald patch at the top of his head, and sat cross-legged on top of several red pillows before pulling out a book called *From Cab Driver to Rich Ruler in Seven Easy Steps.*

"Uh, aren't you going to drive?" Arthur asked.

The man looked up with a *pff* sound that made his big mustache quiver. "Drive? Nobody drives Chuki here. She knows the way. I tell her where we go, and she takes us." He smiled and wiggled his eyebrows. "Very fast."

With a sudden jolt, they took off. Arthur was thrown to one side, all the loose cushions toppling over on top of him. The lava lamp bubbled happily.

Arthur could tell they were going fast. Out of the small plastic window in the front of the tent he could see the sun rising before them. The dark ground disappeared and was suddenly dark water turning orange as the sun rose.

"Can I see that?" Etson asked suddenly. He pointed to a magazine next to the driver.

"The *Historia Today*? Sure. But give it back when finished. I paid five *arrowheads* for it."

"Arrowheads?" asked Arthur.

The driver frowned at him suspiciously. "Yes, five—I don't look down on money, no matter how little!"

Etson handed Arthur a spade-shaped coin that seemed to be made of rock. It looked like the head of an arrow. "We use those for little things that cost less than an hour's worth of work," Etson murmured as he scanned the magazine article.

Griffin snorted at the coin. "Who uses rocks for money? Squirrels?"

Arthur rolled his eyes, then noticed Etson shaking his head at the magazine. "What's wrong?" asked Arthur.

"Just an article on finances. The Society had some money in a risky project investment that went bad a couple of months ago. Quite a few Members lost money on it."

"Did you?"

"No, thank Zeus. But Historia is going to have to find someone else who will be willing to invest now."

Arthur tipped his head sideways to see the cover of the magazine. It contained an old black-and-white photograph of a middle-aged man patting a winged horse. Over part of it, in bright purple letters, was a note.

"Historia celebrates eighty years with traditional daring fun," Arthur read aloud. He raised his brows at Etson.

"Ah, I'd nearly forgotten," Etson smiled. "This is the Society's eightieth anniversary. It's going to be a spectacular year. Every month will bring new contests and games and booths."

Arthur blinked. "Like a fair?"

"Yeah, kinda like that. They've done it once every ten years for the last forty years or so. I've only been to one, but I remember it being a blast. I still have the trophy I won for Alchemy—that's the art of using chemicals to transform matter, you know."

"Contests and games sound like fun," Griffin said, scratching his ear.

With a grin, Arthur leaned back into his cushions. "Sounds like this year is gonna be exciting."

"You bet." Etson winked.

It wasn't long before Arthur's ears began to feel like they were full of bubbles that needed to pop—he yawned, and his ears crackled and cleared. They were slowing down, the shining water below dotted with islands and shores of European countries. They landed with a clobbering clatter.

The driver snapped his book shut. "Ah then. One *presto*, please."

"What?" exclaimed Etson. "That's an hour's worth of work. This trip took ten minutes!"

"Ah, but it was worth one hour. More than! I am giving you a great deal!"

While Etson argued with the driver about fair pay, Arthur

grabbed his bag and slid out of the tent, Griffin jumping down behind him. A chill wind blew at his hair and brought in a salty smell and the sound of waves and seagulls. For the second time in his life, he had landed from an unusual sort of transportation, with no idea where he was.

2
THE FIRST MYSTERIES

Etson glanced at his Telecator watch. Arthur could see its glowing face, which blinked, *Country—Greece; District—Nisos Zakynthos; Population—10,000; Danger—Low.* Etson pushed a button and the screen switched to an ordinary watch face.

"Wow, Greece," Arthur murmured excitedly. "I've never been to Greece before." That, of course, was an understatement. He'd never been *anywhere* before last year. Until then, Wisconsin was the only place he'd known.

"Okay, grab your bag. It's just after nine o'clock." Etson lifted a hand to shade his eyes from the sun glare on the water. "Hm. I don't see anyone. It would be just like Gamble to head off early and not wait for everyone to get here. He's always so impatient."

A shadow suddenly passed over them. Squinting upward, Arthur saw a magnificent white falcon with brown-speckled wings. He automatically frowned. "Gatriona," he murmured. He knew that bird. He had seen her twice over the holidays, spying on him as usual. And he knew whom she belonged to.

"Running late again, are you, Grey?"

Arthur and Etson spun around to see a weathered old man limping toward them, a brown cloak draped around his shoulders. He held a staff of woody vines that clasped a flame-shaped glass full of dancing blue fire above his head. Arthur found the odd staff fascinating. It seemed like it was still growing. And how did that ghostly fire keep burning?

"Oh, G-Gamble," sputtered Etson. "Great to see you—"

"Save it," snapped Gamble, his crooked mouth smirking and his dark eyes squinting behind his spectacles. Gatriona glided onto his cloaked shoulder. He nodded briefly to Arthur.

Arthur gave a half-smile and glanced down at Griffin.

"I don't think anything's gonna change," Griffin muttered. "You watch. Gamble will be the same grumpy old toad he was in Peru."

"I dunno," Arthur whispered back. "It was different last year. Now we know the truth—he's a Guardian, too."

"I'm telling you, he'll be driving you squirrely within a day."

"This way," the old man croaked, and he turned briskly to lead them to the sloping, rocky beach where six fishing boats were moored to the shore. The small boats were painted in bright combinations of blue, yellow, red, and white, reflected as floating blobs of color in the sloshing water. Most of them were full of people.

Arthur saw several hands waving wildly from one of the boats. He grinned and waved back.

"Go on." Etson smiled. "I'll take your bag and catch up later."

Arthur hurried toward the shore, Griffin bounding in front of him. Four young people waited in the boat. Two girls stood waving and another stared off into the distance, while a boy sat in a corner, looking rather green.

The girl with long, fiery orange hair, in which she wore a pair of large pink goggles, beckoned Arthur to the boat. "Howya, Arthur an' Griffin!" she exclaimed in her quick Irish accent. "Did ya have fun on yer *holliers*? I visited Nanna an' Granda an' my little brother out on their farm and it was so much fun to be there at Christmastime puttin' up holly an' candles an' tinsel an' makin' the Christmas seed cakes, though Nanna had to do those over because I burnt them all but I helped make pudding an' we had music an' Nanna liked the time-keepin' apron I made her before we went to the O'Sallies' house for dancin' an' food and it was such a fierce grand time."

"Sounds like fun, Pernille," Arthur grinned. Pernille Hanly was a year older than him and had been with him on his adventures at the Conservatorium, where her father was the Minister of Conservation. She hugged Griffin's neck and kissed his nose.

"We thought maybe you weren't coming back," moaned the sick-looking, sandy-haired boy. His voice maintained its normal crisp English sound in spite of his discomfort. He pushed his glasses up his nose. "You might have been in an accident, set on fire, or eaten by wild, cannibalistic pygmies. Not that it matters. We'll probably all get turned over in this boat by a sea serpent and pulled beneath the treacherous waters to our deaths before we ever leave shore—"

"Esmond has been saying lovely things like this nonstop since we got on," snapped the other girl, who was also English. Besides a nose ring and a half-dozen earrings, she had straight black hair streaked with red and wore high black boots and a torn black dress with white dragon-skull buttons. "Really, I'm ready to wring his little neck."

Arthur couldn't help smiling as he climbed into the rocking boat. "Well, that's how he always is. But what's your excuse, Idolette?" he asked, pointing to her depressing clothes.

She immediately smiled brightly. "Oh, right. I always dress like this when I first get to the main campus. Isn't it blindingly gothic? By the way, you didn't see a packet of Exploding Chewing Gum anywhere on shore, did you?" Idolette was always losing things.

Arthur looked around at his friends. Pernille Hanly, Esmond Falvey, and Idolette. He couldn't believe it had been little more than a week since he last saw them. It seemed like forever ago. Now here they were, Arthur and Esmond starting their second year on the Initiate Team, Pernille her third, and Idolette her fourth. But there was one girl Arthur didn't know.

"Arthur," bubbled Pernille, pointing to the girl at the front of the boat. "This is Nada Bhaksiana. She's new this year and she can speak eight languages, can you believe it?"

The girl turned to face him. She had long, dark brown hair and pale blue eyes in a solemn face. "Hallo," she said softly.

"Hey." Arthur nodded. Griffin wagged his tail at her.

"In a moment," came Gamble's croaking voice from a few boats down, "we'll be moving forward. Everyone remain seated and do not, I repeat, do *not* try to touch the hippocamps."

Griffin cocked his head at Arthur. "Did he say hippocamps? Aren't those giant—"

"Sea horses?" Arthur finished.

They toppled into each other as the boat jolted forward and then glided swiftly away from the rocky shore. They all scrambled to peer over the boat's edge, down into the clear, deep water. Beneath them, large sea horses with stiff, curled tails, two front hooves, and fins like small wings towed the boats.

"Aw, we got a blue one," Idolette simpered. "It's so cute!"

"But Gamble's right," sighed Esmond. "You won't think it's so cute if you try to pet it and it instantly tears off your arm, leaving you with only a bloody stump. These creatures are carnivores—that means meat-eaters, you know—to the highest degree."

Idolette gave Esmond a horrified, mouth-gaping look and then sniffed disdainfully at him as she plopped back into her seat.

Griffin stared into the water, his tail wagging. "The horses are pulling the boats. That one over there is green, and over there is a purple one."

"Well, it's true," Esmond complained to Idolette. "Of course, these have been domesticated, trained to pull the boats without causing damage, but still. You can never be too cautious."

The boats traveled quickly through the swishing water that slapped their sides, and soon the shoreline was lost behind them. Arthur waved to people he knew in the other boats. A few birds passed overhead, their calls mixing with the sloshing of the waves. The ride was a little choppy, but it was otherwise pleasant: the cool wind whooshing past their faces, the cloudless blue sky open before them, the turquoise water beckoning them. Schools of fish glided beneath them, dolphins followed at a distance with an occasional leap out of the water for a better look at the boats, and a long and dark figure dived deeper . . . *Was that a mermaid?*

Arthur turned to blurt this thought aloud, but realized that the new girl, Nada Bhaksiana, was speaking to Pernille.

"I have heard," she was saying, "that there are mysteries at the Main Hall. What are these?"

Arthur listened intently, thinking of the Member at Conservation who had mentioned a mystery here. He smiled as he also remembered the promise he'd made to his friend Sebas—to be sure to go on adventures while here.

Idolette leaned over. "Oh, it's nothing spooky, if that's what you're worried about. Well, I mean, sort of. They say that Homer Siegfried's ghost roams the island, but I don't think that's true. Although the forest is really creepy. Another story is about a beast that lives in the water and can eat people whole. Or eat the whole island. Or something. But I don't think that's true, either."

"Is it so that Madam Siegfried is very strict? That she rules Historia with a tight fist?"

"Well, she's an in-charge sort of person," Pernille beamed. "She has to be, she does. Otherwise Homer wouldnay picked her to take over after him. She's fierce accomplished."

"Is it true some Members opposed her and she threw them out of Historia?"

"Right," Idolette put in. "She doesn't let anyone cross her. It's best not to get on her bad side."

Griffin turned to Arthur. "You'd better behave here, or it sounds like we'll spend a lot of time getting punished."

Arthur shrugged. "I always behave."

Griffin snorted.

"Hey," said Arthur, turning to the others. "Have any of you heard about Historia's eightieth anniversary celebrations?" He noticed that Nada leaned forward with interest.

Pernille's eyes twinkled. "Oh, yes! My da says it's going to be the best one yet and they'll have a list of the competitions out next week an' I only hope there will be some I can do 'cause it sounds like so much fun!"

Arthur blinked. "You mean Initiates can enter the contests, too?"

Idolette waved her hand airily and leaned back. "Of course. Anyone can enter, right? Some competitions will have different levels—you know, like Initiates-only or Masters-only and all that. I can't believe you didn't hear about it. My mum says Dad usually finds a couple of good pieces at the jewelry booths for her."

Arthur raised his eyebrows at Griffin, excitement making his stomach squirm. Griffin's lips pulled back in a doggy grin.

"Don't get your hopes up," Esmond grunted from the corner. "I don't expect Master Gamble will give us any free time for frivolities like contests and games."

Everyone ignored him.

"I heard," Pernille went on, "they always open the celebrations with a real chariot race. Isn't that a gas?"

"Whoa," Arthur laughed. "That would be so cool."

A sudden splash and a scream from the boat behind them interrupted Pernille's reply. "What was that?" Idolette squeaked, whirling around.

Griffin turned to Arthur. "Someone fell overboard."

Esmond muttered, "I expect the hippocamps will devour whoever fell out."

They all leaned over the edge, trying to see what was happening. In the other boat, a girl and two boys grabbed the wet shirt of a sopping dark-haired boy and heaved him back into their boat. He grinned and waved, after squirting out a stream of water from his mouth.

"Oh, it's just Donovan," snapped Idolette. "Why am I not surprised?"

Pernille smiled and shook her head. "He can't help it. He just likes to have fun."

Gamble's boat was in the lead when they came up on two small islands. Standing on each island, like tall torches reaching toward the sky, was an old lighthouse. As they approached, Gamble stood up in his boat and raised his arm high. An object in his hand reflected light from each lighthouse and shone like a star. Then the other boats came forward, passing the tiny islands, and suddenly Arthur saw appear before them a much larger island that hadn't been there a moment ago.

The island was made up of brown and grey rocky hills, pale sandy beaches, and splotches of greenery. At its bottom was a white wall that seemed to follow the entire coast of the island. Like clouds against the blue sky, white buildings gleamed on the higher hilltops. From the crevices peeked blue-domed stucco gazebos and apartments. Everything was smooth and curved like waves. But at the topmost point of the island stood a colossal rotunda of white marble with columns and open porticos. *Like a palace of Roman gods*, Arthur thought excitedly.

"What's all that metal stuff in the water?" asked Griffin.

Arthur shielded his eyes and faced the east side of the island, where large buoys bobbed in the water. Chains dangled between them, blocking off the area. Beyond them, scaffolding stuck out of the water like the skeleton of a giant sea creature. It looked like something was being built there in the middle of the bay.

The hippocamps pulled the boats into a sheltered cove, where a long dock reached out into the quietly lapping water. Arthur grabbed his pack and climbed out of the boat onto the dock. Before him, the rock wall rose sharply up, but a footpath had been cut into it, zigzagging to make the climb easier.

"So, Lisle," breathed Oliver Johnson, a large boy in his fifth year on the Initiate Team, "thought you'd go for . . . a swim . . . in December, huh?"

Donovan Lisle grinned and shook his damp hair. "I just

wanted a closer look at that mermaid. I almost touched her hair. I swear it was like seaweed."

A tall lanky boy gave him a high five, and the other boys laughed.

"Oh hold it down," snorted Idolette, rolling her eyes. "Come on."

Arthur hung back a little to hear the rest of Donovan's story. "That's not all I saw," he bragged. "There was a pit in the seafloor. I could see that far down, it was so clear. It was a big black pit. I'm pretty sure that mermaid would've grabbed me and dragged me straight down there if you guys hadn't rescued me."

From the front of the group, Esmond raised one hand, shoving up his glasses with the other. "What," he demanded, "is all the scaffolding in the water for?"

"Construction," Gamble cawed. "They've been working on an underwater work zone for salvaging artifacts found in the sea and training Investigations divers. Eventually, they'll include an underwater museum. It's supposed to open for the end of Historia's eightieth-year anniversary." He glared at them. "But it's not done."

Pernille grinned at Arthur and Esmond. "Can you believe Historia's been around for eighty years?"

Gamble's falcon, Gatriona, gave a shriek from her place on his shoulder. "Listen up!" Gamble stamped his staff. "I know some of you have a hard time following rules"—he glared at Donovan—"but if you know what's good for you, you'll stay away from the west bay. Otherwise, this team will be minus an

Initiate. Now, what are you gaping seagulls waiting for? Up we go!"

Arthur frowned at Idolette beside him, suspicion kicking in. "Do you know what he's talking about? What's at the bay that he doesn't want us to see?"

Idolette adjusted a dragon-skull button on her dress. "I think it's the sirens. They call it Siren Bay, after all. I was here for my first year, and some kid got his leg torn off."

Arthur turned to Esmond, who didn't waste a moment.

"Sirens are kind of like mermaids," Esmond explained. "Although some references say they have wings. However, they are said to be so hideous that no one in their right mind would approach them. They use their beautiful singing voices to seduce sailors into a trap, such as an embankment or high rocks, where their ships run aground and then the sirens tear them apart."

Pernille shuddered. "Don't have to tell *me* not to go there. I like my arms and legs to stay on my body, thanks."

They marched up the path until, gasping and huffing for breath, they reached a small grove of eucalyptus trees. Two of the trees arched toward each other over a doorway at the path's end. The Initiates gathered in the cool shadows of the trees.

Gamble stepped forward, held out his staff, and knocked once, twice, three times on the bronze door. Everyone waited in silence as the ringing knocks resounded like shots around the rocky island.

At last, the final echo died away. Then, slowly, the door opened, releasing rays of sunlight that poured over them, making them squint. But before their eyes could adjust, the light faded. And a large shadow crept out.

3

WELCOME TO ORIGINS

In the doorway beneath the trees stood two men. One wore a tall, pointed hat and a stern expression. The other man wore turquoise robes and smiled gently. It was he who spoke first. "Ah, welcome, Initiates and Members," he said, his voice soft and calm. "I am In-Su Jung, Minister of Origins. And this"—he gestured to the man beside him—"is Member Sam Cartwright, the steward here." He turned to bow to Gamble, who bowed as well, and they shook hands. "Welcome back, Master Gamble."

"Oh, yeah," muttered Griffin. "I almost forgot Gamble used to work at this location. He was the old steward or something, right?"

Arthur nodded as he and the others followed the two men through the gate and approached the enormous marble building. As they drew closer, Arthur noticed a purple banner that glittered up high with the words, "80th Anniversary of the Historia Society." Minister Jung led them onto the gleaming white portico and gathered them below the banner.

Arthur recognized most of the Initiate Team from last year. They all varied in age, from ten to sixteen, and in how many years they had been part of the team, from fifth-years Oliver Johnson, Thespia Galoopsa, and Tad Weinstein, to the three new Initiates whom Arthur had just met—quiet Miriam Hummad, gruff Oscar Verda, and Nada Bhaksiana. There was Kelly Sullivan, a shy boy who joined at the same time as Arthur and Esmond, and clowny Donovan Lisle was in his third year, along with Pernille. Bridgette Lane and Charda Kuchamann were fourth-years like Idolette.

"Welcome to Elysium Island, our Mediterranean location." Minister Jung gestured behind him. "This is Main Hall, where the Department of Origins is stationed. There are nine hundred Members and Masters who live on Elysium Island, four hundred with Origins and five hundred with the Department of Experiments.

"This island will not be found on any maps outside of Historia. This is because it is securely hidden from prying eyes. It simply cannot be seen unless the security measures are bypassed by use of a special badge. You each will receive a badge that will allow you entrance to certain areas, but it will not let you through the perimeter, so please stay on-site. If you find any questions, I or Steward Cartwright will be most pleased to help you. But come. Your things will be taken to your apartments, and we will leave you to Master Gamble, who will give you the tour of Origins." He exchanged formal bows once more with Gamble and then turned to enter the open doors behind him.

In his oddly Grim Reaper-like way, Gamble stood still, his cloak clutched around him, his staff reaching above his head. He was stonily silent as everyone hushed and any shifting subsided.

Then he crowed, "Lesson of the day!" and everyone jumped.

"Why does he have to be so bloody weird?" hissed Idolette, who had, in her surprise, hit herself in the head.

"If you're going to rock the boat," Gamble snapped, "you'd better know how to swim. Follow me." With a vulture-like flutter of his cloak, Gamble spun around and limped forward, leading the team through the bronze doors into a vast circular room. The floor was of white marble peppered with tiny black flecks. In the center was a large round tile with the seal of the Department of Origins.

Arthur studied the scroll seal with interest. He didn't know much about Origins. "Idolette," he said, "did you say you've been here before?"

"Well, not to this part, right? I had Experiments on the other side of the island a while back. I'm so glad I don't have to go to that department again. Wickedly boring. You'll hate Experiments when it's your turn to go there."

Arthur and Pernille exchanged smiles. Apparently, Idolette had forgotten that it was Pernille's greatest dream to be in Experiments and that Arthur's dad was the Minister of Experiments.

Gamble stopped the group, and they gazed around the circular room. "This entry room is the Rotunda. Main Hall is made up of three concentric rings connected by hallways," he croaked, before leading them on again.

"Concentric," Esmond repeated for anyone around him to hear, "that means circles around each other, a large circle on the outside and smaller circles within it."

"Thanks, Mr. Dictionary," yawned Donovan.

Gamble glared at Esmond, who closed his mouth instead of retorting. "Now," snapped Gamble, "there is only one hall that goes straight through from the entrance to the center and out to the other side. We are about to enter it. This hall is called the Museo Gallery."

The hall they entered had an enormously high, arched ceiling. Arthur felt like he was in a magnificent train station. Light filtered in through elaborate skylights that made the floor, which was the same smooth white marble as in the entryway, sparkle and the stucco walls look rough. But the decor was what gave it the name. The corridor walls were crowded with displays of artifacts and reminded Arthur of a museum.

Pernille tugged on Arthur's shirtsleeve and pointed. "That's a mechanical arrow launcher, it is," she breathed. She wasn't the only one in awe.

"Say, look—is that a Gorgon head?"

"I swear that's a pharaoh's scepter."

"Ew, what is *that*?"

"Is that the crown that King John lost in the thirteenth century?"

"Don't touch *anything*," Gamble interjected.

The great hall held ancient pots, jewelry, paintings, statues, masks of gold and copper and wood, strange animals preserved so well they still looked alive, and tall and short pedestals holding up clay or marble busts. There were statues of gods, and frescoes painted with stories from *The Arabian Nights*, tales of King Arthur, and Odysseus's sea voyages. A spiral mollusk shell the size of a small car glittered silver and copper, and Arthur wondered about the size of the creature that had inhabited it. Other Members stood talking or walked purposefully down the Museo Gallery, some dressed in togas or robes so that Arthur felt like he'd walked right into the days of ancient Greece.

Partway along the hall, another hallway intersected their path. Gamble led them to the right. Along either side of the curved hallway, rows of doors alternated, some open, some closed. "This way we have the Transfer Depot, where most travel takes place and where all Transportals and earth samples are logged and stored. We also have Preservations." He pointed to a door with a small window.

In front of Arthur, Tad Weinstein turned from the door's window and shrugged. Arthur took a turn peering through the window and saw a brightly lit room where two men stood bent over a parchment on a glass table. The scene made Arthur think of doctors performing surgery.

"Here we have Masters Stefanidis and Jolly," said Gamble. "They're among the first to see new documents and artifacts. They analyze each artifact's condition and determine if it needs to go to Repair or directly to Archives. Then they are in charge of scanning each document or artifact and, if it needs to be replaced, ordering a special copy that duplicates it perfectly down to the very fingerprints on it. That is what they call a Scanograph."

One of the men in the room glanced up and waved cheerfully.

"Also," continued Gamble, leading them onward, "we have several laboratories, the Archives, the Room of Repair . . ."

At one point, they passed a door blocked by a thick purply plant. Without stopping, Gamble warned, "I wouldn't get too close to that, if I were you." But Donovan (who seemed attracted to anything he was supposed to stay away from) tried to inspect it as soon as Gamble's back was turned.

Instantly, Arthur shouted and jumped back from the suddenly writhing plant. With tentacles quicker than spider legs, it snatched Donovan and slammed him against the door in a tight hold.

"I ought to leave you up there till the end of the year," Gamble grumbled, glaring at Donovan. "That would save me a whole lot of trouble." But he reached out to tickle a tentacle of the plant and snapped, "Puttydurms."

The plant immediately sprang back into innocent stillness, and Donovan fell to the floor with a *thunk* and a shaky grin.

Idolette shuddered and scooted further away from the door. "Someone could get killed in this place," she muttered.

They continued along the curved hallway, Gamble occasionally pausing to point out rooms or sometimes just to stare at the ceiling for no apparent reason.

"What's that?" asked Griffin. Arthur raised his eyebrows at the dog, but then he heard it too. An odd, buzzing sound. They turned the bend, where the Museo Gallery again met their path. They continued along it, approaching a giant archway, where the buzzing seemed to come from. On either side of the archway, two statues solemnly stood guard—one with the body of a man and the head of a long-beaked bird, and the other with a plump human body and the head of an elephant with a broken tusk.

Arthur gazed up at these—they were twice as tall as Gamble and a bit disturbing, with their hollow marble eyes and grotesque heads.

Esmond pushed up his glasses and reverently murmured, "The Egyptian god Thoth and the Hindu god Ganesh—they protect learning and books. That can only mean . . . "

"And here," Gamble said finally, "we've come to the very heart of Main Hall. None outside of Historia has ever seen the likes of it, not since the days of Alexander the Great. This is the Library of Origins."

"Sweet knowledge of centaurs," whispered Esmond.

The enormous round room was not like any library Arthur

had ever visited. Bookshelves lined the walls, stretching from the floor to the distant ceiling, every inch filled with cubbies containing paper books, bamboo books, cloth books, scrolls, and tablets. In front of the shelves were two long desks, one stretching the length of one side of the room and another along the other side. At the desks Arthur found the source of the buzzing.

Tiny women and men with wrinkly faces, large noses and ears, and glassy eyes moved swiftly about the library. They looked rather like clumps of clay molded by a four-year-old. Arthur recognized them as gnomes and remembered that they could move a distance of five feet in the blink of an eye. The buzzing came from their swift movements.

Esmond gawked, his eyes wide behind his glasses. "They're book gnomes," he whispered to Arthur. "I've read about them. They make excellent librarians because they have the best memories on earth. They each memorize hundreds of books, so if you have a question or need to find a book or even a reference from a book, they can help you right away. You just push a topic button on the desks and the right book gnome will get to you."

Arthur and Griffin followed the others across the library. Hundreds of gnomes flitted between book cubbies, helping Members. Some sat cross-legged behind the desks, drinking from tiny cups and chatting to each other in their strange, rumbly language, while others zipped up thin ladders—which moved without anyone touching them—and retrieved books from fifty feet up.

Arthur noticed an area marked "Drop," where gnomes placed books in baskets labeled with each department name and the books disappeared. Arthur remembered getting a book while at the Department of Conservation. This must be how it had been sent.

The group walked around an enormous wooden column in the middle of the library. It was carved with scenes from stories—Arthur recognized Rapunzel's long hair flowing from a doorless tower, the god Odin on his eight-legged horse, a fierce queen glaring into a mirror, and even a frog caught mid-transformation into a man (Arthur shuddered with the grossness of that one).

At the library exit, the museum hallway continued, and Gamble led them along it until another hall intersected and they went left. Down that way, they saw several map rooms, deciphering rooms, and more laboratories.

At long last, they made their way out into the bright sunshine and cool breeze that came over the sea.

"My stomach's growling," groaned Griffin. "I wonder what's for dinner, or breakfast, or lunch, or whatever our next meal is supposed to be."

"I don't know," said Arthur. "Do you suppose mealtimes are whenever you can get them? Like at the Conservatorium?"

Esmond raised an eyebrow at Arthur. "Obviously, you didn't get the schedule," he said glumly. "Today we have the afternoon meal out on the portico with Minister Jung and the owner of the entire Historia Society, Madam Siegfried herself."

Arthur and Griffin exchanged nervous glances. After all

he had heard about Madam Siegfried, Arthur expected to find someone like his grandmother: strict mouth, prim posture, severely pinned-up hair, and old-fashioned button-up dress. But the woman who waited for them outside was absolutely nothing like that.

Foot tapping and hands in her pockets, a short lady watched them file out. Her eyes were snappy and blue and her smile teasing. She wore a khaki pantsuit, with a red kerchief tied around her neck, and on her head was a curved hat with several pink and red flowers at the back. Beneath her hat, her grey hair was short and reminded Arthur of ladies from old black-and-white movies.

"Welcome! Welcome, everyone. Come out and sit. It's simply divine outside. I'm Madam Agnes Alcott Siegfried, but don't call me all that—just *Madam* will do. Now, after such a long tour, you all must be starving. I trust Master Gamble didn't make the place sound too dull for you? He knows this place inside and out, to the tiniest speck in the corners, but he's more likely to stare at the speck than talk about the adventures going on around you. All right, Gamble?" She shook Gamble's hand heartily, and the old man grunted a greeting.

The Initiates and Members sat down at the prepared tables. Arthur, Idolette, Pernille, and Esmond sat around one table, and Griffin slunk under the tablecloth. Their view was of the open blue sea. The sun was a great pearl nearing the edge of the water.

"Everything's like I remember it," Idolette said, smoothing her black-and-red hair over her shoulder and picking up an olive from a bowl on the table. "It's so beautiful here. I love the sea and the wind. It's like being inside a real film from the cinema, or on holiday, right?"

Esmond sighed. "Except that tomorrow the holiday will end abruptly, rather like life would if you were stabbed in the back, and we'll start our work."

Idolette made a face. "How could I forget? No one can be on holiday when Esmond's around."

Pernille giggled.

Food was brought out: delicious lamb kabobs, olive oil and bread, grapes, and almond-filled honey pastries. Arthur set a plate of meat on the floor, and Griffin licked it clean in about ten seconds.

Before she started on her food, Pernille exclaimed, "Japers, I nearly forgot . . . " and dug in her pack briefly before coming back up with a handful of colorful plastic cards. "When I had a spare moment I found some handy materials and I made these for us over our break," she bubbled, passing them out to each of her friends.

Arthur looked at the two she had handed to him. He immediately grinned.

The Spyglass Squad
Arthur Grey
"The Explorer"

"Pernille, these are great—they're like our own club badges." Idolette positively glowed as she looked up from hers.

"These make it official! We really are the Spyglass Squad, just like that old tosser Chadwick-rat called us last year. But he didn't know we were going to stop him." She smiled dreamily. "I'm the Actress. What are you, Esmond?"

Esmond cleared his throat. "The Bookworm," he muttered.

Idolette burst out laughing.

"I thought it was witty," Pernille said, smiling hopefully, "because that's what Arthur and Sebas called you at first and it's true but it turned out to be a really great role that we need for our squad. I'm just the Mechanic." She shrugged, then pointed to Arthur's second card. "An' there's one for Griffin, too, he's our Scout, ain't that a gas? And look at the blank space on the bottom—this is the great part, I think—we can write messages on the cards and they'll code themselves and decode only when one of us touches it." She gazed ecstatically at each of them.

"That's really amazing, Pernille," Arthur exclaimed. "You've really outdone yourself this time—it's great."

The others murmured their impressed approval, and Pernille grinned from ear to ear, her freckles hidden beneath the warm glowing pink of her cheeks.

While they ate and exchanged winter break stories, Arthur watched Madam Siegfried talking with Gamble and a few other Members. At one point she looked serious. But then she let out a loud cackle and the seriousness broke. "You old coot!" she laughed at scowling Gamble, and Arthur immediately knew he would like this lady. Eventually, Madam Siegfried began moving around, stopping at each table with pleasant cheer, shaking hands and chatting.

"Ah, my dear Idolette. You look like a funeral. Is this in honor of your father?" Madam Siegfried kissed Idolette's cheek.

For a moment, Arthur stared from Idolette to Madam with his mouth hanging open. Then he slapped his forehead. Of course, how could he have forgotten? Madam Siegfried was Idolette's grandmother.

"Yes, I was hoping he'd be out to see me by now."

"Sorry to disappoint, my darling, but he isn't here right now. You'll have to show him your joy at another time." She clapped her hands together and faced the others. "Now who else do we have here? Ah, Pernille Hanly, I'd know that bright hair anywhere. Spanking to see you again. You're taller, dear. Such a lovely young lady now! And your father beams when he tells me about your way with gadgets. I bet you're excited to be getting to Experiments in a couple of years."

Pernille nodded vigorously. "Yes, I can hardly wait but I really like everything I've studied so far."

"Good girl." Madam Siegfried turned to Esmond, who was staring forlornly at his plate. "And you must be Mr. Esmond Falvey," she continued. "I was the Minister of Origins when your father was here. I am quite sad to inform you that he was simply awful in that field." She did not look sad in the least, and a small smile crept onto Esmond's face. "And what is that clown of a brother of yours doing nowadays? Is he homeless yet?"

"No, Madam. He's in Asia working for Conservation. He's quite successful."

"Well, what a surprise! I was sure he'd been a waste of our

time." She winked. "Well, what about you, Mr. Falvey? What field are you aiming for? Not Conservation, I hope. We have enough of those. How about Origins?"

"No—er—yes, Madam. I mean, I'm not sure."

"Well, you let me know what you think of Origins after this year. We could use a few more good Originors, you know."

Arthur was amazed at how Madam Siegfried seemed to read right into each person and know about their families and their likes or dislikes and just what to say to them. He remembered—with some guilty embarrassment—the letter of Esmond's he'd found last year. It had revealed that Esmond's father wanted him to go into Conservation, whether Esmond wanted to or not. Did Mrs. Siegfried know this?

"And you must be Minister Grey's boy."

Arthur sat upright. "Uh, yes, ma'am."

"His name is Arthur, Gran," Idolette said before popping a grape into her mouth.

"Ah, yes, Arthur." Madam Siegfried smiled, and her eyes twinkled as she took his hand and shook his whole arm in greeting. "I'd never have guessed it, what with your darker hair. Though you do have those gorgeous eyes."

Arthur felt his cheeks burn as Idolette and Pernille giggled beside him, and even Griffin snorted from under the table.

"Those eyes belonged to her, you know," Mrs. Siegfried continued with a dismissive wave at the girls. "You are your mother from the nose up. Except for her hair, which was quite fair."

Arthur tried to swallow the dryness in his throat. "Right," he croaked.

"Idolette told me all about your saving her life in the menacing jungles of Peru last spring, and of course everyone was talking about how you saved the alicanto from poachers. Perhaps Conservation *could* use another hand. That's obviously the place for you, Mr. Grey. Conservation. Just like your mother." She looked around the table. "And don't you have a dog? I hope Master Gamble didn't make you leave him in the apartments?"

"Uh, no ma'am. He's here." He shoved Griffin with his foot, and the dog stuck his head out from under the tablecloth.

"My, what odd eyes he has. But I suppose it's not uncommon for some dogs to have two eye colors, is it? Well, he's a nice-looking fellow. Looks like a wolf. Is he wild?"

"Um, not too much."

She opened her mouth to say something else, but stopped and raised her pencil-thin eyebrows at the Hall's double doors, through which the steward now hurried with a harried expression. "Well, what is it, Sam?"

Steward Cartwright bent close to her ear. Since he was right next to them, Arthur could hear what he said. "He's back," the steward muttered. "What should I do?"

Madam Siegfried's face immediately broke into a wide smile. But not before Arthur caught a wrathful spark flicker like lightning through her eyes. "I'll go see to it." Loudly, she called, "Carry on, everyone. Eat, drink, be merry! For tomorrow we work."

Arthur watched her leave. He frowned down at Griffin. "What was that about, I wonder?"

Idolette, who had heard nothing, only sighed dramatically. "She's in her seventies, would you believe it? She looks incredible. I really hope I've got her genes."

Stomach full of food and brain full of information, Arthur began to feel sleepy. It was dusk, the sun almost completely dipped into the sea and the sky a twinkling purple, when Steward Cartwright appeared and announced that it was time for him to show them to their apartments. So Arthur popped a last pistachio into his mouth and headed down the steps back to the path.

They passed neat little gardens of flowers, tall bushes that made cozy nooks with benches, and the occasional statue of elegant Greek gods or tiny wrinkled garden gnomes or large, stern-faced sphinxes. Their way was lit by little lights floating in a stream alongside the path.

"Will-o'-the-wisps," Esmond explained, pointing to the floating lights. "Small spirits that light your path. Though the wild ones may try to lead you astray."

Arthur yawned in reply.

They came to a crowd of white buildings with stuccoed stairs leading from one to another or to roofs or patios in a confusing maze. Behind the buildings, to the west, dark trees huddled together. The apartments flaunted elaborate signs with names of famous gods like Zeus, Thor, Ishtar, and Artemis. The Initiate apartments were more traditionally shaped, each being two levels high, with doors alternately yellow, blue, or turquoise. A warmly glowing lamp shone above each door, and a mailbox hung to the side. Arthur and Griffin were given a badge for number nine in Apartment Odin, along with a handwritten note. Arthur opened the note.

"What flat are you lot in? I'm in Athena," said Idolette.

"So am I," exclaimed a girl Arthur recognized as Charda Kuchamann. The two girls hugged.

Suddenly, a chilling howl rose, echoing from the depths of the forest behind them, followed by a clank and low whispers that might or might not have been the wind. Arthur felt his neck prickle. Griffin's hackles stood up.

"Homer's ghost," muttered Charda.

Esmond clucked his tongue. "Don't be delirious."

"You obviously haven't been to Elysium Island before." Charda shuddered.

"Why?" Arthur demanded. "What's in the forest?"

Tad Weinstein stood beside them, looking toward the forest nervously as he answered, "No one knows. But you won't catch Members going through there to get to Experiments, even though that's the shortest way. They all take boats—or Transportals."

"It's Homer's ghost," Charda insisted. "Everyone knows he died very suddenly, and they say he had a debt he never paid, and his spirit is restless because of it. Isn't that right, Idolette?"

Idolette hugged herself and only shrugged nervously. "I'm going in," she murmured. "'Night."

Kelly Sullivan came over to see if Esmond knew they were

sharing number three in Apartment Odin. "Aren't you staying with your dad?" Kelly asked Arthur.

"No," Arthur replied, folding up his note and pocketing it. "He says his place is on the other side of the island, near Experiments, where he works. So I'll be here. But he'll come up later."

"And Griffin is your roommate, I suppose," sighed Esmond. "I wonder if they gave you two beds or if you have to fight over who sleeps on the floor."

Fortunately, all the rooms were furnished with two beds, so Griffin got his own. Their apartment was one room. Some walls were white stucco and several accented in turquoise, like the door. In a wide arched doorway, a curtain of strings knotted with shells and beads clinked softly in the breeze. On the other side was an open terrace with two chairs, a little table, and two flowerpots.

Arthur stared out of the doorway, the cold wind whipping at his hair. He breathed in and slowly exhaled. "This island feels familiar," he murmured.

"Yeah," Griffin agreed, pausing from sniffing the room corners. "Do you think your parents brought you here when you were a baby?"

Arthur shrugged. "That must be it." He rubbed his eyes and yawned. He felt heavy and tired. After all, he'd been awake for nearly two days straight. "I'm gonna change and go to bed." As he dug pajamas out of his bag, Arthur voiced a thought that had been lurking at the back of his mind for nearly two weeks now. "Do you think Gamble will show me anything about

Guarding? I hoped he would say something after dinner today, but I didn't see him when it was time to go."

Satisfied that the room was in good order, Griffin jumped onto his bed. "I dunno," he admitted. "But I still don't like him. He's very closed. Very secretive. He's like a rude pecking crow—those ones that drop pinecones on your head if you accidentally fall asleep under their tree. Anyway, you remember what he said before—*just learn from Historia for now.* I don't think Gamble's going to be any help at all."

"You're probably right. Still." Arthur had to believe Gamble had a surprise up his cloaked sleeve. He wouldn't really leave Arthur in the dark about his powers. Would he?

A sudden orange glow shone from the place where Arthur had tossed his clothes. "What the . . . ?" He jumped up to inspect. It came from his jeans pocket.

"What is it?" Griffin asked from the bed.

Arthur shook his pants, and a card fell out of the back pocket. It was the badge Pernille had made for him. On the bottom section that used to be blank there was now a messy scribbling that looked like a two-year-old had gotten a little carried away with a marker. Arthur bent over to pick it up. The moment his hand touched the card, the scribble rearranged itself into legible words followed by a symbol of gears: "It's grand to be back with everyone. Nighty-night! From Pernille."

Griffin turned and lay down. "She sure is a funny girl, that Pernille." He let out a contented yawn. "I like her."

Even though Arthur was so exhausted, he didn't sleep well. For a while he tossed and turned. When he finally fell asleep, he had strange dreams. In one, he stood high on a rocky ledge with clear turquoise waves crashing below him, spraying foamy water. He was waiting for something. Then a trumpeting blast, like the cracking of an iceberg or the neigh of a warhorse or the bellow of a bull blew past him. He knew he couldn't wait anymore—it was time to go.

4

LET THE GAMES BEGIN

January first began the Initiates' first week of Origins training. Arthur, Griffin, and Esmond left breakfast in their apartment lounge, meeting up with Pernille on her way from Apartment Isis. They were dressed in the new uniform for Origins—shirts with the Origins scroll logo over one pocket and plain pants or skirts, all in pale, lightweight fabrics. These were very different from the thick, bright clothes they had worn in the mountains of Peru. The biggest difference from life at Conservation, however, was that Griffin was now free to roam with Arthur.

"I see Idolette is missing," sighed Esmond. "I hope she didn't get poisoned by the glazed apples this morning, did she? I never trust apples of any sort. There's nearly always poison in them."

"No," Pernille said with a smile. She gestured over her

shoulder, where Arthur could see Idolette walking with Tad Weinstein, giggling at something he had said.

Esmond shook his head. "I see. She's found this year's homework assistant," he snorted. "Although I doubt she'll get many correct answers from *Tad*."

They reported with the rest of the Initiate Team to the Main Hall rotunda for their first day of work. Just outside the main group stood the girl Arthur had met on his boat ride the day before—Nada Bhaksiana. She appeared to be deep in a foreign-language conversation with a bust of Homer Siegfried.

Arthur leaned toward Esmond. "Does it seem weird to you," he said, eyeing Nada, "that she is talking French to a statue?"

With a sigh, Esmond rolled his eyes. "Arthur, that would be strange, but she isn't speaking French—she's speaking German."

"Whatever. Why would German be any less weird?"

Esmond couldn't help his look of pained patience. "Well, obviously, Siegfried is a Germanic name, you know."

"Who cares?" Arthur sputtered. "She's talking to a statue!"

Gamble limped into the room and stopped next to a stone bench loaded with boxes. The Initiates quieted down in order to get Gamble's notorious "lesson of the day" over with as quickly as possible.

Gamble didn't let them down. "Lesson of the day! Use what you've already got, then use what others give you," he crowed. "What you're given today will help you this year. These tools are an Originor's best friends. You will each come forward and take one from each box." Gatriona perched on a chair, watching them. She shrieked at Kelly Sullivan when he accidentally grabbed two from the same box.

Arthur looked at each new item as Gamble went over it.

"The electronic book is a Translationary. You'll find it useful when you get stuck on the meanings of ancient Greek or Old Norse words. They are extremely expensive to make. Don't break them."

Beside Arthur, Pernille had pulled her large pink goggles down over her eyes and was eagerly dismantling her Translationary.

"Next, you should each have a copy of *The Handy Handbook of Basic Lore* by Ferry Godmotha. I don't really have to explain that, do I? Lastly, you've got a Quick-Preserve Kit for when we touch on ways to preserve old documents and whatnot. Now. These tools will help you as you learn the work of Origins. Do not lose them." He looked directly at Idolette, who rolled her eyes. "Now," he snapped. "Follow me."

Partway down the Museo Gallery they came to Minister Jung's office, where he waited placidly in sky-blue robes. "Ah, young Initiates," he said in his soft voice. "Before you begin, you should know the importance of Origins as a part of Historia, one of the very most important parts. All departments must work together. You came from Conservation, where they study creatures and plants and how to care for and use them for their individual value."

Idolette stifled a yawn. Donovan didn't bother trying to stop his.

"Here," Minister Jung continued, undisturbed, "we help

Conservation by keeping information in lore and myth. This helps them identify creatures and their uses, how to care for them, and sometimes how to locate them. How many of you know the Greek tale of the flying horse Pegasus? Well, using that tale, we were able to tell that this creature enjoys clear spring water above all other kinds, and also what sort of bridle to use to domesticate it. So, as you see, Origins is like a key used to unlock the secrets of other departments."

Arthur's attention wandered. He noticed a large metal slab in the ceiling above. "What's that?" he asked aloud.

Everyone turned to look at him.

"Ah," Minister Jung nodded. "We have not had the need to use those for over a decade. That is one of the safety doors. They can come down in time of emergency to seal off sections of Main Hall."

"Seal off?" repeated Bridgette Lane.

"From fire?" demanded Esmond.

"From invaders?" asked Tad.

"Can they . . . stop trolls?" wondered Oliver Johnson.

The Minister smiled patiently. "Yes, all of those things. They are a part of the protection in place here to guard our most valued treasures from disappearing from history. But to keep them from *becoming* history, we teach them to our children. So, the first thing you will learn is what we call the Two L's: Language and Lore." He gestured down the passageway. "Master Gamble will now take you to the Lore Study."

The Lore Study was on the far side of Main Hall. The Initiates filed into a plain room and seated themselves at the wooden desks. Griffin sat on the floor next to Arthur, his tongue hanging out.

"So this is the kind of thing you do here, huh?" he said, glancing around. "Not very exciting is it? Can I take a nap?"

"Here," Gamble snapped, thunking his staff on the tile, "we keep artifact samples of beginner lore to help your study. Who can name the stories that these pictures come from?" He jerked his thumb toward a pull-down screen.

Esmond pushed up his glasses and raised his hand. But before he could say anything, Nada's soft voice spoke up from behind him.

"The gown of Cinderella, a golden arrow from Robin Hood, and the head of the Trojan Horse." She ended her answer with a polite smile, as if she had just offered everyone a plate of cookies.

Arthur stifled a snigger and pretended to be interested in the pictures as Esmond gave a scandalized gasp and muttered something that sounded a lot like, "How rude."

"The gown of Cinderella?" asked Oscar Verda.

Gamble made a harsh noise like an angry bird and stamped his staff again. "Did you think it was Prince Charming's dress? Of course Cinderella. Now. Are all the stories out there true? Certainly not. But you're here to find out that many have a lot of truth in them." He glared at them all. "What are you waiting for? Get out your *Basic Lore* handbooks!"

Five days a week, the Initiate Team had to study under Gamble's hawkish eye. He set them to memorizing whole sections of stories (all the boys complained when they were assigned "Snow White"), writing papers on the origins of strange artifacts, and stuffing their heads so full of facts about which mask went with *The Iliad* and which creature was first mentioned in the *Epic of Gilgamesh*, that most Initiates immediately decided Origins wouldn't be their career department of choice.

Between lessons and on weekends, Arthur hung out in his apartment's lounge—or sometimes at Athena or Isis—and played *Roman Life* ("You are sold as a gladiator and your arm is eaten by a lion; lose one turn") or *God-Speed* ("Hey, you can't put a Dionysus on a Zeus!") or, more often than he liked, worked on assignments. Each apartment had its own social lounge, styled to suit the building's particular god. So Apartment Odin had lots of polished wood pillars and furniture with complicated carvings that usually included dragon heads or a single mischievous eye, and a bar that served drinks like Wisdom Mead. (The wood gnome who tended the bar refused to let Initiates try it. "Adult Members only," he had sniffed. "Here's a sparkling cherry water.") Initiates also had a curfew of ten o'clock, when the bells tolled and they were booted from their lounges.

It turned out that the Two L's were a lot easier than Arthur expected. He had an excellent memory and enjoyed stories, so memorizing language and remembering details about Aladdin's lamp or the Golden Fleece were no problem. But Arthur was one of the few who thought so. The only other person who was as good at languages was Nada Bhaksiana, and that was because she already spoke eight of them.

It was Sunday afternoon, and the Spyglass Squad was spread out in Odin's lounge, working on an assignment. After nearly two weeks of Origins studies, most everyone was already itching for the year to end. Tales and folklore involved a lot more homework than caring for bizarre creatures had.

Idolette grumbled as she looked over at Pernille's copy of *The Handy Handbook of Basic Lore*. Her own book lay unopened and looked like it had been that way since she got it. "This is such a pain. How are we supposed to remember all that stuff?"

"It's all just words," Pernille agreed, poking her pen at her book. "No numbers or connectors or wires." Arthur couldn't help noticing that her book's margins were covered with doodles of gears and mechanical devices and arrows and notes like "try interconnecting precision coupler" and "change to gross weight" along with fractions and equations.

Arthur shrugged. "It's easy," he said. "I already have the first part of the *Epic of Gilgamesh* memorized. 'He who the heart of all matters hath proven, let him teach the nation. He who all knowledge possesseth, therein shall he school all the people. He shall his wisdom impart and so shall they share it together. Gilgamesh—he was the Master of wisdom, with knowledge of all things. He it was discovered the secret concealed . . . '"

Idolette turned her back to him. "Pernille, let me know when you've invented a brain-transferrer so we can just hook it up to Arthur's brain and get the answers the way he does—by soaking them up without any effort."

"Hey, I put in effort," he exclaimed indignantly.

"Yeah, right." She gathered up her papers and huffed out of the lounge.

Esmond glanced up disinterestedly from where he slouched with his book in a large, cushioned wooden chair. "She's just mad because she doesn't have Arran Whitman to do her work for her anymore." Arran was the pompous boy on last year's team who had often done Idolette's work for her as a way to get in with the Siegfried family.

"I do wish it was more like last year, though," Arthur admitted. "Didn't Gamble once say something about learning things by doing them instead of falling asleep at desks?"

"This is a different type of subject," Esmond put in, not looking up from his handbook. "You can't study everything in the same manner. To learn about the origins of things, you have to read what others said about them and study the things themselves."

Arthur sighed and frowned at a dragon mask hanging on the wall. "I wouldn't mind getting to the 'study the things themselves' part sooner rather than later. But it's not like the stories are completely boring. Right, Griffin?" He looked down at the dog beside him. "Griffin?"

Griffin jerked his head up, his eyes droopy and slobber hanging in strings from his mouth. "Huh? Wha'?"

Esmond smirked. "For once, I'd say Griffin doesn't agree with you."

Griffin was saved from a scolding by Pernille's sudden gasp. "What're they doin'?" she blurted, pointing behind Arthur.

Arthur turned in his chair to see five or six Members

standing around someone hammering two posters onto the wall.

"Is that what I think it is?" Pernille breathed, sliding her chair back and standing for a better look.

Arthur felt his stomach lurch like a Mexican jumping bean. "Let's go see." He and the other three headed toward the bar, where the small group of Members had already thickened to a crowd. Above their heads was the large purple banner reading "80 Years of Historia," and beneath it were two vivid new posters. Arthur could see the largest words at the top of each: MASTERS AND MEMBERS on one, INITIATES on the other.

"Ooh, a jousting tournament in April," exclaimed a young woman. "I'd better tell Herbert—he'll want to enter that."

"Won't it be dangerous?" another woman asked skeptically.

"No, no," gushed her friend. "It's all very safe. The only thing to worry about is the Alchemy competition—last time someone accidentally turned himself into gelatin and had to be carried to the specialists in a five-gallon bucket."

The pair moved out of the way, giving Arthur a clear view of the posters. His eyes darted eagerly to the Initiate Competitions poster.

Month	Event	*Registration Deadline
February	Creature Tricks	1 February
March	Tower Climb	1 March
April	Squire Joust	1 April

THE MINOTAUR RIDDLE

Month	Event	*Registration Deadline
June	Pyramid Build	1 April
July	Archery	1 July
August	Tapestry	1 May
October	Treasure Hunt	1 October
November	Alchemy	1 October
December	Bull-Leaping	1 November

*TO REGISTER, VISIT YOUR NEAREST DEPARTMENT'S ENTRANCE HALL

"How excitin'," exclaimed Pernille, her hands clasped together as she bobbed on her toes.

Esmond shook his head. "It sounds like a lot of accidents waiting to happen," he sighed. "The Master of Medicines is going to have his hands full, to say the least. It's all good and fine for grown-up Members to join the competitions, but Initiates don't have enough experience or strength for these sorts of tasks and—"

"The Squire Joust sounds interesting," Arthur interrupted excitedly. "I've only ridden a horse once ever, though, and that was in a circle around a pen. Do they give you any training, do you think?"

"I think for the Initiates they do." Pernille's eyes sparkled. "What about the Creature Tricks event? That might be fun. And registration's open for that one now."

"You should go for it, Pernille," Arthur said with a grin.

She giggled, her face almost as pink as the goggles in her hair. "Maybe I will."

Esmond shook his head. "No one ever listens to me," he huffed.

"Did you say something?" asked Arthur.

On Monday morning, a large sign in the entrance of Main Hall sparkled and changed colors so no one could miss it.

CHARIOT RACE, 24 JANUARY

In smaller lettering beneath, a notice glowered, "No winged horses allowed."

"That's in less than two weeks," Bridgette squealed, pointing at the sign.

Arthur had a hard time concentrating on the lesson after that, even when Minister Jung joined Gamble in leading the Initiates along the Museo Gallery to inspect several artifacts. Arthur felt nervous about the very idea of signing up for something. But he had the feeling he was the only one.

"I've signed up for everything," Tad bragged to Idolette, who goggled at him.

"Everything?" squeaked Kelly Sullivan.

"Yep. Well, except for Tapestry," Tad sniggered. "Sewing is for girls. But I registered for everything else. I figure it raises my odds of winning at something."

Kelly looked worriedly at Arthur. "I was thinking of maybe going for one thing," he confided, "something that doesn't involve climbing or falling or getting stabbed. Like Alchemy.

At least if I get hurt, I did it to myself instead of someone else doing it to me." He shrugged hopefully. "What about you?"

Arthur shifted his feet. "I dunno. My grandma never let me do any sports or anything. I don't really know how to do much."

"You should go for the Treasure Hunt," Kelly encouraged, his small eyes wide in his freckly face. "I bet you'd be good at that one."

Arthur shrugged. "Yeah, maybe." He glanced around, feeling embarrassed.

"I wish they'd let Initiates do the chariot races," Thespia Galoopsa was grumbling to Oliver and Tad, her fellow fifth-years.

Esmond raised his eyebrows at her and shook his head patronizingly. "Chariot racing takes a lot of upper-body strength," he explained. "Any Initiate would probably get ripped from the chariot and be trampled to death by horse hooves and wheels."

Thespia flexed her rather impressive arm muscles at Esmond, who backed away from her in surprise. "I do chariot laps for fun on holidays," she smirked. "My father is head of the Hippodrome Chariot Club, and we own a fifth-century Byzantine chariot."

Gamble abruptly stamped his staff against the floor and cawed, "Lesson of the day!" Everyone jumped. "Listen while your ears still work, because one day you'll really be hard of hearing."

Now that the Minister had their focus again, he smiled serenely and pointed out an odd contraption in front of them. It got Pernille's attention right away.

"What's it for?" she asked eagerly. "Why did they make it?"

"Ah," Minister Jung said with a careless nod, "we do not concern ourselves with *why*. Here in Origins, it's only the facts that matter, not the why."

Pernille's face fell, and Arthur felt bad for her. *She's the Mechanic, after all,* he thought. *Why things work is what she loves to find out.* Arthur tried to think of something nice to say to her, but his thoughts were interrupted by several gasps behind him. He looked over to see what was so interesting and found himself staring open-mouthed at a towering, curly-bearded man who wore a knitted sweater and had four horse legs attached to his pale brown horse body.

"Hullo, there, Prometheus," Gamble called, as the Minister nodded politely.

"Greetings, Minister, Master Gamble," replied Prometheus. "Greetings, Initiates who have never seen a centaur before."

Some of them managed to close their gaping mouths and murmured good-mornings.

"Are you in the middle of a lesson?" asked Prometheus, his heavily lidded eyes casting dolefully over the team.

"Yes," said the Minister. "They are to choose an artifact and look up all the places where they can find information about it in our many resources."

"Very good then," said Prometheus. "Might I suggest the OctoDiver as an interesting artifact?" He gestured to the large machine behind him. "Alexander the Great himself used one of these aquatic mechanisms in his explorations to help him conquer the then-known world. Some say he invented it. However!" He lifted a finger insistently.

The Minister rolled his eyes. "Not again."

"It's all a conspiracy theory to hide the truth! The OctoDiver was *really* invented by scientists from Atlantis who were researching the lowest places of the earth. Alexander the Not-so-Great-after-all only found it millennia later and tried to take credit for its creation and use it to steal deep sea treasures and—"

"All right, Prometheus," sighed the Minister, with a glance at the wide-eyed Initiates. "This lesson is over. They need to keep moving, you know."

As the week went on, more decorations sprang up around the complex, from bright banners and signs to an entire stadium on the lawns behind Main Hall. And there was so much buzz about the upcoming chariot race that Arthur felt like the entire island was filled with book gnomes. It was quite a job for Gamble and other tutors to keep the Initiate Team focused on learning the basics of Origins.

The following week, the Initiates were assigned to watch the Preservations Team at work. This team consisted of just two men, Zane and Jolly, whose job involved repairing, cleaning, and making Scanographs of documents and artifacts. Days working under those two ended up being some of Arthur's favorites.

Zane Stefanidis was a stocky man with dark hair and eyes. He wore traditional Greek clothes, including a pleated skirt ("It is not a skirt!" he insisted. "It's called a *foustanélla!*"), a vest with trim, and a tasseled cap on his head. Arthur soon learned that, although Zane didn't speak often, once he started, he could go on for a good hour straight, gesturing with his hands the entire time. It didn't take long for all the Initiates to figure out that he had a quick temper, especially if someone called him a Greek.

"Greek?" he would immediately roar. "We are not Greeks, we are Hellenes! Those Romans and their wrong names for everything. When they came, did they bother to ask us what we called ourselves? No! They stormed in and said, 'We will call you Greeks.' They didn't even ask for permission! And now everyone goes around calling us by the Romans' name, without even thinking that maybe we already had a name for ourselves!"

Some people were afraid of Zane, but Arthur liked him. He found that the loud man was extremely friendly if you asked him questions about his country and his family.

"Yes, I have nine children," he explained as he demonstrated the utmost care needed in cleaning a rune-inscribed boulder the size of a pickup truck. "All girls, but two are boys. The first five are married and bring their babies over all the time, as if I run a daycare center. '*Ti!*' I tell them, 'Go raise your own children. I have a job, you know!' But if they have ears in their heads, they don't work. And then my three brothers bring their children over and I say, '*Ti!* Do I run a hotel here? Go cook your own food!' But Mama cooks good food, so what can I say? And my sister brings her lyre and my brother brings his *bouzouki* and my sons bring their *zumas* and my daughters their tambourines, all to make music. So what can we do but have a party?"

True to his name, August Jolly always had a grin on his face. Nothing was ever serious to him. He was originally from northern Canada and was a bachelor, though Zane constantly chided him for this. But Jolly took it in good fun.

"Yeah, eh?" he grinned, popping his strawberry bubblegum bubble and taking off the sunglasses needed during Scanography demonstrations. "Zane's always trying to get me married off to every woman he knows. But I know all about wives, Zane. They hold you on puppet strings, don't they? If you put a toe out of line, they whip you back into shape."

"Yes, but at least I stay in good shape that way."

Jolly roared with laughter and turned to the Initiates. "Never bother trying to tell a Hellenic man that he's wrong, eh? Always remember, there are only two things the Hellenes really enjoy. Good food and a violent argument."

"That is absolutely not true!" Zane shouted, pounding his fist against the wall. "We also love good music!"

"Well, there will be plenty of good music at the opening ceremony tomorrow." Jolly winked. "Wouldn't miss that for a hundred packs of gum. Especially because I have a bet going that Conservation's going to win the chariot race."

Zane grunted and shook his head at the Initiates. "One day his betting is going to go too far. I just hope I am there to see it."

Jolly winked at Arthur, who stood next to him. "I hope he's not," he chuckled, "because he would lecture my ears off about it." He raised his voice. "But it's going to be something else, eh, Zane? You kids bring your binoculars or di-oculars or spyglasses or whatever you have, because you're going to want to see this race as close as you can!"

Jolly wasn't exaggerating, Arthur realized the next day when he and Griffin joined the hundreds of Members thronging up the path around Main Hall.

"Wow," Griffin muttered as they stepped onto the transformed grounds behind the Hall.

It was like a fair. Booths surrounded them every which way, sparkling with color and brimming with jewelry, handmade trinkets, or toys. The vendors' voices clouded the air.

"Real working catapults—get yours here!"

"Vanishing smoke, newly rediscovered. Vanish in a cloud of smoke!"

"Need a laugh? Get your own self-joking parchment. Reveals a different joke every time you unroll it!"

"Holograms—get your holograms! Star in a realistic sports game or build your own mansion. Also comes in Fly-Fishing, Dragon Dodge, and all new Chariot Racing!"

Carts and food stands wafted interesting smells at them as they passed—some good, some that made Arthur feel queasy. One stand had food so pungent that he broke into a sweat just passing it.

Farther down the path, Pernille found them and dragged Arthur forward to see the rows of chariots parked for viewing.

"We've been working on this baby for three years," bragged

one chariot owner. "Just updated the axle system and the shocks."

"Yes, it's hand-painted in the original Roman-era colors."

"It's hard to find parts for the pre-393s these days . . . "

"Indeed, this is an original 746 in great condition. It's for sale after the race . . . "

Arthur sampled food along the way—some Vietnamese food that was so spicy his eyes began watering instantly, Middle Eastern falafel that was green in the middle and made him think of seaweed but was actually really tasty, and even roasted guinea pig, which he'd had before in Peru. Idolette nearly convinced one vendor that she was old enough to have a sample of German beer, but unfortunately for her, Gamble turned up at that moment and gave her a ten-minute scolding.

"Thank the gods this only happens once every ten years," Gamble snapped as Idolette darted off to look at a jeweled hairpiece at another stall and Esmond and Pernille stopped to watch a snake charmer. "It's hard enough teaching you wandering dodos as it is without all the extra distractions." He crossed his arms around his staff, but Arthur thought he saw Gamble's mouth bend upward in the briefest of smiles. "So. You keeping up with your studies?"

Arthur nodded quickly. "It's not hard. I can remember stuff pretty easily."

"So I noticed. Well, if you think that's easy, wait till you get to Special Occurrences. Our kind do well in that field."

Arthur felt his heart stop for a second before launching

into an extra-fast beat. Griffin looked up in surprise. "Do you mean—" Arthur breathed.

"And of course," Gamble interrupted, "with Etson Grey being a natural in Experiments, I expect you'll have an easy time there, too. Might be able to have extracurricular lessons sooner than I thought."

A grin slid up Arthur's face. That could only mean one thing. Guarding lessons. "When?" he demanded.

"We'll see. Maybe—"

But he was cut off by a squeal from Pernille, who appeared next to Arthur and grabbed his arm. "Arthur!" she shouted, apparently forgetting she was right next to his ear. "They're taking the chariots away an' the race is goin' to start any minute so let's hurry an' get good seats so we can watch the race!"

Arthur turned to look back at Gamble, but the old man was gone. Slightly disappointed, he followed after Pernille, Griffin beside him.

Ten minutes later, the Spyglass Squad clambered across the wooden stadium benches to open seats, juggling hot dogs, gyros, fish sticks, and flavored ice cones. Around them, the noise of excited chatter, loud laughter, booming shouts, and echoing claps was enough to make Arthur's head swim. Below them was a sandy track where the charioteers were getting ready.

"I can't believe I let you talk me into coming to this," Esmond muttered from where he slouched on the bench beside Griffin. "This is going to be a bloodbath. Look at those horses. Once they start going they'll be impossible to stop. Someone's bound to get trampled."

Idolette peered down through her antique spyglass. "I was hoping someone would bring winged horses."

"They're specifically banned," Esmond glowered.

"Yeah, that's what would make it so fun, right?"

Esmond gaped at her.

Arthur stared down toward the ten stamping teams of horses as their owners adjusted their gear. "I wish I had some binoculars," he muttered, taking a large bite of his meaty gyro.

"I'll share my di-oculars," Pernille bubbled, holding out a pair of what looked like two binoculars stuck together. "I'll show you how to use them."

As Arthur peered through the lower part of the di-oculars, Pernille adjusted the knobs so his view changed its zoom, its angle, and even showed two views at once. "My mam bought these from a peddler a long time ago," she gushed. "We used them for spying phoenixes in Turkey once."

Using the oculars, Arthur studied the charioteers below. Each team had four horses to a chariot. Every set was decorated differently, depending on which department they represented. Some of the Members looked intimidating, dressed like Roman soldiers, while others wore simpler shepherds' cloaks, and some just wore everyday clothes. One man was wearing a bicycle helmet. The chariots were just as different from one another, some made of painted wood, others of wicker or even bronze. Arthur could see why Jolly would think that Conservation's team would win—their horses wore dragon headpieces and looked like they might breathe fire.

When all the contestants were ready, a Member dressed

like a medieval herald walked onto the track and blew his long trumpet. "Welcome to the opening chariot race of the eightieth year of the Historia Society," he shouted, his voice echoing around the stadium.

Arthur clapped hard with all the other Members and Initiates in the stands.

"On this fourth decadal celebration, we have ten teams competing for the coveted laurel wreath. Number 32 is the Conservation team, who came away with the wreath last decade. Number 40 is Investigations, 26 is Experiments, 34 is Special Occurrences, and 18 is Origins. For the freelancers, we have the Classical Chariot Club sponsoring number 87, the Hellenes Force with number 65, the Thimbleton family with 79, the Wallace Clan with 93, and finally number 51 for the Hippodrome Chariot Club."

"You watch," Esmond warned above the tumult of cheers and applause. "The wheels are always coming off of the chariots in these games and the drivers thrown off and the horses injured. There's going to be a horrible accident in the first five minutes."

Fortunately, Esmond was completely wrong.

There were several close calls, like when numbers 40 and 65 briefly rubbed wheels, giving off a spine-shivering metallic shriek, but they broke apart quickly.

Arthur and Pernille switched back and forth with the dioculars, and even Esmond took a turn. At some point, Esmond pointed out the different rein styles—the Greek method of tying them around your waist and the Roman way of simply holding them in your hands. Arthur was amazed at how the drivers could hold onto the horses' reins at all, with their chariots swaying (or even bouncing) and the waves of dust that poured over them as they raced around the track.

In the end, the Conservation team, number 32, finished the twelfth lap first, with the Hippodrome Chariot Club's number 51 finishing a close second.

"It's so excitin' it just makes you want to go sign up for one of the competitions, doesn't it!" Pernille squealed as she jumped up and down, clapping.

By the time Arthur and Griffin got back to their apartments, they were completely coated in gritty dust and Arthur's skin was pink with sunburn. But it was certainly a race he wouldn't forget in a hurry. Before he went to bed that night, Arthur felt his pant leg grow warm. He dug into his pocket and pulled out his Spyglass Squad card. A message unscrambled itself. "I did it. I signed up for Creature Tricks," followed by a picture of gears as the signature—Pernille. Part of him felt glad for her, that she'd gotten up the courage to join a competition. The rest of him sagged under an invisible weight, wondering if he'd ever mount up his own courage.

5

TRANSLATIONARY TROUBLES

The excitement of the opening chariot race was over sooner than the Initiates wanted, and normal schedules sank back in with the force of a heavy hammer. On a blustery, wet Monday, the Initiates found Madam Siegfried herself waiting for them in the hall.

"Origins was my field, you know. Before I had to start my regular job of bossing people around," she cackled as she led them into the Translations Room.

Madam clapped her hands together as the Initiates took their seats. "Listen up, ladies and lords! I've got a brand-new shiny *drachm* here for someone to earn," she said, holding up a large silver coin with an engraving on it. "Most of you have owned arrowheads or even prestos, but this little beauty is worth eight prestos—that's an entire day's work! You can go to the shops and get yourself a fine set of mini racing chariots or even a Dragon Dodge hologram with this."

Madam sure has talent for getting attention, Arthur thought, sitting up straighter. She had every eye on her.

"All you have to do," she continued, "is tell me who was the first person to discover the existence of the Old Mermish language and where."

Before Arthur could even register the word *Mermish*, both Esmond's and Nada's hands had jerked upward.

"How do they do that?" Griffin muttered.

With a delighted laugh, Madam Siegfried eyed the two Initiates. "How fitting. Looks like I may have to get another drachm." She pointed. "Sir Falvey, answer the first part of the question, please."

"Master Rhubarb Winston," he blurted, and by the way he clamped his mouth shut after that, Arthur could tell it was torture for Esmond not to gush out the rest of the answer.

"Good, good. And Lady Bhaksiana, the second part?"

Nada folded her hands on the desk and blinked once. "He discovered it in an old text hidden in the home of a Romanian lord."

Esmond let out a disappointed grunt.

"Flawless. Well, ladies first, so here's your drachm, my dear. Sir Falvey, I'll get you another one later. Now, let's go over this invaluable tool, the Translationary. I will admit it's not as up-to-date as it should be—old Rhubarb hasn't given us his English translations from Old Mermish yet, for one thing. And since I daresay Rhubarb is one of the few on this planet who knows Old Mermish, we've got to wait for the old coot to finish. Pop-pop now. Everyone get out your Translationary."

Arthur dug his Translationary out of his pack and fiddled with it to turn it on. He waved off Griffin, who tried to peer over his lap at it.

"So, how does it work?" Griffin asked, politely curious.

Suddenly Arthur's Translationary lit up and shouted, "*Woof, ruff!* is the English onomatopoeic equivalent of unknown dog words."

Arthur looked up, his face red. For a moment, the room was dead silent and everyone—including Madam Siegfried—stared at him. Then Madam broke into a cackle, and the whole room filled with laughter. Arthur mouthed, "Good going." Griffin just wagged his tail.

"Looks like we need to include dog language on that thing, too." Madam waved her hand and gave another snorting laugh. "Well, let's get back to work."

They were in the middle of learning to use type or voice to look up words when Kelly accidentally said "hiccup" instead of "Hittite," so that his Translationary began to make hiccuping noises, and no one could figure out how to make it stop.

"There, there, dearie." Madam Siegfried patted Kelly's head sympathetically. "Just go take that down to Member Compter and he'll get that fixed." She opened the door for Kelly to go out, and there stood Steward Sam Cartwright, his hand raised to knock.

"Off you go, Mr. Sullivan. What can I do for you, Sam?"

"Madam," the steward said, "I've got bad news."

Arthur ignored Donovan, who sat behind him typing words like "puke" and "flatulence" into his Translationary, with the volume turned way up, causing raucous laughter around him when the device pronounced them.

"We just got word," the steward continued quietly, "that there was an accident in Egypt. Apparently, a bomb went off. They suspect that the Seeker's Guild was involved."

Madam Siegfried's mouth pressed into a thin, wrinkly line. "I assume it was near one of our sites? Go on, tell me the worst of it."

"Well, two Members were injured, but they'll be all right. The worst is," he cleared his throat and bowed his head, "the Nubian artifact collection was completely destroyed. We lost everything. And," he continued, not looking Madam in the eye, "three more of our investors have decided to pull out of talks."

Her eyes flitted closed and she breathed heavily, her nostrils flaring. In that moment, Arthur knew that all the stories about Madam Siegfried's iron hand were true, and he thought she was going to explode. But she took another noisy breath and unclenched her fist. "There's only one thing to do then. Though you know how much I loathe the very idea."

Steward Cartwright slouched. "Are you sure?"

"I'm afraid so. Call the other investor. That's all there is to it. But you know the drill. Take all the *extra* precautions."

Arthur wondered what she meant. Investors? And one she hated, at that. What extra precautions was she talking about? Arthur turned to see if anyone else had heard.

"Fart," shouted Donovan's Translationary. "The usually stinky emission of gas by a person or animal."

At the Apartment Athena lounge that evening, Arthur worked impatiently on his chart of the travels of Odysseus, waiting for Esmond to finish complaining about Nada so he could tell the rest of the Spyglass Squad what he had heard.

" . . . and she thinks she knows everything," Esmond was whining.

Idolette made a face. "Oh, and that's not ironic or anything coming from you."

Esmond grunted. "I don't pretend to know everything."

"Anyway," Idolette smirked, "I think it's good for you to have someone who knows more than you do."

Esmond's eyes nearly bugged out. "She doesn't know *more* than me," he sputtered.

Arthur decided now would be a good time to interrupt. "Shut up, you two. Listen to what I heard today." He told them about Madam Siegfried's conversation with Steward Cartwright. "What do you suppose she meant about taking the extra precautions?"

"She must be doing this as a last resort," Esmond put in as he carefully folded his completed chart. "She must not trust this investor."

"Oh, that's some helpful news, Professor Obvious," snapped Idolette, flicking her pen at the table and glaring at it as though it had just insulted her.

Esmond sighed and pulled a magazine out of his bag.

"I just hope extra precautions aren't going to interfere with the games," Arthur continued, ignoring them.

Pernille wiggled in her seat. "I'm nervous enough as it is, I am," she admitted. "I do hope nothin' goes wrong. Has anyone else signed up for anythin'? You, Arthur?"

Arthur cleared his throat. "No, not yet. I'm still . . . you know . . . just thinking about it." He glanced next to him. "How about you, Idolette?"

But she was still staring menacingly at her pen. Every inch of her—clothes, makeup, nails, and even hair—glittered poisonous green like a dangerous serpent.

"Idolette?"

"What?" she snapped.

"Geez," Arthur grunted. "I just asked you a question. You don't need to bite my head off."

"Well, I've had enough questions, I think," Idolette huffed. "'Are you studying hard? What did you get on your last exam? What's your paper on? Do I need to talk to Minister Jung for you? What on earth are you wearing?' Blah, blah, blah."

Esmond raised his eyebrows over his glasses. "Your dad?"

"How did *you* know?" Idolette sniffed.

Esmond went back to his magazine. "Mine's the same way."

Idolette blinked. "Oh . . . "

After a few minutes of silence, Pernille gave a jaw-splitting yawn and began gathering her work. "I think that's it for me," she said with a sleepy smile. "I've got to get up early, and I'm beat. See ya."

Arthur glanced at the wall clock decorated with a wreath

of plastic olives and leaves. It was nearly ten o'clock. "I guess we'd all better get to our rooms. You heard what happened to Donovan when he was late for curfew the first week."

"Right. I guess Donovan's finally found his calling in life," Idolette snickered. "Letting everyone else know what punishments we get for breaking rules."

The following day, Arthur thought Idolette was a little nicer to Esmond than usual.

"No, Idolette," Esmond was saying in the most patient voice Arthur had ever heard him use. "Hermes isn't a Mayan god. He's the Greek god of messengers, travelers, and thieves."

And instead of rolling her eyes or telling him off, Idolette corrected her paper and said, "Oh, thanks, Esmond." Probably because she'd realized they had the same kind of demanding dads. Somehow, that made Arthur feel irritated—just a little. *I barely have a dad at all*, he thought.

Arthur ignored Griffin on the floor and hardly paid attention to the list they were supposed to be memorizing—a list of what he was sure was every god and goddess in the history of the entire world. Instead, his brain turned gloomily to thoughts of his own dad. Arthur had spent most of his life living with his grandmother and not knowing his dad at all. *But he worked for the Historia Society and couldn't tell me about it*, a small voice in his head reminded. But Gree's sharp voice had been cold when she said, "Or have you forgotten, Mr. Arthur, that Etson simply *abandoned* you to me eight years ago?"

Gree. What did she know? She thought Etson worked for a

secret government agency. She didn't know about Historia. And she didn't know that Arthur had the power to hide things, that he was a Guardian. She didn't know anything about Guardians at all. Arthur sighed. *Of, course, I don't know much about that either.* He frowned hard at Gamble, willing the grouchy old man to look at him and blurt something about Guardianship. But Gamble just wandered around the room, randomly quizzing Initiates about the different gods.

At long last, Gamble glared at the clock and dismissed the team. "Except for you, Grey."

Arthur's bad mood lifted at once, and he felt tingles raise the hairs on his arms. Was his wish coming true? Had Gamble been able to read his mind? *Maybe he's going to tell me now.* Arthur stuffed his gods diagram into his satchel, pushed past the exiting Initiates, and skidded to the front, Griffin following at a much slower pace.

Gamble took off his spectacles and began wiping them. "I heard your dog was causing a disturbance yesterday."

Arthur's mouth dropped open. "Huh?" He glanced at Griffin whose ears went back.

"You heard me. Your dog was being a troublemaker."

Arthur racked his brain for what Gamble could be talking about. "Oh," he exclaimed. "You mean about the Translationary thing?" Arthur started to grin. "Oh, that was nothing—Madam Siegfried didn't care. No one minded him. It was just an accident—"

"Well, he's to stay off the premises from now on."

Arthur blinked. This had to be a joke. The old man was joking, right?

Gamble slid his spectacles back on and picked up his staff. "The dog's to stay in the apartments or on their property. He may not be in Main Hall for *any* reason."

"But—"

"If you find that too hard to follow, I can arrange for him to be removed from the island completely. Is that understood?"

"I told you," Griffin muttered.

Arthur couldn't believe Gamble was saying this. Over a dumb accident?

"Is that understood?" Gamble repeated sharply.

"Yes," Arthur growled.

"Make sure you remember." Without even a glance at Arthur or Griffin, he thumped his staff on the ground and left.

6

THE INVESTOR

Gamble's unjustness came as a blow to Arthur. He had hoped that maybe he'd actually found a friend in Gamble, but obviously, the old man wasn't trustworthy. As if Arthur didn't have enough on his mind, what with all his work, not to mention the ongoing worry about what competition to choose—he was going to have to pick soon or he'd be the only one not signed up for something.

It took a week for Griffin to stop acting annoyingly superior with his "I told you so" about Gamble's unfairness. "But at least I don't have to stay in one room like I did at Conservation," the dog put in as he scratched his ear. "To tell you the truth, I mostly just fell asleep during all those hours trying to keep track of an Odysseus versus a Ulysses and all that."

Arthur crossed his arms. "You don't fool me. I know you'd rather be with me." He buckled on his belt and shoved his

Translationary into his satchel. "I'll try Gamble today, okay? He just doesn't know it was an accident, that's all. I'm sure he'll change his mind. I gotta go or I'll be late."

As he trudged through lessons and even lunch, Arthur still felt glum without Griffin. He kept feeling like he was forgetting something. His mood didn't lift until Mistress Imogene Featherweit (a bulging-eyed, excitable Origins Master) led the Initiate Team into the Room of Repair for the first time.

"Now this," she said breathlessly, "this is where new documents are repaired. We got this new one in a week or so ago, and it's only just getting ready for display."

Between glass sheets on a table was a collection of papyrus sheets covered with strange writing. Arthur tried to get a look at them, but from the back of the crowded room he could only see that they were stiff and browned, with black and dark red text. Beside him, Nada stood on tiptoes, trying to get a glimpse.

"This lovely piece came to us from a man in Romania who bought a house and found the document in the attic," Mistress Featherweit went on. "He brought it to a museum there where we have an Originor stationed. When our Originor saw the text, she knew it was important and was able to secure it and bring it in to us."

"What's wrong with it?" asked Oscar.

"Amazingly, not much. But there is a section that looks like it's suffered water damage. So the Preservations Team has made a Scanograph, and another team will recreate the ruined section. Does anyone recognize the writing?"

Esmond pushed up his glasses and raised his hand. "The writing looks to be ancient Minoan."

"Nicely done," Mistress Featherweit beamed. "The writing is obviously Minoan, but if you read it, you'll find that the syntax—the way the words are put together to make sentences—is not Minoan at all. It is Hittite. Even more confusing is that this script relates the Greek tale of the Minotaur—you remember that myth, don't you? So we have a mix of Minoan, Hittite, and Greek all in one text."

"But we already know the story of the Minotaur," piped up Bridgette. "Why is this text important?"

"Very good question." Mistress Featherweit clasped her hands with a feverish clap. "It's important because it contains details not in *any other copy*."

"Like what?" asked Arthur, feeling excited. Discoveries always gave him a rush.

Mistress Featherweit looked at them all with her large eyes. "That's the exciting part. *I don't know.* It's a series of symbols we haven't identified yet—perhaps an entirely new language! And so far, we haven't found anyone able to interpret them."

"Ah, so Historia still needs help?" said an unfamiliar voice.

An automatic chill shot down Arthur's back, and he spun around to see who had spoken.

Standing in the doorway was a tall, dark-haired man with an unpleasantly smug face. Arthur felt a blackness creep over him. He couldn't say what exactly about the man made him feel so cold and dark. Maybe it was the glistening scar running across his right eye, which gave him a rather evil appearance.

Maybe it was the dark clothes that gave him the look of a night-time burglar. Or the fact that one of his gloved hands flicked a pocket watch up and down like the twitching tail of a sly cat.

"Um, Mr. B-Berne," stammered Mistress Featherweit. "Um, I-I-I didn't know you were allowed in here."

"He's not."

The room was more silent than a graveyard as Gamble swept inside. He stepped in front of the case enclosing the new text, blocking it from the stranger's view, and thunked his staff down. The two men stared at each other, and Arthur could feel the loathing that radiated between them like scorching fire.

"Well, well," the stranger said coolly. "If it isn't Groundskeeper Gamble. Or were you pretending to be a Master now?"

"Either way," Gamble snapped, "I belong here. And you don't. So *if* you please . . . "

"Actually, I'm glad you brought that up, because—as you will see—I do belong here." The man pulled a parchment scroll from his cloak and unrolled it with a flick before Gamble's face. "Agnes Siegfried requested the assistance of an investor. You do know that Historia can only survive with funding from investors, don't you? Well, I am here on behalf of Lord and Lord Brothers Investors, recommended, as you see right here on this line, by Alexander Siegfried himself."

Gamble glared at the paper as if hoping to set it on fire with his eyes. "Alexander, hoptoads!" he crowed.

"Be that as it may, I am permitted here to investigate the value of this investment. Dull work, I assure you, but it must be done in order to fund your little projects, mustn't it?" He sneered, made a mocking bow, and left the room.

Gamble immediately rounded on the team. "What are you waiting for? Your lesson is dismissed!"

After an uncertain pause, the Initiates began bustling toward the door. Arthur took one look at Gamble's scathing expression and knew this would not be the time to approach him about Griffin. With a grunt, he shouldered his bag and followed the others out.

"Japers," Pernille breathed as they made their way down the curved halls. "Master Gamble looked ready to spit horned serpents, didn't he!"

"I can't believe my dad would do something like this," Idolette frowned. "I bet that's what Gran was so upset about before. She doesn't like my dad's meddling."

Arthur remembered that Idolette's dad was, of course, none other than Alexander Siegfried.

Esmond lowered his book to glance sideways at Idolette. "But isn't he next in line for Historia?" he asked. "If they don't give him some experience in making decisions now, won't he be likely to run the Society into the ground without hope of recovery?"

"I think Gran's afraid he'll do that no matter what," Idolette sighed.

"The real question is," Arthur said with a scowl, "why does Gamble hate that guy so much?"

"Watch out, you lot," warned Esmond, casting a shrewd

look at Arthur. "There's a storm cloud brewing right above Arthur's head."

"Ha, ha, very funny." Arthur pushed through a group of Members. "I mean it. Pernille's right—Gamble was ready to spout serpents and fire and any evil thing at that guy. Does anyone know why?"

Idolette swished her hair (which was blonde today) over her shoulder. "From what I've heard my grandmother say, nobody likes the investors. But I guess we need them for some reason."

Esmond rolled his eyes. "That *some reason* is that Historia needs people to put money into our projects. None of this stuff is free, you know. People who believe our work is important give us money, and when we make money on projects or trades, the people who invested their own money get a return—they get something back. Sometimes it's simply more money, sometimes it's replicas of artifacts or a deal with a museum or—"

A sudden explosion and a shout from Arthur cut Esmond short. Arthur's foot had landed on one of the floor tiles, and before he could finish his step, the tile had turned bright green, opened a slot, and shot something directly up in front of Arthur's face.

"Oh, look, you got a message," Pernille announced.

Hands shaking, Arthur felt his face. "Is my nose still there? Am I bleeding?"

Pernille giggled. "Oh, Arthur, you're funny. It's just the message system. It's not goin' to hurt you." She handed Arthur the envelope that the floor slot had ejected. "It's pretty new still—just invented a couple of years ago, I think. The system recognizes your footprint and alerts you to any messages you have. There might still be a few kinks, but it's ingenious, really it is."

"Oh, yeah, ingenious—if it's supposed to clean my nose off my face." Arthur opened the envelope slowly, hoping nothing else was going to come shooting out at him. He pulled out a piece of paper.

"Who's it from?" asked Idolette.

Arthur read the note. "It's from my dad," he said. "He's here at Main Hall and can meet up for an early dinner today at Apartment Zeus at . . . " Arthur glanced at his watch, "four o'clock. That's in ten minutes." He stuffed the note into his belt pouch. "See you later, guys."

"Hey, you got my message." Etson Grey waved cheerfully from the wide doorway of Apartment Zeus. He clapped Arthur on the shoulder and scratched Griffin's ears, then gestured to the dining lounge.

"Yeah," Griffin grunted, "after it nearly blew us up—I felt you freak out, you know."

Arthur grinned. "That was an interesting experience."

Etson led them through the chattering crowd of Members to find an empty table. "Well, mail is normally delivered to your room, but the Spit-It-Out service is . . . well, just that— spit out in a hurry. It's for messages that need quick delivery. Last-minute. And I'm afraid I'm kind of a last-minute guy," he laughed.

Arthur and Griffin looked around as they walked through

the maze of tables. They'd never been in this building before. There was a lot more gold and glass here, a chandelier sparkled from the high ceiling, a bar hosted a lot more different-colored bottles of drinks, and at one end of the wide room was a raised platform where a group of dwarves played a percussive rhythm with obvious glee.

"Wow," Arthur said, "Zeus is a lot fancier than our apartments."

"Yes, well, only Members stay here, and their guests, usually important ones, so they made it a little nicer. There's a club downstairs for Members, too—but you have to be sixteen or older."

Arthur sat down and ate a grape from the bowl on the table.

"So, how're things going?" asked Etson as he dropped his pack beside his chair. "Still surviving old Gamble?"

Arthur snorted. "I guess. As long as that investor guy isn't around. I get the idea Gamble doesn't like him much."

"Hm," was all Etson said. He cleared his throat and stood up. "Hey, I'm starving. Let's go through the buffet, shall we?"

Griffin sniffed, then nudged Arthur's leg. "I think you're on to something he knows. Ask him about it."

As they left the table, Arthur opened his mouth to ask Etson more about the investor, but he stopped when he noticed a couple of people heading toward the lounge exit. "Speak of the devil," he grunted. The tallest was the new investor. Beside him was a much shorter man with pale hair and a little mustache. He was dressed stiffly in a cloudy blue suit with a diamond-studded tie. A gold watch glimmered on his thin wrist.

"Of course, Master Berne," he was saying in a grandiose voice. "That is exactly what I thought myself. I've often said so. It's a shame more people don't see it our way."

Arthur nudged Etson. "Who're they?" he asked.

Etson raised his brows. "The tall smug guy is Rheneas Berne, and next to him," he said quietly, "is the other Siegfried."

"Alexander?" Arthur asked in surprise. That man didn't look anything like Idolette.

"Yup. He's been Berne's little trumpeter over the last year, parading the guy around like a trophy of some sort whenever he can get away with it, trying to get him an edge inside Historia. What he sees in Berne, beats me. Luckily, Siegfried number two is normally at our Special Occurrences location. Best not to bother with those two." Etson walked quickly on. "Anyway, I hear you guys are going on your first excursion soon?"

Arthur looked up quickly. "We are?"

Etson grinned. "From what I hear, that's one thing Gamble does right. It's good to get out and learn things firsthand every once in a while. I think the plan is for Gamble to take you out and about the second week of March. Won't be too much longer."

As they grabbed plates and got in line, Etson went on, "So how about that chariot race, huh?" They discussed the race as they filled their plates and headed back to their table.

As they sat down, Arthur remembered what he'd wanted to ask. "Is it true Gamble has something against investors?"

Etson glanced around. "Investors, no. *That* investor, yes." He slopped some cucumber sauce onto his flat pita bread. "But

I think just about everyone has something against Rheneas Berne."

Arthur arranged strips of lamb meat on his own sandwich and slipped a few pieces to Griffin beneath the table. "Why? What did Berne do?"

"Well, Berne used to be a Master here at Historia. I don't know the details, but he nearly got us into a big fix some years ago." Etson narrowed his eyes. "In fact, Homer Siegfried had him kicked out, I believe. So, naturally, when he comes back acting like he's got the Society's best interests at heart, no one believes him." Etson shrugged. "Whatever else you can say about old Gamble, you can't say he doesn't care about Historia. And he can't stand anyone who doesn't feel the same way. Thus, he doesn't trust Berne. That's why he didn't trust that Chadwick fellow either."

Arthur raised his eyebrows. "Chadwick? You mean the groundskeeper from Conservation? The one they arrested for selling creatures to poachers?"

"Yup, that's the one." Etson glanced around and lowered his voice. "Historia did a big investigation on him to make sure he was working on his own and not with anyone else. People always get worried when that sort of thing happens."

"How come?"

Etson lowered his voice even more and Arthur had to lean forward to hear him. "In case it's a plot from the Seeker's Guild."

The Seeker's Guild. Arthur stopped mid-bite. He and Griffin exchanged startled glances. "I heard Steward Cartwright tell Madam there was an attack in Egypt by those Guild people."

"That's right. They bother us every now and then out on the field like that—trying to keep us from making discoveries. But it's when something happens on the inside that gets people really worried. In case . . . " Etson swallowed. "In case the Elder is back."

Arthur shuddered. *The Elder?* The name made Arthur think of deep dark halls and long secretive robes. "Who—" he started to ask.

But Etson waved as he took a bite. "Any-ay," he began, his mouth full, "I got su'um fer ya." He swallowed. "Thought you might find it interesting." He dug in his pack, pulled out a newspaper, and handed it to Arthur.

The Maizegrove Bulletin. It was the newspaper from his hometown back in Wisconsin. He unfolded the paper and read the headline: IVOR TREASURE REVEALED. He sucked in his breath, everything else immediately flung from his mind, and read on:

> On Saturday, December 20th, Penelope Riffert of Hartford Lane in Maizegrove solved the mystery that's been on the minds of every Maizegrover for the last twenty years: Did General Jacob Ivor really hide treasure in his mansion?
>
> Ivor Manor on Hill Court of the small town has been rumored to hide treasures ever since its

first owner died suddenly and suspiciously nearly two decades ago. A known explorer, the general was thought to have collected a hoard of valuables that he hid somewhere on his property. But no one had found any hint of it. Until now.

"I never really thought there was any treasure," admits 12-year-old Penelope. "But Arthur did. He's the one who found the rock." Arthur Grey is the grandson of Mrs. Mildred Bernice Grey, who now owns and resides in Ivor Manor. At 11 years old, Arthur mysteriously vanished on Christmas Eve last year, and his whereabouts are unknown. Penelope adds, "I found the rock he left behind. I was scared to do anything with it for a long time, but finally I checked the stair by the attic and there was an old map and I used the clues from that and ended up finding the treasure."

Penelope discovered a number of artifacts and precious stones in

a hollow oak tree on the property
of the old Victorian home. Some
of it will remain in the manor
and can be viewed on the tours.
The rest has been donated to the
Wisconsin Historical Museum in
Madison.

Arthur looked up.

"Pretty crazy, huh?" Etson smiled. "Your grandma gave that
to me when I stopped by to give her your note. Oh well. If
you'd stayed in Wisconsin, you could've found that piddly little
treasure, no problem. But instead, you left and ended up finding an entire city of gold, huh? Obviously, there's no question
about which is the more fantastic," he chuckled.

Arthur nodded and forced his mouth into a smile. His dad
was right, of course. But that didn't mean he did not feel a
hollow pit in the middle of his stomach. *That could've been* my
name in the paper, he thought, staring at the headline. *Me as a*
hero—instead of as some missing kid. Penelope didn't even believe
the treasure was real. But she found it.

Griffin laid his head on Arthur's knee. "Your dad's talking,"
he murmured.

Arthur shook his head and blinked. "Huh?"

"I was just saying—I heard you guys got to check out that
new text they found—the Minos Supplement Text."

"That Minoan text? Uh . . . well, kind of." Arthur pushed
the newspaper away and tried to put it out of his mind. "I didn't

really get to see it before we were booted out because of that Berne guy."

"Oh, that's too bad." Etson took a swig of his Fizzy-Winks Fizzy Soda.

Arthur looked up at him.

"Yeah. They took it off view."

"The text? Are you kidding?" This was turning out to be the worst week ever.

"No joke. I just heard it from an Origins Member. They've put it in high security for now."

Griffin woofed, "I bet it's because of the investor guy."

Arthur nodded slowly. He had the sinking feeling that Rheneas Berne was going to make things rather annoying on Elysium Island.

Over the next two weeks, Arthur felt like life was refusing to get better. For one thing, the Spyglass Squad had lost a member, at least temporarily. Pernille spent all her free time training with a Master for the first of the Initiate competitions, Creature Tricks, to be held on the twenty-first of February. She had selected an amphisbaena (a two-headed lizard that behaved rather like a dog), which she was going to teach to play fetch.

Not that Arthur had time to notice. He had a lot on his mind lately, and not even his fellow Spyglass Squad members could help him sort it out. He'd asked the others about the mysterious Seeker's Guild, but none of them knew anything about it.

As for his longing to know about Guardianship, only

Gamble could help with that . . . and he wouldn't. Not since Rheneas Berne showed up, putting the old man in a constantly distracted and sour mood.

On top of that disappointment, Arthur still felt a stinging ache about the Ivor Manor treasure being found without him—and by Penelope Riffert of all people. "She wouldn't even come with me to stop the thieves," Arthur barked, tossing his papers on the floor. "She stayed in the drawing room and let me go by myself. And then, a year later, she finds my clue and gets to the treasure—which she didn't really believe was there to begin with! I wish I hadn't dropped that rock."

"No point complaining about chewed-up bones," Griffin answered wisely. "You can't change the past."

But that didn't make Arthur feel any better.

By Saturday, Arthur was feeling downright sullen. Nothing seemed to be going his way. He got up late and ate breakfast alone with Griffin in the lounge, wondering irritably where the others were. He didn't bother to look before he went back to his room.

"Are we going to stay here all day?" asked Griffin.

Arthur shrugged. He picked up one of his invisible-ink pens, and his focus jumped to the idea of secrets and hiding things. "Do you suppose it's hard to figure out Guarding?"

"Can't be that hard. You've done it before."

"Yeah, but that was by accident." He stared at the pen in his hand. "Gamble once said Guarding powers are hard to control." He tried to remember what had happened the times he had done it before. It was always when he felt desperate to hide something. *And it always hurts*, he remembered. Using the power made him feel sick and dizzy. Still, it was his power and he wanted to know how it worked.

He stared at the pen in his hand, his heart pounding. Could he do it now—make the pen disappear so no one else could see it? *I've got to hide this*, he thought, frowning at the pen. *It's important. I need to hide it.* But nothing happened. He stood up.

"Maybe if I try it with something that really is important." He dug through his drawer and found the alicanto feather. He looked at it hard and concentrated. *I need to hide this,* he thought over and over. But still nothing happened. With an impatient grunt, he let the feather fall back into his drawer and instead pulled out the book that had once belonged to his mother—*Secrets of the Andes*.

"Do you think if you Guard something, it stays that way? Or does it wear off?" It occurred to him that this book was always lurking at the back of his mind, just out of focus but always ready to be remembered. Was that significant?

Griffin turned from the porch doorway where he had been letting the wind blow his ears back. "I'd forgotten, that's one of the things you accidentally Guarded, huh?" He cocked his head at the book. "I guess you'd have to put it out and see if anyone else could see it."

Arthur gazed at the book, considering it, and then opened his satchel and slid it inside. "Yeah, well, that would be easier if anyone was around."

Griffin sat down and scratched. "Aren't they all at the Creature Tricks competition?"

Arthur felt like something had struck him in the middle of his chest. "Oh no!" he exclaimed. "I totally forgot—Pernille's in this competition." He felt a rush of guilt. "Do you think it's still going on?" He didn't wait for an answer. "Let's go."

Arthur and Griffin hurried down the path toward Main Hall, passing a few Members who had not gone to see the Initiate competition. But before they got to the stadium, a throng of exiting people blocked their way.

"It must be over," Griffin said. "We missed it."

Arthur didn't feel like seeing anyone anymore. Gloomily, he left the main path to find a solitary spot on a bridge over the garden stream where he liked to sit with Griffin when he was feeling thoughtful. He took *Secrets of the Andes* out of his bag and opened it in his lap. For a long while they sat in silence, Griffin pawing reflectively at the water, Arthur with his chin in his hand as he sometimes read, sometimes just stared unseeing at the pages. Occasionally they swatted away the nosy little fairies that liked to flit around the gardens. Twilight crept over the sky, and stars began to pop out.

At last, Arthur set the book aside. He lifted up the locket that hung around his neck and studied the symbols on it. There were eight markings around its face, like a clock, and one at the very center. He wondered how he could find answers about it. He cleared his throat, which felt dry and hoarse from being silent for so long. "I thought about looking these symbols up in my Translationary," he said, "but I don't know where to begin. Is this a language? Is it just random pictures? They mean something, I'm sure of it, but I don't know what." He shooed away a fairy that had landed on his ear.

"That goblet symbol on the left was for the Cauldron," Griffin remembered. "We discovered that in Peru."

"Yeah, but what about everything else? Do you think it's ancient Peruvian writing? After all, Peru was my mom's favorite place, right?" He frowned. "I just wish I had someone to ask." He blew out a frustrated breath. *Good-for-nothing Gamble,* he thought, dropping the locket back under his shirt. Gamble was the only one who might know something about the locket, but Arthur knew the cranky old vulture wouldn't tell him a word. *Not with Rheneas Berne around,* he thought bitterly.

Griffin lifted his nose abruptly and gave a tongue-lolling grin. "Here comes Pernille," he woofed.

Sure enough, Pernille's bright orange hair came into view. She looked at Arthur in surprise. "Oh, hiya, I didnay know you were here."

"Hey. It's okay." He paused, that feeling of guilt pressing on him again.

Griffin nudged him. "Tell her you didn't mean to miss her competition. Go on."

Arthur cleared his throat. "I'm sorry I missed the Creature Tricks. I kinda forgot about it. I . . . uh . . . guess I haven't been myself lately."

Pernille wrinkled her nose. "You haven't? Who've you been, then?"

Arthur cocked his head. "Uh . . . "

"You can't not be yourself, silly," she smiled. Then she shrugged lightly and reached out to scratch Griffin's ears. "It's all right, anyway, I didnay win. It was fun, though. Me mam used to say, 'You haven't lived if you haven't laughed.' And you missed a good laugh," she chuckled. "Thespia tried to train a cockatrice and she got knocked out, and Tad brought a chimaera an' the judges had to rescue him because the serpent tail wrapped him in a body-squeeze and the lion head was tryin' to eat him. An' my amphisbaena tried to fetch one judge's wig instead of the stick I was throwin'."

Arthur finally felt a smile tug at his lips. "I wish I would've seen it."

Pernille moved to sit next to him and her foot kicked the *Secrets of the Andes* book. Arthur snatched it before it could fall over the edge of the bridge. "Japers!" Pernille exclaimed. "What was that? I think I bumped a wisp, though I always thought they were only spirits and how would you bump one then? Did you see something? It was right next to you there."

Arthur looked at the book he had just moved and then back to Pernille, who was peering around the ground as if expecting to find a creature nursing an injured leg. *So the book is still Guarded*, he realized. The thought cheered him.

"I sure hope I didnay hurt anyone," Pernille murmured, straightening. "I guess I ought to get back now. You comin', Arthur?"

He stuffed the unseen book in his bag and stood. "Yeah, I think I will." He grinned. "Thanks, Pernille."

She looked at him with pleased surprise. "For what?"

He shrugged his bag over his shoulder. "Eh. For being you. Come on."

7

DETOUR

As the Initiates headed into their third month of Origins, Arthur felt he was finally used to Spit-It-Out messages, buzzing gnomes, the excitement of spectacular games every month, hearing eerie howls from the forest, being shouted at by Translationaries, and seeing things like stuffed eight-legged horses in the halls. But there were a few things he could definitely do without.

One was Esmond's constant complaining about Nada—her lucky guesses, her unfair advantages, how she didn't follow proper etiquette. Arthur had a hard time sympathizing with Esmond, as he personally didn't really mind Nada. Mostly, she sat around drawing pictures of unicorns or snake skulls and randomly answering questions not addressed to her.

Another problem, of course, was Gamble. That didn't need any explanation whatsoever. And then there was Rheneas Berne, the investor from Lord and Lord Brothers.

It seemed that all the regulars at Main Hall knew about and distrusted Berne, though no one wanted to say anything else about him. Minister Jung told the Initiates, "Mr. Berne is here to learn that the Historia Society is quite valuable and is reliable in any investments. So there will be no need for you to exchange words with him. Simply leave him to the experienced Members."

"Why?" asked Donovan.

"Ah, this is the way of investments."

Even Madam Siegfried warned them. "Don't even discuss the weather," she said nonchalantly. "Don't breathe the word *boo* to the scumbag."

"Are they worried we're going to say something stupid and ruin the investment or something?" grumbled Charda Kuchamann.

Gamble left the Initiate Team more frequently now, constantly giving Main Hall's steward advice on security and care, much to the other man's exasperation. But Arthur suspected Gamble's main reason for disappearing was to keep tabs on the so-called investor. Arthur had noticed that even when Gamble was with the team, Gatriona, his falcon, was missing, probably taking up the watch.

A number of times, their learning was interrupted by the unwanted appearance of Mr. Berne, whether he came in accidentally ("Oh, my mistake, this isn't the restroom. But what is in the Scanographer?") or purposely ("I saw you have a replica of the tenth-century Virupaksha silk banner. What team obtained that?"). Occasionally, he put questions to the Initiates, though usually he didn't bother to look down his nose at them.

At least Arthur's job of avoiding both Gamble and Berne wasn't too difficult, since Gamble always seemed to be just around the corner from Berne. Still, it was annoying.

On a windy March day, the Initiate Team was finishing up a review assignment on Famous Warriors and Their Weapons when Minister Jung announced that they would be taking their first excursion of the year on Thursday.

"Do you think they'll let me take Griffin?" Arthur whispered to Esmond and Pernille as he drew a line on his paper from King Arthur to Excalibur. Idolette was busy getting answers from Tad.

"Probably not," Esmond whispered back. "Master Gamble isn't about to let anyone get away with anything these days."

Arthur looked at Pernille, clearly begging her to have an opinion more hopeful than Esmond's.

She smiled and put her pencil down. "It's true he's been a bit narky lately. But maybe you could try cheerin' him up some way and get him in a good mood and then he'd let you take Griffin along on the excursion."

"I suppose you could ask Minister Jung." Esmond eyed the Minister, who stood calmly at the front, swaying back and forth as he waited for everyone to finish. "Though I doubt that would do any good. He's not one to bend rules for anyone. And he's not even . . . erm . . . narky."

Pernille crinkled her nose and stifled a laugh. "Oh, Esmond, you're funny."

When they were finally dismissed, Arthur found that Esmond was right. Try as he might, Arthur couldn't get Minister Jung to give him permission. In the end, the Minister patted Arthur's head patronizingly and told him he should ask Master Gamble's opinion.

"It's no use," Arthur muttered miserably to the others. "I'll just have to figure a way to get Gamble in a good mood long enough for him to let Griffin come."

Late Wednesday afternoon, Arthur wandered around the Will-o'-the-Wisp Gardens for half an hour before finally bullying his legs into going to Apartment Thor, where Gamble stayed. He had never been inside it before, as no Initiates stayed there.

The lounge was rather misty and decorated with lightshades in the shape of double-headed hammers over lightbulbs that periodically flickered like lightning. Arthur was looking around, hoping to see a friendly Member who might tell him which room was Gamble's, when he overheard the nymph behind the counter talking to someone. He had to listen closely, because she was a wood nymph and spoke in a whooshing whisper.

"I don't think anyone feels very sorry," she said, wiping out a large, lightning-bolt frosted mug. "That Mr. Berne is rather unpopular. I wouldn't be surprised if someone had purposely tricked him into going by the snapper plant so he would get stuck in it. But I heard he's going to go out tomorrow afternoon to get his leg wrapped. He refused to have it treated here by the Master of Medicines."

"Oh, someone feels sorry, all right. Me. I'm sorry he didn't break anything more serious."

Arthur looked up in surprise to find that it was Gamble sitting at the bar, listening to the nymph. Gamble who had spoken. Arthur thought there might have been a trace of glee in the old man's croaky voice. His heart skipped against his chest. This might be the chance he was waiting for. If something bad happened to Rheneas Berne, Gamble would surely be in a good mood.

He waited for Gamble to finish his drink and slide off his stool. "Um, hey, Gam—Master Gamble, sir," Arthur stammered.

The old man raised a bristly grey eyebrow at Arthur and grabbed his staff from where it leaned against the grey-blue wall. "What are you hanging about for?"

"Actually, I'm glad I, uh, ran into you," Arthur hurried on. "It's just, we have our first excursion coming up and I'm pretty excited about it, but I was wondering if—"

"What's this? Have you turned into Pernille Hanly? What are you yapping so fast about?"

Arthur felt his face grow hot. He'd better get right to the point. "Can Griffin come on the excursion?"

Gamble squinted his dark eyes, as if considering. Arthur allowed himself one hard swallow and held his breath. If Gamble wasn't in a good mood now, he never would be. He just had to say yes.

With a dismissive grunt, Gamble muttered, "Fine. Luck's

in your favor, Grey. Bring him. But don't expect to be so lucky again."

Arthur blew out his breath. "I won't. Thanks. Okay." He turned and darted out of the lounge, feeling as though he had wings on his shoes and he could fly.

With how absent Gamble had been the last month, it wasn't much of a surprise when Masters Zane and Jolly met the Initiate Team in front of the Transfer Depot on Thursday morning.

"How's it goin' then, eh?" Jolly grinned, snapping his strawberry bubblegum. "I know you are going to be awfully sad at this news, but Master Gamble is tied up at the moment and will have to meet us later. So we'll be the ones to take you on your first excursion of the year."

Donovan and Tad gave cheering whoops, and several others clapped.

"I promise not to tell Master Gamble that no one cried tears of sorrow," laughed Jolly, as he led them into the Transfer Depot.

The Initiates gazed around with their mouths agape. Along one wall were empty doorways that went nowhere. A sign above each doorway specified which department it directed to, and each was decorated individually. Conservatorium caught Arthur's attention, its doorframe made of lifelike twisting vines and flowers with miniature flying horses, three-headed dogs, and curled-up dragons peeking out. Experiments looked like black iron, with grooves glowing red like molten lava. Investigations was framed in blocks of blue rectangular stone that reminded Arthur of pictures he'd seen of Stonehenge. At the end was Special Occurrences, which was coated in a filmy curtain something like a cloud or glistening rain, but with a rainbow hue to it when it shifted with the moving air. Arthur wondered what countries hosted the other Historia locations.

"This is how Members get from one department to another," Zane said loudly. "By these permanent Transportal doors. But they must be activated by a badge. Don't even think about it," he added with a severe look at Donovan. "Your badges will not work. Initiates have to take the long way."

Against the other walls sat shelves labeled "Location Keys." These were lined with little glass discs that Arthur knew contained dirt for use in the Transportals.

"Now, what does Gamble always say? Oh, yes." Jolly cleared his throat. "Lesson of the day," he crowed, uncannily like Gamble. Everyone laughed. "Always get Transportals in pairs, a going and a return. Don't be one of those folks who takes a trip to the Sahara Desert and then gets stranded because you forgot that you needed to get back, eh? Because then you'll find yourself real thirsty and thinking that sunscreen looks awfully tasty. But don't drink it—it really won't be pretty, trust me. So. We'll take our outgoing trip and our return trip."

Jolly held out his Transportal, an object shaped like a pocket mirror that fit in the palm of his hand, placed a disc labeled "Athens" into it, and tossed it onto the platform at the back of the room. Immediately, the Transportal expanded rapidly into an oval doorway. Through it Arthur could see blue sky and puffy white clouds and a patch of grass, beyond which was a sprawling city. "Everyone got their Initiate badge? Okay then. Let's hop through. Don't mind the wind now. We're off to the Glorious City, the city of Athens."

They went through one at a time, and Arthur felt the familiar sensations of being frozen in midair and the rest of the world jumping up to zoom past him, of suddenly melting like ice on a hot day, and then of being shoved forward onto lumpy grass. He still wasn't quite used to it, but at least he didn't fall on his face anymore.

Athens was a very old city. It wasn't like Cuzco in Peru, where the Spanish had built right on top of old Inca structures. In Athens, the modern buildings—the shops of shoes or coffee or computers—were built up all around the old Hellenic temples and structures. Forlorn ruins sat next to shops, and tourists took photos of ancient temples and then turned around to get a hamburger right across the street.

Zane pointed ahead. "Ah, now the real crown of the Glorious City sits high above, as a crown should," he exclaimed, adjusting the tassel of his hat. "The Acropolis. And that is where we are headed first."

Several of the Initiates had been to Athens before. Idolette, of course, who vacationed all over the world with her parents; Thespia Galoopsa, who was from there; and Nada Bhaksiana, whose parents also apparently traveled a lot.

Even Arthur, who had never traveled anywhere before last year, recognized the Acropolis when he saw it. The most familiar sight was the Parthenon. Nearly every book on Greece included photographs of that large rectangular building with the tall columns.

"Did you know," Esmond began.

"Probably not," interrupted Idolette, who was back on normal terms with Esmond. "And we probably don't care, but I bet you're going to tell us anyway."

Esmond ignored her. "This city could have been called Poseidon instead of Athens. Supposedly, the god Poseidon offered a gift of rulership of the sea to the people here if they would let him be the keeper and protector of their city. But instead they chose Athena to be their goddess. She gave them an olive tree so they would have peace and prosperity as long as it stayed there."

"Rulership of the sea?" Arthur demanded. "I would've picked Poseidon's gift."

"Master Zane," called Pernille as she pointed at a group of children running past, "why do some people wear necklaces that have those blue beads with white on them?"

"Ah!" Zane exclaimed. "Those are to keep away the Evil Eye. Old mothers believe in the spirit that brings sickness and bad luck and even death. Curses from wicked people or jealousy of the spirits—of the gods, if you will. But those necklaces and pendants are meant to keep away the curses."

Behind Arthur, Esmond snorted. "Obviously, old wives' tales."

"Watch it," Zane snapped, "or some old wife will be stuffing beads into that hasty mouth of yours."

It was a fine morning. From the Acropolis they could see for miles around the city. They spent part of the day inspecting the ruins of Athens—with Donovan making frequent jokes about the headless statues and Idolette constantly wanting to borrow Griffin for his camera-collar to take photos of "cute" boys.

"Face that way, Griffin. Now turn the other way, right? Ooh, that guy is totally fit." This lasted until Donovan loudly sniggered to Arthur that he thought they should all get turns taking photos of good-looking boys, at which point Idolette *hmphed* off to bat her eyelashes at Tad.

After noon, they paused to look at souvenirs and then stopped for lunch at an outdoor café with game boards on the tabletops. It was here that Gamble finally caught up to them.

"Where do you think he's been?" Griffin grumbled.

"Hawking over Berne, probably making sure his leg was good and broken. What else?"

In his typical vulture way, Gamble couldn't let anyone rest. "Who can tell me one fact about Greece?" he demanded.

"That it's not Greece," Arthur said loudly. "It's called Hellas."

Zane pounded his fist into his hand. "That is exactly right!" he exclaimed. "That is one smart boy!"

"One smart aleck, you mean," snapped Gamble, but Arthur didn't care. He moved his chess piece against Pernille.

Thespia waved her hand. "The Olympic games began here, about twenty-seven hundred years ago."

"And," added Nada, "the owl and the olive are sacred to Athena, the goddess of Athens."

Esmond muttered, "Didn't I already say that earlier?"

Idolette leaned toward him. "Well, you forgot the part about the owl."

"Hmph."

"Who," Gamble cawed, "can name four sacred items that came from the gods of Greece?"

Esmond's hand shot up. "Artemis's bow."

"Zeus's thunderbolt," piped Bridgette.

Donovan snickered, "Poseidon's fork."

"It's a trident," Esmond corrected with an offended look.

Nada stared off toward the clouds gathering in the west. "Perseus's helmet of darkness," she breathed.

"Good to see you've stayed awake for at least some of your lessons," Gamble croaked. "Now, on your feet, you lot. We've got plenty to see yet. I want to be finished by sundown, unless any of you would like to check out Zeus's thunderbolt firsthand." He nodded toward the dark clouds. "Our next stop is the mountain refuge of Delphi, nearly one hundred miles outside of Athens."

An hour and another Transportal later, the team landed in a much quieter place. Arthur immediately felt like he was in a strict library.

"*Délfoi*," Zane breathed reverently. "Here the god Apollo was honored. He is a son of the great god Zeus and loved music, poetry, and medicine. It was he who helped the Trojan prince Paris defeat the warrior Achilles in the Trojan War. But do not look at Mount Parnassus above us," he groaned. "It does not have nearly as many of the beautiful wildflowers as is usual in the spring." His voice dropped, and he seemed to speak to himself, "That is a bad omen—bad things are to come in this land."

"Well," Esmond put in to those around him, "as the Greek philosopher Plato observed, 'What now remains . . . is like the bones of a body wasted and diseased, with all the rich and fertile earth fallen away and only the scraggy skeleton of the land left and the mountains supporting nothing but bees.'"

Fortunately for Esmond, Zane didn't hear him.

They wandered quietly among the broken stones and pillars. After all the noise and bustle of Athens, this place felt like an old graveyard nestled in the mountains. Esmond said in a hush, "Once people came from all over to visit the Oracle of Delphi and learn answers to riddles or seek out the future."

The Temple of Apollo was the remains of a building from long ago. There were tall columns that no longer held up a roof, bottom layers of buildings, leftover chunks of walls half-buried in grass. They kept their eyes open for other things, too. Griffin caught sight of a nest of tiny winged serpents in the skimpy bushes, and when Bridgette peeked into a crevice in the ground she was startled by a black-faced creature with large, red-rimmed eyes. "Ah, one of the Telchines," Zane said with a bored wave. "Yes, they are hideous, but they are skilled in metalwork. There are some that work for Experiments."

Beyond the temple was the theater, which was just a flat space partly surrounded by curved stair-seating that rose up like a silent stone waterfall. A few bushy trees grew out of the rocky ruin. But by now, Arthur knew that Plato had been right about Greece. Not much grew here.

The Treasury of the Athenians was impressive, though, and stood with two columns and the only roof left in the complex.

The sun was setting and clouds spreading overhead when Jolly suggested they go see a live Greek play, acted out in the old way. "There's a great place where they perform *The Minotaur,* and afterwards we can all eat at the Olive Tree Restaurant. What do you say, eh, Master Gamble?" He winked as he pulled his Transportal out of his backpack.

The play was outdoors, in a space arranged a lot like the empty theater at Delphi. Rows of seats staired down to a platform at the bottom, like a curved auditorium. The first act had just begun, and many seats were already filled, so the team had to spread out. Arthur and Griffin found a spot next to Esmond at the end of a back row.

"They're kind of spooky-looking." Idolette shuddered as she slid in next to Arthur on the stone seat.

Arthur shrugged. The actors wore masks to show the characters they were playing. He didn't think there was anything spooky about that.

"Did you know," Esmond whispered from next to him as a character with a tall trident—obviously supposed to be Poseidon—stalked onto the stage, "that the gods supposedly lived on a diet of nectar and ambrosia? That's what gave them their immortality."

"What's ambrosia?" asked Idolette. "It sounds pretty, right?"

Esmond didn't look at her. "It's a potent alcoholic drink

that's so harsh it would burn your throat and boil your stomach if you tried to drink it."

Idolette turned back toward the stage, but her nostrils flared briefly in a gesture that rather reminded Arthur of Madam Siegfried. The pouty face she made immediately afterward, however, did not.

Arthur knew the basics of the story of King Minos and the Minotaur, so he was able to identify the play's main characters: King Minos of the Minoans, his wife Pasiphaë, his daughter Ariadne, the god Poseidon, an Athenian prince named Theseus, and, of course, the Minotaur.

Like many Greek tales, this was a terrible one involving lies and foolishness and a vengeful god. King Minos found himself the owner of an uncontrollable monster. The people called it Minotaur, "the bull of Minos." Minos had a talented architect build an elaborate maze in which he could keep the beast. And, as a clever plan for his own revenge, he demanded that the city of Athens send young fighters every so often to be put into the Minotaur's maze. These warriors were supposed to find their way out before being attacked and killed by the monster, but not even one of the Athenians survived over many years of this tribute. At last, a young man called Theseus volunteered to go and kill Minos's monster and stop the pointless killing of the heroes of Athens. Theseus was so brave that he caught Ariadne's attention, and she plotted to help the young hero. Before Theseus entered the dark labyrinth that housed the monster, she gave him a ball of thread to help him find his way out again.

Arthur nearly jumped when Idolette grabbed his arm. "What?" he snapped. His heart was still beating fast as he watched the character Theseus make his way through the maze.

Idolette squeezed her eyes shut. "I can't watch any more—those masks really weird me out. And I need to go to the toilets."

"Bathrooms are over there," Arthur pointed out. "Though I'd suggest waiting. I heard Bridgette say earlier the ones she used were really nasty."

"I really need to go."

"Well, go then."

"What—I'm not going by myself! There could be a spooky masked person or something. You come with me."

Arthur snorted. "I'm not going in the girls' bathroom. Ask Tad."

"Tad's not talking to me right now. Just walk me there." Idolette pulled him up. "And bring Griffin."

With a groan, Arthur allowed Idolette to drag him out of his seat. Luckily, they were at the end of their row and didn't need to disturb any of the other watchers. Idolette pulled Arthur up past the remaining rows and across the flagstone court to the bathrooms. "Okay, we're here. You can let go of my arm now," Arthur grunted.

"Oh, right." Idolette released his arm and straightened her sleeve. "I'll be right out. Just wait for me."

"Are you kidding? Look, I can see Pernille from here. Just come over yourself."

Idolette frowned. "Don't you dare leave me. Just wait."

Arthur moaned. "Fine. Hurry up."

"Well, I'll have to fix up a little, too."

"How long is that going to take?"

"Just a minute."

Arthur grunted. He stared up at the purple dusk sky, which was darkening quickly, its orange-tinged clouds turning dark grey. Five minutes passed with no sign of Idolette.

"What is taking her so long?" Griffin grumbled. "What is it with girls and the bathroom? I want to find out what happens to that Theseus guy—does the monster eat him? I'm getting kinda hungry."

At that moment, Arthur noticed Bridgette and Charda hurrying over. "Hey," he called in relief. "When you go back, take Idolette with you, will you?"

"Is that where she is?" said Charda. "We wanted to tell her about the cute boy sitting in front of us."

Arthur rolled his eyes as the girls headed into the bathrooms. "Come on, Griff—" A movement out of the corner of his eye caught his attention. Standing against the other side of the building was someone rummaging through a bag. The shadowed figure looked around suspiciously, pulled down a hat, and then snuck out of sight. Arthur narrowed his eyes and turned to Griffin. "Did that look like Jolly to you?"

Griffin sniffed. "I don't know. Maybe. But the only things I can smell are Charda's perfume and . . . um, smelly bathroom."

"I wonder where he's going." Arthur scratched his head. "Do you suppose he thinks we're missing? Maybe he noticed we weren't at our seats and is looking for us. Let's go see."

They hurried along the stone-paved ground down an open

corridor between the buildings. For a moment, Arthur lost sight of the man, but then he saw him turning a corner. *Where's he going?* Arthur wondered. "Master Jolly," he called. The person paused for a second, but then continued around the corner. *How come he didn't stop?* Arthur wondered impatiently. He beckoned to Griffin, and they made their way past laughing groups of tourists, little café tables, and several other veering alleyways. At one point, he thought about stopping and going back, but his curiosity was too strong. He lost sight of Jolly again for a moment before spotting him ahead, crossing an enclosed bridge toward another alleyway.

Arthur jogged after him. At the end of the bridge, he peered around the corner and skidded to a stop. A number of people lined the street, but there was no sign of a man with a hat. Jolly, if it had been Jolly at all, was nowhere to be seen. Arthur wiped a drip from his forehead. It was starting to drizzle. "Where'd he go? Can't you smell him out?" he demanded, more desperately than he meant.

"Are you kidding?" Griffin's ears went back. "There are so many smells here, how can I pick out one I didn't get a definite whiff of? We don't even know that it *was* Jolly."

Arthur smeared several raindrops from the end of his nose and looked back, suddenly realizing how dark it was. The alley they had come down split two ways, and both looked grey and murky and similar, like a hopeless maze. "Do you know which way we came?" Arthur asked quietly.

But Griffin was distracted. "Who are they?" he whispered, and his ears flattened against his head as he nodded at several people leaning against the walls, looking toward them. They wore sunglasses, even though it was raining and dark. One man grinned and started toward them, calling something Arthur didn't understand.

Griffin crouched low and growled, his hackles bristling. The man said something else hastily and turned away.

"Let's go," Arthur muttered, eyeing the strangers, who were now laughing. He and Griffin turned back, and Arthur led the way down the left-hand alley. He sped up his pace, glancing behind and hoping no one would follow them. But in his hurry, Arthur slipped on a wet marble step and landed hard on his back. Pain shot through his back and then erupted in his left eye briefly before subsiding. He sat up.

Griffin grunted as he got up too. "I wish you'd be more careful. Now I know why I'm always feeling pains—you're a complete klutz."

"Oh, shut up," Arthur grumbled. It wasn't his fault Griffin felt the same pains he did. It was part of being a Fetch. "It works the other way, too, you know. I can feel your pains."

"Ssh!" snarled Griffin. A shadow moved on their left, and Griffin crouched again and growled.

Had one of the shady people in the alley followed them? "Who's there?" Arthur yelped.

A girl stepped out. She was a little younger than Arthur and had dark, curly hair wrapped in a kerchief. *"Ti' ka'nis?"* she asked.

Griffin sniffed and cocked his head. "It's okay," he woofed. "She smells familiar."

Familiar? How could a strange girl in a city they'd never visited before be familiar? Arthur cleared his throat. "Uh, I only speak English."

"Ah, I speak English. Are you lost?"

"Well, I wouldn't say *lost*," Arthur began, but Griffin glared at him. "Okay, maybe we're a little lost. I was just at a play, and I lost my way."

"Of course!" The girl waved both her arms broadly. *Hm, something about her* is *familiar*, Arthur thought. "This part gets people lost easily," she said. "I will show you the way out. I was on my way home from playing with my friends," she went on. "This way is a shortcut. My name is Camilla."

Arthur nodded. Griffin nudged his knee. "The play might be over by now. Ask her if she knows where that restaurant is—the one we're supposed to go to after the play."

"Right," Arthur agreed. "Say," he began, "do you know where we can find . . . " *What was the name of that restaurant we were supposed to go to? It was something to do with Athena, wasn't it? Or a food. Of course.* " . . . the Olive Tree Restaurant?"

"Yes. It's a very good place to eat. Come, I will show you." She beckoned to them and started down the passage with a little skip. She smiled mischievously before commenting, "You must be an Initiate."

Arthur stared at her in surprise. "How do you know—?"

She laughed. "You are wearing clothes of Elysium Island, and you said you were at the play, and want to know where this restaurant is. Like my grandpápa said."

"Your grandpápa?"

"*Né*, of course. Zane Stefanidis."

Griffin's ears twitched. "So that's why she seemed familiar."

"You're Master Stefanidis's granddaughter?"

"*Né*," she smiled. "Yes."

Arthur had a thought. "Do you know Master Jolly, then?"

"Oh, yes!" Her eyes twinkled. "He is very funny and he likes to make big bubbles with his pink chewing gum. He comes for dinner many times when he's not going away to his fancy houses in Italy or Spain. He always brings little toys for me and my three brothers and sisters when he comes. We like him." She stopped. "Look, there he is now."

Arthur looked ahead. She had led them to the restaurant. Arthur noticed the small word "Stefanidis" over the larger words "The Olive Tree." And, just as she said, there was Jolly, along with the rest of their team, heading inside.

"I guess that guy we followed wasn't Jolly after all," said Griffin, and Arthur nodded, feeling his cheeks flush. He had been sure that person was Jolly, but apparently he had nearly gotten himself and Griffin lost for nothing. With some embarrassment, he remembered how wrong he had about the identity of a certain dark figure last year.

A shrill "hyik!" from behind alerted them to Gamble's presence. Arthur turned to find Gatriona glaring at him.

"Where've you been, Grey?" snapped Gamble. "Lagging behind again?"

"Uh . . . I got lost. Coming." Arthur turned to follow the others.

"They'll put on a shadow-puppet show inside," the girl said as she followed along.

Arthur rubbed the back of his neck. "Oh, hey, thanks for showing me the way."

"Okay. I am going to see what Jolly brought for me." She grinned and lightly punched him in the arm. "Good-bye!" She darted through the brightly lit doorway, into the chatter and laughter inside.

More uncertainly, Arthur followed.

8

THE JOUST GHOST

It seemed every month was bringing more for Arthur to think about, and his investigative instincts were working overtime. Were his dreams important? What were Rheneas Berne's intentions against Historia? Why had the mysterious Minos Supplement Text been put away? What did it contain that Berne could use against Historia? And now the newest question: who had Arthur really followed on the night of the play? He tried not to think about the Ivor treasure anymore, as that just made him feel grouchy.

He used the Spyglass Squad badges to call a meeting, hoping they could figure out some answers as a team. But before Arthur could come to any satisfactory answers, Pernille had to go study for their oral exam on Robin Hood, and Idolette had to head out for Tower Climb competition training.

"What about you, Arthur?" Idolette asked before leaving. "Haven't you signed up for anything?"

"Oh . . . uh, no. Not yet. I'm still thinking about it." The truth was, Arthur felt nervous about the very idea of signing up for anything. Maybe it was because he'd never done anything like that before, or maybe he was just stressed. Every time he looked at the poster in the apartment lounge, he felt excited and decided to do it—to sign up for a competition. But the moment the register in the entrance hall came into view (along with the hundreds of Members and Initiates passing through), his heart would leap into his throat and his legs would speed up their pace, taking him right past without giving his hands a chance to stick his badge in.

With March nearing an end, the third competition loomed. Arthur still hadn't mustered up the courage to face registration, which meant he had a week to decide whether he'd sign up for the Squire Joust. And with half the Initiate Team training for the Tower Climb, Arthur felt like he heard about nothing but competitions everywhere he went.

He picked at his breakfast eggs and toast while Pernille and Esmond talked about the upcoming Tower Climb and Griffin stared moodily around the lounge.

"It's fortunate that it's separated by level," Esmond sighed. "Otherwise, the Initiates would never have a chance. I've seen some of the Members training for the higher level, and I'm pretty sure at least two of them are part monkey."

Pernille giggled. "Oh, it'll be fun, though. Idolette is pretty excited. I'm guessin' all her dance and gymnastics lessons will help her do well. What do you think, Arthur? Arthur?"

"Huh?" Arthur looked up.

Pernille reached out to pat his hand and smiled knowingly. "You need to stop thinking about signing up and just go do it."

"Sign up for what?" Arthur grumbled.

"You know exactly what I'm talkin' about. You need to sign up for the Squire Joust. I know you want to."

"She's right," Esmond said glumly. "There's no point telling yourself you're a loser without proving it first. And since the Squire Joust is just for Initiates, there's not much reason why you shouldn't come out of it with some success. Just go sign up for it."

Arthur snorted. "You're one to talk. You haven't signed up for anything, either."

Esmond flushed pink and shrugged, quickly occupying himself with a bite of toast.

"You can do it, Arthur," Pernille beamed. "Just remember, only part of it's about tryin' to win. The rest is about havin' fun."

Arthur pushed his plate away. "I'll think about it," was all he said.

But by Friday, there were four days left to sign up for the joust tournament and Arthur still hadn't done anything. It was Griffin who gave him the most serious wake-up, though.

"Don't let this be another Ivor treasure mistake," he said wisely as he circled the bed. "If you don't do it now, you might regret it later."

On Saturday afternoon, Arthur and the others wished Idolette good luck in the competition and then went to eat lunch on the veranda outside Main Hall. Arthur felt like a million ants were crawling inside his stomach, and he could hardly take a bite. When it was time to head to the stadium, all at once, Arthur made up his mind.

"Go on ahead," Arthur muttered. "I just have to get something. I'll catch up." He nodded at Griffin. "I'll be there in a minute." He rummaged through his pockets, pretending to look for something, until the others had disappeared down the dip in the path. Arthur swallowed hard, then hurried toward the Main Hall doors ahead. He stepped into the cool of the Rotunda and glanced around to make sure it was empty. He stopped abruptly.

Stalking down the Museo Gallery hallway, just disappearing from view, was Rheneas Berne. *Apparently he's better*, Arthur thought. He hadn't seen Berne for several weeks. For a moment, he wondered what the sly man was up to. Then Arthur remembered the fiasco with following that person who turned out not to be Jolly. He shook his head. *Better not get involved. Besides, I have a job to do.*

He took a deep breath and turned to face the registration kiosk. Its dimly glowing screen seemed to smirk at him.

Another glance around the hall, another shaky breath, and then Arthur balled his fists and marched up to the machine. Before he had another chance to convince himself otherwise, he unclipped his badge from around his neck and shoved it into the dark, empty slot. The screen lit up.

"Initiate Competitions List," the machine said in a woman's brisk voice. "Please choose one."

His heart beating like a drum, Arthur stared down the list, looking for the one he wanted. Treasure Hunt caught his eye. He shook his head and looked again. Pyramid Build, Archery, Tapestry, Treasure Hunt, Alchemy. He did not see Squire Joust. "Where is it?" he muttered. "Where is Squire Joust?"

"The Squire Joust competition is full," said the brisk voice. "Please choose another competition."

"What do you mean it's full?" Arthur sputtered. "It can't be!"

"Please choose another competition," the voice repeated.

Arthur could not believe it. He'd finally mustered up the courage to enter a competition, and now it wouldn't let him. "Gimme my badge back," he growled.

"Please choose a competition," said the voice.

Arthur glared at the machine and searched for some button to eject his badge. "Stupid machine," he barked. "Just gimme my badge."

"Please choose a competition."

"I'd do what it says," came a different voice from behind Arthur.

He spun around, smacking his hand on the hard shell of the kiosk. A sharp pain rang through his hand, and then his eye throbbed briefly. He rubbed his hand. Then he saw a woman wearing a green neckerchief and a wide sunhat decorated with dangling ribbons. "Oh, Madam Siegfried," he gulped. "Uh, hi, I was just . . . just checking out the competitions . . . and . . . I, uh . . ."

"Didn't see one you liked?" Madam was smiling, but she narrowed an eye shrewdly.

"Uh . . . well, the one I wanted is full, I guess." Arthur paused, shifting his feet uncomfortably. "I think I took too long . . . to get around to it."

She straightened her hat. "Well, unless I'm mistaken, which does happen on occasion,"—she winked—"there should be five others to choose from."

"Um, right."

Madam Siegfried looked down at the floor, and Arthur saw she was standing right next to the Origins scroll tile. "Do you know," she said, stepping closer to him, "I've been to every single one of these ten-year celebrations. They take place at every location at the same time, so everybody has a chance to get involved. Only one person can win any given prize, obviously, but sometimes a few people manage to break an arm or a leg, and then they have a souvenir cast for everyone to sign." She laughed softly. "But they all come out of it with a feeling of triumph, because they put themselves to a test and they passed.

"I knew a young man once who decided he was not going to enter the competitions. He was very bright, but he was worried about making a mistake in front of everyone—especially a certain someone." Her eyes twinkled. "But, in the end, he figured out what the games are all about: building courage . . . and learning how to fall on your bottom gracefully." She smiled. "So he signed up and won first place in his competition. How's that for a good moral?" She squeezed Arthur's shoulder. "Sometimes it's good to step out of your everyday shoes and put on some different ones—clown shoes for instance. You never know where you might shine, or better yet, help someone else shine." She straightened her hat again and started toward the open doors.

For a moment, Arthur watched her walk away. "Madam Siegfried?" he blurted, his curiosity getting the better of him.

She paused.

"In your story . . . who was the guy who won first place?" But something told him who it was before she even answered.

She smiled. "Why, your dad, of course." Then she turned and left.

Arthur slid into a seat next to Pernille and rubbed Griffin's ears.

"Oh, there you are," she beamed. "Idolette hasn't gone yet, but Charda fell and broke her wrist." She stopped and looked hard at his face. "Are you okay?"

Arthur nodded and even grinned. "I went to register."

Pernille's face brightened. "Oh, good for you, Arthur! I knew it! I knew you had it in you—"

"The Squire Joust was full."

Pernille's smile faltered, and her eyebrows tipped inward. "Oh no, Arthur, I'm sorry." She squeezed his hand.

Arthur shrugged. "I went ahead and signed up for the Treasure Hunt."

Her smile jumped back, and she suddenly flung her arms around him, nearly knocking him out of his seat. "Oh, Arthur, that's grand!" she bubbled. "I'm glad you picked somethin' else."

After the Tower Climb and the presentation of the golden

hair to Miriam Hummad (who had managed to climb the tower in the least amount of time and also dodge the "evil witch" at the top and then climb back down with the Rapunzel doll she'd successfully rescued), Arthur and his friends gathered on the veranda for ice cream.

"You were amazin', Idolette," Pernille exclaimed. "Like an elegant spider zipping up and down the side of the wall."

"Yes," Esmond agreed. "Until you dropped Rapunzel to her death."

Everyone laughed, even Idolette. "Yeah, well," she snickered, "at least I did better than Donovan. He was the slowest. And did you see him try to whack the witch with Rapunzel? And then he tripped on her hair."

When their laughter died down again, Pernille announced, "Arthur registered for a competition, everybody."

"Really?" asked Idolette.

Arthur told them about his registration dilemma and that he'd finally just signed up for Treasure Hunt.

"Well,"—Pernille grinned as she licked her ice cream spoon—"now we've all signed up for at least one of the competitions."

"Except for Esmond," Idolette smirked.

Esmond muttered something incoherently.

"What did you say?" simpered Idolette.

Pernille leaned closer to Esmond. "I think he said 'I did, too.'"

They all stared at him. Then Arthur clapped him on the back, impressed. "That's awesome, Esmond."

Idolette lifted her eyebrows in disbelief. "What did you sign up for? Is there a book-reading contest they didn't tell us about?"

"Ha, ha," grumbled Esmond.

Arthur took a bite of ice cream. "How come you didn't say anything? When did you sign up?"

Esmond cleared his throat and shrugged. "A few weeks ago."

"For which competition?" asked Pernille.

"It's nothing," Esmond muttered.

"No, really," Idolette demanded. "What did you register for? Alchemy?"

"I'm not talking about it."

Idolette looked at Esmond appraisingly. "Is it the Pyramid Build? The Treasure Hunt?"

Esmond crossed his arms sulkily. "I said I'm not talking about it."

"It's the Pyramid Build," Idolette decided.

Esmond sighed and went back to his ice cream.

At that moment, Arthur noticed Steward Cartwright making his way between the tables and chairs along the portico. To his surprise, the man headed straight for them.

"Excuse me, Arthur Grey," he said, and Arthur felt a sudden sinking sensation in the pit of his stomach. But the steward seemed not to notice his unease. "If I could have a word?"

Slowly, Arthur stood, feeling the eyes of the others on his back. He shrugged and followed Steward Cartwright a little distance to a group of unoccupied tables, wondering what he could possibly have done to get in trouble.

The steward cleared his throat. "Madam Siegfried wanted you to know that a spot opened up for the Squire Joust. She seemed under the impression you would be interested."

Arthur blinked. "A spot opened?"

"Yes. The Initiate Charda Kuchamann suffered an injury in the tournament today and had to withdraw her name from the next competition, so her spot is now open. If you are interested, I suggest you register immediately. Otherwise, I'll make an official announcement."

"No, no," Arthur blurted. "I'll sign up for sure. Thanks."

The steward nodded once and headed back to the entrance.

Arthur went back to the others. "Looks like I owe Charda a thank-you."

"Why?" Idolette asked in surprise.

"Because she opened up a spot for the joust. I'm gonna go sign up now."

Pernille grinned. "That's grand, Arthur! Go do it quick."

"I'll be back." Feeling more confident than he had the last time, Arthur hurried through the large bronze doors into Main Hall, where the steward had gone shortly before. He patted the registration machine, feeling rather fond of it now, and slid his Initiate badge in. As he completed the signup, he became aware of voices coming down the Museo Gallery behind him. He tilted his head, listening.

"No, Mr. Cartwright. It's gone. I can't find it anywhere." That was Master Jolly's voice, Arthur thought. He sounded upset.

"You're certain?" asked the steward's voice. "You've looked everywhere? You've spoken to Master Stefanidis about it?"

"Yes. Zane doesn't know either. It's just disappeared."

"This is bad, bad, bad," moaned Steward Cartwright. "We were going to do major research on that. Madam Siegfried is not going to like this news at all. I'll have to tell her straight-away. Although she won't like being interrupted during the Members' Tower Maze competition. I suppose I'll just wait. It isn't like there's anything we can do at the moment. I mean, it could've been gone for hours."

"Unfortunately, yes," Jolly sighed. "I only noticed it when I came in just now. Is there anything I can do to help find it?"

"No, I'm afraid not."

Arthur drew his badge out of the kiosk and headed back outside before the two men could emerge from the hallway. He hurried back to the others. "You'll never guess what I heard," he breathed, and he told them.

"But what was missing?" wondered Esmond.

"They didn't say. But I have a bad feeling I know who stole it."

They all looked at him expectantly.

Arthur frowned. "When I was registering the first time, I saw Rheneas Berne sneaking in. Most everyone else was out for the competitions."

Pernille shook her head. "Mr. Berne? Why would he steal something from Master Jolly and Master Zane?"

"I guess we won't know until we find out what it was,"

Arthur said grimly. "Just, everyone keep your ears open for any clues."

In the end, it was Griffin who came to Arthur with a rather odd answer a few afternoons later. "It was some candle thing with a black beard . . . uh, they called it a Burnt Candle? No, that's not right. A Smelly Burning Candle . . . "

Arthur glared at him. "A smelly burning candle with a black beard?"

Esmond looked up from his book. "An Ever-Burning Candle from Blackbeard?" he demanded.

"Yeah, that's it," said Griffin.

"You know what they say," Esmond went on, going back to his book. "The famous pirate Blackbeard had several Ever-Burning Candles that he placed under his hat to make it look like he had smoke coming from his head."

Griffin scratched his ear. "Yeah, well that was the thing that was stolen. I overheard some Members talking about it in the garden. But," he frowned, "before you go shouting that it was Berne, remember that you were wrong about Gamble last year and then about Jolly wandering off."

Arthur lowered his voice. "We don't know for sure it wasn't Jolly," he huffed. But the guilty bubbling in his stomach told him he really did know, that Griffin was probably right. "Fine," he relented. "I won't say anything . . . yet."

The next day, as he headed for the portico for a lunch break, Arthur's steps were interrupted, for the second time in his life, by an explosion at his feet and the sudden *zip* of a paper envelope shooting up directly in front of his face.

"Your dad again?" asked Pernille as Arthur apologized to a small elderly Member he had knocked over in his surprise.

Recovering his nerves, Arthur tore open the envelope and read the note inside. "No, it's from the Decadal Competitions Board. About the joust competition training. It's a list of Initiate coaches available on Elysium Island."

"I got one of those when I registered," Pernille exclaimed. "That's how I found Madam Grattle to train me for the Creature Tricks."

"And how I found Member Rastoff to help me train for the Tower Climb," Idolette added.

Arthur looked at the paper again. "There're only two names listed on here for jousting. Member Percival Wingham, who's stationed at Experiments, and Member Marc Délicat, who works at Origins." He glanced up. "I guess I oughta try the Origins guy first, huh? It'd be a lot easier, anyway."

"You should probably do it soon, though," Esmond warned. "You've only got twenty-four days to figure out how to joust better than any of the others can."

"Yeah," Arthur said, suddenly worried now that Esmond had put it like that. "I'll go see him right after Gamble lets us go."

True to his word, Arthur headed off later that afternoon to find Member Marc Délicat, who, he had learned, worked in publications. He had to give his name to a young woman nibbling her fluorescent pink fingernails at an extremely tall desk. She gave him a look that plainly said, "I'd rather be watching worms crawl," and told him to wait. She then chewed at her nails some more, rolled her eyes impressively, and left the desk.

It took hardly any time at all, however, for her to come back, accompanied by a tall, thin man with a dangly mustache, wearing a ruffly purple shirt and shiny dark red pants.

"Ah!" the man exclaimed, clapping his hands and looking Arthur over. "You have come to Monsieur Délicat to be taught ze art of jousting! Let us meet tomorrow at ze hour of *set*—that is to say, six—and then we shall determine all. You have come to ze right person."

Arthur left feeling positive he had *not* come to the right person at all. That man could probably teach him how to paint a picture of a joust, but definitely not how to actually *do* a joust. Arthur had the sinking feeling that he was going to end up looking like a fool in front of the entire Origins department.

He didn't feel any more confident the next morning, either. *I'll just have to see how it goes*, he thought glumly. "I won't be back till late," Arthur told Griffin, buckling on his belt. "I have 'ze joust practice.' What are you going to do today?"

"The usual," Griffin yawned, stretching. "Go down to the lounge—they always give me some breakfast down there—then maybe out to the gardens. Have you ever tried to catch one of those will-o'-the-wisp thingies? Just when you pounce on one, thinking you've got it—whoosh!—it vanishes! And you just get a splash of dirty-tasting water up your nose." Griffin shrugged. "So maybe I'll take a nap instead. But not near the forest."

Arthur paused, his hand on the doorknob. "Why not?"

"It's spooky, that's why. I never smell any people scents in there, you know, but there're always noises. There's some kinda ghouls or werewolves or something in there. It's mostly quiet during the day, but it's very spooky and uncomfortable all the same. Plus it smells like cats."

Arthur remembered what Idolette had said on the boat ride to the island on their first day. Something about Homer Siegfried's ghost roaming the island and a beast that could eat people whole. And Charda was certainly convinced that there really was a ghost.

Griffin looked at the clock on the dresser. "Don't you have to go?"

"Oh, great Holy Grails! Yeah, I've gotta hurry. See you."

Arthur ran down the steps and along the path, dodging an occasional Member, his mind abuzz with ghost stories. He skidded into the entrance of Main Hall, and, unable to stop himself sliding, bumped smack into Oliver Johnson.

"Oh, hi . . . Arthur."

"Sorry, Oliver."

"Don't worry . . . I'm fine. I was . . . just finishing my . . . breakfast." He nibbled at the last bite of a pastry he'd been holding, then pointed to the rest of the Initiates, who were gathered ahead. "Master Gamble . . . says we're starting a new . . . unit today."

"Thanks. Aren't you coming?"

"Yup." Oliver licked pastry stickiness from his fingers, and together they caught up to their team in front of a room they'd never been in before.

Gamble stood silently, his hands folded over his tall, woody staff, Gatriona perched on his cloaked shoulder. He looked, as usual, like the Grim Reaper. "You've learned how to use your Translationaries," he snapped (Kelly Sullivan sighed—he still hadn't gotten a good handle on his, and it could frequently be heard snoring or correcting his pronunciation of *Odysseus* to *octopus*), "and you've memorized some of the tales and some of the language. So now you'll see how we get from *Odin* in Old Norse to *Woden* in Old English and then to *Wednesday* in modern English. And you'll work with one of the best."

He opened the door, and Arthur gasped with the others. At the head of a room filled with desks waited the centaur, Prometheus.

"Well, what are you stone trolls waiting for?" Gamble shrilled. "Get in there."

As Arthur entered the room, he gazed at the walls, which were lined with charts of timelines and lists of languages and posters of historians. He found a desk between Idolette and Esmond and sat down, gazing at their new instructor. The centaur seemed to fill the room, he was so large. His hoofed foreleg tapped the tile floor with a loud clack.

When the Initiates were seated and shifting uncomfortably under his doleful gaze, the centaur cleared his throat and spoke.

"Hopefully, you young students will get over my unique appearance in time to actually learn something of value. It is my duty here to study translated and transcribed documents and determine their probable accuracy. I will attempt to teach you the work of a scribe, of the importance of accuracy, of the power a translator wields, and the ease of misusing it."

Arthur tried not to stare at the instructor's swishing tail.

Prometheus looked around at them all. "I encourage you to ask questions when you are curious, as that's the best way to learn. If you never ask, you never learn. Yes, youngling?"

Arthur looked back and saw that Bridgette had her hand in the air. She put her hand down. "Do centaurs know the future?" she asked in awe.

"I'd wondered how long that would take," Prometheus sighed. "No, centaurs cannot predict the future in that way. We have methods for studying the stars and planetary movements that suggest certain events to us—"

"Can you teach us about the stars, then?" asked Tad.

Prometheus sighed again. "That is a job for the Department of Special Occurrences."

"How about battle?" demanded Thespia. "Aren't centaurs fierce warriors?"

"We shall now stick to questions relating to the subject of translations, if you please," Prometheus said, his tail giving an extra hard swish. "So allow me to give you something to ask questions about. I've always found that taking notes helps.

"As you probably do not know, translating an ancient manuscript is not only about the language. Many documents that come to us are not the original, but copies. Whenever something is copied, there are errors and mistakes. There are several types of these errors. Scribal errors are what we call it when the scribe—the copyist—accidentally misses copying a letter, word, or even an entire line, or misspells a word so its true meaning is lost. This is especially true when the scribe didn't know the language of the document he was copying. Thus, we put importance on understanding languages.

"Young Initiate Lisle, if you could not put glue in Miss Lane's hair, I'm sure she would appreciate it. As I was saying, another type of error is, of course, the one done on purpose. A scribe may suppose he knows better than those before him and may add his own details, which might not have been true at the time of the original writing, and so our accurate chronological view of history is disrupted. Sometimes scribes go so far as to add fabricated interpolations. *Inter-puh-lay-shun.* This is a nice word for 'adding completely made-up stories where they do not belong.' In other words, *lies.*"

Esmond frowned disdainfully at Nada, who gazed open-mouthed at her paper, doodling a rather accurate portrayal of Prometheus.

"Yet another type of error," the centaur continued, "is when the scribe believes he is accurately translating a name into more modern form. This is common in place-names. If I am copying a manuscript and see the name *Atenia*, I might assume it is a misspelling or ancient name for the city of Athens. If I change the name in my copy to *Athens*, then the original name of Atenia—which is *not*, by the way, an alternate spelling of *Athens* —is lost forever.

"Now, in order to help you wake up from your drowsiness, I will hand out copies of several documents and instruct you on some ways of revealing the errors we've discussed."

"Wow," Idolette gasped as they all clogged the doorway, each trying to escape the room first. "I think Master Prometheus might be even more depressing than Esmond."

"If you're trying to compliment me," Esmond sniffed, "you're not doing a good job."

"I'd like to stay and hear you guys argue," Arthur interrupted, "but I've gotta go."

"Oh, yeah," Idolette said with a snicker. "You have to learn how to paint jousting pictures." She waved an imaginary paintbrush.

Pernille giggled.

"At least you wouldn't be at risk of impaling yourself on a javelin that way," Esmond offered. "Just don't inhale any toxic paint chemicals."

With them all laughing behind him, Arthur headed the other direction, toward the northeast exit of Main Hall. When he got to the open lawn on that side, he found Member Délicat waiting outside a makeshift paddock in which a green, leathery-hided horse pranced nimbly about.

Arthur approached, blinking appreciatively at the large animal's quick movements.

"Ah ha," called Monsieur Délicat. "Here is our jousting shampion. I have here the riding boots, which will fit you very nicely. Tell me, have you ridden such a creature as Faria before?"

"No," Arthur admitted, watching the horse swing its green head back and forth.

"Zen we have no time to waste if we are to turn you into ze notable Sir Lancelot! I was once a worthy shampion myself, but of course, and now we shall instruct you. Come, come, you will learn to ride Faria. She runs smoothly like cream, and for her gait she is swifter than the arrow. She will not let you down, oh no!"

By the end of his first lesson, Arthur wished he'd had a painting lesson instead, and wondered what he had gotten himself into. The first shock came when he was tossed unceremoniously from the wild green horse and rewarded with a jolting pain that pierced through his left eye as his elbow cracked against the ground. He sat dizzily on the dirt while his teacher laughed and clapped, shouting that he would earn buns of steel before the day was over. Indeed, Arthur lost count of how many more times he fell before he was able to master the art of staying on the creature.

The instructor never stopped talking, even when Arthur was doing nothing more than climbing back up onto the horse. "Jousting has been around for many centuries," he said by way of encouragement. "The lordly knights in their shining armor and bright colors, charging down the track, fighting with lance and sword for the honor of a fair maiden! But, alas, ze kings lost many good knights in this way. And so the fighting became instead a skill of accuracy and quiet strength, and so it is today. And there is still much honor in it!"

Finally, Monsieur Délicat let him call it a day, laughing and calling after Arthur's stiffly departing figure, "Same time tomorrow, zen!"

During lessons the next morning, Arthur was stiff and sore. "I'm supposed to train with him four days a week," he complained to the rest of the Spyglass Squad. He could barely walk and went around bandy-legged, feeling like a plastic cowboy figurine. As for sitting through Translation lessons, well, that was a pain—in more ways than one.

After their first meeting, the Initiates had figured Prometheus was a conspiracy theorist, and now he did nothing to disprove them. He was fond of adding comments like, "Important artifacts are always written about. Unless they are not, which means there must have been a plotted cover-up!"

"One of the hardest issues to come to terms with," Prometheus announced during the next lesson, "is dating a written work. This is a very inaccurate science. I repeat. Inaccurate. Let us discuss a scenario. You have two documents that are both the story of King Arthur. One is in Welsh, the original language of our first tales of the Arthurian legends. The other is in Latin, the language of the Roman invaders. Which is going to be the earliest text? You, sir."

Oliver blinked. "Uh . . . the original Welsh?"

"Incorrect," Prometheus said calmly, as if he had expected Oliver's answer. "In this case, the Welsh was actually copied from a later Latin *copy* of the original Welsh. So the Latin text is older than the Welsh, even though it is not the original language. I see by your drooping eyelids that you all understand the complications.

"Now we will go over how to tell a more original text by finding textual differences, observing possible language modification, pointing out known historical accuracies—or inaccuracies—and known archaeological sites, discerning key date giveaways such as language, spelling, tradition, and place-names. I suggest you open your eyes a bit wider, Mr. Lisle."

Prometheus split them into groups and, oblivious to Esmond's scandalized stare, assigned Arthur, Oliver, Esmond, and Nada to work together. As if to console himself for this forced partnership with his archenemy Nada, Esmond immediately commandeered leadership of their group.

"We're supposed to use place-names to determine the origin of this document," Esmond directed, "so obviously we'll need to use our Translationaries to analyze the name linguistics. It's probable that . . . "

Arthur felt his mouth hanging open and closed it. Then his eyes started to glaze over. He shook himself and tried to listen to Esmond's droning. Next to him, Oliver stifled a yawn. At a desk to his left, he heard Idolette, "Er . . . I guess it looks kind of like Spanish, right?" and Tad's enthusiastic response, "Sure, that sounds good." On the other side of the table, Nada was happily doodling little pictures—on Esmond's paper.

"I think this is an Etruscan word," Esmond was rambling, "so I would say, according to this method, the document originated in . . . " He stopped as he suddenly realized Nada was drawing on his work. With the air of a martyr, he snatched the paper away and shoved it into his pile of books, " . . . in what is now western Italy," he continued through gritted teeth.

Arthur was glad when that lesson was over, though he wasn't glad about the extra homework they received. After dinner, he and Esmond sat in Arthur's room, trying to concentrate.

"Fascinating stuff," Esmond murmured at his book. "It

makes you wonder about the Minos Supplement Text, though. Do you think it really has new information we didn't know about? Why wouldn't others have put it in the copies we have now?"

"Maybe it's really old and no one's been able to interpret it for thousands of years and that's why they didn't bother to copy it down in later copies."

"Or maybe someone inaccurately added it later because they thought it belonged—an interpolation," said Esmond. He paused to glare at the paper Nada had scribbled on, then crumpled it with a vengeance and threw it at the garbage can in the corner before calmly continuing. "It doesn't make any sense. I've checked all the resources on file, and there is nothing that mentions extra symbols. What did Mistress Featherweit say? The document is dated to the seventh century BC? But the language to the twelfth century?"

"Yeah, but Prometheus says dating is still a touchy subject and not dependably accurate."

"He doesn't think anything is accurate."

Arthur shrugged. "Still. Someone lived in Crete, but was obviously Hittite. So, the question is, why were they writing in another language?"

"No, there are a hundred questions, Arthur. We don't know if the writer lived in Crete. All we know is the person knew the Hittite language and was familiar with Minoan letters, and since the language is older than the document, obviously this isn't the original. Maybe he was trying to copy the text from Hittite to Minoan."

"But why?"

Esmond sighed impatiently. "I don't know. You've heard Minister Jung before. We don't concern ourselves with the *why*. Only the facts matter in Origins. Just forget it."

Arthur didn't want to forget about it, but he didn't have any time to spare for questions. Between his jousting lessons, Prometheus's classes, plus Lore and extra assignments, April sped by in a blur. The jousting lessons were especially exhausting. Every failed practice brought critique from Member Délicat, and every successful accomplishment brought higher expectations:

"Use your knees and legs to absorb the horse's movement— you are a fluid rider, not a pencil in a saddle!"

"When choosing a lance, you take in ze size and ze weight. Some like a heavy one so the wind resistance will not move it so much. But for me, I like the lighter lance—easier to carry."

"*Non, non!* You are closing your eyes and so you miss your target and mess up your aim. You must brace with your arms, not your eyes. Your eyes will not fall out when you impact— this I promise!"

"Someday you may have ze beautiful maiden cheering for you as you charge in ze grand tournament! But only after you stop looking like—how do they say it?—like you are having constipation."

Arthur practiced riding while holding an unwieldy javelin. Then he learned how to charge at targets while passing them, knocking down pots lined up on the fences, sacks of potatoes, or a Rapunzel doll.

"It is not bad," Monsieur Délicat remarked, observing the hole in Rapunzel's head. "Not at all bad. You keep up with ze training, and when you are a full Member you will be able to join ze serious tournaments, and under ze exquisite training of Marc Délicat, what a Sir Lancelot you will be!"

Every time Arthur twisted his arm or fell off the horse or cut his finger on his practice armor, his left eye burned with pain, taking him off balance for a moment, and then he would find his injury healed. He tried to ignore it all so Monsieur Délicat wouldn't notice. "Incredibly resilient," Monsieur Délicat had already commented, impressed. Arthur couldn't risk any questions for fear of having to tell about the locket. "Maybe I should just leave the locket here," he suggested to Griffin one evening.

"Don't you dare," was all Griffin had to say on the matter.

Part of Arthur wondered if it was the locket or his Guarding skills that gave him his strange healing power. Another part was sure he knew the answer. He hadn't forgotten his dream: it was the green-cloaked lady who had the healing powers . . . the lady who had the locket.

It was in the last week of practice that Arthur finally felt his arm was strong enough to guide the lance straight, and his instructor set up the poles that held up the rings. Monsieur Délicat let him look at a ring.

"I'm supposed to get a lance tip through that tiny hole?" Arthur didn't think he could get a pencil through that, even if he were standing still. Getting a wooden pole taller than he was to go through that ring would not be easy. He climbed onto

Faria, hefted up his lance, took a deep breath, and urged the horse forward.

At that moment, Arthur finally felt the thrill of jousting, the horse's hooves thundering beneath him, the lance tip glowing in the sun, the rings ahead glittering like treasure. He felt like he could do this for real.

When Arthur hopped down from Faria, two rings on the end of his lance, Monsieur had no critique for him, only a glowing smile.

On the day before the Squire Joust, Monsieur Délicat brought several heraldic coats for Arthur to choose from. Arthur wasn't much for orange, and the red was too flowery, so he chose the blue one.

"Oui!" exclaimed the instructor, "zen you shall do well, for those were my own colors in ze days of my youth!" Arthur wasn't sure if this coincidence made him feel better or worse about his chances of winning.

The following morning, Arthur could hardly eat any breakfast. And when the others bid him good luck and left for the stands, Griffin trailing uncertainly behind them, Arthur felt like he was off to his own execution. When he arrived, Faria was decked out in shimmering blue, with tassels and a braided bridle in blue and gold. Her head armor rested on a hook. Arthur patted her green nose affectionately. "This is it," he said quietly, "last time for you and me." That made his stomach squirm a bit more.

"It is all very simple," Monsieur promised as he helped

Arthur into a light suit of chain mail and the blue surcoat with little golden fleurs-de-lis along the edges, "You will have ze exercises of catching ze little rings with your lance—just like we practiced, *oui?* And zen zere will be ze unseating, when you try to knock your opponent off his seat before he can knock you off. Now, remember the breathing. You take a deep breath . . . and you exhale. . . . Take a deep breath . . . and exhale. . . ."

Arthur felt thankful that he could wear a helmet, not for the protection from getting whacked in the head by someone else's lance, but rather because it would hide his face from all the eyes watching from the stands.

As they waited for the first round, Monsieur Délicat's dangly mustache gave a great solemn twitch. "Zere will be three charges for you to make to spear your rings," he reminded. "Remember your training. You shall do well."

Arthur watched from the shaded sidelines as Tad Weinstein collected one colored ring on the end of his lance, and Thespia Galoopsa swiped all three, while Donovan Lisle barely managed to get one—which didn't even count since he only got it because it snagged on his helmet. Then it was Arthur's turn, and his green horse Faria steered him true, his lance running through all three rings.

The next task was to knock a wooden man off a wooden horse. Oscar Verda and Tad did this in two passes, the others managing it in one pass (except for Donovan, who actually knocked himself off his own horse, sending the crowd into fits of laughter).

Before he knew it, Arthur was handed a blunt jousting

lance and paired against Thespia for the unseating charge. She was twice as big as he was, and if she could steer a chariot, Arthur was certain she could knock him out of his saddle without breaking a sweat. He said so to his teacher.

"*Non, non, mon apprenti,*" Monsieur Délicat chided. "It is not about size, it is about aim and a firm grip."

But Arthur didn't think so as his horse sped him forward across the sandy lane and his lance crashed against Thespia's shield and hers smashed into his with a blow that sent him sideways on his horse, barely holding on.

"Lean forward," Monsieur Délicat called in reminder.

The next pass, Arthur managed to knock Thespia's shield away. He felt more confident at that. Maybe he'd get the title after all and go on to be a jousting champion, followed by cheering maidens and all that.

It was the last pass and Arthur was sure he could do it. *Lean forward, hold the lance steady, keep your knees drawn to absorb the shock.*

He and Faria flew down the lane. He braced his lance and took aim. Four seconds till impact. Three. Two.

Suddenly, behind Thespia, a great white blur sprang up outside the fence, a living creature bounding across Arthur's line of sight. The hair on his neck stood up. It took barely a second, but it cost him his concentration and his aim. His lance sagged briefly, and Thespia's lance hit him square in the chest, shoving him sideways and back, off his horse and onto the sandy ground. He lay still for a moment as the pains in his body eased. The crowd cheered and clapped. No one seemed to have noticed a white creature. No one seemed concerned.

The announcing voice shouted, "The Squire Joust first-place title goes to Thespia Galoopsa, the Yellow Squire!"

Slowly, Arthur sat up, staring toward the other side of the track, searching for some sign of the white blur, for some clue of what it was. His eyes found nothing. Shakily, he stood up, immensely glad that no one could see his damp face beneath his helmet, and traipsed out of the aisle.

9

A Jolly Rescue

Arthur felt slightly irritated at having lost first place in the Squire Joust, but, as Pernille pointed out, second place was still a good title. More than anything else, he was concerned about the mysterious white creature he had seen—and the fact that no one else had noticed it.

He had a hunch about it, but it sounded so ridiculous he only confided in Griffin. "I wonder if it was something from the forest."

Griffin's ears pricked upward. "The haunted forest?" he asked darkly. "Do you suppose it was a ghost?"

"It sure made my neck tingle, whatever it was." Arthur shivered at the memory.

"That doesn't sound good. Ghosts in the forest should stay there and not be roaming around games. Should you tell someone?"

"I dunno." Arthur tried to shrug off his nervous feeling. "It might've been nothing, just my imagination. No one else seemed to notice it. Who would I tell anyway?"

"How about Madam Siegfried?"

"I think she's got other worries right now."

"The Minister?"

"He'd say I have no facts."

"What about Prometheus?"

"Are you kidding? He would say it's aliens trying to steal that OctoDiver or something."

"You're probably right. Well, what about Jolly, then?"

Arthur thought about that. "He'd probably laugh and say it was Gatriona or ask if I'd been getting hints from Prometheus."

"I'm all out of ideas then. But if ghosts come and attack us in the night, it's gonna be all your fault."

But no ghosts or anything else attacked. Nothing unordinary happened at all. In fact, most of the month of May passed uneventfully. The Initiates had a breather from competitions (it was Bard Songs this month, and that was only open to Members and Masters). Gamble had given them a break from memorizing, on condition they attend the Bard competition to see how professionals did it. Arthur mostly forgot about the mysterious white creature, distracted by outdoor wandering, playing games in the apartment lounges, or just lazing around, his brain numbed by warm weather and sunshine.

At the moment, he was lying on his back on a bench in the gardens while Griffin snapped playfully at fire sprites in the bushes, Pernille sat on the grass tinkering with some gears and a tiny motor, and Esmond huddled on another bench with a *Historia Today* magazine he'd checked out from the library.

"Two days till our next excursion," Arthur murmured sleepily to no one in particular.

Esmond responded automatically. "Yes, to Crete."

Pernille glanced up, her eyes large behind her pink goggles. "That's where the Minoans are from."

Arthur opened an eye. He closed it again without saying anything, but Esmond answered the unasked question anyway.

"Yes, the same Minoans ruled by King Minos and whose language the Minos text is in."

Griffin looked over at Esmond. "How does he do that?" he snorted. "Is he part book gnome?"

Esmond lifted his head, eyeing the dog suspiciously. "What did Griffin say?"

"Nothing important," Arthur yawned.

"How rude!" Griffin barked indignantly. "Everything I say is important."

With a huff, Esmond went back to his magazine article. "It must be handy to be able to talk with an animal when no one else can understand."

This time Arthur opened both his eyes. "What's that supposed to mean?"

"He can pass secrets without anyone else knowing. I've often wondered what else he can do . . . ."

A shiver tingled down Arthur's spine. "I already told you guys before," he grunted, sitting up.

"Right, Solstice Magic," Esmond cut in. "You talked to him at exactly midnight on Winter Solstice."

From her place on the ground, Pernille looked back and forth between them, her mouth hanging slightly open.

Arthur shifted uncomfortably. He had once accidentally suggested that Solstice Magic might be the cause of his ability to understand Griffin, and the others had latched on to that idea. No one apart from Gamble knew exactly why Arthur could understand Griffin. No one else knew that Arthur and Griffin could share emotions, pain, and occasionally even specific thoughts. And no one should ever know, Gamble had warned him, not even his friends.

"What're you sayin' that for, Esmond?" Pernille blinked, finally finding her voice. "We already know about it, an' Arthur asked us to keep it secret."

"Sorry," Esmond muttered. "I was just double-checking in case there was anything else to it. We're all friends here and trust each other, right?"

Arthur suddenly noticed the cover of Esmond's magazine. In bold letters, it read, "Solstice Magic Debunked, p 23." He felt his stomach flop as if someone had flipped it like a pancake.

"Of course we do," Pernille beamed, oblivious to the magazine. "Arthur told us about it, didn't he?"

Esmond looked suspiciously at Arthur. "Everything?"

This was getting dangerous. Arthur had to distract their curiosity at once. He would assure them the story they believed was true, that he had already told them everything there was to know.

"No."

Arthur's eyes widened in surprise that it was his own voice that came out of his mouth.

The other two stared at him.

"You didn't tell us everything about Griffin?" Pernille asked uncertainly.

Arthur tried to correct himself, tried to make his mouth say *yes*. But instead, "No," came out again. He swallowed his frustration. "I meant to say . . . ." But it was no use. He couldn't do it.

Griffin was wide-eyed. He shook his head at Arthur.

"I . . . I can't talk about it," Arthur gasped. "Don't ask." He jumped up, nearly kneeing Pernille in the head, and ran, Griffin scurrying after him. He didn't stop until he was in his room and in bed with the pillow over his head.

He couldn't believe it. What terrible luck. How could this be happening to him?

Griffin was quiet for a moment, but Arthur could feel the dog watching him.

"You can't lie," Griffin said knowingly.

Arthur cowered beneath the pillow. He tried to think of the last time he'd told an outright lie. To a tutor, to Gamble, to his grandmother. He couldn't think of a single time. There had been times when he said part of a truth and other people had added their own ideas and he didn't correct them. But he couldn't remember ever actually telling a lie. Was it possible that he just couldn't do it? He couldn't lie?

He squeezed his eyes shut. Was this something to do with

being a Guardian? Could they not tell lies? Had Gamble ever mentioned this and Arthur just forgot?

"I need to talk to Gamble," he blurted. He flung off the pillow and stood up. "Stay here."

Arthur tried Apartment Thor first, and the nymph there said she hadn't seen Gamble all day. Arthur didn't listen to her offer to take a message, but instead bolted for Main Hall, certain Gamble must be there. He'd find him and make the old man listen to his question. But Arthur had hardly started down the Museo Gallery when he stopped.

Voices were coming from the Transfer Depot to the right. He turned in that direction, but another voice from ahead called him, "What're you doing here, Arthur?"

He paused to see Idolette coming toward him, her tomato-red hair spiked, several earrings in a row along her ears, her legs cocooned in fishnet stockings and tall blue boots. Arthur guessed that Mr. Alexander Siegfried was at Main Hall today. They could always tell by Idolette's eccentric outfits when he was around. "I'm just looking for someone," Arthur replied, and he kept walking, hoping Idolette would take the hint. He was in no mood to talk to anyone but Gamble.

But Idolette didn't seem to notice. "I was just talking to Gran," she said, falling in next to him.

"Listen," Arthur began impatiently.

"I really can't wait for this year to be over," Idolette went on with a huff. "What a pain. I don't know why my dad bothers coming to this location. Gran says it's because of that rotten Berne bloke, but I think he's just here at Mother's insistence.

She said I was too involved last year and I need to remember how to live a regular life. As if. But I think . . . "

As she whined on, Arthur tried to think of a way to get rid of Idolette. He needed to talk to Gamble alone. The voices were closer as they approached the Transfer Depot door. Maybe the sight of the cranky old man would send Idolette on her way.

" . . . so why should he care if I snuck out to the pub? It's not like I drank anything. I was with Tad and he's sixteen already. And so I told Gran—" But what Idolette told her grandmother Arthur never found out, because they had reached the open door and Idolette immediately shut her mouth. This was not because Gamble was there, as Arthur had hoped.

Instead, they saw a man inspecting a glass plate of soil in his gloved hand, his black eyes narrowed. It was Rheneas Berne. Before him, his back to them, was Master Jolly.

"I don't know what you expect me to say," Jolly grunted in a rather brusque and un-Jolly-like tone. "I'm a Preserver, not an interpreter. How would I know?"

"Just remember," Berne said silkily, replacing the soil sample, "I'll be watching you. If you are withholding information from—" He cut himself off, noticing the two shadows in the doorway.

All of Arthur's doubts and anger and frustration boiled in the pit of his stomach and suddenly erupted. He stepped forward into the room. "You're no investor," he blurted hotly before he could stop himself. Jolly jumped, and next to Arthur, Idolette gasped, but he didn't care. Who did that Berne guy think he was, threatening Masters and bullying the Society?

Rheneas Berne turned his dark eyes right on Arthur for the first time. Arthur straightened his shoulders and stuck his chin out determinedly as Berne approached him, taking slow, thoughtful steps, his eyes not wavering from the place where Arthur stood. Arthur swallowed, getting the uncomfortable feeling that he was prey being stalked by a panther.

The man stopped two feet from him. His mouth twitched. "And who," he said in a soft low voice, "might you be?"

Arthur cocked his head, trying to understand the look on the man's face. He narrowed his eyes, determined not to let this man scare him. "Arthur Grey."

"His dad's a minister," Idolette added threateningly.

Rheneas Berne's eyes narrowed to slits and his mouth twitched again. "Oh my. A little boy with a minister father. I'd better watch my step, then, or he might run to daddy and tattle on me."

Arthur's ears burned red hot. "I don't tattle," he snapped, irritated at Idolette's interference. "I can take care of things myself."

"I'm quaking," Berne smiled patronizingly.

"You ought to be." Gamble clunked his staff onto the floor behind Arthur.

Berne raised his eyes to look over Arthur's head. "Oh, you again, hm? I'll have to speak to Madam Siegfried about all these interruptions. It will be absolutely impossible for me to give a good report if I can't gather data for funding."

"It'd be easier to gather data if you didn't waste time prancing around, harassing Initiates."

Without another word, Berne smirked, made a little bow, and stalked off.

"Gamble," Arthur began.

"You," Gamble seethed, glaring at Arthur and stamping his staff again with an echoing thud. "You Initiates were told to mind your own business. Apparently, you need help remembering. Tomorrow night you can go see Member Shana about the two hundred handwritten copies she needs to make." Again he thunked his staff on the hard floor. "And Griffin will not be allowed on your excursions anymore, is that clear? Now, you stay away from that menace, you hear me? Let me catch you anywhere near him, and I will have you booted from here faster than you can say 'pain of death.' Is that understood? Just stay away from him!" And he whirled away.

Arthur swallowed his fury. Without even a glance at Idolette or Jolly, he stormed off.

Arthur felt sour and friendless over the next day. Unanswered questions whirled in his brain, making it difficult to concentrate on Prometheus's lesson on Scribe Blunders. None of the other Spyglass Squad members tried to talk to him, but they didn't seem to talk to each other much, either.

After studies ended for the day, Arthur hurried out to the portico café and ate his lemon chicken in a daze, thinking of the note he'd found in his mailbox that morning telling him to meet Member Shana in the Copy Room at seven o'clock to help handwrite copies. It didn't sound like a good time.

He had just slipped the last bite of rice into his mouth when a shadow fell across his table. "What?" he growled.

Esmond cleared his throat and sat down across from Arthur. "I just wanted to . . . er . . . make amends," he murmured.

"Did Pernille put you up to this?"

"No. Well, a little. But I wanted to." Esmond's eyes shifted guiltily. He heaved a breath. "It's like this," he blurted. "I tried to do it—to talk to an animal—an owl actually—at midnight of last Winter Solstice, but needless to say, it didn't work." His hands were clenched so tightly they were turning purple.

Arthur blinked in surprise. "What? But why—"

"It's just like I said," Esmond interrupted, not looking at Arthur. "It'd be handy . . . special. But it didn't work, and it made me think that the magic can't be real after all and there must be something else you didn't tell us about what happened with you. And I got that magazine—though it probably has flaws, it's from 1983, you know—and I was in a foul mood and not thinking fairly and I didn't mean to bring it up and . . . I apologize."

They were both quiet for a moment as Esmond's confession sank in. Arthur briefly considered telling Esmond about his own failure—not being able to keep secrets from nosy people. But he decided against it. At last, Arthur gave a nod. "You weren't off, though," he admitted quietly. "About my not telling everything."

Esmond looked relieved. "Don't worry, I won't ask about it," he said firmly.

"I'd tell you if I could, I just can't. It'd be dangerous," Arthur added as an afterthought.

Esmond looked sidelong at him and shoved his glasses up his nose. "I won't mention it," he said solemnly. Then he added, "And Pernille won't either. She's already said so."

Arthur nodded again, his spirits slightly lifted. "Okay."

The worst over with, Esmond relaxed a bit. "Idolette told us last night that you got in trouble."

Arthur's momentary cheer immediately fizzled away. "Yeah," he growled. "Gamble still has his talent for turning up out of nowhere to hand out punishments, I guess."

"What for?"

"Talking to Berne."

Esmond's eyes widened. "The investor? You talked to him?"

"Well, not much. He was threatening Jolly for not giving him information, and I just said I didn't think he was really an investor and—"

"You're joking," Esmond breathed.

Arthur shook his head. Suddenly, a rush of anxiety splashed over him. He realized how foolish he'd been to open his mouth at Rheneas Berne.

"So, that Berne fellow got you in trouble?"

"No, Gamble showed up. He didn't need any help getting me in trouble."

"This is bad, Arthur. Berne knows you now, and he'll have an eye out for you—not in a good way. He could cause serious trouble, from what we've heard of him. You'll need to steer clear of him at all costs."

Arthur stood up, irritated again. "Look, I've got to get some work done before seven o'clock. I'll see you tomorrow, okay?"

"Right," Esmond sighed, "for our excursion in the morning. See you."

Unless it was noting clues in his notepad, Arthur hated writing. So he dreaded having to help Member Shana. And it was every bit as bad as he'd feared.

The door to the Copy Room was open, so, with a glance at the fireproof door tucked into the ceiling, he entered. The narrow room was stuffed with file cabinets and smelled like wet ink. He couldn't see the walls, which were completely blocked by stacks of paper and towers of ink bottles.

"Come in."

Arthur jumped, startled that he had missed the woman seated at the back, camouflaged between the cabinets and stacks of papers on a desk. She wore large, round glasses that made her look like an owl and had frazzly hair that looked to be full of static electricity. He wondered if it was about to explode.

"You must be the copy boy. Good, good. Lots of copying to do, as you can see. Always busy."

"Don't we live in a technological age?" Arthur groaned. "Why does there need to be so much paper?" His hand already ached at the sight of all the stacks.

"Documentation. We handwrite everything," Member Shana answered, poised with a large quill pen in her hand and a slightly crazed look in her constantly blinking eyes. She looked ready to attack all the papers at once. "Technical advances are temporary at best. Gone in the blink of an eye. Replaced. Easily outdated." She looked up. "I mean, have you ever heard of the Rhymus Catrometer?"

"Uh . . . no?"

"Well, you see my point, then. We'll be working on copying Plato's description of military government. Not a bad job today—only need to make two hundred copies. Ink up." She rolled up her own smudged sleeves, grinning toothily, and brandished the quill pen, spattering Arthur's shirt with ink flecks.

It was nearly eleven o'clock by the time Member Shana listened to Arthur's not-so-subtle hints about Initiate curfew and finally let him go.

Arthur groaned as he slouched down the hall from the Copy Room. His hand was sore, and he had a dozen paper cuts. The words he had written over and over in black ink still floated in front of his eyes. Bitterly, Arthur thought that Griffin had been right—nothing had changed with Gamble. The old man was crotchety and unfair. That's all there was to it. *I'm gonna have to figure out how to Guard by myself. Gamble's apparently changed his mind about teaching me anything.*

His mind taken up with these grim thoughts, Arthur was startled when something squishy touched his hand. "Wha—!" A slimy tentacle grabbed his arm and another slithered around his legs. In two seconds, he was slammed against a wooden door and bound tightly by a gigantic sticky vine. He had walked right in front of the snapper plant.

"You've got to be joking," Arthur grunted as he struggled. "Haven't I had enough unfair punishments today?" He tried to pull his arms free, but he had about as much chance as a tiny ant trying to get out from under a cat's paw. The plant didn't budge. "Great, just great. Hello? Anyone? Help?"

No one answered.

Arthur racked his brain, trying to remember the word Gamble had used to get Donovan Lisle out of this mess on their first day. "Porcupine," Arthur said hopefully. Nothing.

"Plywood?" Nope. Maybe it was a d-word. "Doorbell? Destiny. Dumb dimwit plant!" He struggled uselessly until he was sweating. At last he gave up, resigned to spending the night being squeezed by a plant.

Then Arthur cocked his head. He could hear voices down the hall. He listened, hoping with all his might that it wasn't Gamble coming this way. Or Berne. The voices drew closer.

"Here's a letter for you," said a woman's voice. "I picked it up at the post on the mainland. What a day. Did you hear the rumor? No, of course you wouldn't. I only just heard it before I left the mainland. But it was something about a monster being spotted."

"A monster, eh? Better call Investigations. They don't pay me enough to go looking for monsters." Arthur's heart rose. This teasing voice was definitely Master Jolly's.

"I guess they already have. But it's so close. I heard there was an explosion."

"Probably it was only another earthquake. We get those tiny ones all the time here. Makes me mess up when I shave," Jolly chuckled. A popping sound followed, and the scent of strawberry bubblegum floated along to Arthur's nose.

"Still, I'd be careful till Investigations comes back with a report," the other voice advised. "If the rumors aren't true, they'll know quickly."

"I already know they're not true," Jolly said lightly, and Arthur could hear the grin in his voice. "I've been here long enough to know the goofball stuff people come up with. Take Prometheus, for example, eh? That guy eats a little too much hay, if you ask me—does something weird to his brain. Not enough nutrition—yikes!"

Jolly jumped when he saw Arthur in the dim light. Next to him was a Member Arthur didn't recognize. Jolly recovered quickly and gave a hearty laugh. "Why, Arthur Grey, you look a bit dazed there. Just hangin' around, are you?"

Arthur cleared his throat. "Um," he began, watching Jolly quickly tuck away an envelope into his vest pocket. "I was coming back from helping Member Shana . . . "

"Say no more," Jolly grinned. "That is a painful experience that doesn't need remembering." He stepped forward, reached out to scratch the tentacle that held Arthur's arm back, and firmly said, "Branstock." Arthur gasped as the plant gripped him even tighter. "Oops, that wasn't it, now was it," Jolly chuckled. "Let's try again. How about . . . puttydurms."

The plant immediately released Arthur and sprang back into place.

"Uh, thanks," Arthur muttered as he shakily got to his feet and brushed himself off.

"Don't mention it. I'm pretty sure it happens to everybody at least once. In fact, Lou Grandywine gets stuck in that thing twice a day. But, listen, Arthur . . . " Jolly glanced at his co-worker a few feet away and lowered his voice. "About the other day. . . . Idolette Siegfried mentioned what you overheard from Berne. I just want to let you know it's nothing to worry about. Berne is always going around trying to bully people into getting his way. Thanks for your interruption, though, it sure helped. I'm sorry ol' Gamble was so hard on you. He's right, though. You should stay away from Berne. You all right?"

"Yeah," Arthur mumbled.

"Good. All right, well. Goodnight, Arthur. Get some sleep so you're ready for your big excursion tomorrow." Jolly grinned and continued down the hall with his friend.

Obediently, Arthur headed outside, making his way back to his room. But now he had something else to add to his thoughts: news of an explosion and a monster (even though Jolly apparently didn't believe a word of it), and Arthur couldn't help wondering exactly how nearby "so close" was.

✳

10

DANGER ON CRETE

Arthur was up half the night, wondering first about monsters and ghosts and how the two could be related, and then again about lies and Guarding, which reminded him of what a grouch that old vulture Gamble was and how Arthur wished a monster would come scare the hair off the old man's head, which brought him back to wondering about monsters . . . .

He didn't remember falling asleep. Next thing he knew, he was waking abruptly to blinding sunshine and Griffin barking that he was going to be late for the excursion. After a mad scramble to dress and snatch his things, Arthur barely had time to grab some food before racing down to Main Hall's entrance with a handful of dates and a piece of toast hanging from his mouth.

Gamble wasn't there. The rest of the Initiates stood yawning or else finishing their own rushed breakfasts. *I didn't even have to hurry*, Arthur thought irritably. But then he heard a huffing behind him and turned to see someone jogging toward them.

"Is that Master Jolly?" wondered Pernille. Sure enough, it was, though he was nearly unrecognizable: his clothes—the same ones from the day before—were wrinkled, and his eyes were bloodshot. He looked like he hadn't slept a wink the whole night.

"Are you taking us on the excursion?" Bridgette asked hopefully.

"What? Oh, of course, yes," Jolly stammered. "Gamble had something else to do, so I offered to step in. I hope no one's too disappointed."

"Are you kidding?" Charda exclaimed, and the others laughed.

Esmond leaned toward Arthur. "He looks like he was up all night," he remarked quietly.

"I wonder if it's because of the letter he got," Arthur murmured.

"What letter?" asked Pernille, also leaning in.

Arthur told them about what he had overheard last night. Then he scratched his head, narrowing his eyes at the suspicious thought that popped into his head. "I wonder if that letter was from Berne."

"Let's get off, then, eh?" Jolly called, wiping his brow. "To the island of Crete. First thing we'll check out is the famous Palace of Knossos."

On Crete, Jolly wordlessly lead the Initiates up a hill while Esmond rattled off a constant stream of information like a talking encyclopedia: "Crete is the fifth-largest island in the Mediterranean Sea. . . . It is positioned south of mainland Greece. . . . The Greek name for the island is Kríti. . . . The island has an expansive geological composition, including steep gorges, rugged coasts, and high mountain peaks—"

Nada nonchalantly interrupted, "Knossos is the ancient capital of the Minoans."

Esmond sniffed.

At the top of the hill, Arthur could see the site. A barrier of green trees surrounded the ruined palace. Everywhere inside it were crumbled stone walls, stairways leading nowhere, empty doorways, and flat roofs sitting on wide columns of white or red. As a reminder of the modern world, paths with safety railings zigzagged throughout.

Jolly frowned. "Huh. I wonder why it's so crowded on the road. Oh well. The show must go on. Maybe there's a dancing rhinoceros in a tutu or something. Let's go, everybody."

"Wow," muttered Esmond. "I can't believe it. The Minoan work has been here for five thousand years. We're standing on history. Very possibly the Labyrinth of Minos, where he kept the Minotaur."

Arthur shuddered. He wasn't sure if he was excited or nervous. Something felt strange and made his neck prickle. He looked down at Griffin, then remembered the dog wasn't there. Gamble had made sure of that.

"Hey, what's all the fuss?" Jolly asked a passerby. "It's only an ancient history-entangled site, after all."

The woman looked around. "Didn't you hear? Someone's been wounded badly."

"Wounded? Did he trip down the stairs?"

"No, sir. Says it was a monster that slashed at him."

"A monster?" snorted Donovan. He wiggled his eyebrows. "Did it have a big bull head, too?"

The woman frowned. "So you've already heard, then. Well, good day."

Arthur and the others crowded Jolly. "Did she just say what I think she said?" Arthur clearly remembered that the Historia Member had mentioned a rumor about an explosion and a monster.

"No, no," Jolly waved dismissively. "That lady was only joking. Let's go ask the police up here." They pushed through the crowd to where paramedics were loading a man onto a stretcher and police were keeping the area clear. "What's the news, sir?" Jolly asked the nearest officer.

"Ah, crazy tourist was sneaking around last night after hours and hurt himself."

"See?" Jolly gestured at the Initiates. "The lady was joking. What did I tell you, eh?"

"Yes," the officer continued. "He thought he'd get out of trouble by making up a story of a bull creature stabbing him with its horns. I don't know what he gouged himself on, but, obviously it wasn't a bull horn."

Jolly's smile faltered. "Heh. Obviously. Now, where did you say you found him again?"

The policeman pushed up his hat. "Uhh . . . Well, over there. Inside a lower-level room of the ruin. But everyone needs to move out. Precautions. You can't visit the monument today. Sorry."

"Jolly." Arthur pointed to a print pressed into the dirt.

Jolly stared at the ground for a moment. Sweat had beaded at his forehead and now slowly slid down the side of his face. Quickly, he rubbed it into his hair. Then he began herding everyone away. "Let's go," he called.

"Did you see that print?" Arthur demanded, jostling against several others as they made their way back. "It looked like—"

"Yes, yes. It was probably several prints overlapping. It didn't look like anything interesting. Come on then, everyone."

Arthur frowned, glancing toward the print he could no longer see. He'd been certain the shape looked like a cleft hoof.

The remainder of their trip to the island of Crete was far less involved than the previous excursion to Athens. Jolly pointed out random things like bushes and rocks and acted so flustered and grouchy that Donovan wondered aloud if Gamble was rubbing off on him. He kept checking his wristwatch, as if he just wanted to hurry up and get back to base.

No one argued when Jolly pointed out a small outdoor restaurant for lunch. "We'll break for one hour," he informed them.

It took some time to order food and find seats. Then

Idolette startled everyone with a shrill squeal. "Look, Gypsies! Do you think they can tell our fortunes?" She, Bridgette, and Charda ran off to see, digging in their pockets and purses for coins.

"Fortune-telling is a joke," Esmond grunted, watching the girls line up at the booths. "People's futures aren't written on their palms or predicted with cards. We make our own fates."

"I think it's funny," Pernille smiled, flicking at the straw in her glass. "I got my hand read once."

"What did they tell you?" Arthur asked with mild interest.

"I don't know. I was so nervous that I talked the whole time and the lady telt me I was givin' her a headache and she couldnay read it for me."

Arthur and Esmond laughed, and Pernille giggled too. As he sipped his drink, Arthur glanced around, noticing for the first time that he couldn't see Jolly anywhere. He sat up quickly and searched again.

"Here comes Idolette," Pernille announced.

"Have you seen—" Arthur began.

"How was your fortune-telling?" Esmond asked snidely.

Idolette ignored him. "My name is going to be famous," she said reverently.

Esmond snorted. "Your name is Siegfried—it's already been famous for several centuries. You do know old Germanic folklore, don't you? Siegfried was the hero of the epic *Nibelungenlied*."

Idolette gave him a scathing look. "Don't bother going up, Esmond. I can predict your future myself—you will live the rest of your life alone, miserable, and causing great annoyance to everyone around you." She turned to Arthur and smiled sweetly. "But why don't *you* come get your fortune told, Arthur?"

"What?" he asked in surprise. "I don't need my—"

"Come on. It'll be educational," Idolette insisted, tossing her long black curls over her shoulder and grasping Arthur's arm.

He looked at the others for help, but Pernille only covered her mouth to hide her giggles and Esmond shrugged. So Arthur reluctantly let Idolette lead him to the short line before the Gypsy's table.

"Idolette," he grumbled, "I don't even want my fortune—"

"You have to," she interrupted. She lowered her voice. "The Gypsy told me I'll be brought to harm by a young explorer and I want to find out if it's you."

"What!" Arthur sputtered as they moved forward with the line.

"Well, it's what your Spyglass card says you are, right? The Explorer."

"Don't be a Cyclops. That doesn't mean—"

"Oh, it's your turn now. Go on. And remember what she tells you—word for word." Idolette shoved Arthur forward.

Before him sat a middle-aged woman wearing a tasseled kerchief around her head and beads around her neck and wrists. Her long hair was several shades of brown and blonde, as if she had colored it a long time ago and hadn't kept it up. She did not look at Arthur as she gestured for him to take the seat across from her. On the table between them was a glass globe that appeared to have swirling fog inside it. She was staring at it intently. When Arthur sat down, the woman pointed to the sign behind her.

To his dismay, Arthur saw that the sign was a plank of wood with the cost of one fortune handwritten across it. Irritably thinking that Idolette owed him, he dug in his pocket for the correct change and put it on the table. In a flash, the woman snatched the money, slid it into a pouch around her waist, and then grabbed Arthur's hand to inspect his palm, prodding it with her finger. She did all of this without once looking at him.

"Your path is very complex," she said softly, tracing the lines on his hand. Her voice wasn't old, but it was raspy, as if she had smoked in her younger days. "But I enjoy a challenge."

Arthur looked nervously at his hand and tried not to wiggle even though her fingernail was tickling it.

"There is a beast haunting your near future."

He cocked his head, his heart speeding up. *A beast?*

"And a friend will betray you," she continued. "But the worst betrayal will come from . . . " She stopped and abruptly released his hand. "Put your hands on the crystal ball," she instructed.

Arthur hesitated, staring at the Gypsy's bowed head. "Come from who?" he demanded.

"Hands on the crystal ball," she repeated.

Annoyed, Arthur placed his hands on either side of the glass globe. The mist inside it poofed as if someone had blown a breath of air at it. Then it began swirling faster.

"What do you see?" the woman asked softly.

"Fog," Arthur muttered.

"Do not be angry," the Gypsy chided. "Be careful. Now what do you see?"

Arthur looked again. The grey and white fog blew around in the globe, and for a brief moment, Arthur thought he glimpsed a young man dressed in a cloak and furs, a large wolf beside him. Then the mist shifted and he could make out nothing more. He immediately thought of his dreams about the boy lord and his wolf. Was that what he had just seen? Arthur glared at the woman's bowed head. "I saw a boy and a wolf," he snapped. "Are they my worst betrayal?"

"No. That is from your father. That is all."

Arthur coughed. "What? What did you say?"

"That is all. Thank you."

Arthur was on the verge of demanding that the woman clarify what she meant, but then he heard Jolly calling everyone together. The Gypsy woman also heard and tipped her head upward as if to listen better. And when Arthur glanced back down at her, he sucked in his breath. Her eyes were glazed with a white film and did not focus. She was completely blind.

Swallowing his irritation, Arthur stood up and murmured, "Thanks," and that was all.

Jolly led the team to another site, but Arthur barely noticed, he was so taken aback by what the Gypsy had said. What did she mean by all that bit about his dad? Was she talking about the dream or the betrayal? Arthur didn't talk much to the others or pay attention to where they even were until Jolly, also apparently lost in his own thoughts, announced that it was time to go back and almost threw down the return Transportal right in front of a group of tourists. While Donovan thought freaking out a bunch of tourists would be funny, Esmond pointed out that there would be big trouble for Historia, should anyone see them disappearing through a sudden doorway.

Flustered, but pretending not to be, Jolly found a more secluded area for their departure and dropped the Transportal there.

Back at Main Hall, he said their lesson was over and they could have the rest of the day free.

"That was not a very informative trip," Esmond sniffed as they headed down the path to their apartments. "I didn't get anything worthwhile out of it."

"I did," Idolette announced and turned directly to Arthur. "So? What did the Gypsy tell you?"

Esmond rolled his eyes.

"Uh . . . " Arthur began, feeling anxious.

"My life might depend on it," Idolette warned, "so be honest."

As if I had a choice, Arthur thought irritably. He told them what the Gypsy woman had said, but he left out the part about his dad. He didn't think that needed mentioning, and he rather hoped no one would ask any specific questions. "Did you know she was blind?" he asked Idolette.

"Blind?" Idolette furrowed her brows. "Don't be silly. How could she read our palms without seeing them? What makes you say that?"

"Her eyes were all white—foggy-looking. I dunno. She kept her head down the whole time until the end, and then it was by accident that she looked up. Like she didn't want anyone to know."

"Well, there you have it," Esmond finally put in, apparently unable to keep his opinion silent any longer. "That's just further proof that fortune-telling is completely fraudulent. I mean, a beast haunting your future? Obviously, she heard the story going around about a monster by the palace and thought she'd use it for some drama. And that bit about getting betrayed by a friend—it's an easy thing to say and it happens all the time, so who can prove or disprove it? As for the misty smoke, you can make just about anything out of smoke, can't you. It's all nonsense by tricksters."

Idolette stopped suddenly, and Arthur thought she was going to rip into Esmond about his always being so negative. But she didn't seem to have heard a single word from him. "Maybe," she said thoughtfully, "I'm going to accidentally betray Arthur, and then he's going to bring me to harm as his revenge, thinking I did it on purpose?" She gave Arthur a fearful look.

"You don't even know that she was talking about Arthur," Pernille soothed, patting Idolette's arm.

"But who else is an explorer?" wailed Idolette.

Esmond crossed his arms. "Did anyone listen to a word I said?"

"I did," Arthur said glumly as Pernille waved and consolingly led Idolette toward their apartments. "But don't count on Idolette."

Esmond sniffed. "I won't deny that sometimes I feel very concerned that she's in the lineup to inherit Historia one day." He shook his head. "Anyway. Did you notice that Jolly disappeared while we had lunch?"

Arthur frowned. "Yeah. I'm glad it wasn't just me who noticed this time. Where do you suppose he went?"

"Maybe just the toilets," Esmond suggested, but he didn't sound convinced.

"Do you think that Berne guy is forcing him to find out information for him?" Arthur asked grimly. "He's seemed a bit . . . I dunno . . . "

"Narky?" Esmond offered with a smirk.

Arthur half-smiled. "Yeah. Well, there's definitely something not right. And I bet anything that Berne guy is at the bottom of it. Remember, I heard him threatening Jolly the other day. He said he'd be watching Jolly. And next thing you know, Jolly gets a mysterious letter that has him losing his nerve. We have to figure out how to stop Berne's meddling."

"No, Arthur. We need to stay out of Berne's way. If there's a problem, Master Jolly will tell Madam Siegfried."

"Unless he's worried about ruining the investments for Historia," Arthur protested.

"There's nothing we can do except make more trouble." Esmond gave Arthur a stern frown. "And we'd better not."

11

The Wisdom of Prometheus

Over the next week, the Spyglass Squad had lots to think about, what with Berne's trouble, possible monsters on the loose in Crete, and concern for Master Jolly, not to mention Arthur's and Idolette's disconcerting fortunes. Arthur had frequent nightmares involving the ghostly-eyed Gypsy woman rising from cloudy mist to trap him.

Then there was the Bard competition at the very end of the month, and a week of essays on the role of bards as historians, which drove all else from their minds. Arthur managed to get on Minister Jung's bad side by writing his essay on why he thought bards were probably more like actors than historians and not having any facts to support it (and not being able to lie about not having any facts).

But the first Saturday of June was a gorgeous afternoon, so Arthur and the rest of the Initiates, ready for a break, took their gear down to Olympian Bay on the southeast side of Elysium Island.

"I don't know why they can't let us take a Transportal to get here," Idolette complained. "What's the point in making us walk? Oh, stinky piskies—I forgot my Golden Goddess sunscreen."

"Hey, did you hear?" exclaimed Tad, catching up to them. "The Investigations team reported on the Knossos site." He lowered his voice. "There really is a hoofed beast on the loose."

Idolette covered her mouth.

Esmond shook his head as he adjusted his wide sun hat. "It will probably gouge another visitor or ten and possibly wreak havoc on that historical site before they catch it."

"Do you think it's the Minotaur?" asked Griffin, and Arthur voiced this aloud.

Pernille giggled. "Oh, Arthur, how could it be when the records say the Minotaur lived thousands of years ago? Creatures can't live for that long—even the really old ones like dragons."

"She's right," Esmond agreed.

"Besides," added Nada from directly behind them, "the Minotaur doesn't have hooves, it has human feet."

Esmond snorted. "Actually, no one specifies which parts are bull and which parts are human. In fact, in medieval times, many artists portrayed it with a man's head and bull's body."

Arthur and Griffin hurried ahead so they didn't have to hear Esmond and Nada at their usual battle of knowledge. He could just hear Esmond sneering, "And I suppose next you're going to say that sirens are nothing but your everyday seagull. Well, don't blame me if you get devoured by sirens."

Soon everyone was jogging for the long, white-sanded beach that eased itself into the clear blue water of Olympian Bay.

Oscar Verda and Kelly Sullivan found several canoes in a shed and pulled one out into the water. After about five minutes, however, they hauled it back, both of them soaking wet, having accidentally overturned the canoe and fallen in. They then began a game of Frisbee, which Nada joined.

Arthur and Griffin swam for a while in the cool, bouncing waves before joining Donovan and Tad in digging up five-headed snails and tiny winged turtles.

Esmond didn't go in the water, as he couldn't swim, and instead spread out a towel and read a book. Idolette played for a while before abandoning the boys in favor of sunbathing with several others. Bridgette had to pause often to lather on more sunscreen so she wouldn't burn.

Tired of getting snapped in the nose by little turtles, Griffin ran off to chase birds and dig pits. Pernille built an elaborate sand castle, but Oscar accidentally ran it over while trying to catch the Frisbee. Farther down the beach, Thespia was teaching Miriam Hummad and Oliver Johnson how to play backgammon.

Eventually, Arthur left Donovan and Tad and swam some more. Then he went off to find Griffin further up the beach. He passed the sunbathing girls and overheard Idolette bragging, "Oh, I've snuck into the Talisman Club loads of times and convinced them I'm older than fifteen. Though I saw the steward there once, and I had to leg it quick before he saw me . . . "

When Arthur finally caught up to Griffin, he noticed a large, horse-bodied man wandering down the beach.

"Hey, Master Prometheus," Arthur called, venturing toward him.

The centaur looked out with his doleful eyes and lifted his hand in greeting. He didn't seem quite so dauntingly huge out here in the open as he did in a crowded room. "Young Arthur Grey, I am glad to see you are still surviving your lessons in spite of certain leaders' failure to acknowledge your highly probable opinion regarding bards of the tenth century."

Arthur balked. "Uh . . . thanks. You heard about that, huh?"

"Dear boy, there are few things that don't reach the ears of Prometheus the Centaur."

At that, Arthur brightened. Prometheus seemed to be aware of everything that went on at Historia. "Say, have you heard about the beast they sighted at Knossos?"

"Yes, indeed. Rumors travel much faster than wisdom."

"Some people are saying it's the Minotaur."

"And I suppose others say that creature was killed by the Athenian hero Theseus, and even if it had not been, a creature can't possibly still be alive after so many years."

Arthur cocked his head. "Can it?"

"Dear boy, have they ever found its skeleton? If they had, you would know it is long dead. But if they haven't . . . then who can say?"

Arthur took an excited breath. *Is it possible then? The Minotaur might really exist?* He cast a quick glance at Griffin, then back at Prometheus. "What do *you* think?"

Prometheus looked solemn. "Are you asking me what I suppose to be the truth?"

"Yeah."

The centaur stared off into the sea and said nothing for so long that Arthur began to think he had decided not to answer. Then, "Come with me," he said at last.

Eagerly, Arthur followed him, Griffin tagging along unnoticed, up the hill to a cave with a wide door. Arthur realized this must be where Prometheus lived. They passed a small vineyard of grapevines (the centaur said, "Not *wine* grapes, as I'm sure you know the ghastly story about centaurs and that vile drink." Arthur made a mental note to ask Esmond later).

Inside, Prometheus indicated that Arthur should look beside the door, where a glass case stood like a wardrobe. It contained a long, heavy cloak of a color so deep Arthur could hardly tell if it was red or blue or purple. It shone with bright stars that seemed to twinkle. "That once belonged to a relative of mine."

He seemed to be waiting for Arthur to act impressed, so Arthur cleared his throat and said, "Oh, it's very nice. I've never seen anything like it."

"No. Of course not." Prometheus held out a plate of green and yellow plants. "Snack? They are very nutritious, if a bit chewy."

Arthur managed to politely refuse, and Prometheus decided

to fix up some tea. While Arthur waited, he and Griffin looked around.

Along the walls were paintings of grapevines and sky-maps, posters of star charts, and odd clocks with sun, moon, stars, and planets instead of numbers. On the shelves were journals and books (*The Wandering Woods*, *Startography*, *The Mars Positions*, and *Looking for Peace from Venus* were a few). Over the fireplace mantel were photographs of several centaurs. Arthur was studying one of a fierce-looking young female when Prometheus spoke from the kitchen doorway.

"That is my daughter, Galatia. She lives in more northern places, far too cold for me."

"I didn't know you had a daughter," Arthur said, curious. He didn't know anything about centaur families, seeing as how Prometheus was the only one he'd ever met in his life. "How old is she?"

"One hundred and seven."

Arthur stared at the picture. One hundred and seven? She looked tough, like maybe she could play college men's football, but she didn't look like she could be over a century old. Arthur briefly wondered how old that made Prometheus. He cleared his throat. "Do you see her much?"

"Alas, I do not. Those of us who take to studying amongst humans are seen as outcasts, banished by our kindred, and we must bear our burdens alone. It has been that way since the days when Cheiron taught such heroes as Achilles, Heracles, Perseus, and Jason." He paused to select two books from the shelf and place them on the tray he carried, alongside a teapot and cups containing strainers filled with tea leaves. "But enough about the endearing ways of centaurs. You wanted to know about the Minotaur."

Arthur sat down in the only chair in the room, while Griffin sat on the floor. Prometheus folded his long legs beneath his horse body in his own version of a chair.

"The Palace of Knossos is a ruse," Prometheus said plainly as he poured hot water over the tea strainers. "It is a lie. It is not the Labyrinth of Minos, as some say. The real Labyrinth is a cave now unidentified, according to one translation of the word *labyrinthos*. Here, observe this symbol." He flipped open one of the books to a painting of an axe. "It is a double-headed axe. Did you notice this symbol while you were in Crete? Of course you did. After all, one interpretation of *labrys* is 'a double-headed axe,' and *labyrinth* is sometimes translated as 'the place of the double-headed axe.'

"Now I want to show you this," he continued, opening the other book and holding it out to Arthur. "This is the symbol of the Norse god Thor. You have heard of Thor in your lessons, I take it?"

Arthur looked up from the book, his brow furrowed. "He's the Norse god of lightning and weather, right? He can throw his hammer anywhere and it will come back to him."

"Correct. You might notice that his symbol is also a double-headed axe, or a hammer. Some would have you believe the similarity of these symbols is completely coincidental. However! It is not. There is a link between these two. It is my belief that the link is to be found in one particular item. The sacred *Gjallarhorn*."

"Sorry?"

Prometheus sighed with pained patience. "The Horn of Heimdall. Heimdall is the watchman god of the Norse. He has a horn that he carries as he keeps watch over the rainbow bridge Bifröst, which leads to the land of the gods. Now, do you think it is simply coincidental that the Norse have written about this horn and a double-headed hammer and that the Minoans have a double-headed axe and a man-beast with *horns*? Coincidental? Absolutely not!

"Now, the question is—is there a Minotaur? Many things are possible, but I doubt the existence of that creature. More likely, it was fabricated to divert from the true fact at hand— that the king of the Minoans kept hidden a truly sacred horn, the Horn of Heimdall, the Gjallarhorn, the Recalling Horn. For that is where it was found—in the cave."

Arthur leaned forward. "Cave? But you said the labyrinth cave was never found."

"I never said the cave hasn't been found. I said it is *unidentified*. There are many guesses, but no cave is established as the true Labyrinth. That is to say, no one living knows which cave is the real one."

Arthur's mind buzzed with ideas. "You said no one living. Does that mean it might have been found by someone not alive anymore?"

A small smile crept onto Prometheus's bearded face. "At last, you truly listen. And I see that you are longing to know who it was who actually found the real cave. Don't fear. I will tell you." He sipped his tea. "It was Alexander, King of the Mycenaeans, creator of the vast Greek Empire."

Arthur stared at him, his cup halfway to his mouth. "Alexander the Great?"

"The Great, hmph! Alexander was a king of thieves, stealing many great treasures, the Gjallarhorn being one of them." He put down his cup. "There now. I have told you the little-known truth about the Minotaur lie. Centaurs have always been gifted teachers of humans, though you are slow to learn." He paused and turned a doleful eye to Arthur. "Though, admittedly, I re-member one young human child who attended here many years ago and knew how to truly listen. She was like a silver beam of moonlight, but her eyes were full of sun. Helena Doyle was her name. You know of her, I presume."

Arthur felt a jolt shiver through his body. He cast a glance at Griffin and swallowed the sudden lump in his throat. "Um, yeah. She was . . . my mom."

"Indeed. For she later married a Mr. Grey, didn't she? She was a nice child with a desire to learn and a gift for spreading goodwill. I foresaw her premature death even then, for the stars mourned the coming of that day. We centaurs know how to read the signs." He looked troubled as he eyed Arthur. "And I must say, the signs of your fate are disturbing to me."

Arthur felt his throat go dry. He heard the voice of the Gypsy woman in his head: *Worst betrayal . . . from your fa-ther . . .* "Disturbing?" he said slowly.

"Indeed, signs have a way of presenting themselves in most

confusing ways. But I see the time is getting late, young Arthur. Perhaps you should rejoin your friends." Prometheus stood, and Arthur quickly did the same, nearly knocking over his teacup.

"Uh . . . okay."

"Until another time, then."

As he walked back along the beach, Arthur felt a rush of emotions stronger than the wind that whipped at his face. An ancient horn sounded exciting, but no one knew where it was anymore. He couldn't help remembering his dream from last winter. The green-cloaked lady's voice murmured through his thoughts, "I received word that he has news of a mighty horn in the east."

Prometheus's conclusion that there might've never been a Minotaur was kind of a bummer. What could that mean about the hoofprints Arthur had seen at Knossos? Were they really nothing more than a mess of overlapping human footprints? And what about the man injured by a supposed monster?

Then there was Prometheus's remark about Arthur's own fate. *Disturbing.* What was that supposed to mean? His skin prickled. *First a Gypsy says I'm going to be betrayed, now Prometheus says my fate is disturbing.*

"You heard what Esmond said," Griffin put in, his tail giving a hopeful wag. "Fortune-telling isn't real—even from Prometheus. He said so himself, it's confusing to him, too."

"You're right," Arthur murmured, more to calm himself than anything. He focused on the rest of the conversation. "What do you think about that horn? What did he call it? The

Gjallarhorn—the Recalling Horn. Why do suppose it's called that?"

"Maybe it makes echoes?" suggested Griffin.

"Or maybe if you throw it it'll come back to you?"

Griffin snorted a laugh. "It's a horn, not a boomerang."

Arthur laughed, too. "I guess that does sound stupid. But I can't think of why else it'd be called that. Obviously, there's something special about it, otherwise why would someone like Alexander the Great want it?"

"Maybe it helped him in taking over the world."

"But how?"

Griffin shrugged. "That's the question, huh? And there's only one way to get an answer."

Arthur raised an eyebrow. "And what's that?"

"Go ask Bookworm Esmond."

After Arthur had recounted his visit with Prometheus, Esmond was impressed, though shocked about Arthur's lack of centaur knowledge. "Tell me you've heard the wine tale," Esmond gasped. "I thought it was common knowledge that the centaurs drank wine and became very violent, killing many of their race. It's why there are so few of them left, you know. And the cloak that Prometheus has—why, it probably belonged to the great centaur teacher Cheiron—I wonder if he was a relation?"

Together, they spent their free time in the library (occasionally with Pernille, but Idolette refused to go in there more than she had to). They read up on Alexander the Great, trying to glean any information about his having found a magical horn and what he might have done with it. But their searches were fruitless.

"Here's a story about Alexander and the Gordian Knot," said Pernille, and she read:

> *Alexander of Mycenae came to Gordium in the land of Phrygia, which at that time belonged to the Persian Empire. There the priests told him of a knot dedicated to Zeus. The oldest priest told him that many had tried over the centuries, but were unable to untie it. For whoever could untie the knot would become ruler of all Asia, but at a great price. Alexander resolved to undo this knot, so they showed him to its place. However, try as he might, he could not find an end of the knot by which to untie it. He then took out his sword and sliced the knot so that it came undone. After that, there was a terrible storm of lightning and wind, and all the people were afraid.*

"That's pretty gas," Pernille bubbled. "What sort of knot could it be that it'd be so difficult to untie? I suppose it'd have to be tightly coiled—"

"But there's still no horn in that story," Arthur said wearily.

On Friday evening, Arthur and Esmond were playing a game of darts while Griffin chewed on a dragon bone. Pernille was gone, working for the upcoming Pyramid Build competitions, and Idolette was off with Tad.

Esmond was winning easily because Arthur wasn't

paying much attention to the game. He was thinking about the Gjallarhorn and its link to the king of the Minoans.

Arthur tossed a dart. It landed in a planter. He didn't notice. "That text they found earlier," he said thoughtfully, "the Minos Supplement Text—didn't it have unknown symbols? Wasn't it the tale of the Minotaur?"

"Yes. But remember, they took it off display and no one can view it anymore."

Arthur narrowed his eyes. "I want to see it."

Esmond stopped aiming his dart. "What part of 'they took it off display and no one can view it anymore' didn't you get?"

"Come on."

"Apparently, I need to explain the word *view* to you."

"I'm going to find Mistress Featherweit. Maybe she'll be able to let us see it."

"Wait a minute," Esmond sputtered. "Us? Who said I was going with you?"

"Griffin, stay here—I'll be back."

But Griffin jumped up. "No way. I'm coming."

With Esmond huffing and complaining behind and Griffin trotting next to him, Arthur ran to Main Hall, wondering if Mistress Featherweit would be there. It was nearly dark out, but sometimes Members worked late. After questioning several passing Members, they found her just leaving the Archives. Arthur wasted no time asking permission to view the text, while Esmond clutched a stitch in his side and gasped for breath. Griffin hid behind a large suit of troll armor.

Mistress Featherweit blinked her large eyes apologetically. "I'm sorry, boys, but it's been returned."

"Returned? What do you mean?"

"Well, it was only on loan from the museum, you see. It wasn't ours to keep. Unless we find an artifact or text on our own, we have to give it back to the original finder or holder— in this case, the museum in Romania."

Arthur couldn't believe it. There went his last chance of ever seeing the symbols on the text.

"No, indeed. All we have now is the Scanograph of the document."

With a gasp, Arthur demanded, "What? Isn't that an exact replica of it?"

"Down to the fingerprints, yes. But it's not up for viewing, I'm afraid."

"Thanks, Mistress Featherweit."

As they headed back, Arthur decided, "I'm going to see that text."

Esmond frowned. "Good luck. It's probably locked in a high-security vault a hundred feet below ground, surrounded by curses and troll guards."

Arthur stopped so fast both Esmond and Griffin knocked into him. Arthur slapped his forehead. "Or a plant guard." Why hadn't he thought of it before? He glanced back to make sure Mistress Featherweit was not in sight, then turned back around.

Esmond groaned. "What are you doing now?"

"We passed it on our first day. And I got stuck in it myself. A door with a plant that catches anyone who gets too close to it.

The snapper plant that caught that investor guy nosing around."
Now he hurried. "What do you suppose is behind that door?"

"I suppose you're thinking of the text. But, even if you're right, there's no way to get past the plant."

Arthur didn't say anything, but he remembered the first word Jolly accidentally tried when getting him out of the plant. He bet it might be useful for a different purpose. He kept running.

When they reached the door guarded by the snapper plant, Arthur stopped.

"The coast is clear," Griffin sniffed.

Arthur took a deep breath, firmly said, "Branstock," and reached out to scratch a stiff tentacle of the plant. Immediately, the plant slithered to one side of the wall and hung there like a giant purple octopus. The space that it cleared was a plain wooden door, and on it was a bold sign.

RESTRICTED

(SPECIFIED PERSONNEL ONLY)

Esmond looked about, fidgeting with his fingers. "Are you sure about this?"

Cautiously, Arthur touched the door handle. He looked at the plant to his left, but it didn't move. He shoved the door open and stepped into a dimly lit room with a carpeted floor. All around him were cases of jewels glowing eerily, tablets with inscriptions and even colored decorations, sinister statues and evil masks, rolled scrolls, stretched scrolls.

"Wow, is all this just to hide from Berne?" Arthur whispered.

Esmond shrugged, casting nervous glances at the door. "Let's hurry," he muttered uncomfortably.

They walked slowly through the sporadically placed shelves and stands. At last Esmond pointed at an encased shelf. Inside, placed side-by-side, were several papyrus sheets. The Minos Supplement Text.

"What are we going to do?" Esmond whispered. "We can't inspect it in here—it's too dark, not to mention that every second we're in here, we're at a higher risk of getting caught and hung for crows to eat our eyeballs out."

"You can always take a picture of the text," Griffin put in. He lifted his head to reveal his collar.

"Brilliant, Griffin," Arthur breathed excitedly. He pulled the remote control from his belt pouch. Esmond took Griffin's collar off and held it over the text so Arthur could click several pictures of it. They were nearly done when Griffin suddenly stiffened, his ears tilted.

"Someone else is in here," he whispered.

With a jolt, Arthur realized he'd left the door open when they came in. He tried to wave for Esmond to stop, but it was a *clink* of metal bumping glass that got Esmond's attention. He stumbled to Arthur, his eyes wide. Arthur nodded, sweating.

Without a word, they crept toward the door, Griffin slightly ahead, his sensitive ears twitching. They were hidden behind a shelf of golden masks when Griffin stopped. A tall, shadowed figure slunk past on the other side. It was so close they could hear the swishing of clothes. Griffin turned to Arthur, eyes wide. He didn't speak, but Arthur knew. It was Rheneas Berne.

Griffin and Esmond made for the door, but Arthur hesitated, watching Berne between the gaps in the shelf. The man stayed along the wall, stepping slowly and carefully, looking at the items around him. He stopped when he came to the Minos text. Quickly, Arthur turned and darted out the door.

Esmond was just clasping Griffin's collar back on. Together, they tiptoed down the hall.

"He's seen the text—we have to tell someone," Arthur whispered hoarsely.

"Who?" gasped Esmond.

Not Gamble, Arthur thought desperately, *he'd rip my head off*. He didn't know where Madam's office was or the steward's. "What about Minister Jung?"

They ran down the hall. When they reached the Minister's room, Arthur pounded on the door. Minister Jung opened it; he was still dressed, though he wore silky night slippers. "Yes?" he asked in surprise.

"Minister," Arthur gasped, "the Restricted room—Rheneas Berne is in it—you've got to stop him!"

The Minister stared silently from Arthur to Esmond and lingered on Griffin for a few seconds. Then he stepped back into his room and pushed a large blue button on the wall. It began blinking. "Come into my office," he said calmly. "Please wait here. I will return." He closed the door behind them.

The trio didn't say a word as they waited, each buried beneath worry about what kind of trouble they were in and how much Berne had seen that would make things bad for the

Society. Arthur stared at the blinking blue button, dreading the return of Minister Jung.

It was half an hour before the Minister returned, and he had Steward Cartwright, Master Zane, and Madam Siegfried with him, all looking extremely grim.

"Sit," Madam said bluntly. Her nostrils flared, and her eyes were narrowed to slits.

Arthur and Esmond backed onto a bamboo couch, and Griffin gingerly sat on the rug.

"Explain."

The boys exchanged glances that silently argued over who was going to have to do the talking. To Arthur's relief, Esmond gave up first. "This evening we spoke to Mistress Featherweit," he began in a surprisingly calm voice, "about the Minos Supplement Text, and it made us wonder where it might've been taken. We thought of the plant-guarded door and decided to take a look since we were nearby." He fidgeted. "I don't know if Berne overheard us, but he got to the door, too. We thought he probably shouldn't be in there and ran to tell Minister Jung."

There was a heavy silence.

Arthur could tell by the look on Madam's face that she could see every hole in Esmond's story. To his utter dismay, she now turned her eyes on him.

"So," she breathed through her nose, "you just happened to find the door open with Mr. Berne strolling in?"

Arthur gulped. "No, ma'am." The steward and Zane exchanged glances.

Madam watched him appraisingly. "How did the door come to be open then?"

Arthur stared at his hands. "I opened it."

"How did you do that?" Zane asked sharply.

"I . . . I scratched a tentacle and said the password." He felt rather than saw the swift looks that darted between the four adults.

"How," Madam Siegfried hissed, "did you come to know the password to the snapper plant door?"

Arthur had known this was coming. He thought about saying that he made a lucky guess or that he heard Berne use the password or that Gamble had told him. But none of those things came out of his mouth. "I heard . . . someone . . . use it accidentally when he was helping me get unstuck from the plant one day. He used the wrong password at first."

"And later you guessed it was the password for unlocking the plant?"

"Yes, ma'am."

She eyed him for another moment, then asked the dreaded question. "Who did you hear say the password?"

Arthur hung his head. "Master Jolly."

Zane sucked in his breath. He opened his mouth, ready to roar his disapproval, but received a look from Madam Siegfried and swallowed it, instead settling for looking mutinous.

There was another silence, during which Arthur could hear his own heart beating in his ears.

"Very well. You realize you have caused a great deal of trouble for the Society," Madam said severely. "Your mischief cannot be undone. I am disappointed." She let the word hang in the air for a few seconds, pounding Arthur with even more guilt. "Both of you are hereby banned from being within Main Hall unescorted for the remainder of the year. If you are found here without a supervising Member, you will be removed and you *will . . . not . . . return.*"

They both nodded, their heads down.

"Steward Cartwright will escort you to your apartments."

Silently, they followed the steward out of the office, out of Main Hall, and down the path to the apartments. There, the steward left them and turned back down the path, the will-o'-the-wisps flickering along ahead of him.

Esmond started toward his room.

"I'm sorry," Arthur blurted. "I didn't mean for—"

"See you tomorrow," Esmond interrupted glumly without stopping.

Arthur listened as number three's door opened and shut with an echoing click. He stood still for some time, the water gurgling along behind him, the bushes rustling with the breeze, the occasional fairy's wings glinting in the lamplight. Then he and Griffin trudged to their own room.

By morning, the terrible news of Berne getting into the Restricted room was being whispered by nearly every Member and Initiate in Main Hall. No one seemed to know, however, that Arthur was the one responsible. No one else except Jolly, that is. Arthur noticed the cold way that the Master looked at him during Preservations lessons. Arthur couldn't blame him, and it made him feel even more embarrassed and ashamed.

He and Esmond kept their heads low and didn't draw attention to themselves, staying out of everything that wasn't their business. They agreed not to tell Idolette or Pernille, though this forced Arthur to tell Esmond of his disability.

"I'll have to tell them if they ask me a direct question," Arthur groaned, "because I can't lie."

"How honorable of you," Esmond snipped. He was still upset with Arthur.

"No." Arthur clenched his fists. "I physically can't do it—I can't make untrue words come out of my mouth. In case you haven't noticed all year . . . I can't lie."

Esmond eyed him, distrusting, but slowly the truth seemed to dawn on him. At last, he nodded. "I believe you."

"Don't tell anyone?"

Esmond shook his head. "I won't."

For the rest of June, Arthur stayed out of trouble. The month ended with the Pyramid Build competition, which was the first one to include Members and Initiates in the same contest. The winning Member had made an elaborate six-foot-tall rendition of the Great Pyramid. But Pernille got an honorable mention for her exquisite mechanically opening sarcophagus.

As they headed into July, Idolette busied herself with archery training for the next tournament. The few times Arthur watched her practice, she hit every target bullseye, and Arthur told himself never to make Idolette mad.

One thick-aired day, Arthur, Esmond, and Pernille were

working on an attempt to date several translations of a tale called "Baba Yaga." They lounged around Arthur and Griffin's room, the curtains barely swaying in the nonexistent breeze. Griffin napped on the porch.

Arthur had scribbled out so many decidedly incorrect dates that his paper was more scribbles than legible writing, so he crumpled the paper and tossed it at the garbage can beside the small couch.

"You missed," Esmond said without looking up.

Arthur sighed and peeled his sticky back from the plastic chair to stand up. "Can you imagine," he growled as he bent over to snatch up the crumpled paper and drop it into the trash, "how really exciting things would be here if there was no eightieth-anniversary celebration this year? Then I'm sure the Members would have plenty more time to find really interesting things we could help with—like making a list of every crack on the floor in the Museo Gallery."

Pernille hid her smile. "Oh, it's not all that bad, Arthur. You said so once yourself."

"That's when it was just memorizing. Now there's all this dating stuff that nobody—even Prometheus—cares about. I just can't believe how much paper is around this place."

"Speaking of paper," Esmond spoke up, pointing his pen toward Arthur, "weren't you going to pick up the one you threw?"

Arthur frowned. "I already did."

Esmond narrowed his eyes for a moment, then seemed to remember that Arthur couldn't be lying. "Then what's that?"

Arthur looked at the floor and noticed another piece of paper wedged beneath a corner of the couch. He pulled it out and unwrinkled it. "Oh," he grinned, "it's yours." He slapped it on the table in front of Esmond.

"What is it?" Pernille asked interestedly.

"It's an old paper of his that Nada doodled on, and he was mad about it and threw it at the trash—and missed."

"Poor Nada," Pernille said lightly. "She doesn't mean any harm. She's a really good artist, though. I've seen some of her . . . Esmond, what's wrong?"

Esmond had turned white as he stared at the wrinkled paper before him. "Arthur." He swallowed. "Where are those text pictures—Griffin's pictures?"

Arthur blinked at him for a moment, not understanding. Then, with a start, he remembered. The pictures they had taken with Griffin's camera collar. In the chaos that had followed their exploit in the Restricted room, he had forgotten all about the camera. He wrenched open one of his belt pouches and found the remote for the collar. It had a display screen for viewing pictures.

"What's goin' on?" Pernille asked curiously.

No one answered her until Arthur found one of the pictures and set the remote down next Esmond's paper. They all stared.

"Well, isn't that a gas," Pernille exclaimed. "Some of the symbols in that picture are the same as on your paper. What's this a picture of?"

Arthur looked at Esmond, who nodded. "It's the Minos text."

"How'd you get a picture of it?" Pernille wondered.

"We snuck into the Restricted room."

Pernille's eyes widened and her mouth fell open.

"And probably," Esmond sighed, "there's a *yes* answer to the question you're thinking now, but we'd rather not talk about it, so please don't ask."

Pernille covered her mouth to keep herself from asking.

"So now the question is," Arthur began grimly, "how did Nada know these symbols?"

Esmond frowned thoughtfully. "This text was found in Romania, according to Mistress Featherweit, and it was in cleaning and repair until we got to see it in February. So there was no time for Nada to observe it *before* we all saw it. And after that, it was taken down that very same day to keep Berne from seeing it."

"So the only time she could've seen it was during that one lesson," Arthur said. He paused. "But, hang on, she couldn't have seen it then. I just remembered—she was right next to me in the back of the room, and we couldn't see it from there. So when else would she have seen it?"

"When else indeed?" Esmond wondered darkly.

"And why," Arthur muttered, "does *Romania* sound familiar?"

Esmond studied the paper. "Romania is the country where the first Old Mermish document was discovered by Rhubarb Winston. You probably recall hearing about it during a Translationary lesson with Madam Siegfried."

Arthur vaguely remembered this. "Is that when you had to share answering a question with Nada?"

"Yes," Esmond sniffed.

Arthur snickered. "Madam seemed to think that was a good joke. I remember now—she said 'how fitting' about you guys fighting over who got to answer."

Pernille's fingers parted from over her mouth. "Can I say something now?"

They looked at her in surprise, having forgotten she was there. "What?" said Arthur.

She put her hands down. "Madam wasn't talking about Esmond and Nada. She said that because Nada's family is *from* Romania." Pernille beamed at them.

Arthur suddenly felt his head spinning with a tornado of thoughts. He sat down hard in the chair next to him.

"What?" the other two asked.

But he didn't hear them. He was being bombarded with a rush of images. Madam Siegfried smiling, "The Translationary . . . is not up-to-date—old Rhubarb hasn't given us his English translations from Old Mermish yet, for one thing . . . Rhubarb is one of the few on this planet who knows Old Mermish. . . ." Nada's serene face as she said, "An old text hidden in the home of a Romanian lord. . . ." Mistress Featherweit blinking excitedly: "This lovely piece came to us from a man in Romania. . . . it's a series of symbols we haven't identified yet. . . ." Then Pernille bubbling, "This is Nada Bhaksiana—she can speak eight languages, can you believe it?"

"Pernille," Arthur breathed, rubbing his temples, "what eight languages does Nada speak?"

Pernille blinked and began ticking off on her fingers, "English, of course, and Romanian, German, French, Polish, Spanish, Italian, and . . . and . . . er . . . " She looked up. "I don't know the last one."

Arthur was not surprised. He opened his eyes and took a deep breath. "I bet the eighth language she knows," he said tensely, "is Old Mermish."

12

KNOSSOS PALACE

Esmond's mouth dropped open and Pernille stared.

"What if Nada's family gave that Mermish document to Rhubarb whatever-his-name-is? What if they know Old Mermish?" Arthur nodded to himself. "And what if that excerpt on the Minos text is Old Mermish?"

Esmond narrowed his eyes, quickly working out Arthur's suggestion. "Mistress Featherweit said no one had yet identified the language," he said, "though I doubt they had to time to find someone with a background in Mermish to look at it before they had to hide it away."

Pernille clapped her hands together. "That would explain how Nada knew the symbols without having seen the actual text!"

Arthur jumped up. "We need to find Nada and ask her if she can interpret this picture."

"She stays in Apartment Athena," Pernille offered, grabbing her bag.

Arthur turned to Esmond. "Just a hunch, but it might be better if you wait here with Griffin, so there're no distracting arguments." He raised an eyebrow.

Esmond's lips tightened into a thin line. But he nodded.

Arthur and Pernille found Nada lying in the grass outside Apartment Athena with a large art pad, drawing detailed pictures of insects and fairies.

"Hallo," she greeted them quietly when they stopped next to her.

"Howya, Nada," beamed Pernille.

"Hey," Arthur added. He watched the other girl glide her pencil in light strokes over the paper. "Nada, do you know the Old Mermish language?" he blurted.

Nada didn't look up from her drawing. "Yes."

Arthur's heart sped up, pumping excitement through his entire body.

"I was thinking this morning," Nada said to her paper, "that your dog is so interesting, Artur. His eyes are different from each other, like he must have two personalities inside. I was thinking I would like to draw him one day. It would be a great drawing."

"Sure, Nada," Arthur consented at once, sure this would help him get information. "He wouldn't mind. When do you want to do it?"

She finally looked up, and her pale eyes brightened.

"Tomorrow, if it is sunny. In the lawn. The green of grass would contrast his coloring very exotically, I think."

"Okay, sure. That'll work." Arthur paused as she went back to her artwork with a little more flourish. "Actually," he added slowly, "I have a favor to ask, too, Nada. Since you know Mermish and all that. I . . . uh . . . have a picture that might have Mermish on it, but I don't know what it says. Could you look at it?"

Abruptly, Nada sat up, her long brown waves of hair swinging around her face. "Yes."

Arthur fumbled for the remote and showed Nada the picture of the text.

She looked at it in silence for a moment. "This is the text they put away," she said slowly.

Arthur didn't say anything.

Nada smiled up at him and handed back the remote. "It says, 'The palace of Minos receives the great octopus. Alexander knew the double-axe cornerstone.'"

Pernille giggled, perhaps because of the look on Arthur's face. Whatever he'd been expecting Nada to say, it certainly wasn't that.

"The palace of Minos receives the great octopus. Alexander knew the double-axe cornerstone," Nada repeated, perhaps thinking they hadn't heard.

Arthur cleared his throat and took back the remote. "Uh . . . thanks . . . for that . . . ."

Nada nodded, still smiling. "So tomorrow you will bring your dog?"

"Yes. Tomorrow. See you." Arthur and Pernille turned away and headed back to Apartment Odin. Pernille skipped beside him, not saying anything, but occasionally doing her best to stifle a fit of giggles.

When they got back to Esmond and Griffin, Arthur told the others what Nada had said.

Esmond didn't seem surprised. "It's possible," he sighed, "that she doesn't really know Old Mermish, or that the writing on the text isn't even Mermish at all and she just made that up." He shook his head. "It's also possible that what she said is correct, but that whoever wrote it was completely delusional. And, of course, there's the small possibility that it all makes sense . . . to somebody."

Griffin looked at Arthur. "Prometheus said the Palace of Knossos—Minos's palace—wasn't the real Labyrinth. But what if someone left a clue there about the actual location of the Labyrinth?"

Arthur nodded. As goofy as Nada's interpretation sounded, the link between Alexander the Great and Knossos was too close to what Prometheus had said for him to completely ignore it.

"I've gotta see that palace," Arthur murmured.

Pernille's smile faltered. "At Knossos?"

"But," Esmond protested, "you said Prometheus told you—"

"Whether it's the real Labyrinth or not, it's significant and will have information," Arthur argued. "I've got to see that palace."

Griffin cocked his head. "You remember when we were there last. There were police guards. No one is allowed in there."

"There's no way, Arthur," sighed Esmond. "It would be suicide. You'd better just forget it."

But, as usual, Arthur couldn't. And he knew someone who could help him—someone who had slithered out of many punishments and was good at finding a way into trouble without getting caught. He would see Idolette.

Conveniently, she stayed at Apartment Athena, so when Arthur took Griffin to Nada the next morning, he went to the lounge to see if Idolette was around. He found her sprawled on an overstuffed chair, her eyes closed, listening to the music playing from the speakers in the room. He could tell from the shredded jeans, dark makeup, and array of earrings she wore that her dad must be on the island again. Arthur plopped into the chair nearest to her.

"Just out of curiosity," he began, "what advice would you have about getting some authority to let me in somewhere I'm not supposed to be?"

Idolette raised her fine eyebrows and opened one eye slightly. "That would depend on the authority type and on the place you need to get into. Why?"

Arthur pretended to think about it. "Oh, let's see. Maybe the authority is some police guards and the place might be . . . let's say, the Knossos palace."

Idolette sat up. "Are you thick?" she cried. She glanced around and lowered her voice. "You're not serious." She stared at Arthur's determined face. "You *are* serious." She blew out a breath and shook her head. "What is this, a dare?"

He lowered his voice, too. "No. I need to look around. I'm sure there's a clue about the Horn of Heimdall there, and I need to find it."

"I dunno," she said slowly. "There were a lot of guards around before. It would be hard. And they say that place is a maze inside—you'd get lost."

"You saw the place—it's a ruin. There's hardly any 'inside' to go in."

Idolette tapped her black-painted fingernails on the arm of her chair. "It would be risky. You'd need a convincing excuse and probably a disguise. A distraction wouldn't hurt, either. And a lookout . . . " She looked at him. "No, offense, but you're no good at any of that."

Arthur felt a smile pulling at his mouth. "If we can get to Crete after your archery competition is over with, do you think you could help me?"

"Are you completely off your trolley?" Her eyes twinkled. "Just leave it to me."

The perfect opportunity came the very next week, at the end of a Famous Tales About Dimwitted People lesson.

"Listen up," Gamble crowed, causing Tad's chin to slip out of his hand and hit his desk, and Bridgette to actually tumble out of her chair. "The Minister informed me," Gamble continued, pretending not to notice that he had awoken half the Initiates in the room, "that an artifacts transfer is taking place next Tuesday morning in Crete. I've arranged for you to come along and observe how these dealings work. So be prepared."

Arthur shot a glance at Idolette, who nodded eagerly. The plan was now in motion.

First came the weekend of the archery competition. Idolette easily won the golden arrow award for the Initiate level and was in high spirits, even when her dad came up afterward with a list of things she could have done better.

Three days later, after a disapproving "Don't get caught" from Griffin, Arthur left his room early, his adventure belt pouches filled with his navigational pocketknife, pencils, a notepad, and his usual handy tools. He was so early, however, that only Charda and Miriam were in the entrance hall when Arthur arrived. There was no sign of Idolette. His stomach felt squirmy, like there were a hundred fire sprites bouncing in it. He had no idea if they could pull this off.

Pernille and Esmond arrived shortly after. Pernille beamed as she came up to him. "What's up?"

"What?" Arthur said quickly. "Uh . . . " He closed his mouth.

Esmond immediately frowned. "What are you plotting?"

"Plotting?"

"Yes. If you're not plotting something, then I'm a garden gnome. What are you plotting?"

"What do I have to plot about?" Arthur asked innocently.

"Hm, let's see. I'm recalling a certain conversation about a certain boy named Arthur needing to forget a certain palace on a certain island." Esmond crossed his arms. "And something tells me you haven't forgotten it."

Pernille looked back and forth between them, a look of mixed amusement and concern on her face.

"Okay, you're right," Arthur admitted. He grinned when he saw Idolette coming. "Just do me one favor, okay, Esmond? Pernille?"

"Sure," Pernille agreed. But Esmond eyed Arthur warily. "What's that?"

"If you notice that Idolette and I are gone . . . pretend not to notice."

Pernille's eyes widened. "Oh, Arthur," she whispered. "You're not . . . "

He shrugged off the extra helping of nervousness that crept over him at the tone of Pernille's voice. "It'll be fine. It's nothing dangerous. Just an inspection."

Idolette was dressed rather dully for a change, her hair straight and brown, no makeup, wearing the normal uniform of the Initiates of Elysium Island, and she carried a bulging black purse. For once, she melted into the group.

"Ready," she whispered to Arthur, pulling an empty soft-sided backpack out of her bag for him to take. "You'll need this."

He slung it over his shoulder and shrugged innocently at Pernille and Esmond.

At that moment, Gamble arrived. "Well, what are you lumbering trolls waiting for?" he crowed at them. "I hope you know where the Transfer Depot is after all this time?" He marched them off the short distance to the door and opened it. "In you get."

"What's Master Jolly doin' here?" Pernille asked brightly.

To Arthur's surprise, Jolly had also just reached the doorway and stood uncertainly watching them. He looked terrible—his face unshaven, his shirt wrinkly and untucked, and his features with the pale, soggy look of someone getting sick but trying to ignore it. Arthur quickly ducked behind the others so Jolly wouldn't see him. The Master was probably still upset about the password ordeal.

Gamble gave the younger man a slow, piercing look. "You need the Transportal platform?" he asked.

Jolly shook his head. "No. Well, yes. I just mean . . . I'll tag along with your team if that's all right. I need to check on another transfer nearby. Make sure everything's clear."

Gamble raised a bristly eyebrow. "You don't look well, August," he said bluntly. "Shouldn't Zane go instead?"

"No, no. Zane is busy with another project. I'm fine. It's all fine," he chomped extra hard on his strawberry bubblegum with a sort of finality.

Gamble didn't argue the matter. He shooed the team through a Transportal to Crete, and they landed in the same spot as before. Arthur recognized the ring of trees and the view of the mountains, though everything was browner and drier now. But this time, instead of heading toward the palace, the team filed after Gamble and Jolly in the opposite direction.

Idolette gave Arthur a meaningful look and edged her way to the back of the group. He did the same. Then they crept toward a clump of olive trees and ducked behind it. Arthur saw Pernille glance beside her, where he had been a few moments ago. Her mouth dropped open but quickly snapped shut again, and she faced forward, pretending not to have noticed anything.

Holding his breath, Arthur waited until the group had rounded the other side of the hill. Then, thinking they were already doing better than he'd expected, he and Idolette followed the path toward the ruin of Knossos.

Idolette rummaged through her bag as she walked. "Stop here," she directed. "Let's change before anyone comes." She thrust some clothes and a hat at Arthur.

"Change?" he said, staring stupidly at the bundle in his arms.

"Yes, quick." Idolette was already shimming a skirt over her pants. "And make sure you put the hat on—your face is too young. No one would ever think you're older than ten."

"I'm twelve," Arthur growled. But he found a bush that mostly concealed him so he could change.

When they headed back down the path again, Arthur wore a stiff vest, a clip-on tie, and thick plastic glasses that actually hindered his sight a bit. Idolette had changed into a long black skirt, a matching jacket with brass buttons, and uncomfortable-looking heeled shoes, and was swiftly pinning her hair into a tight bun at the back of her head. Arthur watched in amazement as she then brushed on makeup while they walked and completed her transformation by clutching a threatening-looking black notebook.

"Where did you get all this?" Arthur couldn't help asking.

"I've had these for ages. I mean, you never know when you

might need to pose as an authority figure, right? Now, put that bowler hat on."

Arthur crammed the hat onto his head, jostling the glasses.

Idolette began stuffing their original clothes into the empty backpack. "Right," she said briskly. "So, here's our plan. We're from the British consulate, here to investigate a rumor. Just let me do the talking. No offense, but you're no good at lying."

"Right," Arthur said quickly.

"I'll keep them busy and distracted. You wait for my signal—I'll change my handbag from my left to my right shoulder—and then you go off wherever you need to. I'll try to get rid of the guards and then join you. But I'm guessing we won't have long. Just make sure you walk determinedly—don't prance."

"Prance—I don't prance!" Arthur sputtered. But Idolette only rolled her eyes.

The moment they were in view of the guards, Idolette's back snapped straighter, her walk became swaying but brisk, and her expression turned businesslike.

At the last minute, Arthur remembered that he probably shouldn't be gawking at Idolette like he'd never met her before, so he closed his mouth, tipped his hat down, and tried not to prance.

"Stop right there," demanded a voice, which then repeated the command in several languages.

Idolette slowed and looked the security guard over with a mildly offended expression. "I beg your pardon?" she snapped, and her voice came out slightly deeper than normal, her British accent more pronounced. "I was told you were aware of the investigation and would allow us immediate access."

"Investigation—access?" the man exclaimed.

Idolette leaned back impatiently and pulled an official-looking badge from her jacket pocket. "Amelia Swann, from the British Investigative Bureau of Conspiracy Against the United Kingdom." She waved the badge under the sentry's nose and snapped it back into her pocket. "This is my associate, Benjamin Howl."

The guard balked. "British . . . Conspiracy . . . ?" He glanced at Arthur, who tried to look stern, but only managed to wince.

"Where is your superior?" the fake Amelia Swann demanded.

"Eh . . . I am the authority on duty, Miss Swann, but—"

"I find that difficult to believe, seeing as how no one thought it necessary to inform you of the investigation. Is there someone else in charge here? Where is the general?"

The man's cheeks flushed. "There is no general on duty here. This is a matter of—"

"This," Amelia Swann interrupted venomously, "is a matter of international conspiracy, and your entire country is about to be accused of plotting against the British monarchy, which, I hardly need to tell you is a threat . . . of . . . war." These last words she uttered with all the force of a swinging sword blade.

"You are frighteningly good at this," Arthur muttered so only Idolette could hear. The smallest flicker of a smile crossed her face, but she otherwise didn't break character. Arthur made a mental note to never trust a word Idolette said again, no matter how convincing she was.

"I . . . this . . . " The confused sentry glanced over his shoulder at two of his fellows, who were now looking curiously at him from their station by a half-crumbled staircase.

"So, for the last time, will you kindly direct me to someone who understands matters of international importance?"

The guard tried to regain some of his dignity. "I'm afraid I will have to . . . check the communications," he sniffed. "Perhaps I missed the notice of your arrival . . . ."

"Unbelievable," huffed Amelia Swann.

"This way, Miss."

"Mr. Howl," snapped Amelia Swann—and Arthur remembered just in time that that was him—"wait here until I settle this affair. Unless . . . well, we're going to need the fingerprint-analysis materials, if you care to retrieve them whilst you wait." And she looked pointedly at him.

"Uh, right," Arthur grunted nervously, not sure what he was supposed to do now. Then Miss Swann shifted her purse to her right shoulder. That was the signal. Heart racing, Arthur took a swift look around—which he'd forgotten to do earlier, distracted by Idolette's act. To his right was a low wall he could hide behind. He nodded once to Idolette.

"What is that over there?" Amelia Swann immediately gasped, pointing to the left. The guard spun around to look, so Arthur turned and walked quickly toward the low wall. The other guards were also looking at Idolette and did not notice him, or else they thought the first sentry had given him permission.

Arthur reached the wall, sweating in the hot vest and hat,

dizzy from the thick glasses. He ducked into the shade behind the wall, yanked off the glasses, and peeked around. Idolette was laughing in an embarrassed way, as if she had made a mistake, and the sentry looked slightly flattered.

Arthur let out a low, shaky breath, jerked the bowler hat off to wipe the sweat from his forehead, and jammed it back on before checking his surroundings again and replacing his glasses. How he wished Griffin were here.

He slipped under the railing, off the path, and made his way past partial walls and rubble and steps that went nowhere, heading to the back of the complex. If there were clues anywhere, that's where they'd be. He followed the wall until it ended in a pile of blocks, then dashed to the next wall and hurried along that. Several times he glanced behind, feeling that someone was watching him. But he didn't see anyone. He couldn't help thinking about monsters, especially when he passed low, doorless openings through which he could see nothing but darkness. At last, he reached a squat, partially intact building of smooth rectangular blocks, and he stopped. A shiver shook his whole body, and he knew. This was it.

It took several minutes of searching along the hot bricks, but at last he felt his neck tingle at the sight of an off-colored block at the corner of the partially crumbled building. The sides of it were rounded and concave, like the shape of a double-headed axe. Nada's voice echoed in his head: "Alexander knew the double-axe cornerstone."

He bent over it, yanking off the plastic glasses so he could actually see and setting them down on the dusty ground. He pulled his vest up slightly and felt for the pocketknife on his belt. Finding it, he flipped open the magnifying glass tool and guided it along the right block. There was nothing on it.

This is it, something's gotta be here, he thought desperately. He reached out and felt the smooth stone.

Instantly, something sapped all the energy from his body. He gasped, feeling like an invisible fist had slammed into his stomach and knocked the air out of him. Then his left eye burned so badly that he couldn't see—it pierced his brain. He wanted to shout, to cry out in pain, but he had no breath and all that came from his throat as he collapsed against the wall was a dry croak. Then, suddenly, it all ended.

Arthur sat up, clutching his chest and wheezing, his eye throbbing lightly. He felt weak, but that was all now. And he instantly forgot about it, because he could see that the smooth, blank rectangle was no longer blank. Symbols were engraved on it. He exhaled and quickly yanked a pencil and notebook from his belt pouches.

These symbols were different from the document, he realized that as he copied them. But he would double-check when they got back. All at once, his pencil stopped writing and he sucked in his breath.

Slowly, as if in a dream, Arthur reached into his shirt collar and pulled out the silver locket. "No way," he breathed. The last symbol on the wall was one of the symbols on his locket—the one at the very center. His head spun. How was this possible?

He heard a noise behind him and instinctively shoved the

locket back out of sight as he stood to look around. He wiped away the sweat trickling down the sides of his face.

No one was there. But he'd probably been long enough. He should get back to Idolette. He tried unsuccessfully to slap the dust from his clothes as he headed back.

What did this mean? Last year, in Peru, he'd found out that his locket had the symbol of the magical Aurora Cauldron on it. Now here was this other symbol from the Palace of Minos in Crete. Was this some kind of code? What was the relation between the symbols, and how did the locket connect them?

"Where did you come from?" exclaimed a voice.

Arthur stopped dead. He had almost reached the low wall he'd first hidden behind. Now a guard stood between him and the exit. His stomach plummeted again as Arthur realized he could see the man clearly—which meant he'd forgotten the glasses by the wall. "Uh . . . " he began, wondering if the man noticed the missing glasses. He shoved the notepad into his belt pouch as the guard eyed him distrustingly.

"Step out in the open. Slowly."

Arthur tried to think of a way to get out of this. But he knew that as soon as he opened his mouth, all would be lost.

"Ah, Mr. Howl, I'd wondered what was taking you," came the disapproving voice of Amelia Swann. "Did you get the necessary materials?"

Arthur took in the scene. Idolette approached him, winking at the guard who had stopped him (who immediately thrust out his chest and tried to look taller), while the sentry in charge followed her slowly, his head turning from the entry gate to Arthur, as if trying to understand how Arthur came to be all the way past the steps of the palace. Arthur realized they had only a few seconds before their cover was blown and the guards realized "Mr. Howl" had snuck past them.

"Yes," Arthur said gruffly, hurrying to steer Amelia Swann back toward the guard post and the exit. "From kneeling," he explained at her inquiring look at his dusty clothes.

"How worthless," Miss Swann exclaimed loudly. "Must I do everything myself? I will show you where the materials are so we can be done with this investigation." She paused in front of the head guard and pursed a smile. "I'll be back in a moment."

Arthur passed the opening in the security tape and muttered, "I found what I needed." He glanced back over his shoulder, and his muscles stiffened. The second guard was talking rapidly to his superior, gesturing to imaginary glasses on his face, to an imaginary belt at his waist, and holding an imaginary notebook, then pointing straight at Arthur.

"You, stop!" the sentry shouted.

"Time to duck and dive," Idolette blurted. She kicked off her impractical shoes and tore off down the path in her bare feet. Arthur stumbled, caught himself, and ran after her.

Tourists moved out of the way, hearing the police guards' shrill whistle-blowing. On the plus side, this made the way clear for escape; on the minus side, there would be no taking cover in the crowd. Arthur caught Idolette's arm and jerked her behind a food stand just before they could zip past it. "Let's change," he gasped, his fingers fumbling to open the backpack. He felt sick and weak. "Maybe they won't recognize us."

She nodded.

They raced into a change of clothes, but then Arthur realized a problem. "Your makeup," he groaned. "They'll know you."

"I can't take it off," Idolette wailed. "I don't have anything to wipe it with!"

"At least take your hair down."

She began pulling her hair out of its bun.

Arthur peeked around the food stall and felt his heart stop. One of the guards was right on the other side, talking to a tourist. Idolette peeked out next to him.

"Yes," the woman said loudly. "I saw them go that way."

The guard followed the woman's pointing finger and saw Idolette's head. "There!" he shouted.

"Uh-oh," Arthur gasped. "Run!"

They darted out into the road. Behind them, the guard tripped on a basket of stuffed Minotaur toys and fell, cursing. Arthur and Idolette wove between and around trees and startled people. Arthur wasn't even sure which way the path back was anymore. They were lost. They turned a corner onto a dirt road with a cluster of buildings and a few people walking.

All at once, Idolette shrieked and Arthur spun around to see that someone had grabbed her. He stopped mid-step and flung himself back toward her. "Let her go—" he started to shout.

But several things happened so fast that Arthur had no time to react.

The first was that the guards came into view, still shouting and whistling. The second was the short old man who had grabbed Idolette loudly and happily cried, "Ah, Viola! *Mi Viola!*" and proceeded to take her in both arms and plant a kiss on each of her cheeks. The third was that when he held Idolette back to look at her, she was grinning happily and exclaimed, "*Okhi, grandpápa!*"

By this time Arthur had reached them, and the old man grabbed his arm in an iron grip and yanked him into the shadow of the awning of his building. He rattled something Arthur didn't understand and gestured for them to come in, laughing joyously.

Arthur glanced over his shoulder and saw the guards run past, not even noticing the old man apparently greeting his grandchildren. They ran on.

In the cool of the small pottery store they had entered, Arthur's eyes adjusted to the dim lighting. He stared at the little man who had saved them and who now smiled broadly as he watched them. Arthur realized the man was not as old as he'd first thought. He had a plump, jovial face, odd-shaped yellow-brown eyes, curly greying brown hair with a hat perched on top, and clothes several sizes too big for him—his long pants sagged over his shoes.

"Who is he—" Arthur began.

"Well, I have just saved your lives, *né?*" the small man exclaimed with a wink.

Idolette swallowed and ignored Arthur. "Yes, thank you, er . . . sir."

"You don't know him?" Arthur balked, seeing her embarrassed face.

"No."

Arthur's mouth dropped open. "You are really scary."

"Yes, she is a very good actor," the little man exclaimed, grinning broadly.

Idolette frowned at him. "Maybe, but so are you. Why did you help us?"

The man nodded, his hat wobbling on his head. "Yes, yes, you're suspicious. But no need for it. I saw you and thought I'd help." His smile widened even more.

Arthur's suspicions doubled. He narrowed his eyes in sudden comprehension.

"You saw us?" Idolette asked doubtfully. "We were running pretty fast and only just turned the corner before—"

"No."

Idolette turned to Arthur in surprise. "What do you mean, no?"

Arthur pointed at the man, who was now on the verge of giggles. "He doesn't mean he saw us running just now. He saw us at the palace."

"What?"

"I felt him watching me." Arthur frowned at the man. "Didn't I?"

"Yes!" the little man blurted, and he burst out in a fit of wavering giggles.

Idolette stepped closer to Arthur, and they both stepped toward the open doorway.

"Now, now," the man cried, wiping his mirthful tears away. "Don't you want to know *why* I was watching you?"

"No," Idolette said just as Arthur snapped, "I'd rather know how you got past the guards without them seeing *you*."

The man nodded vigorously again, and his hat wobbled, on the verge of toppling off. He pushed it back onto his head, stifling another giggle. "I'm a good jumper."

They gawked at him.

"It's true," he said humbly, clasping his hands and looking heavenward like a little cherub.

"Thanks for helping us . . . " Arthur began slowly.

" . . . but we have to go now," Idolette finished, and they both took another step toward the doorway.

"Sure you won't stay for tea?" their strange host asked politely, picking up a teapot from a little table next to him.

"Uh, no thanks."

"Crumpets?" He pointed to a plain wooden tray with an assortment of breads and pastries.

"No."

"Scones? Biscuits?"

"No."

"Tarts?"

Idolette raised her eyebrows. "What kind of tarts?"

Arthur glared at her. "No."

The little man blew out his breath in an exaggerated sigh and flung his arms up in defeat. "Fine, fine. I get it. You have to leave. I thought maybe we could have tea and talk about the

Gjallarhorn, but if you're in such a hurry . . . " He looked at their dumbstruck faces and smiled slyly.

"How do you know—" Arthur sputtered.

The stranger held up a small, weathered palm for silence. "Liber."

Idolette and Arthur exchanged glances. "Huh?"

"Liber. It's my name."

"Well, *Liber*," Arthur snapped, "how do you know—"

"Tea?" The little man named Liber shook the teapot temptingly.

Idolette put her hands over her face. "What is going on?" she whimpered.

Liber took that as a *yes* and put the teapot into the glowing embers of his fireplace.

Arthur felt defeated. He watched warily as Liber pranced here and there around the room, grabbing plates and saucers and cups and butter and preserves. "Why—" Arthur tried again.

"Not yet, not yet," the stranger simpered. He wrapped a hand towel around the teapot's handle and pulled it from the fire, then poured hot water into the cups and set them out on the little table. At last he clapped his hands and made a deep bow that toppled his hat from his head. Arthur thought he saw two little nubs of wood sticking out of the curly hair, but Liber swung his hat back in an instant, and Arthur wasn't sure what he had seen.

"Tea is served," the little man smiled. Then he handed them each a cup and a plate with a tart and a cookie, gesturing for them to find seats. He sat down himself, nibbling at a scone. "It's so nice to have guests," he said with the polite, formal air of a party host. "It's a rare treat for me, you see. But as my old mother used to say, always be prepared for a party. It's too bad, though, that you two couldn't be a bit older, because then I could open my wine cellar . . . " He stopped to blink at them. "I haven't poisoned anything, you know."

Arthur looked at his untouched tea and back to their odd host, his brain working furiously. *Wooden nubs under a hat, a bleating laugh, a good jumper . . . .What's he hiding under such baggy pants?* Arthur wondered suspiciously. The more he thought, the more his eyes narrowed. Finally, it struck him. His mouth dropped open. "It was *your* hoofprint I saw last time," he blurted, staring at the little man. "You're a faun, aren't you!"

"Bleh-heh-heh-heh-heh-heh," bleated Liber.

Idolette shrieked and nearly dropped her cup and plate, spilling tea all over herself.

Liber cleared his throat and tried to look dignified. "Now, now. You must be referring to the raised bruises on my head. I was in an accident, you know, and suffered a terrible concussion . . . ." He looked from Idolette's wide eyes to Arthur's narrowed ones and then gave a great sigh. "Fine, fine," he grumbled. "Yes, I'm a faun." He stood and swept off his hat so Arthur could clearly see the little horns on the top of his head, and then he yanked up his pant leg to reveal a hairy little goat-hoofed leg. "Liber Tiberius Glaucus the third, at your ser-her-her-her-her-vice."

Idolette looked faint.

"Uh . . . thanks," Arthur replied uncertainly. "Now tell us why you were spying on me, why you helped us, and how you know about the Gjallarhorn."

"Humans," grumbled Liber. "Always in such a hurry." He raised his voice. "First of all, I wasn't spying on you. I was already there. It's my job to watch that place, you know. It has been since my old mother died sixty years ago." He took a dignified sip of tea. "And before me, my mother watched it when it was only a big pile of dirt, and before that *her* father watched it, and before that *his* father watched it, and before that—"

"Okay, okay, we get it," Arthur interrupted. "Your family watches the Knossos palace. Why?"

"Why?" Liber repeated curiously, as though the answer should be plain. "To make sure someone like *you* doesn't discover the secret."

Something about the way he said "you" made Arthur's heart jump into his throat. He couldn't swallow. He cast a glance at Idolette. She didn't know he was a Guardian—no one was supposed to know about that. Gamble had warned him. He feared the faun would say something. But how could he possibly know?

Liber saw Arthur's look at Idolette. "Hm," was all he said. Then he waved his hand dismissively. "But I saw you uncover the secret. What do you want the Horn for?"

"I don't want the Horn," Arthur said quickly. "I already know it's not even there. It was stolen long ago."

The faun looked hard at Arthur. "Why do you say that?"

"Because . . . uh . . . someone told me."

"That *someone* wouldn't be Prometheus the doom-and-gloom Centaur, would it?"

Now Arthur spilled his tea. "What?" he gasped. "You know Prometheus?" He didn't think he could handle any more shocks today.

Liber gave another bleating giggle. "*Do* I know Prometheus?" He giggled again. "That great old depressing horse-bottomed soothsayer? Of course I know him."

"But how?" quavered Idolette.

"Well, it's not hard. I live here, he lives at that secret island, and," he said loudly above Idolette's and Arthur's protesting gasps, "occasionally he comes over for tea and to talk about the weather." He looked sternly at them. "Centaurs might know all about the stars and planets, little ones, and be all read up on old histories, but they certainly don't know everything."

Arthur leaned forward eagerly. "So you know something about the Gjallarhorn that he doesn't?"

The faun nibbled a corner of his scone and wiggled his furry eyebrows secretively. "You don't think my family could watch that place for centuries and not know what goes on, do you?"

Arthur thought hard. So this goat-legged little man knew about Prometheus and, if not about Historia, at least about Elysium Island. That gave him some credit. And he had saved them from the guards, that was something, too. But then he had made that comment about "someone like you." It was possible that he just meant humans in general. . . . Although he had looked directly at Arthur when he said it. Still, Arthur should try to get as much information from the faun as he could, giving as little as he could get away with. He took a deep breath.

"Prometheus said the Horn was stolen by Alexander the Great, King of the Mycenaeans."

"Oh, he's right about that," said Liber. "That young hotshot did manage to steal it."

"But?"

Liber sipped his tea, his yellowy eyes looking over the top of the cup at Arthur. "But," he said at last, "it was stolen back and returned to the Labyrinth."

Arthur blew out his breath and sank back against his chair. So the Gjallarhorn had been returned. It made sense. *That's probably why I couldn't find anything about what Alexander did with it*, he thought grimly. *I guess he didn't do anything with it—someone else did.* Arthur also realized something else. Liber said the Horn was returned to the Labyrinth—not to Knossos. Apparently, he agreed with Prometheus that the two were not the same. But why would the Horn be put back where it could be stolen again? He looked up to see the faun watching him.

"I wouldn't get any ideas, if I were you," Liber said slyly. "No one else will be stealing it anytime soon."

"No," Arthur said slowly, "because it's guarded."

Idolette sat up. "Not by . . . a M-Minotaur?" she stammered.

Arthur looked inquisitively at the faun.

Liber merely shrugged and sipped his tea.

Suddenly, Idolette gave a shudder. "Arthur . . . what time is it? We have to get back to our team!"

Arthur jumped up. He had completely forgotten that they were not even supposed to be here. "Oh no, we'd better hurry and find them. But you'd better take that makeup off so our guard pals don't recognize you so easily."

Idolette nodded and glanced at Liber. "Do you have a loo?"

"Right through there. Go ahead." The faun waited for the sound of the bathroom door clicking shut, then put his teacup down and narrowed his eyes shrewdly at Arthur. "She doesn't know what you are," he said softly. "But I do."

Arthur tried not to panic. He didn't speak, but gripped his backpack tightly.

"I wonder why Prometheus trusts you," Liber continued, standing up and stepping toward Arthur as if trying to see him better. "I can't imagine he doesn't know about you—him and all his prophecies. He obviously thinks there's something help-ful about you. And it's not as if you have *all* the clues. Still . . . " He was right in front of Arthur now, peering into his face with his golden-brown goatlike eyes. Then his hand snapped out, and quick as a bolt of lightning, snatched the notebook from Arthur's belt pouch. " . . . I'd better hang onto this."

Arthur didn't say anything or try to grab the notebook back. His shoulders slumped, and he felt very tired and weak again.

"Why do you want the Horn?" Liber demanded.

"I already told you," Arthur sighed, rubbing his shaky hand over his face. "I don't. I just wanted to solve the riddle. I just wanted to know. Besides, Knossos isn't even the Labyrinth."

At that moment, Idolette opened the bathroom door and came out, looking plainer with only her normal makeup on. "I'm ready."

"Okay." Arthur sighed again. Their whole adventure had been for nothing now that he no longer had the symbols in his notebook. He wished he could punch that little faun down, but he was too weary, and he didn't want to get kicked by those goat legs. So instead, he simply nodded to Liber and muttered, "Thanks for your help."

Idolette also voiced her thanks, and they started toward the door.

"Oh, look," Liber said suddenly, bending to the floor as if picking something up. "I think you dropped this." He held out the notebook and pushed it into Arthur's hand.

Arthur stared at the notebook, then looked at him and half-smiled. "Thanks."

Liber nodded. "Keep my secrets and I'll keep yours," he said softly. "And always remember—brains over strength, and giving over greed."

Arthur cocked his head at the serious look on the faun's face. "Uh . . . okay. I will."

Liber waved from the doorway, grinning. "And visit again if you're ever in the area," he called cheerily. "I always like having guests!"

"Oh, Arthur, you shouldnay done it," Pernille scolded later that afternoon in the comfort of the Odin lounge. "That was dangerous."

"Indeed," Esmond added. "You could've been caught or kidnapped. You could've gotten yourself killed or Idolette injured. And, Idolette, I'm surprised at you after all that fuss you made about the Gypsy saying an explorer was going to put you in harm's way or whatever that rubbish was."

Idolette's eyes widened. "Oh, I'd forgotten about that," she breathed, staring at Arthur. "Do you suppose this is what she meant?"

Arthur felt slightly ashamed of convincing Idolette to help him. "It had to be done," he said shiftily. "I got very good information. Plus, we got to meet a faun."

"Yes, you mentioned it," Esmond grimaced. "What was he like?"

"Creepy," Idolette sniffed at once.

"Creepy?" Esmond made an offended face. "You meet a creature with the magical power to give you endless happiness or to cause you to fall into eternal sleep and all you say is he was creepy?"

"Well, he was! He was completely off his trolley! You should've seen his little horns, and his laugh was absolutely like a goat's . . . "

For a short while Arthur sat silently, not listening as the two argued and Pernille giggled at them. All at once, he gestured to Griffin and got up, unnoticed.

"We're off to see that Nada girl, aren't we," said Griffin as they started out the door.

Arthur patted the belt pouch where his small notebook rested, keeping secret the symbols on the wall at Knossos.

"Yup." In silence, they followed the path to Apartment Athena, waving to Tad and Donovan and then Charda and Bridgette, whom they passed on the way. Before they reached their destination, though, Griffin sniffed the air, stopped, and turned around, nodding at a bushy enclosure where Arthur now recognized the top of Nada's brown hair peeking over the edge. "Hey, Nada," Arthur called.

She looked over and smiled pleasantly by way of greeting.

They found her with her usual art pad, which was today covered in doodles of hollow-eyed skulls, sword-stabbed cloaked figures, and nasty demon creatures.

"What did you think of the transfer of the skull today?" she asked serenely.

"Uh," said Arthur, who didn't think anything of it, as he had missed the entire thing.

"It wasn't so interesting as I thought it could be," she went on, "but I'm supposing Master Gamble didn't mind. Hallo, Griffin," she said abruptly, holding her hand out as if she were a queen and Griffin a knight who should kiss it. Griffin settled for sniffing her hand instead, and she smiled and patted his head.

"I actually wondered," Arthur coughed, "if you could take a look at something else and see if you can tell what it says."

Nada rubbed Griffin's neck. "Probably."

He took out his notebook, flipped it open, and handed it to her.

"No picture this time?" she said calmly. She continued to

pat Griffin with one hand and studied the page in the other. "Hm, isn't that interesting . . ."

Arthur hoped she couldn't hear his heart beating loudly against his chest. "What is?"

"The symbols you haf here. Here is octopus again. But these I don't know. This one is for Knossos. That one for a guard." She looked up at him. "There is no sense here. Just random symbols. Doodles." She smiled.

"Okay, thanks," Arthur replied, taking back his notebook. He felt disappointed. After all he and Idolette went through to get those symbols, he wished they would've been more obviously useful. "Thanks for your help, Nada. I guess we should get back now. I'll see you tomorrow."

She nodded and went back to her drawing. As he and Griffin left, Arthur glumly guessed he could go back to "lying low" again.

13

A LIBRARY LESSON RUINED

The month of August was slow going. When Arthur found a chance to tell Prometheus about meeting Liber the Faun, the centaur gave a long sigh and replied, "Fauns are far too careless with information, and their giddy ways are not to be trusted." Arthur decided against mentioning Liber's opinion about centaurs not knowing everything.

Arthur secretly wondered what Prometheus had told Liber about him that would cause the faun to think that Prometheus trusted him—especially after Prometheus's comment about Arthur's "disturbing" fate.

As for Initiate lessons, Preservations was often a joke nowadays. More than a few times, Zane had to lead the team alone because Jolly had taken ill at the last minute. On the days when Jolly did show up, he looked awful and taught worse.

The name *Rheneas Berne* was murmured darkly by the Initiates as the cause of Jolly's unhappy appearance.

Outside it was hot, and the Initiates (and many Members) spent any free time at Olympian Bay, soaking their feet in the cool, clear water or burying each other in the smooth sand. Arthur noticed that Esmond didn't join them very often, probably because he didn't like water. But since Esmond was usually sensitive about such things, Arthur didn't mention it.

So it was quite by accident that he found out what Esmond was really up to.

Griffin claimed to be tired of going to the beach every weekend, so instead he and Arthur visited some of the booths that were still up around the stadium. Arthur didn't have any extra money, though, so they could only look. Arthur was just inspecting one of the hologram games, wondering if he should ask his dad for one for his birthday, when a voice behind him spoke.

"Hello, Arthur."

He jumped and spun around. "Oh, hi, Kalila." He grinned at the older girl, Kalila Sheridan, who had been on his team last year. She was dressed in a turquoise toga that complemented her dark skin and made her look like an exotic queen. "I didn't know you were here at Main Hall. Didn't you finish last year?"

"I finished Initiate training, yes. Now I am working on my PASS. I am trying to get my apprenticeship for Origins."

"PASS?" Arthur wondered.

"Placement Approval for Specific Study. It's where you write an in-depth paper on a subject to prove you're ready to be an apprentice in a specific department."

Arthur scratched his head. "Oh yeah, right. I didn't see you at orientation, though." They began walking.

"No," Kalila said, "I didn't have to go because I already went through as an Initiate. I'm usually in the library, though sometimes I get a chance to go to the Talisman Club to meet up with people. I've been really busy with work. I'm doing my PASS on my theory about a connection between the Holy Grail and King Midas—you know, the king with the 'golden touch'."

Arthur suppressed a grin. *I'd have to say it's a pretty good theory*, he thought, remembering how close he'd come to actually finding the Grail last year. "Wow, that sounds interesting," he said aloud. "So if you've been here the whole time, I guess you've probably heard about the supposed escaped beast on Crete, huh?"

"Yes," Kalila said slowly. "There have been two injuries and one missing person so far. But no one from Investigations has actually seen a beast."

Arthur paused. *Two injuries? A missing person?* His brain whirled. He had the feeling Liber hadn't been quite honest. How could the Minotaur be injuring people if it was in the Labyrinth and Knossos wasn't the Labyrinth? Something wasn't adding up. Arthur took a deep breath. "Do you know anything about the Minotaur?"

Kalila smiled. "Caught up in the rumors, are you? I learned about Minotaur myths my first year, so it was a long time ago.

But you can try the gnomes in the library. Ask for a *Greek myth* gnome."

"Greek myth. Okay, thanks a lot. I'll try the library."

After that, they chatted about the competitions so far, and Kalila mentioned that she had seen the Squire Joust and was impressed with Arthur's skills. She herself had competed in Archery for Members and won a bronze arrow. "But that was it for me," she said with a shrug. "I am so busy. But did you see the tapestries?"

"Tapestries?" asked Arthur. "Oh, you mean for the next contest?"

"Yes, the Tapestry competition. They will put them up in the rotunda next week for the official judging. But I saw the judges taking some of them to the judging room. I can't believe how amazing Esmond's is. Will you please compliment him for me?"

Arthur balked, mouth open. "Esmond's?"

Kalila nodded. "Yes, Esmond Falvey from the Initiate Team. There was a tapestry with his name. That is the same Esmond?"

Arthur recovered from his shock. "Yeah. Yeah, I'll tell him for you. Thanks again for your help. It was nice to see you. Good luck on your PASS."

"Thank you. I will need all the luck I can get."

As Arthur and Griffin headed back to their apartment, Griffin snickered, "So *that's* why he wouldn't tell anyone what he signed up for. Wait till Idolette finds out. . . ."

Esmond was alone in his room when Arthur and Griffin knocked.

"Why didn't you tell us you registered for Tapestry?" Arthur demanded the moment Esmond opened the door.

Esmond's face grew red. "W-what? Who told you that?"

"We ran into Kalila Sheridan today, and she said she saw yours."

"Oh." Esmond crossed his arms, his mouth pouty.

"Well?" Arthur frowned at him.

"Well what?"

"Is yours any good?"

Esmond shrugged. "I guess I'll find out at the judging next week. There's only one—it's for Initiates and Members together, so I doubt I'll get anything, but . . . " He shrugged again. "I had to sign up for something." He paused, then blurted, "Don't tell Idolette."

Griffin snickered.

Arthur shoved the dog. "I won't," he promised—then, getting an idea, quickly added, "if you help me find something in the library."

"Hey," Griffin barked sharply. "You're not allowed in there without Member supervision."

Esmond glanced from the dog to Arthur. "I'm guessing he just said this, but, you do remember we've been banned from Main Hall without a Member, don't you?"

"Yeah. But, I'm sure we can follow someone in easily."

"I don't believe this."

Arthur crossed his arms. "I want to try a different tactic—looking up anything the library has about horns, especially the Minotaur. I've been doing a lot of thinking, and there's no coincidence that there was an explosion and then rumors of a creature start popping up. Maybe it was just Liber—the faun who helped us—but somehow I don't think so. I'm beginning to wonder if Knossos wasn't the Labyrinth after all," he muttered. "And the mystery of how the Mermish language is mixed up in this is really bugging me." He raised his brows. "So?"

Esmond groaned. "If I don't go with you, I suppose you'll tell Idolette what competition I signed up for."

Arthur shrugged. "Probably not. She'll find out next week anyway."

Esmond raised an eyebrow. "You're not a very good negotiator."

"Are you gonna help or not?"

Esmond sighed. "I can't believe I'm doing this."

Armed with his notes, and leaving Griffin at the apartments, Arthur hurried with Esmond to Main Hall where, to their luck, they found Arthur's jousting instructor, Monsieur Délicat, heading up the wide staircase to the bronze doors. Under pretense of being interested in further jousting lessons, they tagged along with him. At the library, however, they cut off his story of the joust he failed when he was five years old, and left him to continue on his own.

Arthur approached one of the two long, ornate desks and found an open place to stand. He studied the panel of buttons in front of him and pressed the one marked *Greek Myth*. A book gnome appeared in front of him so fast that Arthur wondered if it hadn't dropped from the ceiling.

"We need information on Minotaur myth," Esmond said. "Any date, any author. We'll start with the first ten."

The gnome buzzed off, and Arthur was glad Esmond knew his way around the complications of this library. Within three minutes the book gnome returned with a stack of tablets, scrolls, and books. "Funny you should ask about the Minotaur," he rumbled in his deep, earthy voice. "Someone else was looking that up recently, too."

"Who?" Arthur asked in surprise.

"I don't remember. Here you go." With that, the gnome was gone.

Esmond narrowed his eyes. "He was lying. Book gnomes have the best memories on earth. He knows exactly who asked, but he isn't going to tell us."

Arthur frowned. Who else would be so interested in Minotaur myth? Maybe someone who had seen the Minos Supplement Text? "Berne," he growled.

Esmond shrugged and picked up the stack of books. "No proof."

Arthur gritted his teeth but said nothing and followed Esmond to a table. There, he set his mind to concentrating on the materials they'd received.

They had pored over the resources for a half hour when Esmond gave a great sigh. "What exactly are we hoping to find?" he asked as he gazed down at a tablet in front of him.

"Well," Arthur said, "let's say the Minotaur and the Horn are truly linked. Either Prometheus is right, and there's no bull-man because the Horn and the bull signify the same thing, or else what Liber suggested is right and the Horn is guarded."

"Well then?"

"So, the question we have to answer is, if there really is a beast around, how do we tell if it's the Minotaur?"

Esmond tapped the tablet. "But how *could* it be? The Minotaur would have to be thousands of years old, for one thing."

"I thought about that, too." Arthur pointed at Esmond. "And actually, you gave me the answer at the play we saw on our first excursion."

Esmond thought for a moment, then raised his eyebrows. "Ambrosia? The gods' drink of immortality?"

Arthur nodded eagerly. "I bet such a beast could handle that kind of powerful drink."

"It's possible," Esmond mused. "So that would be how he could go on living, but what about food?"

"Liber." Arthur cocked his head. "The faun said his family's been watching over Knossos for a gazillion years. Why would they do that? Unless the palace had something worth watching—that they needed to take care of?"

"I see what you're thinking." Esmond tapped the tabletop. "What if the faun's family leaves food for the beast?"

"Exactly. So there *could* be a Minotaur."

"But what about Theseus? You're forgetting the story. The hero Theseus killed the Minotaur inside the Labyrinth."

Arthur shook his head. "What if he only said that to make himself look brave? If nobody else could enter the maze and get out alive, how could anyone say otherwise? You've read the other stories about Theseus, too—he wasn't exactly the most honest guy."

"I see what you mean. But people visit Knossos all the time. How could they miss seeing a frightening creature like that?"

"Because," Arthur said simply, "Knossos isn't the Labyrinth."

Esmond rolled his eyes. "Then why exactly would Liber's family be keeping an eye on it?"

Arthur lowered his voice to a whisper. "Because it *leads* to the Labyrinth."

Esmond frowned, silently staring up at the vast ceiling. At last he concluded, "You think the explosion last month opened an entrance between the Knossos palace and the Labyrinth . . . enabling the Minotaur to leave the Labyrinth?"

"Well, that's what I think we should try to find out."

Their search revealed some old examples of Cretan coins with the Labyrinth symbol on them. Arthur couldn't help wondering at their straightforward shape. "Those labyrinths are very winding, sure, but in the story, why would Theseus have needed a thread from Minos's daughter Ariadne just to go around in a couple of circles? Was he stupid?"

Esmond shrugged. "Stories don't always remember all the details. But listen to this bit about the Labyrinth from the eighth book of *Metamorphoses*: 'Daedalus, celebrated for his skill in architecture, laid out the design, and confused the clues to direction, and led the eye into a tortuous maze, by the windings of alternating paths.' This makes it sound like the Labyrinth was an actual maze, instead of the classical seven-circuit ring path these symbols make it out to be. I wonder which is right?" He frowned and repeated, "Confused the clues to direction . . . led the eye . . . " He shrugged.

By the time they left the library, it was getting dark. Arthur's stomach growled, but he felt cheered by what they'd found.

Arthur and Esmond had just reached the Rotunda when they stopped short. There, in the entrance, was Alexander Siegfried, accompanied by none other than Rheneas Berne.

"Ah," Berne sneered at the sight of them. "If it isn't the boy with a minister father."

Arthur felt his ears grow hot as Mr. Siegfried looked at him. Then he wondered if Mr. Siegfried knew they weren't supposed to be in the Hall without an adult. His stomach gave a nervous turn.

"What are you boys doing here so late?" asked Mr. Siegfried. "Where's your team?"

After a desperate look from Arthur, Esmond cleared his throat and stepped forward. "We were just studying, sir, and realized how late is was, so we're heading back to the apartments."

"Well, don't let it happen again," warned Alexander Siegfried.

"No, sir." Esmond and Arthur started quickly for the open doors and escape.

"Wait a moment," called Berne. "What do you have there?"

Arthur froze, for Berne was pointing his black-gloved hand at a paper hanging out of Arthur's back pocket—the paper he'd copied the symbols of the Minos text on. He looked at Esmond for help.

"It's our notes for a research project," Esmond put in.

But Arthur could see Berne's eyes glinting with interest. "Where did you find that symbol?" He turned from Esmond to Arthur. "Do you know what it means?" He stared at Arthur, and his dark eyes gave a twitch.

"Yes," Arthur muttered angrily.

Berne raised an eyebrow and his lip curled mockingly. "And what does it mean?"

Arthur struggled between the yearning to prove he wasn't stupid and the sense to keep his mouth shut. But the man's sneer was more than Arthur could ignore. His mouth opened. "The octopus."

Immediately, Mr. Siegfried chuckled. "What nonsense! I think you'll need a few more years of Origins studies before you can interpret symbols."

But Berne did not laugh along. "What language is it?" he hissed at Arthur.

Arthur swallowed, wishing he'd kept his mouth shut.

"What language?"

"Mermish." He was breathing hard. They had to get away. He was ruining everything!

Esmond groaned, and Berne's quick eyes darted to him. "I will look into it," he threatened. He turned to Mr. Siegfried. "I wasn't aware your facilities had access to Mermish translations."

While the man's back was turned, Arthur grabbed Esmond's arm and hurried out the doors.

"That was a disaster at best," Esmond moaned as they jogged down the path. "I knew we shouldn't have gone in. I just knew something like this was bound to happen . . . "

Arthur couldn't speak. He knew he had just made even more trouble for Historia now, and he felt awful. If Madam Siegfried found out . . . But at the same time, he had just received undeniable proof that Berne was interested in Mermish symbols. The way the man's eyes lit up at the sight of his notes was a bad sign. Arthur decided he needed to help make things right. He needed to warn someone what they were up against. Grimly, he remembered Etson telling him who cared about Historia more than anything else. He'd have to tell Gamble.

To Arthur's frustration, he couldn't find any sign of Master Gamble over the rest of the weekend. He had to wait until after their next Languages lesson. He waved the rest of the Spyglass Squad off and waited for everyone to leave the Lore Study before he could get Gamble on his own.

"Berne wants to find the real Labyrinth," he blurted.

He could actually see the color rising in Gamble's face, as if the man were being filled with boiling purple liquid. Arthur rushed on, "I know he saw the Minos Supplement Text, he's the one who stole the Ever-Burning Candle from Jolly's office, I'm positive he's been in the library looking up information on the Minotaur, he's been threatening Jolly, and he's interested in the symbol translations of that text. You've got to—"

"I thought," Gamble cut in menacingly, "you were told to *stay—away—from—investors!*"

Arthur winced. "I'm just trying to help protect—"

"What goes on with Historia property," Gamble hissed, "has *nothing* to do with you. You are *not* a hero here. You are an

Initiate. Although, I'm *this* close," he shoved his nose right in Arthur's face, "to putting an end to that!"

Arthur bristled. He was trying to help, and everyone was treating him like a toddler. "This isn't fair!" he shouted.

"Don't talk to me about fair," Gamble snapped. "Lesson of the day—life's not about fair. It's about choices. It's what we deserve, not what we want."

"Well, what did I do to deserve this?" Arthur barked.

"You're being nosy and insolent." They glared at each other for several seconds. Finally, Gamble straightened and breathed calmly, though Arthur could still see the old man's hands shaking around the staff he clutched. "You're *this* close," he muttered, narrowing his eyes. "Watch your step, Grey."

Arthur was furious. *I've got to do something to stop Berne*—the phrase spun constantly at the front of his mind, and he barely focused on any of his studies. All his waking moments and even his sleeping ones were filled with ways to get rid of Berne, most of them involving sharks and giant octopuses.

The next weekend, Arthur was snapped back to reality as he walked toward Main Hall with Pernille, Idolette, and Tad to see Esmond's tapestry.

"Arthur!" someone called.

He turned and froze. For a moment, he only stared at Etson Grey, a feeling of gloom washing over him as thoughts of the Gypsy's fortune and Prometheus's "disturbing fate" jumped forward in his brain. Then Arthur shook his head. *Don't be stupid*, he scolded himself, *that's all nonsense*. He forced his mouth into a smile. "Hi, Dad!" He fell back from the others to wait for Etson to catch up. "I didn't know you were going to be here."

"I decided last-minute," Etson smiled. "You know me."

They headed into Main Hall with the other groups. Inside, about twenty banners and tapestries hung along the high-ceilinged walls. Arthur was amazed. They were stories told in woven pictures. He could make out scenes of battles, of detailed castles, of galloping horses, of fire-breathing dragons, of shining swords.

"There," he blurted, impressed. "That's Esmond's." The hanging banner entitled *Yggdrasil* bore Esmond's name and a large second-place ribbon. It showed a large tree with a shiny eagle at its top and a dark dragon curled at its roots, with various scenes taking place on the branches. Arthur recognized it as part of Norse mythology.

They admired it for a while before moving on. Then Etson grew serious. He cleared his throat. "You, uh, haven't been having any trouble with Gamble lately, have you?"

Arthur blinked. "What do you mean?"

Etson gazed up at a banner of three witches around a bubbling cauldron. "I got a message from him yesterday."

Arthur's mouth dropped open. So *that's* why Etson was here. He couldn't believe Gamble would deal such a low blow—tattling to his dad! "It wasn't my fault," he sputtered, trying to keep his voice low. He launched into an angry explanation about Rheneas Berne's behavior and Gamble's constant popping up to punish Arthur for absolutely nothing. "After all everyone says about that Berne guy," Arthur seethed, "you'd think they'd want to find a reason to get rid of him so he stops bothering Historia. But Gamble tells me to mind my own business." He frowned up at Etson. "Do I have to listen to him?"

Etson crossed his arms. "Well, Berne is up to something, obviously." He paused. "But Gamble does have a point."

Arthur slouched. "So, I should just pretend nothing's going on?"

Etson tapped his chin thoughtfully. "Here's the thing," he said quietly. "A friend in Investigations once gave me a bit of advice. He said, 'Open all doors; just close them quietly behind you.'" He shrugged.

Arthur furrowed his brow. "Open all doors?" Was Etson saying it was okay to keep an eye on Berne as long as he was quiet about it?

As they headed back out, blinking in the sun, Etson stretched and turned to Arthur. "I discovered a new treat the other day—I don't suppose you'd be interested in some Fizzy-Winks ice cream?"

"As long as it's not gonna spray at me," Arthur grinned.

Fifteen minutes later they were settled at a table on the veranda with bowls of crackling ice cream, trying to talk around the popping in their mouths. Arthur started to tell Etson about his explorations on Crete.

"Hm," Etson said skeptically. "I don't know if it's a good idea to go wandering around where there are rumors of horned monsters. Gamble could get you in big trouble for that sort of thing."

Arthur shrugged. "But I had to find out if Prometheus was

right, didn't I? I mean, what if there really is a magical horn that Alexander the Great used?"

"Well, if Historia could manage to find an artifact like that, I'm sure it would certainly encourage other investors to come to our aid, but . . . " He made a face. "How do I put this nicely . . . . Prometheus is a quack."

Arthur laughed.

"I mean it, kid. The guy's off his rocker. He's studied too many conspiracy theories—everyone says so. He thinks Alexander the Great and the lost island of Atlantis are at the bottom of every unexplained mystery in any legend and myth. I wouldn't take what he says too seriously. He's a nutcase, loopy, mad as a March hare. And that's putting it nicely." He winked.

Arthur forced another laugh, but he felt an anxious shiver vibrate through his body. He couldn't let himself believe Prometheus was wrong. Not after everything he'd learned and pieced together so far. Again, he remembered the word *betrayal*. He shook himself in frustration.

"Anyway," Etson went on easily, "something else I thought might interest you, Origins just found a world map from the fifth century, and it includes mention of an island with 'a horned bull that attacks newcomers.' What do you think of that? They're transporting it next Tuesday. Though it's all hush-hush. You won't get to see it, I'm afraid, since they'll probably do it overnight to retain secrecy."

Arthur sat up. "An old map that mentions the Minotaur?"

"Yup. They'll probably sell the Scan for a hefty profit. But it's like I said, nobody will get to see it. Agnes doesn't want anything going wrong—Historia's having a hard time, and any more trouble would really be bad."

"What are they doing to keep it safe?" Arthur demanded, thinking about the stolen Ever-Burning Candle.

"I'm sure they'll have guards while it goes between stations. It'll need to get cleaned up, and Zane will Scanograph it. Anyway, remember what I said about staying out of trouble," he added. "I don't need Gamble snapping at my throat, if you know what I mean."

Arthur nodded absently. He remembered one thing Etson had said, anyway: *Open all doors; just close them quietly behind you.* He began to make a plan.

14

THE SPIRAL OFFICE

By the time Arthur got back to the apartments, he had made up his mind to follow his dad's advice. "Griffin, wake up. I've got a job for you. Before Tuesday, you need to find out where Rheneas Berne stays."

"Huh?"

"You heard me. My dad said a new map is being transported in. And you know what that means." He frowned. "Berne is going to intercept it."

"Why?"

"Are you joking? For one thing, the Society kicked him out, remember? He's trying to get revenge. For another thing, the Minotaur myth is involved. He's going to try to steal that map."

"And what are we going to do about it?" yawned Griffin.

Arthur rolled his eyes. "Stop him, of course."

Griffin sighed. "I was afraid you were going to say that."

"You're going to watch his room and follow him the moment he leaves on Tuesday night. We need to do everything we can to stop him from getting to that map and ruining Historia."

While Arthur had lessons, Griffin learned that Berne roomed in Apartment Zeus. On Tuesday evening, Griffin was to watch the door after Berne retired to his room for the night. He would howl when Berne left his apartment, and Arthur would be nearby in the bushes, ready to get Gamble from Apartment Thor. That would show the grouchy old toad that Arthur was right about Berne.

But Arthur waited so long for Griffin's howl that, before he knew it, he was waking up to morning light and a fairy trying to pick his nose. And to Arthur's frustration, the frantic voices of several Members hurrying down the path informed him that the map had indeed been stolen during the night.

He didn't waste a moment, but ran from his own hiding place to Apartment Zeus, where he found Griffin asleep behind a planter near Berne's door.

"What are you doing!" Arthur scowled at the droopy-eyed dog. "You missed him!"

Griffin shook his head. "Huh? That's not possible," he yawned. "I was here the whole time and never heard a thing. But I'll tell you what—this whole floor smells like cats."

"I don't care what you smell. I care what you *didn't* smell. The map's been stolen! You didn't stop him."

Griffin laid his ears back. "But . . . I didn't hear anything. . . ."

"Maybe he used a sleeping dust on you or something." Arthur pulled out his pocketknife and opened the magnifying glass tool. "I need to look for footprints or a trace of sleeping powder or some other clue. Do you suppose we could break into—"

Before Arthur could finish his sentence, the door beside him sprang open. Griffin dove back behind the planter, but Arthur had no time to hide. He was standing in front of Berne's room with his magnifying glass aimed at the door, and Rheneas Berne now glared at him with his lip curled back.

"You again, is it?" he sneered. "I admit this is beginning to irritate me. I thought I told Agnes Siegfried to keep disruptive nuisances out of my way. I see I will have to remind her yet again." He stepped past Arthur, shutting the door behind him, and stalked off down the stairway.

"Not good," Griffin muttered, poking his head out from behind the plant.

Arthur spent the rest of the day worrying, expecting every footstep across Main Hall to bring a Spit-It-Out message from Madam Siegfried telling him to pack his bags at once and leave the Society. *I guess I didn't close the door very quietly*, he thought bitterly.

As the Initiates headed toward the portico and dinner that afternoon, Pernille asked Arthur what was wrong (he was wincing with every step, fearing that a letter would fly out of every next tile). But Arthur's mouth was so dry he couldn't speak, and he only shrugged in reply. It was during supper that Steward Cartwright found him and informed him he was to come along to see Madam Siegfried.

Esmond and Pernille exchanged anxious glances, and Idolette blinked at him in surprise.

His head bowed, Arthur scraped back his chair and followed the steward into the Hall and down the Museo Gallery. He silently argued with himself: *If I get out of this, I'll mind my business from now on. . . . Why won't anyone listen to me? . . . I just don't want to go back to Ivor Manor. . . . Gamble's going to ruin Historia. . . .*

By the time Arthur looked up, he found that the steward had led him into the library. To his surprise, they stopped in front of the huge column at the center of the enormous room. Steward Cartwright lifted his hand to knock slowly four times on a section of the decorated wood, and immediately a doorway cracked open in the column.

"Madam Siegfried is expecting you." The steward gestured Arthur inside.

Slowly, Arthur looked up at the long purple flag that hung down just inside the doorway and shone with gold letters announcing, "80 Years of Historia." Beside it began a long banner that ran the length of the wall before curving out of view. It was woven like the tapestries of the competitions, and Arthur wondered if Esmond had used this for inspiration. It began with the year 1929 and an image of a man putting down the first stone of a building. The stone was labeled "Historia Society." He realized the banner must show the history of the Society.

Arthur started down the narrow, winding hall, staring up at the tall, wood-paneled walls. He felt like he was walking uphill and realized he was spiraling up toward the center of the enormous column. As he walked, he glanced at the long tapestry, noting dates with things like "Conservation becomes its own department," "Initiate Program begins," and "Scanographer invented by Han Cobalt."

All at once, the hallway dead-ended at a closed mahogany door that was rather taller than normal doors. Hung on it was a stained-glass sign that read,

THE SPIRAL OFFICE

MADAM AGNES ALCOTT SIEGFRIED

OWNER OF THE HISTORIA SOCIETY, HONORABLE MAGE,

GRAND MASTER OF SCROLLS

He raised his hand and knocked. The door was so thick that the knock barely made a sound.

"Come in," came the voice of Madam Siegfried, and the door swung open.

Arthur stepped into the office.

Like the hallway, the small room was round, probably in the very center of the library column. It was decorated formally with large, dark pieces of furniture, oil paintings on the wall, and a jackal-headed Egyptian statue behind an oversized chair.

At a large, curved desk sat Madam Siegfried, looking down at a piece of paper. Her glasses rested at the tip of her nose in a way that reminded Arthur sharply of his own grandmother. She glanced up.

"Ah, Mr. Grey. Come in." As Arthur approached, the door

closed behind him of its own accord. Madam removed her glasses and rubbed her eyes.

"Have a seat."

Without a word, Arthur sat in the oversized chair, feeling uncomfortable that the jackal-headed statue was peering over his shoulder. He glanced at an open tin on the desk. There were several pieces of chocolate inside.

Madam gestured to the tin of candy. "Orange chocolates. Special fancy of mine. Would you like one?"

Arthur shook his head.

Madam pursed her lips for a moment, as if wondering where to begin. "Do you know," she said at last, "I knew your mother." She nodded at Arthur's startled look. "Yes, indeed. I had just become head of Origins at the time. Everyone knew Helena Doyle, as she was back then. She was one of Homer's favorites and still managed to be liked—Homer was very obvious about who his favorites were, and sometimes they were disliked, you see. But not Helena. She commanded respect because she always gave respect."

Arthur squirmed restlessly, wondering why Madam Siegfried was telling him this. Did she want him to know his mother wouldn't be proud of him for having to sit in the Spiral Office? He stared at his shoes.

"Well, I suppose you know why you're here," Madam sighed.

Arthur swallowed. He avoided looking at her eyes, which he could feel probing him like a stethoscope.

Madam Siegfried grabbed a small cloth from somewhere on her enormous desk and began wiping her glasses. "Mr. Grey,

I must ask you to let Rheneas Berne alone. I trust you realize the gravity of the situation."

Arthur couldn't help himself. "But what about the map?" he blurted.

"That is not your business. There is nothing you can do."

Arthur felt like he heard that a lot. "I just don't trust him."

Madam gave a harsh laugh. "Trust him? Neither do I. Believe me, no one dislikes the man more than I do. But you are to stay away from Mr. Berne. If you annoy our investors, they will take their money away and leave, and we will not be able to run the Historia Society anymore."

Arthur cleared his throat. It couldn't be as bad as that, could it? "Can't you get another investor?" he asked.

"If only it were that easy." Madam smiled bitterly and set her glasses down. "No one wants to work with us these days. It seems all our luck has dried up. So we take what we can get until things get better. And thank heaven that old Homer isn't around to see it."

Arthur tilted his head, finally looking at Madam. Why would she be thankful that Homer Siegfried was dead?

"I see the question in your eyes." She smiled wearily. "So I'll let you in on a little secret. Old Homer did not want Historia working under the demands of investors." She gestured to a tall painting on the wall. The balding man in it had a neat, wiry beard and was dressed in old-fashioned traveling clothes, a desert scene in the background. "That's Homer Siegfried, as I'm sure you recognized. When he started Historia, he had nothing but a collection of ancient texts from the Library of

Ashurbanipal that he found on the black market. He put his life into Historia, running it until he died over ten years ago. He was my father-in-law. That is to say, I married his only son."

Arthur stared at the painting. Homer Siegfried looked like a nice guy. He remembered Idolette saying that Homer hated his grandson Alexander, Idolette's own dad. Distractedly, Arthur wondered what Madam thought of her son.

"If there's one thing Homer wished to do away with, it was greedy investors," Madam Siegfried continued, shaking her head sadly. "The whole reason he began Historia was so people could search for the truth without having any strings attached—without the rules, lies, and pressure of money-hungry and power-craving funders. Unfortunately, even Historia falls on hard times, and we've had to resort to the things Homer hated. That is why I say it's good Homer's not here to see it. He would be devastated."

Madam Siegfried raised her eyes to look around the room. "Do you know," she said quietly, "that I was in the very first group of Initiates to go through Historia? I have been here for an extraordinarily long time. This is my life as much as it was Homer's."

Arthur looked back at Madam and was surprised to see tears pooling in her eyes. "Is . . . is there anything I can do?" he murmured awkwardly.

"I'm afraid not. Unless you have an immense fortune or an exotic artifact to donate?" She smiled. "No? Then all I can ask of you is that you stay away from Mr. Berne and leave him to more experienced Members. That's the best way you can help,

Sir Grey." She looked hard at him, and her eyes were again steely. "Promise you'll stay out of Berne's way for me."

Arthur swallowed the bitter lump in his throat and nodded.

"I know it's hard. Goodness knows, I'd love to kick the man down the stairs one of these days. But, alas, we can't all have our wishes." She winked. "Very well. Off you go, dearie."

Arthur stood up to leave. Then he stopped and stared. On the wall behind his chair, behind the jackal, was a framed pencil drawing that looked out of place in this fancy, stuffy office. It resembled a curved axe. *An axe, or maybe . . .* Arthur pointed at it. "What's that?"

"Hm? Oh that was old Homer's. All of this was, actually. I never changed the office when I took over. Though I keep telling myself I need to rip out this carpet—it's terribly tacky." She chuckled. "Well, goodnight, then."

Arthur nodded again and left the office. His mind was whirling with ideas. The drawing was a symbol he recognized from his locket and from the wall at Knossos. He suddenly knew what it was. *The Horn.*

So Homer Siegfried had known about it somehow, whether from the palace or from the locket, Arthur had no idea. As he hurried around the hall, Arthur searched his belt pouches and found his Spyglass Squad card. He began scribbling, "Meeting—now—in Odin," and a magnifying glass for his signature.

By the time he reached the lounge, the others had gathered. "I've got something to show you guys," he announced firmly. Griffin gave him a wincing glance, knowing what was coming, but Arthur was determined to go through with it. It was time to trust his friends. He slid the chain over his head and placed the locket on the table between them. The others leaned in to look at it.

"Is that yours?" murmured Idolette. "It's pretty."

"Is it mechanical?" Pernille wondered.

"I don't recognize these symbols," Esmond began, but suddenly he stopped. "No, wait a minute. I've seen that one before . . ."

Arthur nodded. "That's right, Esmond. That is the symbol for the Aurora Cauldron—better known as the Holy Grail. You and I saw it on a pendant in Peru."

Esmond's mouth opened in awe. "Where did you get this?"

"It was my mom's. At least, I think it was. Last year I discovered it's got the Cauldron symbol, and now I know it's got one of the same symbols that's on the Knossos wall—the Horn symbol." He looked meaningfully at them all. "I need to find out why. Why are two symbols for magical objects on this thing?"

"And," Esmond put in, "what does that mean about the rest of these symbols?" He looked sharply at Arthur. "Could it be Mermish? You said that the symbol was on the wall?"

"It was," Arthur confirmed, "but it was one of the symbols Nada didn't recognize, so I don't think it's Mermish."

"Does it have to do with Griffin?" asked Idolette, picking at her purple nails. "Didn't you once say something about finding both of them at your old house?"

"Yeah, but I don't see how it can be related."

Pernille carefully picked up the locket. "Does it have any information inside?"

Arthur shook his head. "It doesn't open."

"Do you have the key?"

Everyone stared at her.

"Here," Pernille said patiently. She pointed to a tiny hole at the bottom. "This looks like a keyhole."

Arthur snatched it back and looked. "You're right!" he gasped. "I'd never noticed before. I always just thought that was part of the designs." His excitement immediately deflated. "But I don't have a key."

"Maybe we could force it open," Idolette offered.

Esmond gave a horrified gasp. "You would risk injuring an obviously ancient artifact!" he cried.

Arthur had to agree. "No force," he said firmly.

"I'm not sure we can do anything right now then," Pernille said brightly. "We don't know what the other symbols are and we can't open it."

Arthur felt let down. But what had he expected? Some sort of miracle?

"I wonder," Esmond asked, "what makes you say this center symbol stands for the Gjallarhorn?"

Arthur shrugged. "It seems right, doesn't it? The shape of it, the sacred object theme, the fact it's on the palace wall." He suddenly remembered why he had gathered them all in the first place. "And it's in Homer Siegfried's old office." He rounded on Idolette. "He was your great-grandfather. Do you know anything about the drawing in his office?"

Idolette shook her head. "Homer died when I was really little. And he and my dad hated each other. I don't know anything about his life, really."

Griffin spoke up. "Homer's involved somehow. They say he died suddenly, that his ghost supposedly roams the island—and you even saw a white ghostly creature—and Homer had a drawing of the Horn. It's all very suspicious."

"Yeah," Arthur muttered, "but what does it all mean?" He stared off. "What did Homer know? And who else knows . . . " Before anyone could answer, however, a shadow fell across their table.

"It's nearly ten o'clock," said the squat dwarf from the bar. "That's curfew for you babies, you might remember. You all better clear out, or there'll be mischief!"

They separated for their own rooms. "Pernille's right, though," Griffin sighed as he settled on his bed. "Without a key, there's nothing we can figure out about the locket. And even if you're thinking this might have something to do with whatever got that Berne guy so unpopular," he added shrewdly, "you promised Madam Siegfried you would stay away from him."

Arthur grunted. "Sometimes I really wish I couldn't understand you," he grumbled.

True to his word, Arthur resisted his constant urges to go anywhere near Rheneas Berne. Though it wasn't like he had much choice. The Initiate Team was working overtime on memorizing parts of the *Kalevala*, making new papyrus pulp to repair old scrolls, comparing Greek and Latin text translations, labeling ancient cities on maps, and writing essays on artifacts from the Gallery.

At the end of September, Arthur and the other Initiates attended the Members' hippocamp race, a brutal contest of speed, treasure collecting, and vicious seahorse fights. Several riders were injured and sent to the Master of Medicines on stretchers.

After that big event, Arthur and more than half the other Initiates, including Idolette, began brushing up on their clue-spotting skills for the upcoming Treasure Hunt.

The Hunt was an extremely difficult race through a vast maze. The Initiates had to find various treasures by discovering and using clues set out in its paths. Outside, the stadium seats had been arranged above a dome of one-way glass so that the spectators could watch the competition, but couldn't give hints to the players. It was all the more competitive because the contestants got to keep whatever they found, and whoever came out of the maze with the most treasure was the winner.

To his own delight, Arthur was the first to find his way out, the most successful in collecting treasure, and the only one who avoided getting burned by dragon fire, being bitten by a snackertack plant, or needing rescue from the flicker swamp by the emergency standby team. When Madam Siegfried handed him the first-place golden fleece, Arthur had to keep from laughing at Pernille, who jumped up and down at her seat while clutching Esmond's arm—which he was trying to wave. As a double reward, Etson, who had come to watch, bought

Arthur the new Dragon Dodge hologram he'd wanted, while telling everyone he saw, "That's my kid!"

Then, before the Initiate Team could relax, they were bombarded with lectures about the SCROLL projects that would end the year. Minister Jung reminded them that their futures depended greatly on the results they got. "These will be assigned at the beginning of December," he warned them. "And after them, Historia's eightieth-year celebration will conclude with the twelfth and final competition, which will be most spectacular: the Bull-Leaping Contest. This in turn will be followed by the opening ceremony for the new Poseidon's View water station at the Winter Solstice celebrations."

But when December rolled in with its colder winds, something happened that finally distracted Arthur from his promise to Madam Siegfried.

Idolette, Pernille, and Arthur, along with Griffin, enjoying their last bit of freedom before SCROLLs began, had been hanging out together in each of their apartment lounges in turn. Esmond (who, Idolette proclaimed, did not know how to enjoy himself) remained in his own apartment. The other three had just gotten told off for play-sword-fighting in Idolette's apartment, and they decided to try Apartment Isis instead. They had just stepped out the door when a particularly chilling shriek arose from the nearby forest. It sounded closer than normal.

"Actually," Idolette shuddered, "I'm really tired. I think I'll stay in." And nothing the other two could say would make her change her mind.

"She won't admit it," Pernille sighed as she walked along the path with Arthur, "but I really think she believes it's Homer's ghost. I keep tellin' her there are no ghosts, but the idea of it bein' *his* ghost just scares her."

Arthur cocked his head. "But Homer was her great-grandfather."

Pernille shrugged. "It's true, but she thinks there's bad blood between him and her because of her da."

Arthur gazed toward the forest. It looked black under the purple-tinged sky. "I never mentioned it," he said slowly, "but the reason I lost the joust was because of some white spirit."

Pernille glanced at him to see if he was joking, and he explained. "Japers," she murmured. "What do you suppose it means? Is there really a ghost?"

"I dunno—"

Griffin suddenly froze, and the other two stopped to look at his twitching ears. Arthur felt goose bumps rise on his arms, as if a cold wind had suddenly blown over him.

"Voices," Griffin murmured.

They listened. "It's not ghosts," whispered Pernille. "It's Madam Siegfried and Minister Jung. An' Steward Cartwright," she added.

The voices were quite close, on the other side of a tall hedge where the path forked toward Apartment Zeus.

"I hate to hear you say it, Madam," came the steward's voice.

"Well, goodness knows, I hate to say it. But it's the truth."

Arthur and Pernille looked at each other, curious.

"Something will come up," Minister Jung offered. "We must believe this."

"I hope you're right, In-Su. But unless a miracle happens before Solstice, I'm afraid Historia won't be here much longer."

Pernille covered her mouth, her eyes wide.

"After the map theft," Madam went on angrily, "we just can't get any investors on our side."

"And what about Lord and Lord Brothers?" the steward snapped. "Have we been entertaining that impertinent Mr. Berne for nothing?"

"We can't depend on them after all these accidents and thefts. Most likely they'll pull out like the rest."

"Still," the Minister put in, "Mr. Berne seems to desire giving Historia a chance."

"But the longer he stays," grumbled Steward Cartwright, "the more bad things happen. I don't suppose Master Jolly is the only one who suspects a connection. . . ."

"August Jolly needs to be more careful what he says," huffed Madam. "I know it's difficult, but we need to stand back until Solstice and see what happens. Make Mr. Berne see Historia as a worthwhile investment. If we can't, we're doomed." She sighed heavily. "As things stand, we'll open the water station as planned, but we might have to cancel the final celebrations. Looks like the Society's eightieth anniversary might be its last."

Arthur, Pernille, and Griffin stood still until the adults wandered out of earshot.

"Oh n-no, Arthur." Pernille wrung her hands. "What's goin'

to happen now Historia's in such trouble an' there's nobody to help?"

"There *is* someone to help," Arthur said forcefully. "Me. I'm not going to let Historia down like this! And neither are you."

"But what could we—"

"You heard Steward Cartwright—Jolly thinks Berne is making the problem. But everyone else is too afraid to do anything about it. Homer Siegfried didn't even want investors in the first place," Arthur muttered, remembering his conversation with Madam Siegfried. He thought hard. "Maybe if we offer our help to Jolly, he can think of something to do to get rid of Berne and save Historia."

"I dunno, Arthur," Pernille said slowly. "He's seemed awfully uninvolved lately. . . ."

"Well, apparently Madam's told him to keep quiet. Not to mention, think of all the trouble Berne's been causing him. That's one reason I really think he'll be on our side." Arthur's mouth twisted in a smirk. "He's gotta hate Berne as much as we do."

15

POSEIDON'S VIEW

The next day, the Initiate Team fidgeted and shifted anxiously in the Translations Room, warily eyeing the wide-mouthed vase that Minister Jung held and waiting for him to give them the dreaded details of their Origins SCROLL. Once they were all assembled, he bowed to them.

"Welcome to the start of your Somewhat Complete Review of Life and Legend for the Department of Origins. If you find you have any questions, I or Master Gamble will be most pleased to help you.

"Your task will give you opportunity to reveal knowledge you have gained during your year of study here. It will be challenging, but if you perform well, you may be able to return to Main Hall after your Initiate Training and be involved in the incredible discoveries we bring to light here."

Behind Arthur, Donovan muttered, "I'd rather have a date

with Medusa." He mimed being turned to stone with a horrified look stuck on his face.

"Each of you," the Minister continued, "will come forward and randomly choose the name of an artifact from this vase. Your task will be to determine the origin country of your artifact and its approximate date, to interpret any language or symbols on it, to determine what legends it is found in, and finally, to describe what process you might use to clean and preserve the artifact. You will have two weeks to complete your task. You may use any resources in the library. Please form a line in front of me."

When it was Arthur's turn to choose from the vase, his fingers found a piece of parchment and unfolded it as he walked away. "Tale of Taliesin," he read. What a relief! He'd already had to memorize parts of this tale and thought he might even have a few notes on it that he'd copied from Esmond. "Well, that won't be too hard."

A few Initiates began their projects right away (Esmond, for example). But most felt there was no rush. Arthur decided to find Jolly on his way to the library. He knocked on the door of the Preservations room, but no one answered. Disappointedly, he turned to leave, then heard the familiar *snap!* of a bubble popping. He spied Jolly walking down the hallway, his nose in a *Historia Today* magazine, not looking where he was going.

"Hey, Jolly!" Arthur called.

The man jumped and looked around like a scared rabbit. "Oh—Arthur," he breathed, wiping his forehead. "It's only you. Everything going all right?"

Arthur cleared his throat. "Uh, not entirely, no. It's about Historia's money trouble. Can we talk?"

Jolly eyed him suspiciously, but he got out his key card and unlocked the Preservations door. Arthur followed him in.

"It's like this," Arthur blurted. "I know Rheneas Berne has been threatening you and trying to get you to give him information he shouldn't have. So if I've figured a way to help Historia get its reputation back and get rid of Berne, could you help?"

Jolly's stare made him look like he'd just been smacked in the head with a frying pan. "Uh . . . " he croaked. "Well, I mean . . . " He broke into a weak smile. "Sure."

"Great! So, here's what we've got." Relieved, Arthur slid his satchel off and began pulling out papers. "This is all to do with the Minotaur and a sacred horn."

"The M-M-M-Minotaur?"

"Right. See, we've figured out that he's probably real and his lair can be reached through some part of the Knossos palace, but we don't know how exactly. I figure, he's guarding the Gjallarhorn, so if we leave that alone, he might not care about anything else. If we can just prove the Minotaur actually exists and prove where the real Labyrinth is, that's sure to get other investors interested in Historia again, right?"

Jolly was staring open-mouthed at the papers Arthur had spread out. "What *is* all this?"

Arthur glanced at the mess and began pointing. "Well, that's a picture of the Minos Supplement Text, and that one's my sketch of the wall at Knossos, and that's the translation of both of them, and, uh, those are notes about some Norse gods. It's all to help prove the Labyrinth and the Minotaur are real." He looked up hopefully.

Jolly clasped his hand to his forehead. "You did all this?" he asked weakly.

"Yeah—me and the others."

"Others? Who else knows about any of this?" He paused. "Not Rheneas?"

Arthur frowned. "No, not him. Just me, Pernille, Esmond, and Idolette."

Jolly looked at him sharply. "Idolette Siegfried?"

"Yeah." Arthur thought he saw the question in the man's eyes. "She hasn't told her grandma any of it, though. Not that she'd listen," he added with an encouraging nod at Jolly. He wanted Jolly to know that even though Madam Siegfried decided to ignore him the Spyglass Sqaud was with him on this.

Jolly seemed to get Arthur's hint. He stared at the papers in front of him. "Arthur . . . " He looked around nervously and lowered his voice. "About Berne . . . I know for a fact he collects exotic creatures, and probably artifacts, too. It was a few years before I came here, but he was in Investigations here at Historia, only they kicked him out because he stole something from us. Now he's back to get revenge. He's going to try to destroy Historia," he breathed, and he looked shocked at the sound of it.

Arthur felt his anger toward Berne boiling up. "So?" he prompted. "Will you help us find the Labyrinth so we can get rid of Berne?"

For a moment, Jolly was silent. "If you're going to get Rheneas Berne out of this . . . " He turned to Arthur with a relieved grin. "Arthur Grey, you can count me in."

Arthur let Jolly hold onto his notes and sketches and hoped the man would be able to make something of it all, because at the moment Arthur had no time.

The following week was grueling. Everyone spent a lot of time in the library or wandering gravely down the Museo Gallery while scribbling notes about their SCROLL topics. By the time the weekend came, no one wanted to think about SCROLLs anymore. So when Gamble offered to take them to preview the Poseidon's View water station, he was met with unusual enthusiasm.

Once they rounded the bend in the path on the east end of the island, the bay came into view, and Arthur could see the spot where all the construction scaffolding had been the first day they arrived. Now an impressive new water station gleamed in the sun. Over it, with hollow eyes staring out across the shining sea, stood the statue of a tall, bearded figure wearing a crown of coral and holding a conch-shell horn in one hand, a long trident in the other. His legs rose up from the real water, and Arthur felt like he was looking at the actual Greek god of the sea, Poseidon.

Inside were rooms full of diving suits and exploration equipment, and parts of the hallways were nothing more than huge, fortified, transparent tunnels that snaked out into the Mediterranean Sea. In the water outside were massive mechanical arms and platforms for examining shipwrecks and other sunken artifacts. One window already overlooked an old, rotten-looking ship waiting to be studied.

"What's that over there?" asked Idolette, peering through Pernille's di-oculars, which she was borrowing (having lost her own spyglass). "It's like a black hole in the sea bottom."

Donovan looked over her shoulder. "It's a lair of water demons," he said in a spooky voice.

Gamble thumped him on the side of the head. "Lesson of the day—if you don't know, don't speak!" He gestured out with his staff. "It's a sea trench, nothing more."

Arthur stared toward the gaping darkness far out in the water. His neck tingled.

"What's . . . in it?" asked Oliver.

"I wouldn't know, would I," snapped Gamble. "Merfolk, most likely. Leastways, they won't let anyone near it."

"Merfolk?" squealed Bridgette.

In the excited babble about merpeople that followed, no one but Esmond, Idolette, and Pernille noticed when Arthur smacked his hand to his forehead with a sudden gasp. "I know why the Labyrinth doesn't make sense—why Theseus would've needed a 'thread' to get out," he whispered excitedly. "It's like a Slinky!" He grinned at them expectantly.

"Er . . . What's a Slinky?" demanded Idolette.

Arthur rolled his eyes. "Come on, you know. It's a toy, like . . . " he struggled for a word, "like a spring."

"Ooh, I think I've seen those," Pernille bubbled. "They're an American toy like long springs, and they can walk down the stairs and—" She cut herself off, her eyes wide. "They're shaped in a *spiral!*" She made a downward spiraling motion with her finger. "That's it, Arthur!"

Esmond glared at them for a moment, then blinked as if a light had just snapped on in his face. "So you're saying you think the spiraling labyrinth symbols are really showing the view of a downward spiral from above? The Labyrinth cave doesn't just go around . . . it goes *down?*" He nodded thoughtfully. "And Theseus would've needed some sort of help-line to pull him up out of the Labyrinth. That would make more sense."

"But where could such a thing be?" wondered Idolette.

Arthur's thoughts were interrupted by Thespia's loud voice. "Isn't there one of these inside the Museo Gallery?" She was pointing toward a section blocked off by yellow construction-warning tape, where a large, round, gold-colored machine stood propped on a tangle of eight flexible legs.

"Yes," Gamble answered as he led the group over for a closer look. "The OctoDiver. We found those in a pair. One is kept in the Gallery, and this one is going to be of service here in the new facilities." He patted the round aquatic machine as if it were a pet.

"Didn't Prometheus say something about how Alexander the Great stole this?" asked Donovan, knocking on it with a resounding clang.

"I'm glad to know your ears work after all, Lisle," Gamble snapped. "Now let's move on. The rest of the site is still under construction until next week, so you won't be able to go any further until the official opening."

They started to follow him back the way they had come. But Arthur paused, noticing that Nada was standing motionless, staring at the submarine as if daydreaming. Then, she abruptly turned and smiled knowingly at Arthur. She pointed at the OctoDiver. "What do you think? I think it resembles a giant octopus," she murmured.

At that, Arthur felt as if he'd received an immense electrical shock, and images crashed in front of his eyes:

Prometheus shouting, "Alexander the Not-so-Great-after-all only found it millennia later and tried to take credit for its creation and use it to steal deep sea treasures . . . ."

Nada murmuring, "The palace of Minos receives the great octopus. Alexander knew the double-axe cornerstone."

Prometheus confiding, "I will tell you who actually found the real cave—it was Alexander, King of the Mycenaeans, creator of the vast Greek Empire."

Liber saying, "But the Horn was stolen back and returned to the Labyrinth."

Nada interpreting, "This symbol is for octopus. This one is for Knossos. That one for a guard."

Pernille reading, "Alexander resolved to undo this knot, so they showed him to its place. However, try as he might, he could not find an end of the knot by which to untie it."

"That's it," Arthur breathed. "Nada!" he exclaimed, grabbing her hand to shake it vigorously. "You're a genius!" He hurried to catch up to the rest of the team, his heart racing. He was bursting to tell the others his theory. He waited impatiently, trying to get the Spyglass Squad away from the rest of the group. But they were too spread out, and he couldn't risk anyone else overhearing.

It wasn't until the end of the day, when they were gathered in a corner of the Isis lounge with mugs of hot chocolate, the others still going on about the water station and end-of-the-year and other unimportant nonsense, that Arthur was able to talk freely.

"It's like this," he interrupted excitedly. "The OctoDiver is the Gordian Knot."

After a brief silence with everyone staring at Arthur stupidly, Idolette gave a derisive laugh. "Do we look thick to you? The OctoDiver isn't made of string."

Arthur was quivering with excitement. "No, but it was used *instead* of string. The Gordian Knot wasn't real—it was just an analogy, a half-remembered story to prove a point, that Alexander the Great cheated! It's like the string that Theseus needed to get out of the Labyrinth. The idea of a string is a trick, it's really the OctoDiver!"

They stared at him. Idolette uncertainly, Pernille curiously, Esmond with a look of having just had half a lemon stuffed into his mouth.

Then, brightening, Esmond raised his hand. "I see," he said, "it's like with the knot. In the stories, the Gordian Knot was supposed to be untied, but Alexander cut it. A hero was supposed to use a line to get out of the Labyrinth, but Alexander used an OctoDiver."

"But," mused Pernille, "that would mean the Labyrinth had to be underwater."

Griffin sat up. "Old Mermish!" he barked.

"Yes." Arthur rushed on, "Remember the Minos Supplement Text—the clue on it was written in the Mermish language. The merfolk would know about it if it happened underwater. And don't forget that in the stories Poseidon was involved—the Greek god of the sea."

They were all silent, their eyes wide.

"The Labyrinth is within our reach," Arthur whispered. He looked at them all.

"But," Esmond interrupted. "None of us knows how the OctoDiver works. It's not as if we could just get in it and find the Labyrinth. There's probably some sort of coordinates or code that it would need."

Pernille brightened. "Like the symbols from the Knossos wall?"

"Hm," said Arthur. "That's an idea. We'd have to compare them to the OctoDiver."

"We should tell Master Jolly," Idolette put in. "He might know how to work the submarine."

"Besides, he has all our notes with the symbols on them," Arthur reasoned, glancing at the throne-shaped clock on the wall. He wanted to go find Jolly right now, but he saw with a sinking sensation that it was nearing curfew. "I guess I'll ask for them first thing tomorrow," he said reluctantly.

Arthur hardly slept all night, he was so excited by the prospect of rediscovering the Labyrinth even as Alexander the Great once had over two thousand years ago. Alexander the Great, a legendary hero—or thief. It didn't matter really, he was a legendary conqueror! To find the maze that only a few people in all of history or legend had ever found—that would be monumental. *And maybe, just maybe, the Gjallarhorn could be there*, Arthur thought with a shiver.

He rolled over and pushed out the image of Liber demanding, "Why do you want the Horn?" He didn't want the Gjallarhorn, he only wanted to help Historia, and finding the location of a mythological site would help for sure, he knew.

The moment he heard the seagulls calling in the morning sun, Arthur jumped out of bed, gulped down a hurried breakfast of yogurt and toast, and ran to the Main Hall entrance to wait for Jolly.

"Master Jolly," he called, barely able to keep his voice low.

Jolly was sleepy-eyed and tousled as they walked down the halls together, but he grew more and more wide-eyed as Arthur explained his theory about how to get to the Labyrinth. Finally, Jolly stopped dead.

"So, I need my notes back," Arthur rushed on, "so we can compare them to any symbols in the OctoDiver."

Instead of looking pleased or excited, Jolly gaped and ran a shaky hand over his face. "Arthur," he groaned. "I can't give you the notes."

Arthur immediately felt a chill run over him.

"I can't give them to you," Jolly said miserably, "because someone stole them from my office last night."

16

STUCK ON A JOURNEY

The news that all of their notes and hard work were missing was a blow to the Spyglass Squad. Arthur knew exactly who had stolen them. But the worst of it was that he could do nothing about it at the moment. He had three days to complete his SCROLL assignment, and he had only finished two of the four tasks. But a burning desire for revenge seared through him every time Rheneas Berne walked by with his smug smirk.

By Thursday evening, Esmond and Pernille had handed in their assignments. Pernille babbled on about the weekend's upcoming ceremonies while Arthur and Idolette tried to concentrate on finishing their own work, with less than a day left.

"I've never seen a bull-leaping," Pernille said. "I wonder if it's dangerous."

"Highly," Esmond snorted. "It was a ceremonial sport on Crete, they say. There's a large painting of it inside the Knossos palace ruins. Imagine bull-fighting, only add having to do gymnastics over those impaling horns without being gouged by them."

Pernille wrinkled her nose. "Maybe they wear armor."

"Doubtful. It would make leaping rather difficult, I should think. Still," Esmond added thoughtfully, "it makes one wonder . . . "

"What about?"

"About the Minotaur." Esmond frowned, staring off. "Leaping over a bull, instead of trying to fight it." He shrugged as if it were nothing.

Arthur glanced up from his work. "That kinda reminds me of what Liber said—brains over strength or something."

Esmond opened his book back up. "Anyway, it's highly probable that there will be injuries."

"I'm sure for the competition they'll make it safe," Pernille put in. "I cannay wait to see it. Did you ever find my di-oculars, Idolette?" she asked.

Idolette flushed. "Oh, er, no. I forgot to look. I'll do it tomorrow for sure."

"That's fine." Pernille smiled. "So long as I have them in time for the events on Saturday. They were my mam's, ya know."

When they decided to turn in for the evening, Idolette waited for the others to get ahead of her before she grabbed Arthur's arm to stop him.

Arthur looked at her worried face. "What?" he demanded.

Idolette wrung her hands. "I lost Pernille's di-oculars!" she wailed. "I mean, I think I know where they are, but . . . "

Arthur shook his head and blew out a breath. "No way."

"I know. I think I left them in the water station." She looked at him pleadingly. "You're good at finding things. Can you help me?"

He knew Pernille was fond of those oculars—her mom's and all. She'd be upset if they were gone. He sighed. "I guess I'd better. It'll have to wait till tomorrow, though." He waved his papers. "Gotta finish SCROLLs."

She nodded. "Tomorrow, then."

It was early afternoon when Arthur finally handed in his project, feeling he could do no better on it. Idolette waited until the actual deadline announcement from Minister Jung before she gave up. By that time it was late afternoon, and the two of them hurried down the long walk to the station, talking about the Labyrinth and the celebrations, or abusing the very thought of Rheneas Berne, but generally avoiding the disconcerting subject of their SCROLLs.

Their trip down to the shore, however, was for nothing. The Members there turned them back due to the construction going on.

"We haven't seen any di-oculars," an impatient, burly Member told them as he shoved them back out the glass doors. "We'll set them aside if we notice them. Now run along and play."

"I'm Madam Siegfried's granddaughter, you know!" Idolette shouted haughtily at him, flinging her matte blue hair over her shoulder. But the man had already shut the doors.

On the way back, Idolette grimly resolved to find Pernille in Main Hall and tell her about the di-oculars being lost. Since Arthur couldn't go without supervision, he suggested Idolette also find Jolly and ask him to meet them about the clues so they could start devising a plan. Idolette agreed and headed off. Feeling a bit frazzled, Arthur returned to his apartment lounge.

Several hours passed, and Arthur found himself in the middle of a losing game of chess against Esmond, with Griffin trying to help. "Move your knight," Griffin urged.

"He's not allowed to tell you how to play," Esmond said with a slightly shocked look. "That would be cheating."

Arthur curbed his sharp reply as Idolette flew into the room, followed closely by Pernille. "What's up?" Arthur demanded, noticing their anxious looks.

Idolette plopped into a chair. "We can't find him," she blurted.

Arthur raised his eyebrows. "Jolly?"

Pernille nodded. "We even asked around, we did, but no one's seen him an' Master Zane said he thought Jolly looked sick earlier today an' then no one's seen him after that. He's just disappeared."

Griffin looked up at Arthur. "Sick? Do you suppose this has anything to do with Berne?"

Arthur eyed the clock on the wall. It was ten minutes till nine o'clock. "I think we should warn the Members at the station to watch out for Berne," he said, rising from his seat. "I don't think he knows the clue about the code, but we can't take any chances. Someone should probably go to Jolly's apartment, too, and make sure he's okay. Because if Berne got to him, he might've cracked and told about the code for the OctoDiver. Maybe check Main Hall again, too. I wouldn't put it past Berne to poison him or something."

They split up, since they were short on time before curfew. Griffin, Arthur, and Pernille ran toward the station, while Esmond headed toward Apartment Zeus and Idolette went to check Main Hall.

When Arthur arrived at the Poseidon's View, only the emergency lights were on and no one was there. "That's not good," Arthur muttered. "Where are the Members who were here earlier?"

"Do you suppose anyone's inside?" Pernille pulled on the door, and to her surprise it opened right up. She looked at the door latch. Her nose wrinkled and brows furrowed. "Look, it's been taped over," she said slowly, "like someone wanted to keep it from locking."

Arthur cocked his head. "Why would anyone need to do that? Wouldn't they have a key?"

Griffin's ears went back. "Unless it was someone who's not supposed to be able to get in."

Pernille held the door open. "Let's see if anyone's here an' we can ask them. Maybe we'll see my di-oculars, too."

"I don't smell anyone," Griffin put in.

The three entered slowly, peering down the long, quiet hall. It felt eerie: a low humming noise throbbed through the floor, dark water moved outside the lower glass walls, and the pale blue glow of the emergency lights cast odd shadows.

"Where did Idolette have the oculars last?" Arthur whispered as Griffin began sniffing along the wall.

"I let her use them when we were looking out to the south," Pernille whispered back. "After that, we went down further."

Arthur looked toward the end of the hall, where the OctoDiver stood in dark shadow behind the yellow construction tape. He tried not to think that the glass window on the front of the OctoDiver looked like a freakish giant eye watching them. At least the window was curtained on the inside, so it was more like a closed eye.

They headed that direction, inspecting the floor and behind cabinets as they went. Finally, Arthur pointed to the OctoDiver. "I see them," he exclaimed. "They're over there."

Sure enough, Pernille's di-oculars were sitting on a panel protruding from the machine, reaching just over the construction tape.

"Oh, thanks, Arthur!" Pernille took the oculars affectionately and placed them in her bag.

Arthur glanced back toward the entrance far behind them and decided it was time to take a small risk. "Listen," he blurted, "while we're here, I'd like to look inside the submarine to see if there are any symbols to control it." He saw doubt cross Pernille's face. "I wouldn't ask if it wasn't important. You're good with mechanics, Pernille. Do you think you could figure out how to get it open?"

Her face brightened. "Maybe." She ducked under the yellow tape to have a look while Arthur kept watch on the door at the other end. "Amazin'!" came Pernille's voice from the other side of the Diver. "I think there's a sort of bilge tank underneath to let in water for submersion and all around the entire surface it's infused with solar power lines an'—"

Arthur blew out an impatient breath. "Pernille, does it open?"

"Oh, right . . . "

After about thirty seconds, there was a hissing of air and grinding of gears, and the back section of the round submarine rose up. Pernille's freckly face appeared in the gap, beaming.

"Great work, Pernille," Arthur breathed. He glanced at Griffin. "Stand guard, okay?" He and Pernille entered the OctoDiver. Pernille's eyes were wide, her lips open in a small O as she gazed around the large space they had entered. It was lit only by the bluish light from the hallway outside. There was room enough for three people to stand without being squished, though they'd have to watch their heads at the edges, where the walls arched inward. On the right was a chair anchored at a curved control console with charts and gold and brass levers, knobs, and panels. Beyond the console was the heavy curtain that blocked the view outside. Along the left wall were hooks holding ropes, lanterns, and other tools. At the back of the room was a closed door.

Pernille sat gingerly on the chair, blinking. "Do you suppose Alexander the Great really sat here?" she whispered.

"Probably," Arthur replied distractedly. He gazed at the controls. "Do you see any symbols?"

Pernille inspected for a moment, then chose a panel to her left and pried it open. Beneath it was a square keypad. Arthur looked at Pernille. "Symbols," she said. "But are they the ones you thought they'd be?"

He studied them. "Yes, some of them are. But there are others, too."

"Do you suppose they're for a password?" asked Pernille. "Or are they like coordinates? I would dearly love to find out how it works. Do you suppose the legs act as a rudder? The solar lines on the outside must power it somehow, but what are they connected to? The Mycenaeans didn't have electricity. . . ." She was already under the console with her goggles down.

Arthur rolled his eyes. "Just hurry up, okay?" He decided to have a look at the closed door at the back. Warily, he gripped the handle and yanked it open. It was just a storage room containing a couple of wooden crates and two large tanks. At the very back was a small, thick, round window looking blearily at the wall outside. There was barely enough space for a person to stand. He shut the door.

" . . . so these levers and wheels must control the diving process, and if this connects to the tendrils outside," Pernille was rambling from the floor beneath the controls, "they could be controlled completely by hydraulics and—"

A low growl startled them both. Griffin leaped inside. "Someone just came into the building."

Pernille scrambled up from the floor.

"Do we have time to get out and hide?" Arthur demanded.

Griffin shook his head grimly.

"Quick," Arthur gasped, "shut that door, Pernille!"

The two of them tugged at the OctoDiver door and pulled

it down. "Not all the way, Arthur," Pernille quavered, "or we'll lock out our air and won't be able to breathe." So they left the metal door open a crack. Pernille was right. After a few seconds, the room felt stuffy. The only light came through the crack from the blue emergency lights.

Arthur snatched his flashlight from his belt and clicked it on. He edged toward the storage door at the back and opened it just in case they needed to hide further. He hoped not—he didn't really want to squish into that closet. *Please hurry up and leave*, he thought.

But Griffin suddenly jumped away from the cracked-open door, his ears back. "They're coming this way," he yipped.

Panic choked Arthur's voice. Wordlessly, he grabbed Pernille's arm and tugged her into the closet. She resisted for a moment, eyeing the tiny space in terror, but gave up as Griffin dived in before them. Pernille squatted behind the large crate, and Griffin lay as flat as he could at the base of the nearest tank. Arthur had no choice but to stand in front of the door, which he held open just a sliver. He switched the flashlight off, engulfing them in darkness. Then they were silent but for their ragged breathing.

Arthur's heart rate doubled as he heard the outer door open with a churning of gears, and a whip of air pulled on the door he held barely open. Blue light filled the space and flashed through the crack in the doorway, blinding him for a moment. Then he felt the sudden vibration of walls and floor around him, and cool air began filling their closet hideout. The OctoDiver had come alive. Arthur pressed his eye to the crack. The outer room was now lit with a yellow glow from the top half of the walls, and the curtain that had blocked the window at the front was pulled back so Arthur could see straight out the clear window into the hallway. Inside the OctoDiver, a hooded person was shutting the large outer door. A Member badge stuck out of a slot in the control console, though Arthur could not make out the name on it. *Whose badge has Berne taken?*

Then the man sat down at the chair and stared at the open panel Pernille had forgotten to shut. Arthur held his breath, hoping Berne wouldn't find the panel suspicious, and hoping even harder that he did not know about the symbol code.

But to Arthur's horror, the man in the chair pulled out Arthur's own notepaper with the symbols from the Knossos wall and began pressing the symbol buttons in the panel. *No!* Arthur thought desperately.

All at once, Arthur was thrown back against the window behind him, causing both his head and left eye to erupt with pain. The door clicked shut as the floor began to rock one direction, then the other, as if it were the back of a large animal that was getting up. When he regained his balance and sight, Arthur turned his flashlight back on. Griffin's eyes glowed eerily from the corner for a moment before Arthur held the light on Pernille. She was pale, and her lips were sealed tight.

"We're moving," Arthur whispered hoarsely, and Pernille merely gave a slight nod. *At least there's air now*, he thought. *This machine must have some way of getting in air once it's turned on.* He wondered if that's what the large tanks were for.

For a few minutes, Arthur could see nothing but dark wall

rushing past the little window as he tried to hold still amid all the jolting and rocking. Then, without warning, the OctoDiver stopped. "What's it doing—" he started to ask. But before he could finish, they were all tossed sideways and then slammed backward as the OctoDiver tipped and dropped onto some hard surface with a loud clank that rang through the walls. Then they began rolling back and forth in chaotic motion. Arthur was just feeling he might very well throw up, when they came to another sudden stop that slammed them against the wall. But with hardly a pause, they were moving again. From his window, Arthur could see a light blaring ahead of them, illuminating the area outside.

"Pernille," he gasped. "Look . . . "

Slowly, she squeezed past the crate to cram herself next to Arthur at the little window. She gave a frightened squeak. "We're underwater!"

All around them, shadowy water pressed them in. They were moving along the sandy floor, passing boulders and sea plants, fish, sharks, water serpents with glowing eyes. A small octopus sailed past.

"We're heading for the sea trench," Pernille breathed.

"Of course," Arthur groaned with a sickening lurch of his insides. "Of course we are . . . "

As they approached the dark, gaping hole in the seafloor, Arthur could see about a dozen creatures zipping out of it. They were mostly human in shape, but they had scaly tailfins for legs, some silvery, some mossy green, a few purply. Their hair was long, feathery, and green-tinged, flowing like dancing seaweed. Some of them had beards. Their skin had a blue tint to it, and their hands were webbed.

"Merfolk," Arthur whispered in awe.

The merfolk waved rusted weapons at the oncoming OctoDiver, but they didn't seem willing to get close to it. Finally, just as the submarine drew near enough that Arthur could see the creatures' eyes—large, protruding, and lidless—the merpeople threw down their weapons and scattered like a frightened flock of seagulls.

Arthur heard a chuckle from the outer room.

"Did you see who it is?" Pernille whispered, shuddering. "Who's driving?"

He shook his head. "But he managed to steal someone's badge," he whispered back.

"We need to send a message," Pernille blurted. She rummaged through her bag, accidentally elbowing Arthur in the cramped space. "Oops, sorry. But we need to let the others know what's happened to us. Maybe they can help." She pulled out her Spyglass Squad card. "I'm going to send a message to Idolette and Esmond."

"Will it work down here?"

"I hope so," Pernille answered with some of her old cheer. "Though I've never tested it from so far away." She began writing on the card. "I'm tellin' them that we're goin' in the sea trench and for them to tell Minister Jung right away that someone brought us here by accident and we can't get out without them an'—" She stopped and looked up with a frown. "Oh,

I don't have enough space for all that. Well, they'll figure it out, I think."

Then they fell into uneasy silence as the OctoDiver entered the sea pit and blackness swept up around them. Arthur held his breath.

The submarine leaned forward for a moment, then rocked slightly to one side for a bit before shifting to the other side.

"You were right, Arthur," Pernille whispered. "We're going down—in a spiral." She looked at him, her eyes round.

From his uncomfortably squashed position on the floor, Griffin gave a small woof. "We're going to the Labyrinth."

They descended for what felt like twenty minutes. Arthur felt clammy and shaky. They were deep in the earth—how deep, he didn't want to think. Just when he was wondering if they would keep going until they hit the center of the planet, the trench leveled out and headed back upward. With a jolting crash, the OctoDiver leaped out of the dark waters and landed on solid, dry rock.

Arthur turned off the flashlight and they listened at the door, holding their breath. The vibrating of the OctoDiver died down, and they heard the outer door give a squelchy hiss as it opened. Arthur began to feel their air dissipating. They needed to get out of this room. He waited a few more moments, then risked pushing the closet door open a crack. Cold, wet air leaked in. He put his eye to the crack, but he couldn't see anything—the room was dark. He opened the door slightly wider.

"Where are we?" whispered Pernille.

"In a cave, I think. Hold on—there's something there." Arthur squinted out the window and saw a light bobbing ahead. It was growing smaller. "Whoever that is took a lantern and is going that way." He strode to the control console. "We've got to get back and tell someone what's going on." He yanked out his Initiate badge and slid it into the empty slot. But instead of the submarine coming back to life like he'd hoped, the slot simply spewed Arthur's badge out, barely missing his face.

Pernille shook her head at the slot. "Apparently, only certain badges will work on it. We're stuck until whoever that was comes back."

Arthur frowned down the passageway, struggling with what to do. Berne had a badge. They needed it. And they needed to stop Berne from doing any more harm. Arthur made up his mind. He reached for a lantern. "Well, then, our only way of escape is getting away, isn't he? We need to find him."

With a shudder, Pernille gripped her satchel. "Shouldn't we stay here till he gets back?"

"What if there's another way out of here and he doesn't come back? Remember, if this somehow connects to Knossos,"— Arthur shook his head—"then we'll be stuck forever. Besides, if that's Berne, he's obviously not supposed to be here, and is probably up to no good. How can we tell the Minister about this if we don't know what Berne's actually doing?"

Pernille blinked uncertainly.

Suddenly, Griffin spoke up. "Does anybody else smell sugary fruit?"

"Huh?" Arthur sniffed. "Sugary fruit? I dunno. A little,

I guess." He looked at Pernille. "Do you suppose anything grows down here?"

She shrugged and gave a weak giggle. "If it did, I don't think it would be anything that smelled nice—more like nauseating fumes."

Arthur lit the lantern and held it up. All three of them immediately gasped.

The light revealed an enormous hallway floored with flagstone tiles, one side of it lined with towering, deep-red columns, the other bordered by a smooth wall decorated with fresco-style paintings, one of a dazzling woman with wild hair, her arms and dress flowing as if in a dance. The hall ended in a flight of eight steps leading upward to a landing, where it took an abrupt right turn.

"The Labyrinth," Arthur whispered, his heart pounding. It really existed, and they were in it. He took out Griffin's camera-collar remote to take photos of the amazing wall. Who was the lady in this painting? Could it be Ariadne, the daughter of King Minos? Abruptly, he shook himself back to the task at hand. Every moment they stood there, their key was getting further away. "Come on."

Griffin sniffed the air again. "I don't like the smell," he growled. "It gives me a bad feeling."

Arthur felt it, too. It was a poisonous sort of sweetness. It reminded him of something. Still, they had no other choice. "Are you ready? Let's go."

They followed the hallway in silence, gazing at the decorated walls and pillars as they walked, occasionally pausing to take a photo. After the sharp right at the top of the steps, the hall took an immediate left. Then Pernille walked into a wall of spiderwebs. "Oops," she exclaimed, brushing web out of her face.

Directly behind them came a grinding noise. They spun around to see a wall sliding into a new place, leaving them in a cloud of dust.

They stared at each other in horror.

"A moving maze," Pernille gasped.

"This is *not* good," muttered Griffin.

"No," Arthur breathed. "Not good at all. If the walls move, there's no way we'll find our way back."

They stood in silence as the gravity of their plight set in. After a moment, Griffin tilted his head. "Hang on. What about your navigational pocketknife?"

Arthur's heart leaped. Of course! It had saved him once before. He fumbled at his belt pouch and found the navigation tool. "Maybe if we keep track of where we go . . . " But to his dismay, the projected map only blinked halfheartedly a few times, gave a discouraging buzz, and disappeared. He tried again with the same result.

"There must be some substance in the walls that blocks the signal it needs to read the area," Pernille offered brightly as she looked around.

Arthur took a deep breath as he replaced his knife, trying not to panic. But he couldn't help thinking that if his map didn't work, it was likely the Spyglass Squad message hadn't either. He frowned at Griffin, whose ears lay back anxiously.

"Okay," Arthur began in what he hoped was a calm voice, "so that doesn't work. Do you think you could smell our way back out if we keep going?"

Griffin snorted. "I don't know what good it would do if there are walls blocking the way we went. Last I checked, none of us could go through solid walls."

"Arthur . . . "

"So we can keep going," Arthur went on, not hearing Pernille, "and possibly never find our way back *or* forward. Or we can stay here and *definitely* never find our way back or forward, but maybe Rheneas Berne might find us . . . "

"And do what?" Griffin asked worriedly.

"That depends on whether or not he sees us before we see him," Arthur frowned.

"You'd better think of some more ideas, because so far yours all stink."

"Arthur!"

He turned to find Pernille inspecting the wall behind them, her pink goggles over her eyes.

"Look at this."

Cautiously, Arthur and Griffin approached. Before they reached her, Arthur stopped and stared in amazement at the two Pernilles crouched at the wall in front of them. "What the—"

She grinned. "It's a reflection!" she said happily. "The wall is a mirror. And it isn't the only one. That one is, too. They make it difficult to tell where you are because the walls appear to be situated differently than they really are, so this didn't actually move—it just let down the mirror over itself—probably when I ran into the spiderweb—which isn't a real spiderweb—it's manmade, amazin' isn't it!— and if we can manage to ignore the distortions an' focus on the true path an' avoid backtracking, we should be able to get on without too much trouble."

Arthur and Griffin gawked at her.

"Do you know the story of the Minotaur?" she asked patiently.

Arthur swallowed and nodded hesitantly.

Pernille smiled. "Then I think we'll be okay." She pointed at the wall, and Arthur realized some of the walls had scenes painted on them. This one was of a small, horned goat-man presenting something to a white star. On the opposite wall was a scene of man wrestling with a bull-faced monster.

"So, you think . . . " Arthur hesitated, looking from one wall to the other. "You think we just have to follow the walls with the right pictures and they'll lead us the right way?"

"It seems so. Do you know which is part of the correct story?"

Arthur scratched his head, thinking. The voice of Liber whooshed through his head: "The Horn was stolen back and returned to the Labyrinth." Finally, Arthur pointed to the left wall. "I'm going to guess the story is running backwards. That's the Horn being returned to the Labyrinth. The next one down is Alexander the Great blowing the Horn." *And what did that do?* he couldn't help wondering.

Holding up the lantern, Arthur led them up and down stairs, around sudden corners, along a twisting and turning backwards-story trail of Alexander the Great retreating up the spiral trench in an OctoDiver, of Alexander taking the Gjallarhorn, of the Mycenaean king arriving in his OctoDiver. They passed several graphic scenes of the Minotaur running people through, a scene of a man painfully transforming into a bull, of that same man taking the Horn and getting caught by trident-wielding Poseidon, of Daedalus building a maze-like palace, of a woman with flowing snakelike hair dancing the path that would become Daedalus's maze, of the god Thor throwing down his mighty hammer (or was it Zeus throwing his lightning bolt?), of the armor-clad Heimdall blowing on the Gjallarhorn, its call bouncing back off the cliffs around him, a vast glowing army gathered behind him.

They were mostly able to ignore the confusing mirrors by avoiding the fake spiderwebs and concentrating on the story Arthur had been piecing together over the entire year. Every now and then, Griffin stood still while Arthur took a photo of the unbelievable scenes. They only made a couple of mistakes that called for backtracking along their route.

At last, they turned a corner and the paintings ceased. The passageway had opened so wide their light didn't even reach its walls.

Griffin walked along sniffing, constantly cocking his ears for sounds. A small *snap!* echoed faintly. At once, he stopped and growled. "We're not alone. And now I know what that smell is."

Arthur raised his light, and a shadow jumped out to their

right. "Who's there?" Arthur yelped as Pernille clutched his arm.

"Well, well," chuckled the stranger. "If it isn't Arthur Grey, here to set me straight again."

"You!" Arthur shouted angrily as he too finally recognized the scent of strawberry bubblegum.

Pernille blinked in surprise. "Master Jolly?"

For, of course, the man who now stood in front of them, grinning nastily, was August Jolly. "That's right, Pernille. It's me." He snapped a bubble.

"But . . . aren't you sick?" Pernille stammered.

Jolly smiled, pleased. "I guess you must have talked to Zane, eh? He's not the brightest sometimes."

"You liar!" Arthur growled. "I trusted you!"

Jolly frowned. "No need to name-call. I'm just trying to look out for myself. At the end of the day, it's every man for himself, Arthur. The Society put me in a tight spot with all its money troubles, and now it's going to help me get back out."

"What do you mean?" asked Pernille.

"Never you mind at the moment."

But Arthur felt like a lightbulb had flicked on in his head. He remembered sitting on a pile of cushions on the Borak Express, Etson Grey frowning at a magazine and commenting that "quite a few Members lost money on a risky project." Then he remembered meeting Master Zane's granddaughter in the confusing streets outside Athens and her saying that Jolly had fancy houses all over Europe. "You lost all your money," Arthur blurted, "and now you can't pay to keep all your stuff."

"I think we have other things to think about." Jolly smiled broadly, a slightly mad look in his eyes. "Your helpful notes got us all this far, but now we've got a bigger mountain to scale, if you get my meaning."

"I get your meaning," Arthur snarled. "You've had my papers this whole time. Nobody stole them—you lied about that."

"Well, I couldn't have you suspecting me when Rheneas Berne deserved the blame so much more. As I said, every man has to look out for himself. But that doesn't matter. What matters is that we all get out of here alive, which means we need to work together."

Arthur glared at him. "Work together? We've been doing all the work. How did you even know we were here?"

Jolly shook his head and clucked his tongue patronizingly. "I saw the open panel in the Diver and heard the closet door close. But I wasn't worried—I knew you were the only other ones who knew about the OctoDiver being involved. You told me so yourself. Even I can put basic clues together," he laughed. "But let's not lose focus.

"I'm sure I don't have to tell you what's on the other side of those doors ahead." Jolly gestured to the end of the room. Their eyes had adjusted enough now to see several wide steps that led to a set of gigantic double doors.

"The Minotaur . . ." whispered Pernille.

A feeling of dread swept over Arthur, making his legs feel like they had turned into rubber bands. Up till now, his attention had been on getting to their captor. He had forgotten that somewhere ahead lurked the great beast of myth. "If you made it this far, you probably know how to get past the Minotaur yourself," he said, trying to sound bold. But he heard his voice crack.

Jolly smiled sarcastically. "You heard me say this before, Arthur—I'm a Preserver, not an interpreter. I can't make anything of these notes that you didn't explain. So if you want to get past that monster, you'll have to work with me."

"Why can't we just go back?" Pernille suggested meekly.

Jolly laughed heartily, as if this were all a great joke between friends. "No one's going back until I get that horn." He smiled at Arthur's pale face. "Oh, yes, Arthur, because that's exactly what I want. It's actually thanks to you that I know about the Horn at all. So for that, you have my gratitude." He nodded pleasantly.

Arthur felt sick to his stomach.

Griffin crouched next to him. "I can take him out," he snarled. "I'll get his badge and we can get out of here."

Arthur shook his head. He didn't want to risk Jolly hurting any of them. He felt queasy. He couldn't believe he'd gotten his friends in trouble yet again. Vaguely, he wondered if Esmond or Idolette had received Pernille's message. But he remembered, with an even further plummet of his insides, that the message couldn't have worked. "What do you want us to do?" he asked, his voice hoarse.

"That's more like it," Jolly grinned. "I need you to figure out what the beast wants in exchange for the Horn."

"You want us to go in there?" Arthur yelped.

"Yep."

"And if it rips us apart?"

Jolly shook his head. "Tsk, tsk. Such morbid thinking. Just try not to make it mad, and you should be fine."

"What if we have to fight it?" Pernille asked, pale. "That's what Theseus had to do in the story."

"Well, you're in luck," Jolly smirked. "According to Arthur's detailed notes, the story of Theseus isn't a true one." He gestured them forward. "It's that, or I have to open the door and invite him to come out here and devour you. But I'm a nice guy. I don't want to hurt anybody. I'll let you pick for yourselves."

"That's really nice of you," Arthur snapped. Renewed anger shook his whole body.

Jolly merely shrugged.

Arthur stood still, breathing heavily, trying to calm himself. There was no escape. His anger, his fear, his regrets were all nothing. There was only the set of doors before them. He nodded at the other two, and they shakily strode forward to the steps ahead. He wished painfully that he'd thought to ask Liber a lot more questions. Too soon he was standing before the giant bronze doors, Griffin and Pernille on either side of him. His heart pumped furiously as his eyes darted over the door, trying to find something helpful in its engraved images.

He knew the doors were going to open when he pushed on them—there was no way he could be lucky enough for them not to. The question was, once they opened, what would be in there . . . and what would it do to them? He searched his brain for any memory of Liber's conversation, for any information from the piles of library books he'd gone through, for any of

Esmond's random points on the Minotaur—anything at all that might help him deal with what awaited them.

"We don't have all day," Jolly called impatiently. "Are you going, or do I have to take matters into my own hands?"

Arthur closed his eyes and reached out. He pushed lightly on the doors, and they glided inward without a sound.

17

RELEASE OF ASTERION

Arthur opened his eyes, but quickly closed them again and ducked as a cloud of screeching black objects flew at them. *Bats.* At the opening of the door, more than a dozen torches sprang to life along the walls, lighting a large room with enormous columns of deepest red. Tiled over the expanse of the floor was a large eight-point star with a smaller star at its center. Standing upon the center star was a pedestal displaying an object that gleamed in the torchlight. Arthur couldn't see what it was, but he had a good idea.

Before any of them could even think about moving, the room began to rumble, and between them and the pedestal, a tile slid back to reveal a hole in the floor. Arthur could do nothing but gape as a monstrous, horned bull head rose out of it, followed by a hugely muscled body kneeling on the tile that pushed it up into the room.

The Minotaur.

Even Griffin cowered. There was no way they could fight such a creature. It would rip them apart without even blinking.

As if she had read his mind, Pernille gripped Arthur's arm, her eyes wide in her pale face. She licked her lips and whispered, "Don't try to fight it. Yesterday, Esmond put it right, he said, 'Leaping over a bull, instead of trying to fight it.' Even Liber telt ya, 'brains over strength.' An' I think they're right."

Arthur barely heard. He was too busy staring wild-eyed ahead.

Before them, the beast rose from his knee. Hot, stale animal breath exploded from his nostrils with great grunts, blasting their hair back and making them shudder in abhorrence. He was tall—Pernille could've stood on Arthur's shoulders and still only reached the Minotaur's chest. All three of them standing side by side weren't even as wide as he was. His body was like a man's, only with sinewy muscles like a full-grown bull. He wore no clothes except for a skirt around his waist that reached to the middle of his thighs.

Arthur felt paralyzed, staring in horror at the monster, his stomach churning, his whole body quivering. He couldn't even swallow. His eyes were glued to the part-man, part-beast creature that stared back at them with dark, animal eyes.

Then the Minotaur opened its mouth, and a voice, deep and gravelly and oppressive, bellowed out of it.

Beware stranger, lest your greed
Lead you to your death.

Patiently draw in your breath
And listen carefully.

Riddles three now answer me
Then I'll ask one more.
Correctly heed all answers four
And truth will set you free.

The voice stopped, and Arthur felt as if a spell had been broken. He was able to move. He licked his lips and tried to swallow. For a moment, he was frozen only by amazement that the beast spoke in their own language—or was it some magic in this place that allowed them to understand it? But he had to think. So they had to answer riddles—four, by the sound of it. He wasn't sure if that would be any easier than a fight. But he looked at Pernille and at Griffin and gave a weak nod to the beast.

Still staring at them, the Minotaur opened his mouth again, and again his frightening voice grunted.

What starts a master down a trail
is not what brings his end.
It's one step further that he finds
this monster that's within.

Arthur sucked in his breath. Incredibly, those words had a familiar ring to them. *A man may start down a road with good intentions . . .* Like a vision, it came back to him—his dream and what the green-cloaked woman had said. He knew the answer.

"Greed," he blurted without realizing it, and his voice sounded tiny in the cavernous room.

Next to him, Pernille gave a squeak, and terror crashed over Arthur. He looked swiftly at the Minotaur. What had he done? What was the punishment for a wrong answer? Sweat seeped from his forehead. Would they be attacked?

But, to his immense relief, the monster didn't advance on them. Instead, he gave one slow nod with his great bull head and took a step backward, away from them. Then he spoke again.

> *Much have I seen, much have I lost,*
> *Much have I learned from the gods.*
> *And you should fear*
> *She who deals*
> *Only in what you deserve.*

Arthur took a deep breath, his relief sucked away. This riddle had nothing to do with his dream. He'd had a brief hope that it might be that easy. But no. It was something to do with gods—or a goddess, more specifically. Who was a goddess who gave what you deserve? He mentally shuffled through the myriad of god and goddess names he'd had to memorize over the entire year, searching for one that fit. Then, out of the corner of his eye, he was distracted by the sight of Pernille stepping forward.

She blew out a shaky breath. "Justice," she said firmly,

and looked hopefully at the beast. They waited, not daring to breathe.

The Minotaur gave another slow nod and took another step backward to stand right in front of the pedestal. Again he spoke.

> *I go out as one, but I return as many.*
> *I crush men, bringing disaster to my master's enemies.*
> *I cut through earth and air,*
> *And in water am most powerful.*

One thing that could become many things? Arthur scratched his head. Maybe an army? An army was one thing made of many people. And armies could bring disaster. *But they aren't most powerful in water*, he thought with a grimace. What could it be? He felt a wet nose push his hand. He looked down at Griffin.

The dog blinked at him earnestly. "The pictures on the walls," he whispered.

The pictures? Arthur tried to pull the fresco scenes up in his mind. He remembered Heimdall's horn blowing, its echoes bouncing off the walls; a god slamming down a mighty hammer. . . . Then he realized. This wasn't a one-answer riddle—it was three answers.

He balled his fists and faced the Minotaur. "The horn blast of Heimdall goes out as one voice," Arthur said, "but it comes back with many echoes. The hammer of Thor crushes men." He stopped. With a jolt, he realized he only knew two of the answers. What was the third thing? What could cut through earth and air and was powerful in water? He turned desperately to Pernille.

Her face was pale, but she actually smiled. "And the lightning bolt of Zeus can cut through earth and air, and its electricity travels through water," she said.

Again, the Minotaur nodded slowly and took a step back so he was beside the pedestal. Arthur's skin prickled. Three riddles so far—they had answered three of the four riddles. This was beyond his wildest hope. They just might get out of this alive, after all.

> *I can make mountains of your molehills*
> *or cut your mountains down.*
> *I can open doors or close them.*
> *I can serve you now or later.*
>
> *I can take you right or left.*
> *You can face me or disregard me,*
> *But you will always have me.*
> *Though I will always haunt your past,*
> *still I will always be before you.*

To Arthur's dismay, Pernille looked inquiringly at him. He shook his head. *Make mountains or cut them down.* What could do that? *Serve you now or later.* So something that was strong but could serve. *Though I will always haunt your past, still I will always be before you.* What could be behind and in front at the same time? Arthur felt a drop of cold, clammy sweat slide down the side of his face. He glanced at Pernille and could see that her face was screwed up in desperate thought. But he just had no clue. He felt a terrible turn in his stomach. What would happen if they couldn't answer?

Then an angry voice resonated behind them, echoing off the pillars and walls.

"Choice!"

They spun around to see Jolly standing in the doorway. His face was a mixture of anger and fear and pride. "The answer is choice," he repeated. "Though it's a lie."

The Minotaur took a final step back so that he was now behind the pedestal, no longer blocking it.

"Sometimes you really don't have any choice," Jolly hissed as he stopped beside Arthur and Pernille. "Sometimes you're forced to do what you don't want." He grabbed Arthur's arm and shook him hard. "Go up there and get that Horn." Then, his eyes gleaming madly, he released Arthur and pulled a knife from his belt and flipped it open. "Or I won't have a choice." He grabbed Pernille and looked threateningly at Arthur.

Think! Arthur told himself, but his mind was a whirl of confusion. He felt dizzy. *Think—save Pernille!* Arthur backed away toward the pedestal. He glanced at the Minotaur, but the creature had not moved. *Think . . .* Arthur stepped slowly toward the star at the center of the floor until he could see the Horn that rested on the pedestal. It was breathtaking, white like a pearl from the sea, with carvings over it of lightning bolts and chariots and clouds and waves. He could feel ghostly tingles reaching out from the beautiful relic, almost like voices were whispering from within it. But before he could do anything other than look at it, Pernille's voice rang out behind him.

"Don't!" she shouted. "Power, greed, justice, and choice, Arthur! *Correctly heed all answers four, and truth will set you free.* If we're greedy and choose to take the power of the Horn, Justice will be right behind. Think of Alexander the Great! He died soon after taking the Horn, and the power he tried to gather completely fell apart."

Arthur stopped. He stared at the Horn resting on its pedestal. It could help save Historia, he was sure of it. *But greed can make one go too far,* a voice reminded him. The green-cloaked lady with the locket had said that. Arthur knew it was true. How many heroes had taken things that they didn't need? What always happened to them? Heracles, Odin, Alexander the Great? They all brought destruction—to themselves, to their friends, to whole nations.

Arthur shook himself, suddenly aware that he was in the Labyrinth, sweat dripping down the sides of his face. He looked over his shoulder at Griffin. Even Alexander the Great hadn't been able to change his fate once he took the Horn. Arthur clenched his fists, finally thinking clearly. Jolly was greedy, but he wouldn't really hurt Pernille, Arthur knew that now. He forced his body to turn away from the pedestal and its prize. "The fact is, I *do* have a choice," he blurted angrily. "And so do you. I won't take it."

For a moment, Jolly stared at Arthur with a dazed expression. Then, all at once, his eyes went wild with rage and fear.

To Arthur's shock, Jolly looked almost as much like an animal as the monster behind them.

With a scream, Jolly shoved Pernille aside and rushed at Arthur, who tumbled out of his way. Jolly lunged at the pedestal and snatched the Horn with both hands, knocking over the marble stand. It barely missed Arthur's head as it crashed to the hard floor, exploding into a hundred glistening pieces. Arthur flung his arms over his head as hard chunks pelted him.

"I choose success," Jolly breathed heavily. "I choose riches. Now get out of my way!" He turned and fled.

"Stop!" Arthur shouted, jumping up. He looked helplessly at Pernille and then at Griffin. Before he could turn his gaze to the Minotaur, the floor shook beneath his feet, throwing him back to the ground. It rumbled again, and one of the tall red pillars shook and teetered. "Look out!" Arthur gasped as the towering pillar began falling, bringing a chunk of rock the size of a house down from the ceiling.

"It's justice!" came Pernille's frightened shout.

"We've got to stop Jolly!" Another deep rumble threw them down, and to Arthur's horror, the quake wrenched open a crack in the tiled floor just inches from his feet, separating Arthur, Pernille, and Griffin from the doorway and escape. He tried to get up, feeling like a surfer on a wildly tossing ocean.

The room shook violently again, and Arthur stumbled, struggling to stay away from the gaping hole. "Pernille!" he shouted. She was several feet behind him and could not get up to help him. He looked back to find Griffin, but the ground beneath him gave a great lurch and he lost his balance on the tile. He was flung forward, flailing as he tried to grab some-thing—anything—but it was too late. The yawning dark hole was swallowing him into its depths. . . .

To his astonishment, his body came to a painful jerking halt, suspended at the brink of the gap. He looked up, and his mouth fell open. A broad-chested man clad in nothing but a pleated skirt held Arthur by the scruff of his shirt. The Minotaur—only he was *human*. But how? The stranger gave an effortless tug and heaved Arthur onto the solidness of the tiled floor.

"How did you . . . " Arthur gasped, "What happened to your . . . I mean, what did . . . " He stared at the stranger's deep eyes. There was still something slightly untamed about them.

"Arthur!" barked Griffin as he made his way toward them, with Pernille steadying herself against his back.

"Who are you?" Pernille goggled.

The large man looked down at his own hands, as if ponder-ing that very question himself. "Asterion was my name once," he muttered, and his voice was deep and hoarse. "I tried to steal the Gjallarhorn and was punished, turned into a horned beast-man to guard what I had tried to steal. I was the Minotaur, though I had no memory of it until now." He looked at Pernille and bowed his forehead to the ground. "You put together the clues of the riddles, connecting the four answers together, and caused the spell to break. My mind is now free from my imprisonment."

For a moment, Arthur, Griffin, and Pernille merely stared.

Then another fierce rumble shuddered through the room, and another piece of the ceiling collapsed at the other end.

"Quickly," exclaimed Asterion. He grabbed Pernille's arm. "The spell is broken and the magic is leaving this place. It is destroying itself. Come! The gap is widening. I will throw you across so you may escape from this place."

"But—" Pernille began. She had no say in the matter, though, because the huge man picked her up as if she were no heavier than a kitten and tossed her across the fissure in the ground. She landed unsteadily on her feet and braced herself with her hands against the floor, then glanced over her shoulder at them in shock.

Without a word, Asterion grabbed Griffin and heaved him across the way.

But when he turned to Arthur, Arthur held up a hand. "What about you?" he demanded. "How are you getting across?"

"There is no time," the man said, suddenly weary. "I cannot live now. Already, I feel my strength leaving me. My human body won't survive the ambrosia that has kept me alive for so long. But listen to me now, and I will tell you how to escape. You must follow the paintings with axes—this is a shortcut, and it will take you to the faun, to Liber. He will know of the fall of the Labyrinth by now and will meet you and take you to the Knossos palace exit. Tell him that I remember his family's kindness to me, and I thank him."

Arthur stared at the man in horror. He seemed much smaller than he had a few moments ago. "But," Arthur began.

Asterion grabbed Arthur's shoulders. "It is finished!" he

roared, and with his last strength, he flung Arthur away from himself, across the widening gap in the floor.

For a wild moment, Arthur saw nothing but pitch black beneath him, felt nothing but a blast of heat from below. Then it was past, and he landed hard on the rumbling tile. He felt frozen in his kneeling position, shock running through his bones. Suddenly, Griffin was yanking at his pant leg, pulling him up. Dazed, Arthur looked back across the crumbling floor. Asterion was on his knees, shrunken, weak, coughing. Arthur looked up at a noise and saw a huge chunk of ceiling falling away, right above Asterion. He started to shout, but Pernille grabbed his hand and yanked him from his stupor, toward the doorway.

The three ran down the halls, leaping stairs and crashing into the walls of the writhing Labyrinth, narrowly avoiding the giant boulders dropping around them. They kept their eyes open for any scene with the Labyrinth axe painted into it and never spoke, but only pointed whenever they caught sight of an axe. Their only sounds were heavy panting and an occasional squeal or shout when danger barely missed them.

They had just reached the opening of several branching hallways when a voice startled them from the right. "You have very little time."

Arthur whirled around and saw the little goat-man waiting for them, clutching a lantern in his extended hand.

"Ah, why am I not surpri-hi-hi-hi-hi-sed," Liber bleated when he saw Arthur's face in the light.

"I can explain," Arthur gasped.

"No time. Where is the Minotaur?"

Pernille pointed behind. "His name is Asterion, he turned into a man," she blurted. "He said he couldn't live anymore and helped us get out, but . . . but . . . " she faltered.

Liber bowed his head in sorrow. When he lifted it, there were great tears pooling in his yellowish goat-eyes. "Then it is finished. Come, we must escape from here before we are trapped." He turned to lead them down the right-hand hall.

A sudden tremor rippled through the ground, and Arthur fell back. Pernille stumbled into the wall. Above them, Arthur saw a red-stained pillar tipping, crashing over sideways, right toward where Pernille had fallen. *Help her!* he thought—but the words didn't have time to reach his lips.

The pillar collapsed with an enormous boom, dust and debris flying everywhere. Arthur scrambled back, coughing and choking. "Pernille!" he hacked.

"I'm okay," Pernille's voice squeaked. "Griffin pulled me back just in time." She paused. "Can you get over this?"

Arthur pushed against the column blocking the way to the right tunnel. It wouldn't budge. He was separated from the others and the way out. "Liber!"

"Listen to me-hee-hee-hee-hee," came Liber's voice. "I will take these two on. There is one other way of escape, though it's longer. It will take you back the way you came in. You must hope your ride in is still there."

Arthur could hardly breathe. He had nearly forgotten about Jolly and the Horn. Had the lying backstabber escaped already?

"Take the center hallway," Liber continued. "Follow

the scenes in order. Go quickly. Don't stop—or you'll be de-heh-heh-heh-heh-head."

"Liber," Arthur blurted, desperate to honor the Minotaur's last request—in case he didn't make it. "Liber, Asterion said he remembers your kindness and he thanks you!"

The faun gave an echoing bleat. "Go now!"

"Please get them out safely," Arthur shouted, and he turned and sprinted down the hall. He glanced at the painted scenes on the walls, making sure to follow the right path. He had to get to Jolly. He had to stop him!

Finally, he recognized the first hallway. He was almost to the place where the OctoDiver was parked. He ran harder, ignoring first the sharp pain in his side and then the throbbing in his eye. Before he knew it, he was splashing into several inches of water that filled the tunnel. He passed the painting of the dancing woman—it was cracked in half. Ahead, he could just make out the shadow of the Diver in the open cavern. The water had risen around it. Clambering into the open door of the OctoDiver was Jolly. And he had the Gjallarhorn.

Arthur pushed through the water rising first to his knees, then up to his waist. "Stop!" he shouted desperately.

Jolly saw him. With a hardened look, he grabbed the handle for the door to shut it. But it was difficult to do with one hand gripping the Horn and the Diver rocking as it rose with the still-swelling water.

Arthur lunged and grabbed Jolly's foot, splashing water as he fell forward. The man's hand slipped, losing its grip on the door handle. "You're stealing!" Arthur shouted at him, not letting go of his jerking foot. "You're following the wrong path—you're making the wrong choice!"

"I don't . . . have a . . . choice!" Jolly shot back, still trying to shake Arthur off his foot.

"We always have a choice," Arthur snapped. "Didn't you listen to the riddles?"

Jolly didn't answer, and Arthur suddenly felt a sharp whack to his head—Jolly had hit him with the Horn. Arthur fell back with a splash, and water sloshed over his head. He choked, struggling to right himself. Smearing back his wet hair, he bobbed around, looking for Jolly.

The man was again working on closing the door. He used two hands this time, while still trying to hold the Gjallarhorn. But just as he jerked the door down far enough to shut easily, his hand, wet from the sloshing water, lost its grip on the Horn. The ivory relic hit the waves and began to sink.

"No!" Jolly roared in fury. But he could not get his prize without leaving the safety of the OctoDiver—the flood was already threatening to sweep the submarine away. He looked wildly at the place where the Horn had disappeared and then at Arthur struggling to stay above the water. "See what you did!" he screamed. "Now no one will ever find it again. And you lost your life for nothing at all!" He slammed the door shut with a clanging crash.

Arthur felt numb as he watched the Diver's lights sputter on and its legs begin to rotate into position. Jolly was going to leave him there to die. He could not escape without the OctoDiver. In a last effort to do something—anything but sit here paddling pointlessly for dear life—Arthur heaved a great breath and dived.

The greenish water was flecked with debris from the crumbling cavern, but he could just see the white of the Horn as it sank. He swam for it. By the time he reached it, his lungs were burning for air and his eye seared in pain. His fingers closed on the end of the Gjallarhorn and he flipped around, trying to make his way back up. But the water kept going and going all around him—no direction was up. He could barely see a thing, and he was in terrible pain. Agony filled his lungs, shot through his muscles, blazed in his eyes. He didn't think he could hold his breath anymore.

He didn't have any thought to spare for the large dark creature that suddenly appeared in the bleary water, heading straight for him. The last thing he knew was that he was a goner.

18

THE DONATION

Light pierced Arthur's shut eyelids. He ached. His chest felt on fire, and his sides and eye ached. He realized he was coughing and water was spewing out of his mouth. But he could breathe. He tried to speak, tried to ask what was going on, but all that came out of his mouth was more water.

"Lie back, boy. One of these days you'll stop making me run around trying to rescue you."

That cawing voice was familiar. *But how . . . ?*

He struggled to open his eyes. A sliver of light blinded him. He blinked.

"He's going to be okay, right?" came a girl's anxious voice. "I told you we had to hurry."

"I'm sure he'll be so fine, he'll be back to mischief before he has time to learn his lesson." There was a pause. "What do you think, Grey? Can we catch that two-timing, good-for-nothing scoundrel?"

A third voice answered. "You bet. These things have pressurized cables installed. I'll just tangle up his rotors and he won't be able to go anywhere."

Arthur blinked again, and the shadowy figures began to clear up into three people. "Idolette?" he coughed. "Gamble? Dad?"

"Oh, Arthur, you are so stupid!" shrieked Idolette, throwing her arms around him, nearly choking him. "Do you know you almost died? You were just floating in the water and there was barely enough space left in that tunnel to open the door without getting flooded! We were almost too late, though we really tried to hurry, right? It took me forever to find Gamble when we got Pernille's message, and you wouldn't believe how slow he was about it. But luckily your dad was there and he knows about Experiments stuff, right? So he got the OctoDiver from the Museo Gallery running and we came to find you."

Arthur pushed her arm off and leaned up on his elbows. "What about the others?" he gasped. "Pernille and Griffin might still be inside!"

Gamble raised a bristly eyebrow at him. "Esmond told us about a possible entrance from the Knossos palace. He and Zane took a Transportal that way to check it out. I sent Gatriona with them."

Arthur sat up, panic seizing him. He gazed around, realizing his hands were empty.

"Looking for this?" Gamble asked. He held up the ivory horn.

With a sigh of relief, Arthur collapsed back to the floor. He immediately sat up again, anger rushing through his whole body like a tidal wave. "And what about Jolly?" he spat.

"Oh, don't worry about him," said Etson from the control console. "We had to pass him on the way down to find you, but we've caught up now, and it looks like he's broken a rotor and his speed's gone down. Now we've got that punk right where we want him. Everybody hold on."

A sudden jolt shoved the OctoDiver backward, and a cable shot out through the water at the other OctoDiver in front of them, entangling itself in the rotating legs and causing the submarine to tumble wildly.

"Bingo!" Etson exclaimed. "We'll just tow him up, shall we?"

"Carry on," snapped Gamble.

Idolette shook her head, her blue hair swaying. "I never would've thought it, right? Jolly? He was always so nice. How could he do this?"

Gamble cast them a sidelong glance. "Lesson of the day. Can't have your head full of money and full of brains at the same time." He frowned sourly and said nothing more.

They reached a deserted shore of Crete, where they found Zane waving to them. "I've got them here. Everyone is well," he called. His face was set with an unhappy mixture of anger and grave sorrow. "I take it all back," he added quietly to no one in particular, "I did not really want to be here to see his betting habit go too far."

Liber was there, standing back in the shadows. Esmond looked pale and only nodded weakly at Arthur, but Pernille jumped on his sopping wet figure, squeezing him tightly. "You're all right!" she squealed. "Though you're a bit wet," she added, looking down at her own clothes, now damp from hugging him. "What happened?"

"Tell you later," Arthur grunted, rubbing Griffin's head. "Are you guys okay?"

"Yeah," said Griffin. "Thanks to that Liber character. But it was all I could do to keep going through all the pain I felt. What was happening to you?" he demanded.

Gamble interrupted. "You lot should know," he said grimly, "exactly what happened." He frowned toward the OctoDivers, where Etson and Zane were now busy tying a wild-eyed Jolly up. "You see, we found out that Jolly gambled a lot of money in some of Historia's investments."

"And then Historia began having all the investing trouble," Esmond guessed.

"Right. So he lost most of his money. He's always liked living the high life—he's got three houses across Europe, and he likes to party. So the loss hit him hard. But that's not it. Since he's one of the first to see artifacts, he began giving tips on where they'd be taken next or even sold their secrets. On top of that, to make up for the money he lost, he made a deal with some explorers. He'd give them information on an untouched drowned treasure site if they'd pay him. But it all went wrong when the explorers used dynamite and ended up blowing a hole right into the Minotaur's lair. When they discovered there was a monster down there and one of their men was badly injured, they refused to pay Jolly for his information and even threatened to find out who he really worked for. So he had to come up with new ways to get his money. He even went so far as to try to convince Rheneas Berne to pay him for information."

Gamble thunked his staff against the ground as Etson joined them. "He thought it wasn't fair, and so he made a foul choice to make it more to his liking." He frowned at them all. "Let this be a lesson to you. Easy money is never free. There'll always be a price to pay."

Etson sheepishly scratched his neck. "Speaking of Berne, he knew Jolly had something up his sleeve and tried to trick Jolly into giving it up so he could tell Madam Siegfried. Today, Berne found a bunch of papers in Jolly's office and realized that Jolly was after a relic horn. He advised us to keep an eye on Jolly and even suggested he might be using Arthur. But by then it was too late—no one could find Jolly."

"We came in right during their meeting," Idolette interrupted. "Gran, Minister Jung, Master Gamble, Master Zane, and Minister Grey were all in Gran's office. We'd gotten the Squad message, and we told them what had happened."

"So we came as fast as we could," Etson finished. "And not a scratch too soon."

From behind, they could hear Jolly shouting, "I had to do it—I had no choice!" Zane was none-too-gently dragging him back into one of the OctoDivers. Gamble turned to Etson.

"Zane will take him away in that one. You taking the other one back?"

Etson nodded. "And you've got a Transportal to get the kids back, right?"

Gamble held up the device.

Etson ruffled Arthur's hair and waved to the others. "See you back at base, then."

"Let's get ready," Gamble snapped, throwing the Transportal down.

As the rest queued up beside Gamble, Arthur quickly turned to find the faun, who was still backed away from the others. "Liber," he began, holding out the Gjallarhorn.

Liber stepped forward and shook his head. "As the great Socrates said, 'He who isn't content with what he has, wouldn't be content with what he'd like to have.' I don't need it." He shrugged. "The girl Pernille told me everything that happened. You won it fairly. And what's more, you put together the warning clues and set Asterion free." Liber eyed him. "Apparently, Prometheus was right about whatever he saw in you. Still, you're more of a troublemaker than I'll ever be." He gave a bleating laugh that made Idolette shriek behind them.

Arthur looked uncomfortably at the Horn in his hand. He thought he had learned its lesson. You should think before you act, because nothing—not power, not money—was worth making other people suffer. Brains over strength, giving over greed, as Liber himself had said. "What are you going to do now that the Minotaur—I mean, Asterion—is gone?" he asked.

"Meh." Liber shrugged. "I don't like selling pottery much.

I like dancing, though. Perhaps I can be a dance instructor somewhere with cooler weather?" He grinned.

"Whatever you do," Arthur advised with a smile, "make sure you are kind to your guests."

Liber gave another bleating laugh. "Ah yes, I do love to have guests!" He surveyed Arthur fondly. "You're a good one—for a human," he teased, "and even for being one of *them*. Just never let it go to your head. And don't worry, your secret is safe with me."

"Thanks for all your help," said Arthur. He stuck out his hand, but Liber skidded forward and wrapped him in a wooly hug. Then the faun leaped back and skipped off into the darkness of the night, his little cloven feet clacking against the hard ground.

"You coming, Grey?"

Arthur traipsed to the Transportal, where the others had already disappeared and Gamble waited, tapping his foot impatiently. "Yeah," said Arthur, and he stepped through.

They were met outside the Transfer Depot by Madam Siegfried herself, as well as Minister Jung. Madam was relieved that everyone had survived, though when she cast her gaze on Jolly a short while later, there was nothing but pure loathing in her eyes.

After Pernille and Arthur gave a brief account of their side of the story, Madam Siegfried let them go. Gamble took Pernille to the Master of Medicines to get her cuts and scrapes bandaged, and the others were released to return to their apartments. Arthur, however, hesitated. Now that he was safe again, a feeling of shame had begun to creep over him like a dark cloud.

Madam took a few steps down the hall and then paused. "Why, Sir Grey," she said gently, "is something wrong?"

"It's just . . . " Arthur muttered. "It's just that I let you down."

Madam Siegfried pursed her lips. "Actually, in a way, it was I who let you down," she admitted with a heavy sigh. "I let all of Historia down. I was so busy feeling sorry for our end that I didn't pay attention to who was actually ending it." She looked sadly at him. "After all this time, I should've known better than to fall for the illusion that there was nothing I could do. I wanted things to go on being the way they always were. I should have paid more attention to the clues you tried to give me. I'm sorry I let you down."

Arthur felt his ears growing warm. Somehow, getting an apology from Madam Siegfried seemed an embarrassingly indecent thing. "Is Historia still in trouble, then?" he asked quickly.

"I'm afraid so. Rheneas Berne has confirmed that Lord and Lord Brothers is still interested in supporting, but I just don't see how we can turn our situation around. It's a great pity the Labyrinth has been destroyed."

Griffin nudged Arthur's leg and cocked his head meaningfully.

Arthur's eyes widened. He looked at the ivory horn still clutched in his hand and then dug the camera-collar remote out of his belt pouch. "Madam Siegfried," he said slowly. "What if the Society found an ancient relic and could publish a story about its finding?"

Madam eyed him curiously. "Well, that would be a happy day, but . . ."

Without another word, Arthur held out the two objects. "Here's the Gjallarhorn. I'm donating it to the Historia Society. You can ask Prometheus the Centaur, and he'll tell you all about its history. And that remote has pictures from the Labyrinth. You can use those, too."

Madam took the Horn and remote gently, sputtering her thanks and amazement and confusion. Arthur merely grinned. "Tomorrow is the celebrations and the opening of the Poseidon's View, right?"

"Well, I . . . yes, I suppose it must be . . . it can be now . . ." She was still staring back and forth between the Horn and the remote in disbelief.

"Okay. See you then." Arthur and Griffin grinned at each other and headed toward their apartment.

There wasn't much left of the night, and tired though they all were, Arthur, Griffin, and the rest of the Spyglass Squad just couldn't sleep. They exchanged messages on their Squad cards (Pernille from the medicines ward) until daylight began creeping over the sea with golden glitter. At last, they each said goodnight—good morning—and drifted off to sleep for a few hours.

The end-of-year celebrations were a spectacular event.

When Madam Siegfried came out in a festive hat to announce the day's agenda, she put in a bit about Arthur donating the Gjallarhorn to the Society and said she was sure they would be able to recover from their money troubles.

They began with the much-discussed Bull-Leaping contest. That was a slight disappointment, though, because the bull did nothing but nap during the entire contest, not caring the least that half a dozen people were trying to look brave as they leaped over it.

Afterward, Minister Jung introduced the Initiates' graduation ceremony. Opening a scroll in front of the audience, he announced in his calm, uninterested voice, "Having completed their year of Initiate Training, these Initiates are now awarded their Medal of Origins.

"Nada Bhaksiana, Miriam Hummad, and Oscar Verda."

The clapping of many people echoed around the stadium and reminded Arthur of the Gjallarhorn.

"Esmond Falvey, Arthur Grey, and Kelly Sullivan."

Arthur bowed to the Minister and accepted his medal. It was in the shape of the Origins emblem: an open scroll with the words *Initiate of Origins* inscribed across it.

"Pernille Hanly and Donovan Lisle," Minister Jung continued. "Charda Kuchamann, Bridgette Lane, and Idolette Siegfried." After these last three accepted their medals and the applause died down, the Minister was handed a set of large gold awards, which he paired up with the Origins medals. "We are pleased to honor these next Initiates with their Quite Useful Evaluation of Studied Training medal, as they have finished their training as Initiates, and we now send them with good wishes into their year of PASS. Congratulations to Thespia Galoopsa, Oliver Johnson, and Thaddeus Weinstein."

"It feels weird," Kelly whispered next to Arthur as they clapped. "Every year, the oldest ones leave us."

"But every year," Pernille added, beaming, "new Initiates join us."

After the ceremony, Minister Jung led the Initiates down the path to the eastern shore. The wind rushed along with them, flapping their turquoise Origins robes around their legs and whipping their hair over their faces.

A large crowd had gathered in front of the water station. Arthur could see Madam Siegfried before the entrance, where a suspended waterfall oscillated in the doorway. Minister Jung joined her, and she handed him a large, colorful shell.

"I now declare the Poseidon's View open for Historia use," she proclaimed.

The Minister faced the waterfall curtain, put the shell to his mouth, and blew into it. With the sound of wind on the waves, the watery curtain spread apart to reveal the water station doors.

A thunder of applause rose up from the Members and Masters. Then, chatting happily, the crowd moved forward slowly to tour the newly completed station.

Arthur, Griffin, and the rest of the Spyglass Squad followed along, joking and talking about their Solstice plans, teasing Arthur as he turned red every time a Member grabbed his hand to shake it and thank him for his donation.

"For the holiday, Dad is taking me to Paris, where Mother's waiting," Idolette announced, adjusting the thick-rimmed glasses she wore today. "I'll never come back to this island if I can help it. Unless I'm vacationing on a yacht. But why bother then, right?"

Pernille smiled. "The rest of us still have Experiments yet to get to. That'll be fun, won't it?"

"As fun as riding a harpy," Arthur snickered.

She shook her finger teasingly at him, then turned to Esmond. "How's your mam, Esmond?"

He cleared his throat. "She's still not well, you know. But she can write letters for herself now. Of course, she thinks I'm at a special academic school since my father doesn't think she should know about Historia, but she doesn't mind. I'll spend the holiday with her since Dad will be visiting my brother in Sweden—he was re-stationed there over the summer. It'll be nice."

"What about you, Pernille?" asked Idolette.

"The norm," she responded cheerfully. "My little brother won't find out about Historia for a coupla years yet an' he misses me when I'm gone. My da is going to try to take a holiday too and we'll stay with my granparents." She grinned at Arthur. "An' how's about you? You've got a birthday comin' up."

Arthur scratched his neck. "Yeah, I guess so. Not sure what we're doing yet, though. I'm sure my dad'll think of something." Part of him almost wished he had a stationary place he could go home to. *No, it's much better to be on the move than stuck in one place*, he scolded himself. He straightened and looked up.

Abruptly, he held out an arm to stop the others. At their curious frowns, he nodded ahead to where Nada Bhaksiana stood alone, staring out a glass wall over the turquoise water.

"Howya, Nada," Pernille greeted brightly.

The other girl glanced over. "Hallo." Her small smile broadened when she noticed Griffin. "You know, his picture came out very nice," she said to Arthur. "It was just as I imagined in my head."

Arthur grinned. "That's great, Nada. Listen, thanks for the Mermish interpretations. We never would've found the Horn without your help." He glanced questioningly around at the others and they all nodded—Esmond grudgingly. "Nada, would you like to be part of our club, the Spyglass Squad?"

Her eyebrows lifted in mild interest over her serene blue eyes. "What does it do?"

"Well, I guess we make discoveries." Arthur checked the others for approval. Since they were all grinning, he supposed it was a good answer.

"Thank you for the invitation," Nada said politely. "I think your Squad is just right, though. A quad is four, you know, and you have four in your Squad already."

Arthur cocked his head. "Are you sure? It's no big deal if we have more than four people."

"I think so," she smiled.

But Arthur thought he saw her glance at Esmond, and he had an idea that she knew Esmond wasn't keen on her joining. He shrugged. "Maybe you can be our consultant, then."

Her smile widened a little. "Okay." Then she abruptly

grabbed his hand, startling him. "Since you like to make discoveries," she said, "when we first met on the boats coming to Main Hall, Idolette tells me about ghosts on the island. Did you know yesterday some Members found a white tiger in the forest? It was stolen from a zoo, they think. Mr. Berne offered to capture it. I think that must be the ghost on the island."

Arthur nodded. It came to him that Jolly had mentioned Berne collecting exotic animals. He wondered if this cat would be an addition to some weird kind of zoo.

Griffin muttered, "A white tiger? That must be why I smelled cat so much. And white? That must be the thing you saw at the joust." It certainly seemed to fit.

"Thanks, Nada," Arthur said. "Are your parents coming to pick you up?"

"Yes. And my three sisters and my brother."

"Well, see you in a couple of weeks, Nada." The others added their farewells, and then the four of them and Griffin continued down the busy corridor.

They had only gone a few steps when something else caught Arthur's eye, making his heart leap. He stopped, and Esmond bumped into him.

"What's up?" asked Pernille.

Arthur looked over her head, into the crowded corridor. For a fleeting moment, he thought he'd seen a worn-out Panama hat bobbing amongst the robes and jackets shifting and bumping through the hall. "I'll see you guys outside," he said distractedly. He and Griffin pushed their way through the throng toward the front of the building. Then they saw him.

Near the glass wall, his hands in the pockets of his dingy traveling coat, his face hidden in the shadow of his hat, a short man stood looking around the room with interest. Arthur's face broke into a broad grin. "Hobbs!" he shouted.

Investigator Nicholas Hobbs turned, a twinkling smile on his face. "Well if it ain't the hero o' the day—Ahthur Grey." He ruffled Arthur's hair and beamed. "I came fer all the celebrations and was hopin' I'd run inta ya whilst I was here. Had a good year, have you? Tell ya what, I fancy a roasted kebab, what ya reckon we take a waltz outside?"

Glad for the chance to catch up with his old friend, Arthur led the way out of Poseidon's View. As they walked and munched on samples from food tables, he told Hobbs all about his time at Origins, and then Hobbs talked about his own adventures in Asia since they had parted last year.

"But here's a treat," Hobbs grinned, wiping his mouth on his sleeve. "Startin' next February, I'll be in Egypt for a bit. What do ya make o' that, eh?"

Disappointed, Arthur looked down. He pictured Hobbs waving his hat from atop a dusty camel in front of a giant pyramid. "Egypt, huh?" he said, trying to be cheerful. "I bet you'll have fun there."

"Don'tcha know, then?" Hobbs exclaimed. "You're in Investigations next, and we're stationed in Egypt."

At that, Arthur's grin jumped back up. "We're going to Egypt, too? That's great! Then you can help keep me out of trouble."

"Nah." Hobbs laughed and slapped Arthur on the back. "I can show you where the funnest trouble is!" He winked.

Just then, someone behind them called, "Master Hobbs!" He looked over and waved, then turned back to Arthur with a pleased smile. "Great seein' ya, Ahthur. You're doin' well, mate. I'll see ya 'round—if not later today, you know it'll be soon." He squeezed Arthur's shoulder, tipped his hat, and headed off.

The official Solstice celebration had begun directly after the Poseidon's View opening, and now Members browsed through the booths of food and trinkets set up for the last competition. A few chariots were still for sale (Arthur heard Donovan begging his dad for one). A group of merfolk serenaded the shore with incessant, high-pitched songs that sounded an awful lot like what Arthur had always been told were whale noises. Several bards performed ballads throughout the complex—as far away from the mersongs as possible.

Arthur and Griffin bought a couple of gyros and sat on the steps of Main Hall to eat. Arthur had felt a little hollow after Madam Siegfried's donation announcement. It made him realize he had found—and actually held—something that heroes of long-ago days once touched, and that he had given it up. He didn't even know what its power was.

"You did the right thing," Griffin comforted. "There will be other discoveries, of course."

"How do you know?"

"You heard Hobbs—next is Investigations, and you're

bound to get into something there because—how did Gamble put it?—you are nosy and insolent." Griffin snickered.

Arthur grinned and shoved him. His grin immediately faded, however, when he noticed the white falcon perched on a hanging planter above him. Griffin stuck his tongue out at her, and she shrieked at him.

"Not being insolent, I hope?" crowed a voice behind Arthur.

Arthur and Griffin jumped. "Uh . . . hi, Master Gamble," Arthur said uncertainly.

The old man leaned against his staff and stared silently out over the crowds for a while. Arthur stared out, too, wondering if he should try to thank Gamble for coming to the rescue yet again. He decided against it—Gamble didn't need his ego pumped up any more. Finally, tired of the silence, Arthur remarked, "You know, I just realized, today's not even the real Winter Solstice—that's not till Monday. Why do we have celebrations early?"

Gamble looked sideways at him. "Some people like to spend Solstice with their families. This way we celebrate as a team, have a big to-do and all that nonsense, and then Members can do as they like for the actual Solstice Day."

Arthur cocked his head, suddenly curious. Gamble was human—mostly, anyway. What did he do during holidays? "Do you have any family?" Arthur wondered aloud before he could stop himself.

Gamble's face immediately went blank. He stared off with a glazed look, and his mouth sagged a little. He might have been turned to stone for all the life that seemed to be in him. Arthur glanced uncertainly at Griffin.

Then it passed, and Gamble came back to life. His eye twitched and he frowned. "Not anymore," was all he said.

Curiosity surged through Arthur. Gamble was obviously hiding something dark and mysterious. Arthur wanted to ask what happened, when it happened—did it have anything to do with how his own mom had died . . . But Griffin gave him a warning look, and he grudgingly guessed he'd better not push it. After all, Gamble could still make things miserable for him next year. Glumly, he thought about getting up to join Pernille—he could see her talking animatedly with one of the chariot owners. Or maybe he'd look for his dad.

"You probably ought to know," Gamble said suddenly, startling Arthur. "While Rheneas Berne is out of the fire with some people, he's not with me."

Arthur felt his heart speed up. Was he going to find out the truth about Berne's history? "Why not?"

Gamble gave a slow, raspy sigh. "Rheneas Berne was an Investigator and always will be. Likes to put his nose where it doesn't belong. There was a time," Gamble muttered, "a dangerous time when he got very close to discovering Guardians. To learning about our powers. Very close." He frowned severely at Arthur. "If our secret gets out, it'll be the end of us, you hear me? The end of our kind."

With a shudder, Arthur nodded bleakly.

"That's the real reason I separated you and your dog," Gamble went on with a huff. "The reason I wanted to keep you out from under Berne's nose. He needs to not be reminded of Guardians. No one should know about us." He thunked his staff against the step.

Arthur and Griffin exchanged glances. "Wouldn't it be nice if he would just tell us these things at the beginning?" Griffin grumbled. Arthur shrugged. The mention of Guardians had brought another thought bursting to the front of his mind, and he was determined to get an answer. "Can you lie?" he demanded.

Gamble looked down his nose at him, and his mouth twisted into a smirk. "Ah. Found out about our powers did you?"

"Powers?" Arthur scoffed. "Weakness, you mean."

Gamble frowned. "Those who twist words don't have power over them, boy. Why do you think there are so few of us in the world? Words are powerful, and they can obey us—for good or for bad. But you have to know them and not take away their meaning. Lies make you lose power."

Power. For a moment, Arthur considered asking Gamble about the silver locket. *Don't be stupid*, he scolded himself. *I shouldn't show it to any more people. Besides, Gamble wouldn't know anything about it anyway—it's got to do with artifacts, not Guardians.* Though he couldn't shake away the memory of the wolf-boy from his dream suggesting that the lady with the locket was a Guardian. He looked hastily at Gamble, hoping none of his thoughts could be read on his face. As much as he wanted answers from this old man, Arthur still felt cautious.

After all, he still knew very little about Gamble, and there were plenty of rumors about his sanity.

Griffin shook his head knowingly. "You'd better wait till he can prove he's not a psychopath before we really get to trusting him." Arthur shrugged.

"Next year is Investigations for you," Gamble continued. "Boy, I am *not* looking forward to the kinds of trouble you'll be able to get into with that."

Arthur couldn't help a half-smile.

Gamble held out his arm, and Gatriona flapped down onto it, her white feathers standing out against his dark cloak. "Guess it can't be helped now. Berne or not. I'm going to have to come up with extra lessons to keep you out of trouble, that's for sure." He made a grimace, but Arthur thought he caught a hint of a smile on Gamble's oddly shaped mouth.

Arthur's thoughts jumped to the idea of being able to call Griffin from anywhere and having him come instantly, of being able to keep things safe by hiding them, and who knew what else. "Do you mean it this time?" Arthur demanded, not caring that he sounded disrespectful. "Are you really going to teach me about being a Guardian?"

"Don't have a choice, do I? You are a nosy and insolent tot!" Gamble crowed. "Always into trouble! Get on with you! Go and take advantage of the last celebrations before you're sentenced to exile with that nuisance of a father of yours."

Arthur and Griffin jumped up and ran down the steps to join their friends. "You were right," Arthur said to Griffin as they headed toward Idolette, Pernille, and Esmond. "Gamble hasn't changed one bit."

Griffin's tongue hung out and his tail wagged. "Nope," he grinned. "But neither have you."

ABOUT THE AUTHOR

V. K. FINNISH has been writing adventure stories since middle-school and still loves it, even after trying out other jobs like cake-decorating, office-managing, editing, and sales. Besides writing, Finnish has always enjoyed reading history, hiking, traveling, and taking photos. All of those things can be done quite easily in the Rocky Mountains, where the author lives with family and too many pets.

WWW.VKFINNISH.COM

CPSIA information can be obtained at www.ICGtesting.com
Printed in the USA
LVOW05s0351170713

343126LV00003B/258/P